the Coldest Touch

the Coldest Touch

ISABEL STERLING

RAZORBILL

RAZORBILL

An imprint of Penguin Random House LLC, New York

First published in the United States of America by Razorbill,
an imprint of Penguin Random House LLC, 2021

Visit us online at penguinrandomhouse.com.

LIBRARY OF CONGRESS CATALOGING-IN-PUBLICATION DATA:
Names: Sterling, Isabel, author.
Title: The coldest touch / Isabel Sterling.
Description: New York : Razorbill, 2021. | Audience: Ages 12 and up.
Summary: Elise, a mortal girl who feels the death of anyone she touches,
and Claire, the vampire assigned to recruit her to the Veil, must work together
to stop a paranormal killer even as they realize they might be falling in love.
Identifiers: LCCN 2021027516 | ISBN 9780593350430 (hardcover)
ISBN 9780593350454 (trade paperback) | ISBN 9780593350447 (ebook)
Subjects: CYAC: Death—Fiction. | Vampires—Fiction. | Bisexuality—Fiction.
Ability—Fiction. | Supernatural—Fiction. | LCGFT: Novels. | Paranormal fiction.
Classification: LCC PZ7.1.S7443 Co 2021 | DDC [Fic]—dc23
LC record available at https://lccn.loc.gov/2021027516

Manufactured in Canada

1 3 5 7 9 10 8 6 4 2

FRI

Design by Rebecca Aidlin
Text set in Adobe Caslon Pro

For Jaimee, who listened to me spin stories long before I was any good at it.

Prologue

A girl made of stone and masks and broken glass sits alone at her desk. In her new apartment. In a town far from home. The girl is used to being alone. Used to wanting things she cannot have. A family. Friends who care about *her* more than the favors they request.

Love.

But she doesn't have those things, doesn't remember if she ever did. She's been lonely longer than she's been seventeen.

And she's been seventeen for so many years she's lost count.

The girl ignores her silent heart and focuses on the task at hand. On her laptop, she opens a secure link and flips through the file of a girl who has everything. Photo Girl stands among her family with a bright smile and laughter in her eyes. She's victorious atop a podium with wet hair and a gold medal around her neck. She kisses a boy on the cheek while his arms wrap tight around her. Comments under the post declare them #RelationshipGoals. She's with him again, glittering crowns on their heads and a flower pinned to his suit. Photo Girl's life is everything the lonely girl wants for herself.

But then the family photos and smiling selfies cease, and a series of newspaper clippings follows.

SUDDEN STORM SENDS LOCAL MAN OVER BRIDGE

CAR PULLED FROM RIVER, BODY STILL MISSING

MEMORIAL SERVICE FOR NICHOLAS BEAUMONT, 21

The next images make her recoil, but she carefully commits each one to memory. A grieving family greets mourners beside a closed casket. A twisted, broken guardrail and muddy tire tracks. Photo Girl on her knees beside the river, hair stuck to her face as she screams.

The smiling portrait of a young man no longer among the living.

She didn't know about the dead brother, not until she'd already accepted the case. The death doesn't change her mission. Even so, seeing the stories in black and white makes something uncomfortable shift and knot inside her.

But there isn't time to care about the people in these photographs. She has a job to do.

So, she tries on an array of personalities. Becomes a dozen funhouse versions of herself until she forgets who she is inside. She'll wield her charm as a weapon and her smile as her shield.

And when she meets Photo Girl, when she sets eyes on this creature with hair the color of sunlight and eyes like the ocean, she will be ready.

1

Elise

I don't belong here.

Though I've visited three times in as many days, I still feel like an intruder as I maneuver through the tiny shop's narrow aisles. Heart & Stone Metaphysical is located in downtown Elmsbrook, where stores shorten their hours and sit mostly vacant while the local university is closed for the summer. I wish I'd known about this place then. Now, in the early days of September, the shop is full. The new college students are only two years older than me, but it feels like a lifetime.

Their gazes linger as I pass shelves of carefully wrapped lies and impossible promises, like they know I'm trespassing in their world of magic and make-believe. The two white men who work here seem nice enough. Over the course of a few visits, I've overheard enough conversations—and asked enough questions—to know they believe in the hope they're peddling.

So far, I've avoided knowing their deaths.

In the center of the long, rectangular store, one of the men offers advice to a young woman looking for the best stones to banish unwanted attention at work. He rattles off a list of black rocks: tourmaline, onyx, and smoky quartz. He seems at home in this world of magic and make-believe. He chose this life.

I was cursed into it.

At least, that's the only logical conclusion after a summer of medical tests and therapy appointments didn't solve anything. When I turned sixteen last April, I lost *everything*—my brother, my spot on the swim team, and eventually, my friends. My heart clenches as the memories try to surface, but I force them under. I won't fall apart in public, not again.

Tugging the sleeves of my sweater down far enough to cover my palms, I check the list of supplies on my phone. As much as my rational mind wants to deny everything this shop stands for, science failed to uncover the source of my problem. I have no choice but to test the magical, the paranormal, the strange.

With the help of the internet, and a couple awkward conversations with the men who work here, I've cobbled together the best of what the metaphysical world has to offer. Bay, fennel, and nettles to break hexes. Selenite to cleanse my so-called *energy field*. Plus five different kinds of salt, and enough candles to burn down the house if I'm not careful. All of that, yet each time I review and refine my plan, there's something else I need. Buying supplies for the ritual has already used up most of my savings, but I'm afraid to leave anything out. If I'm going to do this, I'm doing it right.

As if there's a *right* way to dabble in make-believe.

Careful not to get too close to the woman scanning the bookshelves, I approach the back counter. Beneath the glass sits an assortment of handmade jewelry, but I'm not interested in a necklace or a hunk of sparkly rock. Instead, I focus on the display of pendulums swinging from a wooden stand.

Except . . . the list on my phone doesn't specify what kind of pendulum to get. Would it make a difference if I used an amethyst pendulum instead of one carved from wood? I bite back a sigh. Why can't one part of this process be simple? My frustration almost sends me sulking out of the shop, but I have to try. I already tried faking migraines, but the X-rays and MRIs I had this summer found nothing.

They couldn't explain why I see death everywhere I go.

"Trouble making decisions?"

I flinch away from the soft voice and turn to find a white girl standing close beside me. *Too close.* She's wearing jeans and a plaid shirt rolled up to her elbows, the pale skin of her forearms flawless beside the green fabric. I pocket my phone and tug my sleeves all the way to the base of my fingers.

"What?" I finally ask, heart beating too fast as I put more space between us. I didn't hear her, didn't notice her get so close. She could have touched me. She could have—

The girl points to the display of pendulums, cutting off my panicked thoughts. "These are great for making decisions." She smiles, but the quick sweep of her gaze contradicts that warmth. It feels calculated, like she's examining me.

I return her stare, cataloguing the soft cascade of brown hair that falls past her shoulders and the deep black sunglasses perched on top of her head. She seems about my age, but I've never seen her around town before.

"They can also help find what you've lost," she offers, still smiling. Still standing too close.

"I know." The words come out stiff and harsh, and my cheeks flush with heat. "They supposedly do a lot of things."

I pluck one of the clear quartz pendulums from the rack. Based on my few weeks of intense research, colorless stones are supposed to work for most rituals, sort of like a universal blood donor. Except . . . for magic. The quartz should work well enough to open chakras, and—more importantly—close them.

"Supposedly," the brunette echoes, and follows me away from the display case. I can't read her tone, can't tell if she's agreeing with me or mocking me.

At the wall of bulk herbs, where dried plants are stored in large glass jars, I pause. The girl stops, too, lingering beside me. With the pendulum clutched tight in one hand, I try to focus on something other than my new shadow. Soft instrumental music filters through the store, and there's enough incense in this place that it's nearly a breathing hazard. But I can still sense her standing beside me. *Just get the supplies and get out.*

I scan the labels and grab the jar of dried witch hazel.

"Interesting choice," the girl says, leaning over my shoulder and making me flinch. She must notice my discomfort, though, because she steps away. "Are you looking for protection or divining for true love?" A conspiratorial grin tugs at her blood-red lips.

Something about the easy way she smiles picks at my defenses. In another life, one where this curse hadn't destroyed everything, I might have returned her grin. Now I just want her to leave me alone. "How is that any of your business?"

She glances at the floor like she's embarrassed. "Sorry. I don't mean to be nosy." When she looks up again, her expression is softer and less teasing. "I'm Claire," she says, and holds out a hand.

"Elise." I ignore her outstretched palm and adjust my grip on the supplies. She doesn't leave, and I don't know what she wants from me. I don't have time for whatever this is. The new moon is tomorrow, and it's my chance to fix everything. The friendships I smashed to pieces this summer. The distance I have to keep from my family. The terrible curse ruining my life.

"Nice to meet you." Claire drops her hand, and the smile finally slips away, uncertainty taking its place.

Guilt tugs at my heart, which makes no sense. I don't know this girl. I don't owe her anything.

"All set?" One of the shopkeepers suddenly appears beside me, hands reaching for the jar. "I can take that to the front for you." His fingers slide against mine as he takes the pendulum and witch hazel.

Pain and fatigue crash into me, and I shut my eyes. In my mind, I see an older version of him, gray hair clinging in thin wisps to his head. It's hard to breathe. Impossible. Each gasping inhale refuses to fill my lungs, and my brain gets fuzzy. Then everything is cold, and the hospital machines are screeching that he's gone.

When he finishes collecting my things, his fingers slip away from mine. The moment the contact is gone, the vision fades. I gasp for air, lungs expanding again the way they should, but I can't stop my hands from shaking. I didn't want to see him die. I didn't want to know, didn't want to *feel* it.

"Another small bag for the herbs?" he calls on his way to the register, and it's all I can do to nod. My voice is trapped in my throat, tears threatening behind my eyes.

I remind myself to breathe, forcing one deep inhale then another. It takes every bit of control not to cry, not to think about all the other deaths I've seen. The lives I've failed to save. My heart clenches tight, and I see my brother's face.

Nick is gone, and it's all my fault.

"Are you okay?" Claire reaches for me, face etched with concern.

"Don't touch me." I jolt away from her approaching fingers and knock into the shelves. Jars rattle dangerously, but none of them fall. "I have to go." My tone is harsh, but I don't apologize. I'll never see this girl again, anyway.

I leave her standing beside the herbs and hurry to the counter to pay for my things. I slide over exact change, grab the small bag of supplies, and head for the door.

Before I can escape, there's this tightening in my chest. A prickle of cold against the back of my neck. I glance over my shoulder and find Claire watching me. Studying me. A shudder trembles across my skin, and I push open the door, slipping into the warm afternoon.

I have a ritual to prepare.

2

Claire

The moment Elise slips out of the store, I dissect our inter-action. I don't know what to make of her presence in a place like this. Nothing in her dossier pointed to an interest in the para-normal. Yet given her reaction to the scrawny man who touched her—and the way she kept a deliberate distance between us—I'm positive the witches found the right person.

But what was she doing *here*? Has she embraced her gift? Does she think other types of magic are at her fingertips, waiting to be discovered?

When the lead shepherd talked me into rejoining their team, when they talked me into taking *one last case*, I thought I'd find the grieving girl from the file. I was wrong. Elise isn't the same girl she was before, smiling and aloof, but there's a spark in her I didn't expect. A fire in her ocean eyes.

And she's getting away.

I move silently through the shop and slip behind the counter where the owners are bundling dried herbs. It would be easier if I could corner each of them alone, but I'm strong enough to handle two humans at once.

The paler one notices me first. "You can't be back here." His tone is kind but unapologetic.

"Oh, I'm sorry." A flutter of guilt moves where my heart does not, but I ignore it. I grab each man's forearm and stare into their eyes, waiting for the moment their minds belong to me. When I feel the familiar pressure in my head, I hold tight to the sensation. "Do you know that girl?" I keep my voice low so I don't alarm the mortals shopping in the aisles.

"Not well."

"She's come in a few times."

"If she ever visits again, call me immediately." I make the men memorize my number. "What is she trying to do?"

"She's been asking about chakras and how to close them."

"She asked me about curses."

"Is there anything else?" Impatience tightens my grip. The longer I delay, the harder it'll be to track Elise. The men shake their heads, so I release them. The compulsion will settle into the back of their minds, only activating if Elise steps into the shop.

If she doesn't, these men will never feel my influence again.

Outside, the bright afternoon sun assaults my senses, weakening my muscles and blurring my vision. A dull ache blossoms at the back of my skull. With a groan, I slide my sunglasses onto my face. The witches on our research team developed special lenses that block the worst of the sun's effects, but this pair is getting old. I haven't worked a daylight shift in ages, so I didn't realize their effects had faded.

There's no time to get a replacement pair, so I turn left and stalk through the busy streets. At first, I'm surprised by the amount of traffic on a Monday afternoon, but then I pass a bookshop with a large LABOR DAY SALE! banner in the window. It explains the crowd, but that doesn't help with the growing headache or the pressure throbbing along my gums. I mentally flip off the blazing sun and consider telling Wyn to give this assignment to someone else.

But then I remember Wyn's final argument. *You know what this girl means to the Veil, Claire. If you succeed, Tagliaferro and Guillebeaux will owe you for a change.*

Wyn made it seem simple, but shepherding is never easy. Not everyone takes well to the rules of our world, and unlike the men in the shop, I won't be able to compel Elise. Her gift makes her immune to paranormal manipulations, but that's not even the worst part of this case. Infiltrating her world means going back to high school. I'd rather die.

Again.

Ahead, I finally spot Elise, her blonde braid swinging in a gentle arc across her back. She slips through the crowd, careful not to brush into anyone. Splotches of sweat speckle her thin gray cardigan, yet she keeps the sleeves pulled all the way to her fingers.

Part of me wants to sprint after her and explain everything— she clearly has no idea how to control her rare gift—but she was more guarded than I expected. I'll need to go slow, build at least a little trust, before I explain the paranormal world and her place within it.

Still, as I watch Elise dodge around a small child with tiny pig-tails on top of her head, I can't help but feel a twinge of sympathy. I remember the bone-deep fear that flooded my newly heightened senses when I realized humanity was my past, not my present. I'll never forget the dead girl on the floor, the taste of blood in my mouth, the panic that drove Rose away.

Rose, who stole my life and never bothered to explain what I'd become.

The ache in my jaw intensifies, and I squeeze my hands into fists so tight each of my knuckles pops. *Rose.* I've been chasing her for so many years I've lost count, but she's always one step ahead. Every time I think I've found a new lead, the trail disappears like smoke in the night.

You know what this girl means to the Veil.

Wyn's words are in my head again, and I remember the panic at headquarters when Elise's predecessor went missing. When it became clear she had died and passed the gift to someone new. Convincing Elise to embrace her power, convincing her to serve the Veil, is vital to our continued survival. Wyn was right about the reward, too. If I succeed, Tagliaferro and Guillebeaux, the Veil's leaders, will finally owe *me*. They'll have to help me find Rose.

I smile despite the pain pulsing through bone and muscle and marrow. I'll find her.

And then I'll tear out her slender throat.

Up ahead, Elise turns west, away from the downtown area. I keep plenty of space between us, but I don't let myself lose sight of her golden braid for more than a second or two. When we pass into a residential community, the sidewalk traffic thins to nothing. Storefronts give way to green lawns, and the scent of sweat and exhaust fades to burning charcoal and sizzling burgers.

Now that we're alone, now that it's clear Elise is simply headed home, I let more space stretch between us. I lose sight of her when she turns north into an even more expensive neighborhood, where she lives with her surgeon father and real estate agent mother. The moment she's out of sight, my phone buzzes against my leg. I ignore it, since the only creature who bothers to call me is Wyn.

Despite their centuries of experience, Wyn never cultivated a sense of patience.

The buzzing eventually stops, and I silently thank whoever planned this neighborhood for the tree cover. Though shade is a poor substitute for the dark of night, it's better than facing the direct assault of the sun. The pounding in my head relents. A little.

My phone buzzes again, and this time, I pull it out. As expected, Wyn's name glows in the middle of the screen. I consider ignoring them, but apparently, they'll just keep calling.

"I've been in Elmsbrook less than a day. What could you possibly want?" Even though there's more than enough space between Elise and me, I keep my voice low. She can't know I'm here until I *want* her to know.

"You were supposed to call after you settled into your apartment." Wyn's voice sounds far away, like they have me on speaker. "You promised not to miss check-ins."

"And before that, I promised I'd never shepherd again." I'd meant it, too, when I left Wyn's team ten years ago. I didn't expect them to lure me back with promises of revenge. "If you don't trust me, why the hell did you beg me to do this?" My voice is harsh, but they deserve it.

Wyn sighs. "You're the only one young enough to pass as a student."

"So glad you believe in me."

"You're also one of the best damn shepherds the Veil ever had," Wyn adds, albeit begrudgingly.

Down the street, Elise turns off the sidewalk and approaches a two-story house with gray siding and white trim. The shrubbery out front is carefully sculpted, the grass as neat as all its neighbors'. She punches a code into the lock, opens the door, and slips inside. I'm vaguely aware of Wyn rambling on about protocol and precautions as I slip closer to the house and pause across the street.

The navy blue front door is fitted with panes of glass, and through them I spot Elise darting up a staircase with the supplies she bought at the occult shop. I wonder again what she plans to do with the pendulum and witch hazel, and I kick myself for not asking the shop owners if she'd purchased anything else.

I'm tempted to knock on the door when I notice more movement inside. A white woman with dark red hair follows Elise up the stairs. Her mother, probably, though she's dyed her hair since the funeral.

"Are you even listening to me? Claire, you can't—"

"I found her," I say, cutting off Wyn mid-rant. "She's not alone, though." I run through a dozen different scenarios, ways to show up at her house uninvited and ditch the mom long enough to tell Elise everything she needs to know. None of them work. Trust takes time. Patience. Setting the right foundation is essential.

"And?" Wyn prompts. "Have you made contact?"

A plan comes together piece by piece. "Tomorrow," I say as I start the trek back to my apartment. "I'll make contact at the academy."

3

Elise

Mom is in the kitchen when I get home.

I slip inside, close the front door as quietly as I can, and race to the stairs with my supplies. I only make it three steps before Mom calls out. The downside of the *open floor plan* she loves so much.

"Elise? Is that you?"

"I'll be down in a minute!" I hurry up the rest of the stairs, no longer quieting my steps. My parents aren't particularly religious, but I'd rather shave my head than explain the magical properties of witch hazel to my mom. She would only worry, and she's had enough of that.

At the top of the stairs, I turn right down the hall. My chest constricts as I pass Nick's room. It's unavoidable, just like the way my fingers brush against his door. The habit started when Nick left for college three years ago, and it didn't stop when he—

My throat closes, as if my body thinks that will stop the words in my head. I missed Nick so much when he went to school, but that was nothing compared to this new crater in my chest. It's been five months since we lost him—since *I* failed to save him—and the pain only grows and grows, like a black hole slowly consuming my life.

Inside my room, I lock the door and go to my closet. Mom

usually doesn't snoop, but I don't want to risk it. Not with the collection of herbs, crystals, and candles I'm hiding. Reaching for the box under the pile of discarded jeans—

Merrrrowww!

I jolt back and swallow a scream. "Damn it, Richard!" The three-year-old calico saunters out of the corner. She meows more politely and tries to nibble on my fingers. "Why are you such a jerk? I'm the one who feeds you." I scratch under her chin with one hand and lay the witch hazel and pendulum inside the box with the other supplies.

Just one more day.

The thought soothes some of the ache in my chest. I spent all of August researching for this ritual. It's going to work. It has to.

"I don't suppose you could help?" I ask the fuzz ball, petting the patchwork of orange, gray, and white fur along her back. In response, Richard turns and nips at my fingers hard enough to hurt. When I wince, she jumps over my lap and scratches at the bedroom door.

"You are such a traitor, Richie." I stand and strip out of my sweat-slicked shirt and sweater, ignoring the cat's pleas to escape. Mom has the air-conditioning cranked, and the cool air kisses my skin until I shiver.

Though it's a tiny problem compared to the weight of this curse, I'm tired of dressing in soft cotton armor, with sleeves pulled down to my fingers. Central New York summers are muggy and hot and terrible, especially when you're stuck in sweaters all the time. I never thought I'd say this, but I'm actually looking forward to winter.

But tomorrow . . . Tomorrow everything will be different. I'll be free of this curse, free to wear my favorite T-shirts again without fear.

"Elise? Dinner's ready." Mom shows impressive restraint by knocking instead of barging in. "That cat better not be scratching my carpet."

"I'll be right there!" I grab the nearest long-sleeve shirt and tug it on. In the mirror, I find my hair a mess, flyaways that Mom will definitely try to smooth against my head. With quick fingers, I undo my braid and grab the brush from the top of my dresser.

The door handle jiggles. "Why is this locked?" Mom's voice is tight with worry. "Elise Beaumont, what are you doing in there?"

"Getting changed. Hang on." I adjust the pile of clothes covering my magic supplies.

"Open the door right now, young lady. Or I'll—"

I reach the door and pull it open before Mom can finish. Despite the cat's earlier whining, she lingers in the open doorway like she can't decide if she actually wants to leave. Mom, on the other hand, looks pissed. She's still wearing work clothes, a charcoal pencil skirt and white blouse, and her face is nearly as red as her salon-colored hair. I toss my brush on the bed. "See? I was just changing. Nothing scandalous, I promise."

Mom narrows her eyes at me, the same blue-green eyes Nick and I share. *Shared.* The correction churns like acid in my stomach. We both looked a lot like Mom, with golden hair and thin noses. After the accident, after we lost Nick, Mom started dyeing her hair a fiery red. She claimed it was to make herself more memorable with clients, but I think it was too hard to see Nick in the mirror. It's a miracle she can still look at me.

Dad doesn't.

Mom props one hand on her hip. "If you're doing drugs again, so help me." She stalks into the room and sniffs the air. "I'm not afraid to get you tested."

"I'm not doing *drugs*."

"Funny. That's what you said right before we found your vape pen."

Shame burns my cheeks. There wasn't *supposed* to be anything illegal in the cartridge. The seller said it was an herbal mixture meant to cure visions, not create them, but there was definitely something medically—not magically—mind-altering about that stuff.

"Don't worry, I learned my lesson." I reach up and start working my hair into a tight braid. "I was hot from my walk and needed to change. That's it, I swear."

She studies me a second, but then her posture softens. "Here, let me help with that."

"It's fine, Mom. I got it."

"Don't be ridiculous." Mom reaches for me, but I flinch away. Pain flashes in her eyes, which makes me feel like shit. I don't want to hurt her more than I already have.

"Sorry," I say, sitting at my desk. "I'm just nervous about school tomorrow." It's a dangerous kind of lie, the type that skirts too close to the truth, and I brace myself for the hurt of her touch.

"I know last year ended on a sour note." Mom runs her fingers through my hair and starts on the French braid. I try not to tense, but between the thickness of my hair and the length of Mom's fake nails, her skin doesn't touch mine.

A relieved sigh escapes my lips, but then I really hear her words. "*Sour?* Dean Albro threatened to expel me." Which was bullshit, honestly. After Nick . . . School didn't seem that important. I was seeing death everywhere, and I needed to find a way to fix it. I couldn't tell my parents—they'd never believe me—so I cut a few classes. Got behind on homework so I could research. Faked terrible migraines to convince doctors to order all sorts of scans. I scowl at the wall while Mom works on my hair. "He said if I couldn't 'get over it' and 'focus on my classes,' I should drop out and go to Elmsbrook High instead."

"I'm sorry, baby. I know you don't want to switch schools." Mom pauses, my hair held tight in her fingers, but then she's working again. "Dean Albro promised to give you a clean slate this year, but he emphasized that Elmsbrook Academy doesn't alter their standards of achievement, no matter how real the reason you're struggling is."

I suppress a bitter laugh. *Struggling.* As if that could explain the horror of seeing Nick die. His was the first death I felt unspool inside my head, and I was there, hours later, when he actually drowned. Every agonizing second of his death is seared into my brain.

It was the world's worst sixteenth birthday.

"All set," Mom says, and I carefully pass her the hair tie around my wrist. She secures the end, and I have to smile. This is the closest we've been in months, the closest I've been to anyone without pain tearing through me. "Come on." She bends forward and wraps me in a hug, pressing her cheek against mine.

Images unfurl like a poisonous flower, vivid and painful, inside my head. Every part of me freezes up, and then I see her. Mom. Wrinkled and gray and alone in a hospital bed. Her weakness is echoed inside me, limbs heavy and going numb. My heart rate slows, each beat a struggle. Finally, hers stops altogether.

And then so does mine.

Panic tears at my chest as the seconds pass and my heart doesn't beat. But then Mom stands and pulls away, taking her touch with her. I gasp as my heart starts again, racing to make up for the beats it missed.

"You okay, Ellie?"

"I'm fine." I stand quickly, pain and grief intertwining inside me, making my body tremble. It's always like this. Every single time. I've tried to focus on the good things—that she's old, that she gets to live a long life—but Mom is always *touching,* and every time it's the same. Her heart gives out while she sleeps. Alone in a hospital bed. Dad nowhere in sight.

Probably because he dies first.

I hate the thought the second it arrives, but I can't push it away. I don't know for sure—Dad hasn't touched me, hasn't hugged me, since we lost Nick—but I looked up the statistics. Husbands usually go before their wives. Not knowing is the only good thing about him hating me. He hasn't said it, but I know he blames me for Nick.

Which is fine. I blame me, too.

"Come on," Mom says. "Your dad and I grilled burgers." She turns and steps into the hall, leaving me standing by my desk, the fatigue in my muscles still fading. Her death lingers like a fog, and every time I blink, all I see is her dying in that bed.

Just one more day, I remind myself. *One more day until the ritual that fixes everything.*

I raise my chin and follow Mom down the stairs, trying very hard not to cry.

In the morning, I wake before the sun, lace my shoes, and run. The first mile, my brain is filled with all the things I want to forget. Memories of diving into the river after Nick. Mom's constant worry and forced happiness. The heaviness of knowing how my best friends are going to die yet being powerless to stop it. I try to focus on tonight's ritual, on my curse-free future, but even that makes it hard to breathe.

So, I run faster, push my legs harder until there isn't room for anything but the sound of my breath and the pounding of my shoes against the pavement. When I make it home, the three miles have left my body spent and shaking, but it worked. My mind is crystal clear.

I shower and dress in the bathroom Nick and I shared. Even after five months without him, after three years of him away at college, I still expect Nick to knock on his side of the door, begging me to hurry up.

These days, it's Richard pawing at the door while I braid my hair. She cries like she misses me, but I know she just wants extra treats. When I glance back at my reflection, I sigh. My braid came out a little crooked this morning, but I let it fall over one shoulder, like it was intentional.

Back in my room, I grab the final piece of my school uniform. I'm already wearing the navy blue trousers and white dress shirt, but I still feel exposed. Despite expected highs in the seventies, I pull on a green cardigan and nestle the sleeves in my palms.

Armor complete, I turn to leave and catch sight of the picture on my nightstand. It steals my breath every time I see it, but I can't convince myself to take it down. Nick is in his soccer uniform, the ball tucked under one arm. It was supposed to be a serious portrait for the yearbook, but something off-camera made him laugh, and the photographer captured the essence of my brother: goofy and caring and eager to make others smile.

Mom gave me the framed photograph when Nick left for college. I was only thirteen, and I was mad at him for leaving, even though I was proud that he made the college team.

Now, all I have left of him is that picture and the cat currently meowing at me.

"Come on, Richie. Breakfast time."

I touch Nick's door and continue downstairs, careful not to let Richard trip me. Dad is in the dining room when I pass through to the kitchen and toss a frozen bowl of eggs and veggies into the microwave. I feed Richard while my breakfast cooks, stealing glances at Dad. He doesn't look up to greet me, though. If anything, he shuffles the newspaper higher to block me from view.

Dad was never a hugger like Mom, but he used to tell work stories and sing along to the radio while he cooked. Nick would sing, too, voice purposefully off-key just to annoy me. I'd roll my eyes, but inside I was laughing. I'd do anything, trade anything, to have those mornings back. I even miss Nick's wobbly, dying goose of a falsetto.

The microwave beeps, and I pull my breakfast out with careful fingers. I consider eating in the kitchen, standing by the counter island, but make myself go to the table. "Morning, Dad."

He mumbles a half-formed greeting in response before letting silence settle between us. Dad's a surgeon, but even though he wears scrubs at the hospital, he still dresses up before he goes in. Today, he's in a black suit and tie, his face clean shaven. He looks nothing like the rest of our family, beyond our shared pale skin. He's all dark hair and dark eyes and wide shoulders. The silence stretches into a chasm I fear I'll never cross.

I didn't know it was possible to miss someone who's in the same room as you.

"Anything interesting in there?" I ask, trying to bridge the distance.

"The soccer team won." For a moment, Dad sounds like his old self. But then he clears his throat and shuffles the paper, turning away from the sports section. He reads it every day, like it's a time machine to a better past, like one day Nick will be in there again, photographed scoring the winning goal.

I try to eat my eggs, but they taste like ash on my tongue. My brother's absence is a physical thing. The wound he left behind is puckered and red, infected with guilt and regret and a million toxic *what if*s.

What if I'd been faster?

What if I'd made him stay home that night?

What if this curse inside me caused the accident?

I lose what little was left of my appetite and stand, tossing the rest of my breakfast in the trash. Richard is still eating, and I swear she sounds like a malfunctioning blender as she chews.

Above, footsteps tell me Mom will be down soon, and I know she'll try to fuss with my hair if I don't escape. With everything else today, I can't stomach seeing her death. I don't know how many times my heart can stop with hers before it forgets to start beating again.

Dad doesn't say anything when I leave the room, and I don't either. I grab my backpack from the bottom of the stairs and pause with one hand on the door. Guilt digs into my chest, and I suck in a deep breath. "Bye, Mom! Love you!"

Then I'm gone, slipping out into the blistering sun. September is a strange month in this area. It's hot and muggy today, but it could plummet to fifty tomorrow and be back into the eighties by the weekend. Sweat trickles down my spine, but I can't risk removing my cardigan. It's only a short walk to school, and then I'll be in crowded halls where any exposed skin is a risk.

Just one more day. Tomorrow, everything will be different.

Doubt tries to creep in, but I push it down and repeat the mantra in my head, over and over, until Elmsbrook Academy peeks over the horizon with its stone turrets and waving flags. When I crest the final hill and start my decline, a sea of classmates in navy blue, forest green, and bright white shirts mingle on the manicured lawns and freshly washed white stone.

The distance between us shrinks and shrinks until I'm amid the storm.

My body tenses as people shuffle past. Someone screams behind me, high and shrill, and dashes across the courtyard to embrace a friend. A pit of jealousy forms in my chest, and I scan the crowd. I remind myself that my classmates are more than a minefield of violent deaths waiting to explode inside my mind. They're people with the rest of their lives stretching out before them.

Unfortunately, I forgot that over the summer. When I first experienced my best friend's future death, I couldn't stand the sight of her. It hurt too much, knowing how I'd lose her. Seeing how young she was. But she still has life to live. She's still *here*, and I can't let this curse keep us apart. *Especially* now that I have a way to end it. I search the crowd until—

There.

Maggie, a petite Korean American girl with dark hair that falls past her shoulders, stands near the stairs that lead to the school's grand entrance. Seeing her for the first time in months knocks the wind from my lungs. My brain tries to supply images of her—slipping, falling, head cracking against the cement around a pool—but I push them away. Maggie is alive and smiling and happy. She wears the blue-and-green checkered skirt and white blouse version of our uniform, and she's traded out her old black-rimmed glasses for a pair that's deep red.

I move carefully through the crowd, happy memories replacing her death. Maggie and I have been best friends since we were four years old and our parents signed us up for the same swim class. *Minnows for life*, we'd promised as we climbed the ranks to dolphins and eventually taught the new minnows—including her much younger half sister, Vivi. Maggie and I trained together for twelve years, spent the night at each other's houses, and stayed up late dissecting the vague social media posts of our respective crushes.

It feels weird, how blissfully *ordinary* our lives were.

But then this summer, my boyfriend—my *ex*-boyfriend—ruined everything. I made the mistake of telling Jordan about the curse. He wanted to believe me, but he didn't. And after I broke up with him, he told Maggie.

Jordan wasn't trying to hurt you, a voice inside says. *He and Maggie are friends, too.*

The three of us were friends long before Jordan and I started dating. Hell, Maggie's the one who brought Jordan into our friend group and made him an honorary minnow. His family moved to Elmsbrook when we were in sixth grade and his dad became the new adjunct law professor at the local college.

I should have known Jordan would go to Maggie after I stomped all over his heart. I should have known that Maggie—who likes facts and evidence and digs until she finds the truth—would get my secret out of him.

The space between Maggie and me shrinks, and I swallow

down my nerves. Sweat spills down my spine and collects along the waistband of my slacks. I can't lie my way out of this one, not with her.

"Elise?" Maggie notices me before I get all the way there. The laughter falls out of her eyes, replaced by something I'm afraid to name. Curiosity? Disgust? I don't look close enough to be sure.

Another two steps and I'm standing before her. "Can we talk?" My gaze flicks past Maggie to where a few other girls from the swim team are lounging in the shade. Karen and Jenn, who used to invite the team over for horror movie marathons. Grace and—

Ugh, Kaitlyn.

The new team captain—a title that was supposed to be *mine*—left increasingly hostile comments on my Instagram page after I quit. According to her posts, I single-handedly screwed our relay team out of the state title.

I clear my throat and focus on Maggie. "In private?"

Maggie starts to respond, but Kaitlyn pushes away from the wall and comes to stand beside her. She rests her arm around Maggie's shoulders, and the gesture almost seems . . . protective. "Whatever you have to say to Maggie, you can say to all of us."

"This doesn't involve you." I cross my arms, but the motion is more armor than challenge.

"Doesn't it?" Kaitlyn tilts her head, and there's this angry glint to her eyes. "You ditched Maggie like some shitty ex. You can't waltz back in like nothing happened. The team can't afford any distractions this year."

Guilt tears at my insides, but this is about so much more than the team. "Maggie, please? I just need a minute."

My best friend glances from Kaitlyn to me to Kaitlyn again. She hesitates, and it hurts, even if I deserve her mistrust.

"Forget it." But my broken voice is stolen by the tolling of bells, telling us it's time to get to class. I pivot on my heel and hurry for the stairs, but I feel Maggie's gaze on my back with every step.

Inside the school, the halls echo with laughter and the shuffle of hundreds of bodies hurrying down the marble walkway. The air-conditioning cuts the worst of the heat, but my cardigan is already clinging to my sweat-slicked skin, further fueled by the bitter mix of embarrassment and grief. I know I screwed up this summer, but I can't believe Maggie would confide in *Kaitlyn*, of all people.

I hope she didn't mention any of the things Jordan told her about my curse . . .

The bells toll again, the sound deep and resonant as it moves through the school. I pick up the pace, but someone jostles my shoulder. I stumble, and a hand presses to the small of my back. Fingers graze my bare wrist.

My head fills with screaming tires and shattering glass and then there's pain *everywhere*.

I yank away from the touch, some tall lanky white boy I don't recognize. He raises his hands, apologizes, and dashes off again, leaving me gasping for breath. I don't even know the kid's name, but I know his death. What the hell did I do to deserve a curse like this?

Just one more day. One more. You can do this.

I adjust the straps of my backpack and hurry into my classroom. I have trig first period, and I slide into a seat at the back of the room as the bells die away. My heart is still racing, the last of the boy's death slowly bleeding out of my muscles. When my name is called, I manage a steady "Here," and ignore classmates' pitying stares.

"Claire Montgomery?" The math teacher, Ms. Parsons, calls the name a second time and looks up from her list to scan the room. "Miss Montgomery?"

The heavy wooden door swings open, and a dark-haired girl in the school's skirt and blouse waltzes in. "I'm sorry," she says, voice lyrical and rich like honey. "I got turned around."

"Miss Montgomery?" Ms. Parsons confirms.

"Claire," she says. "Yes."

"While you're up, you can pass out the syllabus and find a seat."

Claire picks up the stack of papers, and her body moves with impossible grace as she weaves through the rows. When she slides a syllabus onto my desk, I mutter a half-hearted thank-you, but she doesn't leave.

She's smiling when I glance up. "We have to stop meeting like this."

At first, I don't know what she's talking about, but then I see past the school uniform to the confidence of her posture. The perfect cascade of her brown hair. The easy grin. She's the girl from Heart & Stone Metaphysical, the one who pestered me about the supplies I was buying.

What is she doing here?

4

Claire

High school is even worse than I remembered.

While the teacher details the course objectives, I watch Elise. Her golden hair is braided again, this time falling over one shoulder instead of down her back. Here among her classmates, there's no spark in her eyes. When she catches me staring the second time, a challenge in the rise of her brow, I look away and watch the clock tick down.

Elmsbrook Academy—no matter how different from other schools I've attended, small and exclusive as it is—won't be immune to my . . . particular appeal. Once the bells ring, I'll be surrounded. The popular ranks will swoop in, assessing and cataloguing to determine where they'll place me in their social hierarchy. No matter what I do, I always make it to the top.

Guilt forms like an old scab, and I mentally pick at it until it bleeds. Part of me hates these games. My foolish heart—too young, too fragile—wants to help Elise. I imagine stopping her after class. Pulling her into a private space to share all the secrets I know. I could shepherd her back to the smiling girl she was before and leave her free to choose her own future.

Except . . . this isn't a normal shepherding case. Elise doesn't have the option of a normal life. The Veil *needs* her, and until I know more, until I've established a connection, I can't risk her putting up walls and pushing me away. Fully trained, Elise will be the Veil's most powerful asset.

Which makes her *my* ticket to destroying Rose.

The bells ring, and I'm surrounded by teens eager to show me to my next class. They crowd in close, talking over each other, and it's hard to breathe around so many thudding heartbeats and exposed throats. Their combined pulses, erratic and out of sync, are so loud they nearly drown out the flood of questions.

"Where did you move from?"

"Are you going to try out for the school play?"

"How long have you been in Elmsbrook?"

Their eyes are bright with the desire to hold my attention, but it's not because of anything I've done. My kind always has this effect on humans. Our presence draws them in like sheep to the slaughter. Hunger gnaws at my insides. I should have fed last night, but I stayed up late reviewing Elise's file instead.

I stare past the gathered horde and watch Elise slip out of the room. She moves like a ghost, flitting through the world without touching anything.

The petite brunette beside me must notice my stare. She leans close, pulse hammering in her pale white neck, and pitches her voice to a conspiratorial whisper. "Have you heard about her brother?"

I shake my head and stand, letting the girl lead me out of the classroom.

She slips her arm through mine and steers us through the halls. "He died last spring."

"Really?" I fake surprise, and there's this sudden tightness in my chest, like my body wants to grieve for a young man I never knew. Or, perhaps, it wants to grieve for the sister he left behind. I remember the photo of Elise covered in mud, screaming beside the river that swallowed her brother whole. "That's so sad," I say, and shove the feelings down. Having a brain that's stuck at seventeen, a brain that's too quick to feel, too quick to hurt, is a nightmare.

"It was awful." The girl squeezes my arm, and I'm very aware of her brachial pulse pressing against me. She introduces herself, but I don't register her name. She won't matter beyond this moment. "Everyone loved Nick."

"Especially his sister, I bet. I don't think I caught her name." The lie, like so many others, slips easily from my lips.

"Elise Beaumont." My guide sighs dramatically. "She used to be friends with everyone. There were even rumors that the swim coach wanted her to try out for the next Olympic team."

"And now?" We're near my next classroom, but I drink in each detail. I fit the pieces against what I already know, assembling a puzzle of my target, searching for a way in.

The girl shrugs. "She quit the team and won't talk to anyone, not even her friends. I heard her grades tanked so hard the dean almost kicked her out."

"So, what then? Everyone abandoned her because her brother died?" A harsh edge enters my voice, and I force my expression to soften. I'm not supposed to react. I'm not supposed to *care*. "Has anyone tried talking to her?"

"I wouldn't bother," says a voice behind us. A Black boy, not the one from the homecoming photos, steps into view. "All her friends tried, but she wouldn't talk to anyone. She even broke up with her boyfriend."

A flush of emotion travels through my starving body. *Boyfriend.* I remember him from the photos, tall with brown skin and a flower pinned to his suit. Her kiss upon his cheek.

Before I can ask anything else, though, the bells chime.

"Sorry!" The girl backs away. "We're late."

I don't say goodbye or watch them leave. I'm too busy piecing together a new plan as I take my seat in class. By the time the period ends, I know what I have to do.

All morning, I collect Elise's former friends like chess pieces and prepare my board for battle. I smile at the right times. Lean in for the juiciest bits of gossip. Elise is always on the periphery of my mind, but I can't make my move until all the variables are exactly where I want them.

So, I collect my knights and my rooks and prepare my move against the queen. In every class, I find the swimmers and dazzle them with charm. By lunch, I've secured a place at their table.

Elmsbrook Academy offers an obscene variety of food, so no two people are eating the same thing. There's made-to-order stir-fries. Salads topped with fresh salmon. Vegan and gluten-free options. I was going to skip lunch altogether, but I wanted to fit in. That, and the blood-red slice of filet mignon called my name. The flavors explode on my tongue, but the food can't tame the hunger that puts pressure on my gums.

I try to follow their conversation, but it means nothing to me. It's all swim times and back strokes and which boys are cutest. I don't care about any of that. Especially the boys.

Across the polished mahogany table, a Korean American girl pushes her pesto risotto around with a spoon. "What do you think Elise wanted this morning?"

"Elise?" I try not to sound too interested, but I'm not sure I succeed.

"Forget about her, Maggie. Unless Elise plans to rejoin the team, whatever fake-ass apology she cooked up doesn't matter."

The swim captain, Kaitlyn, flips her blonde hair and settles her attention on me. "I don't suppose you swim, do you? We need a solid anchor for the four-by-four."

"Sorry." I shake my head and steer the conversation back to Elise. "Why'd she quit?"

Kaitlyn stabs at her salad. "Elise doesn't give a shit about us. She couldn't handle the pressure of being captain, either."

"You know that's not why," Maggie says, and there's fire in her tone. "She saw her brother drown. I overheard Coach saying she might have PTSD over it."

"Whatever," Kaitlyn says.

It was clearly meant to dismiss the entire subject, but Maggie keeps going. She turns to me, thick red glasses framing her brown eyes. "I've actually been looking into Nick's death for the school paper. He's her brother." Her voice catches, and I wonder how well Maggie knew him. "There's this theory going around that he faked his death."

"Really?" I perk up. Wyn didn't mention anything about that. "Why?"

She leans closer. "I haven't found any evidence yet, but when the police pulled his car from the water, he wasn't inside. They didn't find the body when they dragged the bottom of the river, either."

Grace, a white girl with light brown hair that falls all the way to her lower back, nods. "It's true. My dad led the service at our church." She glances at Kaitlyn for approval before continuing. "He said there wasn't a body. They still had a burial, though."

Strange. The newspaper clippings mentioned the body was missing, but I hadn't thought much of it.

"Why does everyone assume he's dead if there's no body?" It's been several months now, but the police reports listed him as presumed dead almost immediately. "Wait. You're writing about her brother for the paper? Isn't that . . ." I search for the right word when Kaitlyn scowls at me. I don't understand why she seems to hate Elise so much. It can't just be the swim team, can it? "I mean, his sister still goes to this school, right? Won't an article about her dead brother be hard for her to see?"

Kaitlyn scoffs. "I doubt Elise even reads the paper. No one does."

"I do," Grace says, but Maggie shakes her head.

"The article isn't the point. I know Elise. Not having Nick's body wrecked her. If our places were reversed, she would do the same for me." Maggie shifts back to sit normally in her seat, no longer leaning across the table. "And . . . there was a witness at the river who saw him go down with the car. He never came up."

Our table goes silent after that. Even Kaitlyn doesn't have a snide remark to add. After a half-dozen heartbeats, Grace says something about needing to work on her backstroke, and the conversation moves on. They talk about which classes will be hardest, debate who their coach will put in the vacant relay spot, and gush in painful detail about which boys got the hottest over summer break.

This place is my personal hell.

When the bells chime to signal the end of lunch, Kaitlyn is the first to stand. "I can't believe they make athletes take a gym credit. I'm still sore from practice last night."

I follow her to the tray return. "You have gym next period, too?"

She looks at me like I'm a tiny bug she wants to squash. "We all do. We're split up by year. All the junior girls have the same gym period."

"Really?" I must sound too excited, because Kaitlyn rolls her eyes. I don't care, though. If all the junior girls have gym together, that means Elise will be there, too. This could be my chance to get her alone. I run through my options, search for a way to steal a private moment, even if it's only a few minutes.

"Hey, Kaitlyn? Could I talk to you a sec?" I call after her, infusing my tone with every bit of charm I have.

Even she isn't immune when I put on a good show. "Yeah?"

"Just us?"

Kaitlyn waves the rest of the team on, and when we're alone, I take hold of her arm and stare deep into her brown eyes. There's this moment of pressure, of futile resistance, and then her mind belongs to me. "While we're in gym class today, you will trip Elise."

Eyes blurry and unfocused, she nods. "When?"

If I were a few decades older, my compulsion could operate at the back of Kaitlyn's mind, constantly scanning the environment for the ideal time to surface, rather than going fully dormant. And without a clear and obvious activator—like I had with the men at the occult shop—I'll need to trigger it myself.

"Wait for my signal," I say, releasing my hold on Kaitlyn. She blinks as her consciousness resurfaces, and she covers her confusion with a smile. I ignore the guilt and twinge of sympathy that burns my lungs. These methods always feel slimy, but Wyn will want an update tonight, and I *will* have something.

No matter what.

━━━

Ten minutes later, we've all been assigned lockers, and I've compelled the gym teacher to give me the same uniform everyone else had with them. As I dress in the required navy shorts and heather gray T-shirt, Kaitlyn and Grace chattering about some nonsense behind me, I spot a flash of golden hair.

I look up in time to see Elise dart through the room, bare arms crossed protectively over her chest. She turns at the door, like she can feel me staring, and her eyes widen when she sees me among her friends. But then someone approaches, and she hurries out of the room.

Moving faster than I should with people around, I finish tying my shoes and chase after Elise. I follow her into the gym, where there's a volleyball net set up in the center of the room. As the teacher splits us into teams, I'm struck by how archaic it feels to schedule classes by binary genders.

A touch on my elbow pulls me from my thoughts, Maggie gesturing for me to join her and Grace. On the other side of the net, Kaitlyn and Elise are teammates. Kaitlyn glares at her former captain, but her anger has nothing to do with my compulsion. She won't feel those effects until I give her the signal.

When the game begins, everything moves so slowly that I want to tear off my skin. I force myself to keep pace with my team, even missing a ball or two, but my body rebels at being held back. It takes more effort to move this slowly than to run at top speed.

I'm too damn hungry for this.

On the other side of the net, Elise moves with the confidence of an athlete. Except her sure steps keep her away from everyone else. As soon as anyone gets too close, she shrinks back. She's an island unto herself, and avoiding the rest of her team makes it almost impossible for her to interact with the ball.

Not that anyone seems to care. It's only gym class.

The ball arcs over the net toward me, and I set it up for Maggie, who has an excellent vertical jump. She sends the ball flying over the net. Elise calls the shot and backs up quickly. I tug on the mental thread that connects Kaitlyn and me, and despite my guilt, the compulsion makes Kaitlyn hook her foot behind Elise's ankle.

Everything moves in painful slow motion as Elise loses her balance and falls. Her body slides several inches across the polished floor before finally coming to a stop.

The teacher blows her whistle to pause the game. "You good, Beaumont?"

Elise nods and tries to stand, but the salty tang of blood hits the air.

Pain explodes in my mouth, unbearable pressure then splitting gums. I fight against the desire to react, swallow down saliva and hunger, and the effort makes my whole body tremble.

"You're bleeding." I duck under the net, glaring at Kaitlyn— who did a far more effective job than expected—and kneel beside Elise. The agony in my jaw intensifies when she lifts her arm and reveals red dripping down her pale skin. "You need the nurse."

I reach out to help Elise to her feet, but she scrambles away and stands on her own.

"Don't touch me." She articulates each word so harshly they're practically a growl. Then she turns and leaves, pressing a hand against her bleeding elbow.

"Elise, wait!" I call, but she's already halfway across the gym.

"Oh, let her go." Kaitlyn covers her confusion with a smirk, the thread of compulsion dissolving now that she's fulfilled the command. "She's fine."

"She's *bleeding*." Even more importantly, Elise is about to be very alone. Though I didn't want her to get hurt, this might work better than expected. I abandon the game, ignoring the teacher's request to stay—and the *What the hell, Kate?* Maggie whispers to her captain—and slam through the double doors.

In the hall, I follow Elise's scent to the locker room. My jaw aches, and the freshly spilled blood blots out all sense and reason. My body begs me to drink, to take just a little to slake the fire in my throat. I grab the nearest locker and squeeze tight, trying to bury the monster inside and let my rational mind surface.

This hunger still feels alien after so many decades frozen in this existence, and I promise my withering veins that I will feed tonight, that I'll give them everything they crave.

Finally, the pain in my jaw subsides enough for me to swallow, and then I'm moving again, turning the corner to the row of sinks.

I find Elise examining her injured elbow in the mirror. When she spots me, she drops her arm and glares at my reflection. I've never been more relieved that that particular myth—the lack of reflection—isn't true. "What do you want?"

"To help," I say, stepping forward. "You're hurt." Though it's uncomfortable, I stop breathing to block the scent of her blood.

"I don't need your help. I didn't yesterday at Heart and Stone, and I don't want it now, either." Her tone is so hard it's almost brittle. She turns and tries to maneuver around me, but I'm not letting her get away. Not when I finally have her alone. Not when Wyn is breathing down my neck for an update.

"Wait." I grab her wrist and hold very, *very* still as Elise's entire body goes rigid. A heartbeat passes. Then two. Three.

Elise relaxes into my touch, the tension in her body melting away. She turns to look at me, her blue eyes wide with shock and relief, the little bit of color draining from her fair skin. "How . . ." She doesn't finish the thought, but I can guess why the words dried up on her tongue.

She can't see my death because I'm not among the living. Not really.

I offer a smile that's all softness and warmth, a smile that's more *me* than anything else I've worn today. "It's okay to let someone help you." I release her wrist when the heat of her blood draws dangerously close to my fingers. I turn and grab a paper towel from the automatic dispenser. "May I?" I wait for Elise to nod before touching her and gently wipe the blood from her skin.

Elise winces when I dab at the cut, but she doesn't pull away. I feel the weight of her attention as I work, but I don't look up. I give her the space she needs to grow curious.

Curiosity is a shepherd's most valuable tool.

When I've done the best I can, I toss the paper towel and press a fresh one over the wound. "You should still see the nurse." My throat is tight with pain, and I don't know how much longer I can stand this close to her blood without losing myself.

And if I falter, if I let my teeth pierce her skin, I could forget about convincing the Veil to help me find Rose. They'd run a stake through my heart for the smallest taste, and if I really lost control and killed their favorite asset?

They'd let her successor unravel me.

I suppress a shudder and guide Elise's free hand to put pressure on the paper towel. "Hold this." We stand there together, unmoving for a long time. Skin on skin on skin. Eventually, she shivers from the cold of my body, and I let go. "Come on. I'll go with you."

Elise nods, a bit of her sunlight hair escaping its braid. She watches me, a thousand questions held in her eyes. I wait for her to ask them, to pepper me with theories, but by the time we reach the nurse's office, she hasn't voiced a single one.

5

Elise

I didn't see her die.

That thought circles on an endless loop while I ice my elbow in the nurse's office. *Why didn't I see Claire die?* I know I'm not cured—I saw the nurse's death when she handed me the ice—so it has to be something about *Claire.*

She's still with me, sitting in a chair that faces my small cot. I want to reach for her hand. I want to feel her cool, soft skin and make sure it was real. Make sure I can feel her touch and nothing else—no pain, no fear, no weakness.

No death.

"You don't have to stay. I'll be fine." While part of me is drawn to her, a louder instinct doesn't trust this strange girl. Did she do something to block her death from me? She seemed to know a lot about herbs and stuff at the metaphysical shop.

Claire studies me with an intensity that makes my face burn. "Do you *want* me to leave?"

Her words feel like a challenge, and before I can make a conscious decision either way, I'm shaking my head. "You don't have to go." My words tumble over each other in their rush to get out. "It's just . . . I don't want you to feel obligated to stay. You can go back to class if you want."

A single dark brow arches up her forehead. "You think I'd rather be playing volleyball in a hot gym?"

I smile, the movement stiff and foreign, like my face forgot how to do anything but frown. "I guess not." I catch myself staring at her and shift my focus to the ice I'm holding. "You were good, though. Did you play at your last school?" The words are empty and hollow compared to all the things I want to ask, all the other theories racing through my head.

Maybe she had a near-death experience and fate doesn't know what to do with her. Maybe she's some kind of witch and can block other magic. Maybe she has the same curse I do, and our powers are like inverted waves that cancel out the effects.

I dismiss that last idea. If she saw death the way I do, she wouldn't have touched me in the first place.

Claire tilts her head to one side. "Is that *really* what you want to know?"

Shit. That heat in my cheeks turns into an inferno. *Can she read my mind?* The thought should feel ridiculous—I'm a girl of science, the daughter of a surgeon!—but it's so hard to know what's real anymore. Before my sixteenth birthday, if someone had told me I'd develop a psychic power, I would have laughed in their face.

Yet here I sit, predicting death like it's the most natural thing in the world.

"Can I ask you something?" Claire says when I take forever to respond. She's leaning against the wall now, like she doesn't have a care in the world. This version of her reminds me of the girl she was at Heart & Stone, dressed in jeans and a plaid shirt, picking apart my purchases.

"Sure."

"What's your deal with Kaitlyn? She clearly tripped you on purpose."

God, where to begin? I adjust the ice on my arm, the cold leaving my skin numb. "I used to be on the swim team with her. I was . . . I was pretty good. Kaitlyn's upset that I'm not swimming this season."

"Upset enough to intentionally injure you?" That arch in her eyebrow quirks higher.

"She probably thought it'd be funny, not painful. Besides, it's not that bad." My arm stings, and it'll probably bruise, but the cut looked a lot worse than it was. It doesn't need stitches or anything.

Claire worries at her lower lip, and it's the first time she's ever looked remotely unsure of herself. Somehow, it's more endearing than her usual bravado. It feels more real. More true.

"Is there something else?"

"It's nothing. I just . . . I heard about why you quit." She shifts on her feet and flicks her focus from the floor to me. "I'm really sorry about your brother."

The ice I'm holding can't compare to the sudden frost that surrounds my heart. It's nothing compared to the freezing river that pressed against my skin and stole the breath from my lungs. Nothing compared to the memory of Nick, his face full of panic as he pounded uselessly against the car window, unable to break out.

Unable to breathe.

His lips forming words I couldn't hear. *Go. Please, Ellie.*

It's my fault he was even crossing the bridge that night. Nick only came home because I'd complained about spending my birthday alone. Our parents were out of town for a medical conference where Dad was speaking, and Nick showed up to surprise me with cake.

No one could sing happy birthday as painfully out of tune as Nick.

The memory makes me smile, but then the rest of the night comes rushing in. Having my first vision when he passed me a piece of cake. Letting him drive back to college despite the storm. Panicking and stealing Mom's car to follow him. All of that, and I still failed. I couldn't break the window. I couldn't get him out.

Nick is gone, and there's no one to blame but me.

"Hey." Claire's voice is impossibly gentle, and she comes to sit beside me on the cot. She takes my hands in hers, and the comfort of her deathless touch makes the tears spill down my cheeks. "I'm sorry. I shouldn't have said anything."

I squeeze her hands, the first real anchor I've had since that sudden April storm. "No, it's fine." Reluctantly, I let her go and dry my cheeks on my wrists. "I don't know how much they told you, but my brother drowned last spring." My throat tries to close, the emotion so thick it's hard to breathe, but I swallow it down.

One more day, I promise myself, even though fixing the curse won't bring my brother back. *One more day.*

"Shit, I'm sorry." She shifts on the cot until our bare knees touch. She's cool as stone against my hot skin.

I shrug. I never know how to respond when people say they're sorry. *Thank you* makes it seem like I should be grateful, but that's not how I feel. At all. I'm angry all the time. At Mom for acting so normal. At Dad for ignoring me. At whatever god gave me such a terrible ability.

At myself.

"Anyway, Kate thinks all of that is a shitty reason to quit the swim team."

"Kaitlyn can fuck off."

A startled laugh bursts out of me. "I thought you liked her. I saw you with the rest of the team in the locker room."

Claire grins. "Been keeping an eye on me, Elise?"

Heat swirls in my belly, but before I can say anything, the nurse comes back. "Feeling better?"

"Yes, ma'am." I hold out the bag of ice, but Claire takes it and hands it to the nurse, saving me from another round of nausea and exhaustion.

"You girls can head back to class," the nurse says, glancing between us like she's trying to understand who we are to each other. But then she turns and dumps the ice in the sink, tosses the bag, and disappears into her office.

"Thanks for that," I say, even though I can't tell Claire *why* her gesture means so much. How could I possibly explain that she just prevented me from experiencing the nurse's death?

"Anytime." Claire stands and holds out a hand for me.

Cautiously, I accept her help. I'm rewarded with a blissfully empty mind as I untangle my legs and stand. I end up close to Claire, so close I have to look up to meet her gaze. She's a couple inches taller than me, probably five eight or so. My breath catches in my chest, and I realize with a burning embarrassment that I'm still holding her hand.

I try to step back, but her grip tightens. "I know what you can do," Claire whispers suddenly, leaning close. Her soft hair slips over her shoulder and caresses my cheek, sending a thrill of goose-bumps down my arms. "I know what you see when you touch anyone who isn't me."

A terrible hope swells inside me, blotting out the fear that whispers at the back of my mind. "You do?"

The bells chime through the school, but we stand frozen in the nurse's office. When they finally stop, I'm the one who's tightening the hold between us. "How? How do you know?"

Claire steps back, hazel eyes examining my eager expression. "Find me after school. At the edge of the soccer fields, near the woods." She puts another step between us and reaches for the door. "I'll explain everything," she says, and slips into the hall, disappearing into the current of students.

"Wait!" I chase after her, but I'm still in my gym clothes, arms and legs dangerously exposed. I'm buffeted by the swell of people, hands grazing my arms as students try to maneuver around me. I'm overcome with a cascade of deaths.

Car accidents.

Heart attacks.

A sudden fall.

And when my head finally stops spinning, Claire is gone.

⸺

The rest of the afternoon, I don't hear a single thing my teachers say. Not a word. Instead, Claire's voice is on a loop, saying that she'll explain, that she understands what I see inside my head. The surge of hope makes me dizzy, the promise of answers intoxicating.

How am I supposed to give a shit about ancient history, or even the biology class I've been looking forward to since ninth grade, when Claire is somewhere in this building with the answers I need?

Unless it was all a trick.

That worry rolled in last period, like storm clouds blotting out the sun. What if she lied? What if she's some con artist who's good at reading body language?

What if Maggie or Jordan told her?

My best friend and my ex are the only people who know every-thing. I told Jordan because I thought he would understand. I had to tell him something after avoiding him for weeks, dodging calls and hiding in the library during lunch. I was afraid to touch him. Afraid to know how I'd lose him.

So, one evening in early June, I told him everything.

Jordan said he believed me, but he didn't believe enough to be careful. He still reached for me, still touched my hand. Instead of the comfort he was trying to provide, he gave me his death. I saw him old and wrinkled, dying quietly in his sleep, lying beside someone else.

Someone who wasn't me.

While my English teacher rambles on about the boring classics we'll read this year and the types of essays we'll learn, a different kind of grief overtakes me.

Logically, I knew Jordan and I might not be a *Forever Couple*, but part of me had always hoped. Jordan celebrated my swim vic-tories louder than anyone else. He let me pick new shows for us to watch. And despite being more of a dog person, he'd find the perfect cat videos to make me laugh. He even helped me start an Instagram account for Richard.

It wasn't just me, either. My whole family adored Jordan, even Nick. The two of them spent most of winter break last year play-ing video games while I helped Dad bake an absurd number of cookies.

Seeing Jordan die was awful, but I expected to see that. It's comforting to know he'll be super old, that his death won't be painful like some of the others I've felt. But having proof that we were going to break up? Really *knowing* that he and I wouldn't last forever? It hit differently than all the deaths I'd seen. That future felt more tangible, more real.

It seemed pointless to stay together after that. Why wait until things soured or we grew even more attached? Better to end things before he forgot about my curse and held my hand or tried to kiss me again. I didn't want to see him die over and over and over.

Even though breaking up was the right thing to do, it wasn't easy. I couldn't flip a switch and turn off my feelings. The last few weeks of school were awful, seeing him in the halls, his brown eyes full of sadness. I'd already lost so much—Nick, my dad, my team. Losing Jordan felt like the final straw.

So, I spent the summer hiding at home, running until my lungs ached. With time, my broken heart went numb. But what if Jordan's heartbreak didn't dull like mine did? What if his heart went cold? What if he told Claire about the curse to get back at me?

A small, stubborn hope whispers that it could still be real. That Claire might have the answers I've wanted for months.

When the final bells chime, the stubborn hope wins out. I have to meet Claire and find out what she knows, even if there's a chance it's a trick. While everyone else heads for the main entrance, I move against the current toward the rear exit that leads to the soccer fields. Dodging around my classmates makes me slower than I want, and I'm careful to pull my sleeves all the way to the tips of my fingers.

I'm done seeing death today. *Done.*

As I near the locker rooms and gymnasium, the scent of chlorine is so thick I'm afraid I'll choke on it. *Just a little farther. The exit is right there.*

"Ellie?" Jordan's rich baritone chases after me. "Ellie, wait!"

No, no, no, no. My heart flutters erratically in my chest, but I force myself to stop. I can't give Jordan any reason to grab my hand. Slowly, I turn to face my ex, the boy I loved with all my heart until I forced myself to let him go. He looks good, even in his school uniform, and I hate that I notice. His hair is different than I remember, the fade tighter on the sides but longer on top so that his curls spill over his forehead. His brown skin is dark from a summer spent lifeguarding, and his eyes are as warm as ever.

He smiles when he catches up to me, the expression full of light and hope. "Are you rejoining the team?"

"What?" I don't know what he means until I realize where we are, where it looks like I'm headed. Swim has always been a constant for Jordan—for *us*—no matter how many other hobbies he cycled through. I always loved how passionate he got about each new obsession, from digital art to drums to a very brief excursion into coin collecting, even though each hobby never survived more than a few months before he moved on.

I used to worry our relationship would be the same. That he'd get bored of dating me after a couple months, but he didn't. We were together so long I started to hope I would become the other constant in his life.

But then this curse ruined everything, and I broke both our hearts.

"No, Jordan," I say, the words weighing heavy on my shoulders. "Swim is over for me. I can't—"

"Right. Of course. Sorry." He rubs a hand across the back of his neck. "Sorry," he says again, "this isn't how I thought this would go." Jordan looks down at me, and god, I forgot how tall he is, six feet of pure swimming speed. When he used to hug me, it felt like being burritoed in warmth. Even fresh out of the pool, Jordan is always a million degrees.

"I'm late. I have to . . ." My words trail off, and I gesture toward the exit at the end of the hall. I should have gone a different way— should have avoided this entire area.

"Sure, sure, okay. Cool." He's rambling, his words overlapping like they do whenever he's nervous. "It's just . . . Can we talk? It doesn't have to be now, you've got stuff to do, but I missed you so much this summer, and I— Can we please just talk sometime? Soon?" He's so earnest, and he's keeping a safe distance between us even though I can see him itching to hold my hand. My heart starts to break all over again.

"Jordan . . ."

"You're late, Wallace. Get— Elise? What are you doing here?" Coach Cochrane, a white man in his forties with dark hair streaked through with gray, appears from his office. He has a clipboard in one hand and a stopwatch hanging around his neck. "Tryouts were last month, Beaumont. The roster is already set."

Could this day get any worse? I hold up my hands. "I'm not trying to rejoin the team, Coach. I'm meeting someone on the soccer fields." The admission draws a confused, hurt look from Jordan, but I focus on Coach. I need to get out of here. Fast. I don't know how long Claire will wait before she takes off. "Good luck this season."

"The team misses you, Beaumont, but we understand why you had to step away." He gives me this pitying smile that makes my insides squirm. Besides, he's wrong. Kaitlyn is plenty pissed, despite my absence being the only reason she made captain. That, and the fact that our only senior swimmer moved to Florida last spring.

"We'd love to have you back next year. If you're up for it," he continues.

"Thanks," I say, because what else am I supposed to tell him? I can't control the panic attacks I get whenever I think about being underwater. Besides, losing the team—wasting the years I spent cultivating my speed and form—hurts me more than any of them. "I really should go, though," I say as I back toward the exit.

"Elise, wait." Jordan steps forward like he's going to chase after me, but Coach puts a hand on his shoulder.

"Locker room. Now." Coach nods toward the closed door. "I wanted you in the pool for warm-ups five minutes ago."

Jordan's expression falls, and it's like someone punched him in the gut. My heart twists. "I'll call you tomorrow," I promise, even as I'm making my escape. "We can talk then."

He lights up at the suggestion, which makes me feel awful for suspecting he would use Claire to hurt me. And that means Claire might have *real* answers about this curse, about my future, and I can't delay a moment longer.

6

Claire

Overhead, the blazing sun inches west across the sky, casting shadows in the least helpful direction. The light makes my muscles brittle and my jaw ache, but I can't retreat to the woods. It'll be hard enough to gain Elise's trust without skulking out of the shadows like a total creep. I didn't expect her to take so long after the final bells to get here.

Isn't she desperate for answers?

Between my growing hunger and my waning strength, I'm irritable and short-tempered. Which is *not* the first impression I want to make as Elise's official shepherd. If I want to convince Elise to leave the mortal world and dedicate her life to the Veil, I need to be patient and trustworthy and—

My phone buzzes in my skirt pocket, cutting my thoughts short. I pull out the phone, unsurprised by the name on the screen.

"Impatience doesn't suit you, Wyn."

A car door clicks shut before my mentor responds. "I waited until the end of the school day, didn't I?"

"I'm not sure I'd call that restraint." I wince as a breeze carries the scent of fresh blood to me. My insides twist with pain as I glance at the soccer field. One of the players has a bloody nose, and it takes all my concentration to keep my canines from lengthening.

I stifle a groan. "If you had waited another twenty minutes, I'd have something to report."

"Oh?"

"She's supposed to meet me any second now." I watch the school exit, but I still don't see Elise. "We had a moment alone in the nurse's office. She knows I have answers. She'll be here." I say that last part to calm my nerves as much as Wyn's impatience.

"A *moment*?" Wyn's tone takes on a suspicious edge. "What kind of moment?"

Embarrassment over previous failures twists into shame and then hardens into anger. "I will happily return to Abigail and the other trackers. If you don't trust me, you can shepherd Elise yourself."

Except . . . I don't want to leave. Not really.

Something changed when I was in the nurse's office with Elise. Hearing her story, hearing the hurt over losing her brother laced through every word . . . I cared. For a moment, I wanted to rescue Elise from the pain of her past and the lonely future the Veil requires. She feels like a person now, instead of an asset.

It's a subtle, barely there change, but it complicates everything.

Before Wyn can call my bluff and actually kick me off the case, I spot Elise exiting the school.

"She's almost here. I have to go."

"Claire—"

"I'll call you once it's done."

I hang up and rearrange my emotions. If I want any chance at revenge, I can't let myself feel like this. I can't care about whatever future Elise imagined for herself. She has a new one, a better one, ahead of her now. I just have to spin it so she understands how important she is.

Once she finds out the truth of her gift, she'll be curious. New paranormals always are. They want answers and details—so many details—about their gifts and their place in our world. A world that's so much stranger than they ever imagined. I'll give Elise all of that and more. She'll have a purpose that's so much bigger than either of us.

Elise fusses with the end of her braid as she approaches, but there's a spark in her blue eyes that doesn't look like excitement. At first, I don't understand the expression, don't get why she's not smiling. Then I notice the angle of her brow, the bitter tang of sweat and caution. There's an anger in her that surprises me.

I adjust my strategy as quickly as I can.

"You came." I say it lightly, injecting uncertainty into my tone. It feels false, wrong somehow, to play these games with her. Of course she came. There was never any doubt, not really.

She studies me, releasing her braid to tug at the edges of her long sleeves. Carefully, she pushes them up to her elbows. Elise never takes her gaze off mine, like she's issuing a challenge. A dare. "If this is some kind of sick joke—"

"It's not," I rush to reassure her. "I promise."

"If it is," she says again, hands curling into fists. "I'll make sure you regret it."

There's nothing she could do to hurt me, yet I find myself intrigued by her promise. By the anger she embraces so freely. I adjust to this new reality, try to piece together the best way forward.

I hold out one hand, palm up, and wait.

Elise stares at me a long time before resting a hand gently against mine. She tenses when our fingers brush, but a moment later, she relaxes into me. Something shifts behind her eyes, and

I wish I could peer inside her head and unwrap every thought.

"If I was lying about what I know, we couldn't do this." I hold her hand in both of mine. "See?"

"How?" she asks, voice broken and pleading. Her anger is forgotten. "How is this possible? Why don't I see anything?" When I don't respond immediately, she squeezes my hand as the first tear slips down her cheeks. "You promised to tell me everything. *Please.*"

Though I shouldn't allow it, my young heart whispers impossible things to me, and I wipe the tears from her cheeks. "I will, Elise. I swear. I always keep my promises." I lower my hand and hold both of hers. Elise's skin is warm with life, yet her fingers tremble. "Once you know, you cannot unknow."

She doesn't look away. "Tell me."

I take a deep breath, savoring the moment where the entire world balances on the precipice of great change. The moment Elise will shift from confused mortal to one of the most powerful creatures on this earth. In the space of a heartbeat, her life will change forever. I drink in this last second of the girl she is now. I drink in her *Before*. The girl with sunlight in her hair and the ocean in her eyes.

"You, Elise Beaumont, are the Death Oracle."

7

Elise

"I'm a *what*?" I yank my hand from Claire's grip. The sun is hot overhead, but her words leave me cold all over. I thought having a name for what's happening to me would feel better, but somehow, this is worse.

"The Death Oracle," she says again, like the title itself should explain everything. "It's an incredibly rare and special gift."

"You think this nightmare is a *gift*?" A bitter laugh punctures the space between us. How can she possibly think predicting death is anything but awful?

"Elise . . ." But she sounds uncertain now, and I latch on to the silence between us.

"How do you even know that I'm this . . . This—"

"Death Oracle," she fills in again, like she's stuck on a loop.

Her lack of clarity is infuriating, and I try to assemble a puzzle with too few pieces. She promised me answers, but she's only given me a name I don't understand. "Are you one, too?"

Claire shakes her head. "There's only ever one Death Oracle in existence at a time."

A frustrated scream claws up my chest and gets trapped in my throat. "Stop repeating yourself and explain this to me." I close the gap between us and take her hands in mine. "If you're not like me, how is this possible? How can I touch you and see *nothing*?"

She watches me a moment, her icy fingers curling around the back of my hands. "The Veil sent me here to help you. I know your . . ." Claire pauses and seems to select her next word with care. "Your *ability* must be terrifying, but that's only because you're untrained. If you let me help you, I can teach you to control it. I can teach you to harness your power into something great."

I start to pull away, shoving aside a rush of questions. I don't care who sent her. I don't want to know how they found me. All I want is my *life* back. I want to hug my mom without seeing her die. I want to kiss a cute boy without seizing up with pain. I want Maggie back, with no secrets between us. But then I think of Nick, and—

Nick.

His name thunders through me with each beat of my heart, and a whole world of possibilities unfurls before me. If what I've experienced is only the beginning of my power—if it's the un-trained, untested parts of this so-called gift—what else can I do?

"Can I bring him back?" Instead of letting go, I hold tight to Claire, to the proof that there's so much more to this than I under-stand. "If I let you teach me, can I bring him back?"

"Bring who back?" she asks, but there's this thread of warn-ing in her tone, this note of caution. She knows *exactly* who I'm talking about.

I say his name anyway.

"Nick. My brother. If I do what you say, if I become the Death Oracle, can I bring him back?" The world is a blur of color—green and blue and the shining brown of her hair—and it takes a mo-ment to realize the sudden watercolor is caused by tears. I let go of her hands and scrub the wetness from my face.

But her silence stretches on and on, and I feel like I'm falling.

"It's not possible, is it?"

Claire shakes her head. "I'm sorry."

"Then screw this." I turn and start the long trek back to school. I don't know why I bothered coming here. I already have a plan. The new moon is tonight, and the ritual *will* work. I'll close my third eye and get rid of this curse for good.

"You can't ignore your power."

"Then give it to someone else!" I whirl around to face her. "If I can't have my brother, I don't want it."

"But—"

"Do you have any idea what it's like? Do you know how much it hurts to see death every *single* time someone touches you?" I ask, cutting her off again. "Did the Curtain or the Shade or whatever tell you that I can physically feel it? Every pain and ache and weakness. Every time my mom touches me, my heart *literally* stops beating. Do you know what that's like?"

She goes silent again, her lips parted like she wants to speak but can't find the right words.

"Stay the hell away from me." I retreat toward the school, glaring at her the entire time. Daring her to say something. To try to stop me. When there's half a soccer field between us, I finally turn my back on the strange girl. The collapse of such a sudden, bright star of hope leaves me feeling bruised and tender all over.

Suddenly, Claire appears in front of me and grabs my arm. Tight.

"How did you do that?" My heart beats faster and faster until it's hard to breathe. "Let go of me."

"I need you to listen, Elise. This isn't just about you." Her eyes flash red, and an animal-like fear coils around my spine. "If the

Death Oracle—if *you*—fall into the wrong hands, the entire paranormal world could descend into chaos."

A terrible chill settles over my skin. *She's not even breathing hard.* "How do I know *you* aren't the 'wrong hands' I'm supposed to avoid?" Claire has no ready reply, so I push past the growing terror and yank out of her grip. I don't need her or her vague warnings. I have a ritual to prepare. "Tell the Cloak to find someone else."

I turn and head for the school, but she grabs my wrist again. "Elise, wait!"

As she pulls me back, I twist toward her and punch Claire as hard as I can. My knuckles connect with her jaw, and pain explodes through my hand. But it's enough to distract her.

When she reaches up to touch her face, I run.

8

Claire

I fucked up. Big-time.

Elise's fleeing form shrinks until she disappears into the school. I rub my jaw and head for the woods. Rusty instincts urge me to follow Elise, but I've been a shepherd long enough to know better. I already pushed too hard. I should have let her go the first time she turned away.

At least the shade of the trees is a calming balm against my skin. My vision sharpens, and the terrible fatigue fades from my muscles. The dark of night would provide even more relief, but my strength is still compromised.

I really, *really* need to feed.

My phone buzzes, and a growl rumbles deep in my chest. How the hell am I supposed to tell Wyn that I scared away the Death Oracle? I could blame the sun or the decade away from shepherding, but the simple truth is that I fucked up.

And now Elise wants nothing to do with me or her gift.

A string of vicious profanities fills the woods as I grab my things and walk back to my apartment. Instead of her title, I should have led with the best parts of her power. There must be someone whose death she'd like to delay.

This whole thing would be so much easier if Death Oracles

could be compelled. Since they can't, I was supposed to get her to trust me the old-fashioned way. Instead, I sent her running like a freshly risen rookie.

Wyn will *not* be happy when they find out.

The phone finally stops buzzing, but I pull it out and turn the damn thing off. I need a new plan before Wyn calls back. I need to salvage this fucking wreck of a disclosure before Elise does something impulsive.

I rub my jaw again. It doesn't hurt, not really, but it proves that Elise won't sit on the sidelines and wait to be saved, that's for damn sure.

The woods don't bring me all the way to my place, and when I emerge, I walk on the opposite side of the street to take advantage of shadows cast by two-story houses. This neighborhood is nothing like the one where Elise lives. None of these houses have seen a bit of care in decades. It's all dingy brick facades and peeling siding.

My landlady—an elderly widow who goes to bed by seven each night—lives on the first floor of a mid-nineteenth century Victorian. She's let the place fall into complete disarray. One side of the house clings to a faded purple hue, remnants of a long-forgotten paint job, while the front has gone gray from a half-hearted attempt to prime the wood. The carpeting and appliances in my upstairs apartment are painfully outdated and only semi-functional.

I fit the key in the front door and let myself into the entryway. The narrow space shares a wall with my landlady's kitchen, and it always smells like whatever she's cooking. Today, it's roasted chicken and potatoes. I climb the rickety stairs to my apartment, but when I get there, I freeze.

The door is open, even though I *know* I locked it this morning.

I'm not worried about intruders—there isn't much that could

hurt me—but I can't spend my night tracking a thief. I need to feed, and there's homework to do. I focus my blood-starved senses, but there are no signs of life inside.

I ease open the door and step over the threshold into my kitchen. There's no whisper of breath or beating heart. All I smell is the lingering scent of spiced body wash and stale cigarettes from the previous tenant. I inch across the old, cracked linoleum and slip into the living room. Sudden movement makes me duck, and a bright yellow pillow smashes into the wall. The tattered fabric bursts, raining white stuffing all over the ripped carpet.

A growl rumbles in my chest as all my violent instincts rise to the surface. I whirl on the intruder, ready to tear out their throat, only to find someone I've been trying to avoid. "Damn it, Wyn. I liked that pillow."

Wyn brushes brown hair out of their eyes and flops onto my sagging couch. They're dressed in their usual formal attire—black suit, impractically white shirt, and a vivid red tie—but Wyn must have abandoned the jacket somewhere along the way. "You've been avoiding my calls. What else was I supposed to do?"

"Oh, I don't know, wait an hour. Shepherding takes time." I drop my backpack on the floor and collapse onto the loveseat, hanging my feet over the armrest. I *really* don't want to report my failure in person, but there's no avoiding it now. "Please tell me you didn't kill the landlady."

Wyn presses a hand to their chest, feigning shock. "Who do you think I am?" When I give them a withering look, they only smile. "I told her my cat had been hit by a car, and when she stepped outside, I compelled her to invite me in."

"You're a monster." I tip my head back to stare at them upside down. "That's incredibly cruel."

"But effective. It works on everyone." Wyn rolls their shirt-sleeves to their elbows, resting thin, pale forearms against their thighs as they study me. "Why are you in such a mood?"

"I'm not in a *mood*," I say, and press one of my remaining pillows tight against my face. Which I realize, too late, only proves their point.

Wyn sighs. "Let me guess, Elise got scared when you told her you're a vampire."

Vampire. The label—and all the stereotypes it conjures—only irritates me further. All the movies and literature of the past several decades make it out to be some romantic, albeit tortured, existence, but I didn't ask to be this way. By Veil law, I shouldn't exist at all. Vampires aren't supposed to turn humans younger than twenty-five.

Rose either didn't know I was underage, or she didn't care, when she took my human life and left me with . . . this.

I let out a pathetic groan when Wyn yanks the pillow from my face. "I didn't get far enough to tell her what I am," I admit. "Elise should have been excited to learn more about her power. At the very least, she should have been relieved."

"She wasn't?" Wyn knits their brow, seeming curious instead of disappointed.

"Not at all." I sit up and face them fully, sifting through memories of the failed conversation. "Well, she wanted to know if she could resurrect the dead. When she realized she couldn't, she stormed off."

Wyn laughs, the unexpected sound reverberating through the small space.

"What could possibly be funny about that?"

"Now you know what it's like to work with someone as dramatic as *you*."

I smack Wyn on the shoulder. "Asshole."

"Don't sass your elders," they say, still laughing.

Though Wyn was turned at twenty-five, they're not referring to human years. Wyn has been a vampire since 1782. I was turned at seventeen, in 1937, which means I'm practically a child by vampire standards. It also doesn't help that I can't claim a bloodline, since Rose never bothered to properly introduce herself, but at least that part Wyn understands. They don't know their bloodline, either.

Being a too-young orphan, I had to fight like hell to be taken seriously by the Veil. I worked harder than all the other shepherds—and then trackers when I switched roles—until I was the best. It's been a long time since I failed so spectacularly.

Not since Fiona.

Shame and regret creep around my heart. Fiona was a lot like Elise, a mortal teen with a rare, paranormal gift. The Veil sent me to shepherd Fiona when her flair for summoning fire started to attract the wrong kinds of attention. I taught her to control her power, to respect and follow Veil laws. I even thought I could convince Fiona to accept the occasional mission to help further our interests. That part wasn't required, not with her, but it would have raised my profile among my peers.

For two years, I guided her, and for two years, my foolish teenage brain ignored all the warning signs. The pointed questions. The impossible promises. I did the worst thing a shepherd can do.

I fell in love.

When everything went sideways, when Fiona killed a tracker and tried to hurt me, too, the Veil forced me to end her life.

Leadership never knew I loved her—they only knew I'd failed. Luca Tagliaferro, an Italian vampire turned at the start of the tenth century, seemed satisfied by the outcome. Henri Guillebeaux, the

French co-founder of the Veil, was mostly sad to lose what he called *an amusing gift*.

After Fiona, I swore I'd never shepherd again. I wanted to leave the Veil altogether, but Wyn convinced me to stay, saying orphans like us couldn't find a better family. I transferred to tracking and spent the next decade hunting paranormals who broke our laws, bringing the worst offenders to Tagliaferro for sentencing. It was a simpler life. Brutal and violent, but simple.

But then the previous Death Oracle went missing, and Wyn dangled a rare opportunity in my face. Shepherds who successfully train new Death Oracles are always well-rewarded for their efforts. Riches. Prestige. Decades-long vacations from Veil duties.

All I want is a little revenge.

"All right, enough moping." Wyn reaches out a hand and hauls me to my feet. "What's your next move? I know you have one."

"I don't know." My voice comes out like a whine, which just makes me more annoyed. Wyn is like an older cousin who sneaks me into bars and encourages me to party, but when I know I've disappointed them, I spiral.

Wyn levels a glare at me. "Yes, you do. No other shepherd relates to teenagers like you." They poke a finger against my temple. "Now, use that semi-mortal brain of yours."

I swat Wyn's hand away and scowl. My brain may be stuck at seventeen, but it's not *mortal*. It's hard to think when there's hunger gnawing at my insides, but I force myself to pull apart everything that happened today. Everything she said. Every pointed silence. Every brush of her fingers against mine. No. I shake that last thought away. I can't afford another mistake like Fiona, not with someone as important as Elise. As important as the *Death Oracle*.

"She needs time," I say at last. "Pushing the issue got me nowhere, but she knows I have the answers she wants. If I keep my distance for a few days, she'll come looking for them." Plus, if she tries anything weird, the men at the occult shop will call to warn me.

"Fair enough. So long as you don't give her *too* much space. There are already rumblings in the tracking division that vampires have noticed Hazel's absence."

I wince at the mention of the previous Death Oracle. The Veil isn't popular with all of our kind. Plenty of vampires resent the Veil's control, despite how necessary that control is to keeping our world secret and safe. If enough vampires find out that Hazel is gone and her replacement isn't fully trained, we could have a war on our hands.

"Anyway." Wyn steps back and adjusts their tie. "After such a big day, I assume you're hungry?"

My jaw aches and my canines lengthen at the suggestion. "Starving, actually."

"Perfect. I drove past a college on the way here. I'm sure we can find a party to crash."

"I can't. I have homework," I say, ignoring Wyn's pointed look. "I can get a pizza delivered."

"And you'll what? Drink from the delivery guy?" Wyn shakes their head. "Unacceptable."

"But my homework—"

Wyn's brown eyes flash red. "You don't actually *need* to study. Just compel the teachers into giving you perfect grades." Wyn pushes me toward the bedroom. "Now, get changed so we can find you a pretty girl to take the edge off."

9

Elise

Pavement flies beneath my feet. Wind tugs at my hair. Yet with every step, her words echo through my head.

You're the Death Oracle.

I near my street, but at the turn, I go west instead of east.

If you fall into the wrong hands, the entire paranormal world could descend into chaos.

This can't be happening. It can't be *real*. I adjust the backpack slamming against my ribs, and my thoughts change course. If magic isn't real, how can I see the things I do? How did Claire catch up to me so quickly? Why don't I see her death when we touch?

If she isn't like me, *what* is she?

My muscles burn, and my lungs ache with each hard-won inhale. I'm running faster than I can sustain, but it's not fast enough to slow my mind. One question shouts louder than the rest, over and over and over.

Why me?

Out of the billions of people on earth, how am *I* the one cursed with this? And if I really am the only one, how did Claire find me? Do I give off paranormal pheromones? Has someone been watching me my whole life? Are my parents part of the paranormal world, too? Was Nick?

I don't have answers—for any of it—and that only makes it worse. This is supposed to be a world of science and logic and reason. Of cause and effect. Instead, I'm trapped in a dark, twisted fairy tale.

As I push my body to the razor's edge of its limits, the physical discomfort eventually drowns out my thoughts. Half a mile later, I link up with my usual route and force my legs to carry me home.

The house is empty when I punch in my passcode—my birthday, 0421—and unlock the front door. Dad must still be at the hospital, and Mom's probably showing a house. Even Richie doesn't come to the door to greet me, and I hope she hasn't gotten herself locked in a closet somewhere.

It wouldn't be the first time.

At the top of the stairs, I touch Nick's door and duck into my room. I drop my bag to the floor and peel out of my sweaty uniform. My back already aches. My quads and calves, too.

In the shower, I try to keep the panic at bay. *Just a few more hours until the new moon ritual. Just a little longer, and this will all be over.* Doubt tries to creep in, but I shove it away. I won't let some girl I barely know turn me into a Death Oracle. I can't even imagine what her training entails.

Or what I'm supposed to do *after*.

I dress in an old swimming T-shirt and a pair of leggings, braid my hair, and pull out my supplies. Candles. Salt. Baggies of dried herbs and the quartz pendulum. I take a deep breath. *I can do this. Just a few more—*

The doorbell rings, the soft chimes echoing downstairs. A cold chill runs over my bare arms. *If Claire followed me home, I* . . . My thoughts falter. I have no idea what I would do.

Cautiously, I leave my room, press my fingers to Nick's door for luck, and go downstairs. Whoever rang the bell isn't visible through the bit of glass, but only Jordan and my dad are tall enough to be seen there, anyway.

The person abandons the bell and knocks. "Come on, Elise. Answer the door."

Maggie's voice melts the tension from my muscles. I open the door, and my heart lurches to see her standing there. She still smells faintly of chlorine, her wet hair pulled into a bun.

"Hey," she says, a note of caution in her voice. A layer of uncertainty that isn't supposed to exist between us.

Uncertainty that I caused.

"Hi, Maggie." I don't know where to go from there, though. This morning, I had planned to explain everything, but *everything* is so much bigger now. So much stranger. Where would I even begin?

"So . . ." Maggie clears her throat and sits on the wicker bench beside the door. For as many summers as I've known her, that seat has been her favorite. "This morning, you said you wanted to talk?"

Betrayal flickers in my chest, but I can't blame Maggie for her earlier hesitation. Though I'd never admit it out loud, Kaitlyn was a little right. The way I abandoned Maggie was beyond shitty. But I have a plan now. A way to be friends again without seeing her death. I have to fix the hurt I've caused, no matter how complicated.

Except . . . I don't know where to start.

"So," Maggie says when I've stayed silent too long. "I saw Jordan at practice. He said he ran into you in the hall. That you promised to explain what's been going on?"

I wince and step out onto the porch, closing the door behind me so Richie doesn't escape. I never should have said that, but seeing so much hurt and hope in Jordan's eyes tugged hard on my heart. "You know how he gets with that sad face he pulls."

"But it's not just him," Maggie presses without missing a beat. "You wanted to talk to me this morning, too. So, let's talk. I can tell there's something going on."

"There's nothing—"

"Yes, there is! I'm worried for you. I've *been* worried, but I thought you needed space after Nick and . . ." She pauses, voice thick with hurt. After several deep breaths, she brushes tears from her face and holds my gaze with hers. "Something is clearly *off* with you. We were supposed to be minnows for life. And minnows—"

"Don't keep secrets," I finish, sinking down to the floor. I pull my knees to my chest and rest my forehead against them. "You won't believe me," I mumble against my leggings.

Maggie climbs down from the bench until she's sitting across from me, her skirt fanned out over her legs. "I'll believe almost anything if it explains why my best friend has been ghosting me since June."

She reaches for my hand, but I flinch away. Maggie pulls back. "This is about what you told Jordan, isn't it? The death thing?"

The way she says it—without a hint of sarcasm or judgment or doubt—nearly breaks me. Tears spill over my cheeks.

"Ellie, please. Tell me what's going on. I can't help if I'm kept in the dark."

My heart lurches, and I bury my face in my hands. Telling Jordan was such a disaster—and he so quickly spilled everything to Maggie—that I decided it was safer if no one else knew. I tried to figure this out on my own, but nothing worked. Hopefully, a magical approach will have better luck.

No, not hopefully. It will. It has to.

"Please?" Maggie asks again. Her voice breaks, and the last of my resistance washes away.

"It's horrible," I finally manage, my words broken and my throat tight. Once I start, though, I can't stop. I explain the visions in my head, how they happen every time someone touches me. I tell her the way I feel every death like an imprint on my body. I tell her how Mom dies.

How Jordan dies, too.

"He's really old, and he looks happy." I brush away the drying tears, my throat raw and my nose so clogged I can't breathe. "But the person he's with . . . it's not me. How was I supposed to keep dating him when I knew we were going to break up? When I couldn't even hold his hand?"

"Did you try gloves?" Maggie asks, and she seems so sincere that a laugh bubbles up my chest.

God, it feels good to laugh.

The feeling doesn't last, though. There's more she needs to know. "Remember that day we fought? When you grabbed my wrist, I saw your death, too. You—"

"Nope. Absolutely not." Maggie shakes her head and covers her ears. "I don't want to know. Not now, not ever."

"Are you sure?" It feels wrong, somehow, to know her future and not tell her.

"Positive. I don't want that hanging over me the rest of my life." She shudders and hugs her arms around herself. "What do we do? I'm not letting you ice me out again." Maggie tries to play it off like a joke, but I hear the real hurt under her words.

"I'm really, really sorry about that, Maggie." Guilt picks at my heart. "I didn't know what else to do."

Maggie waves away my apology. "Just don't let it happen again. No more secrets. Deal?"

The lingering hurt in her voice stings, but I nod. "Deal."

"Good. So, what's the plan?"

"I've been looking for a way to get rid of it." I tell her about the faked migraines and medical tests. All the research and the trips to the occult shop to create a ritual to close my third eye. How having a plan made me realize how much I'd messed up by pushing her away.

"And you're sure all those herbs and things will work?" Maggie sounds skeptical, but at least she's still here. She hasn't run off. She hasn't tried to touch me.

I shrug. "I've tried just about everything else." For a moment, I consider telling Maggie about Claire—about how she thinks I'm a Death Oracle and wants to train me—but things are already weird enough. If the ritual succeeds, none of that will matter anyway.

"Fair enough. When does this all go down?"

"Tonight. It's the new moon, which is supposed to be good for breaking curses," I say, and when Maggie raises an eyebrow at me, I laugh. "I know, I sound like a character in those horror films Karen and Jenn made us watch."

"And definitely not one of the characters that makes it through alive, either. You wouldn't survive the first thirty minutes with a plan like that." Maggie shakes her head, but then her face lights up. "They're planning another movie marathon this weekend, actually, if you want to come."

"Won't that be weird?" It stings, the sudden reminder that Nick's death did more than take *him* from me. Watching him drown stole so many other parts of my life—so many pieces of my identity. "Those nights were just for the team."

Maggie sighs. "I guess." She glances back at the front door. "Where are you doing the ritual?"

"In my room?"

"Really." My best friend gives me a look that so clearly says *Are you serious right now?* "And how do you expect to pull that off with your mom home? There's no way you can burn candles without her knowing."

"I'm not going to miss my chance," I argue, but Maggie's right. Especially after the vape pen incident, Mom has been on high alert for any weird smells. Plus, Richie is bound to be a pain in the ass. If she's locked out of my room, she'll sit outside the door and scream. And if she's in the room with me? She's likely to catch her tail on fire.

I don't know why I love that cat so much. She's such a nuisance.

The thought of going another month with death following me around like a shadow is unbearable. Especially with Claire trying to convince me to join some cult. "It has to be tonight."

"Do it at my place," Maggie says, scrambling to her feet and grabbing her bag. "I'm at my dad's this week, so Vivi won't be around to snoop. Plus, he's working a double in the ER. He won't be home until super late."

"Are you sure?" Guilt and shame burn inside me. I was such a terrible friend for such a long time. I don't deserve Maggie's help. "How do you even believe me? I barely believe any of it, and I'm the one living this nightmare."

"Look, when we said 'minnows for life,' I meant it." Maggie opens my front door and heads for the stairs, leaving me scrambling after her. "If you say you're psychic and want it to stop, I'm going to help make that happen."

We get to the top of the stairs, and Maggie goes quiet as we pass Nick's door. She even seems to hold her breath until we're safely tucked in my bedroom. I open my closet door, and Richie blinks up at me, the carpet around her scratched to hell. I shoo her away and grab my ritual things.

I text the family group chat and let my parents know I'm going to Maggie's place. Dad won't respond, but I'm sure Mom will be thrilled that I'm being social again. Her reply is almost instantaneous—a string of confetti emojis with a reminder to be home before eleven. I pull on a hoodie, slide my phone in the front pocket, and double-check that I have everything.

Once I'm sure things are ready, I turn back to Maggie. "I'm all set."

"I do have one condition," Maggie says after we've passed Nick's door again.

"Anything."

Maggie flashes a wicked grin, and I regret agreeing before she's said a word.

"You have to invite Jordan to help."

———

Maggie's dad provided the Miller to her hyphenated Sullivan-Miller last name back when she was adopted. Things always seemed fine—at least to us kids—but when Maggie was eleven, her parents got divorced. Ms. Sullivan moved out, got remarried, and had Maggie's half sister, Vivian, a year later.

It's not until I step into Mr. Miller's place that I realize how long it's been since I was here. Maggie always seemed to invite

Jordan and me—or me and the other swim girls—to hang out on Mom Weeks, despite Vivi toddling around. At first, I don't understand why Maggie never had us come here. It's not like the place is a disaster or anything. It's actually really clean, which is impressive considering all the long hours Mr. Miller works at the hospital as an ER nurse.

On the walls, he even hung pictures of him and Maggie. Mr. Miller is white—both of Maggie's parents are—and he keeps his head shaved even as his beard gets progressively bigger in each photo: first a mustache that looks like it's straight out of the '70s, then a goatee, and finally a full beard kept neatly trimmed.

In all the photos, Maggie is smiling, but she looks . . . stiff. Uncomfortable. After the divorce, neither of her parents would talk about what happened, but Maggie hates platitudes and missing facts. She went searching for answers. It took her a couple years, but when she was thirteen, she found out her dad was having an affair with another nurse at work.

It feels weird to be here now, following Maggie through the house. She never told her parents that she found out, but as I step into her room, it's clear she keeps a *lot* from her dad. Her room is practically sterile. There aren't even pictures of us on the walls. Although, I realize with a twinge of regret, that might be my fault, not his.

This isn't just about me, though. Her bed is neatly made, and there isn't a pile of dirty clothes in the corner. At her mom's, Maggie's room is an explosion of color, clothes shoved haphazardly into drawers, her bed unmade and covered in decorative pillows.

"Will this work for the ritual?" Maggie asks, straightening the edge of her boring blue bedspread. "We could use the basement instead if you need more space."

I glance down at the carpet beneath my feet. "The basement has wood floors, right?" I ask, trying to conjure a memory of the last time I was here. "That will probably be easier to clean."

"Yeah, this way." Maggie leads me down to the large finished basement.

As we push furniture out of the way, I wonder if Maggie's parents originally chose this house thinking Maggie would need a place to hang out with her friends. Does her dad notice that we never visit anymore? I consider asking Maggie about it as we work, but things still feel . . . precarious between us.

Fixing our friendship will have to wait until after the ritual, though. I pull out my supplies and put half the bay, fennel, nettles, and witch hazel in a bowl with liquid coconut oil and let the herbs soak. As I'm reaching for the first jar of salt, the doorbell rings.

"That should be Jordan," she says, heading for the stairs. "Do you want to tell him, or should I get him up to speed?"

I fumble with the jar of salt, but thankfully, it doesn't fall. I wasn't thrilled about inviting Jordan to help us, but I owed Maggie, and it was her only request. "Could you do it?"

Maggie nods and disappears.

One crisis at a time. First the ritual, then I can fix everything else. I take a deep breath and draw a huge circle on the floor in salt, leaving a gap for Jordan and Maggie to enter. Once that's set, I trace over the circle with the second half of the dried herbs.

While I work, I'm hyperaware of the conversation happening above me. I light candles and set them within the perimeter of the circle, but fear creeps across my skin as I think of Claire. She found me at Heart & Stone. She found me again at school. What if she follows me here, too?

The stairs creak as I'm stripping out of my hoodie, Maggie

returning with Jordan in tow. My ex pauses outside the circle and shoves his hands in his pockets, like he's afraid he'll reach for me. The stiffness in his posture makes my chest ache. Two summers ago, before we were dating, Maggie, Jordan, and I spent so many nights in his backyard, the three of us jumbled together in the hammock while his dad grilled us dinner.

Jordan lets out a low whistle. "Are you sure this is a good idea? It looks like a horror movie in here." He rocks up onto his toes and shudders. "My mom will kill me if she finds out about this."

"Trust me, I'm not telling *any* of our parents." I point to the gap I left in the salt circle. "If you want to help, you can come in through there. If this is too weird, for either of you, it's okay to wait upstairs."

"I'm not leaving," Maggie says, stepping through the gap. She glances over her shoulder at Jordan. "Stop being a baby and get in here."

Reluctantly, Jordan follows her into the circle. "Just for that, Maggie, if demons follow me home, I'm sending them right back to you."

Maggie rolls her eyes, but my stomach flips to see them together like this. To be part of their banter again. I wish I could bottle up memories like this and keep them forever.

Jordan stops a couple paces from me, hands still in his pockets. "Anything you need, Ellie, I'm here for you."

The sincerity in his voice, the warmth, stirs something in me, but I press it down. I won't let our hearts get tangled back together just so fate can rip us apart. There's no point acknowledging the way he's looking at me, like he wants to kiss away every hurt and worry and pain. I won't let myself admit that part of me wishes he could.

I clear my throat. "Someone needs to close the circle. The salt and herbs are there."

"Do I just pour it where there's a gap?" Jordan asks, picking up the supplies.

"Yeah. Just make sure you're on the inside of the circle when you do it."

"On it."

"What can I do?" Maggie pulls a thin pair of winter gloves from her pocket. "I found these upstairs. I thought they'd make it safer if you needed help."

The gesture soothes some of my nerves, and I pass her a hunk of selenite shaped like a wand. She squeezes my bare hand in her gloved one. Through the fabric, the warmth of her touch nearly breaks me. *You're almost there. Focus.*

"I need to spread the herbs along as much of my skin as I can. While I do that, can you run the selenite through my aura?"

"Your aura?" Maggie raises a brow.

"Look, it's only going to get weirder. If you want out—"

"No, I'm here. I'm in this." Maggie soothes the skepticism from her face. "How am I supposed to know if I'm doing it right?"

"I was planning to wave it around my body like those metal detectors at the airport." I mimic the motion I mean. "The guy at the occult shop said it's best to start at the top of the head and work your way down."

"Umm . . . I think I did this right?" Jordan says from the edge of the now-closed circle.

"Looks good." I hold up the bowl of herb-infused oil. "Could you hold this for me?"

Jordan hurries over, and the candle flames make shadows dance across his face. I remind myself to focus and get to work. I dip my fingers into the bowl and scoop out chunks of oily leaves. As soon as I spread them along my arms, my skin prickles. The earthy, herbal scent clings to my lungs. Maggie, meanwhile, holds the bit of selenite and brushes it down the length of my body.

As we work, I repeat my desire over and over inside my head. *Save me from this awful plight. Cleanse these deaths from my sight.*

"I think that's good?" Uncertainty pitches Maggie's words into a question.

My fingers scrape the bottom of the bowl, and I put the last of the herbs across my forehead. "Me too."

"Now what?" Jordan asks.

I pick up the pendulum from the top of my bag. "Now, Maggie closes my third eye."

"I do what now?"

"You close my third eye. It's one of the major chakras. Here." I point to the space at the center of my forehead, just above my brow line. "I'm going to lie down, and you'll hold the pendulum above my third eye. If you ask it to close the chakra, the crystal will spin counterclockwise. When it's done, it'll fall still."

This time, it's Jordan who looks at me like I've completely lost touch with reality. "How do you know all this?"

"Lots of really weird research." Carefully, I lie down at the center of the circle and close my eyes. When nothing seems to happen, I peek over at my friends, who haven't come any closer. "If you don't want to do it, I can—"

"No. Sorry," Maggie says, coming to kneel beside me. "I can do this."

"It won't hurt if she messes up, will it?" Jordan asks.

"Trust me, it can't hurt more than this curse." My words are met with an uneasy silence, until Maggie finally sighs.

"Okay, let's do this." She raises the pendulum over my forehead and closes her eyes. When it starts to spin, counterclockwise just like the articles said, I let mine shut, too.

I hadn't planned to do this with others, but there has to be extra power in being together, right? Even though it feels weird, I crack open one eye. "Do you want to chant with me?"

Maggie nods. "Sure."

Jordan fidgets but stays close. "I guess."

"Okay, here goes. For science," I say, though neither of them laughs. I take a deep breath and ignore how silly this whole thing feels. I never played make-believe, even as a kid. "Save me from this awful plight. Cleanse these deaths from my sight."

"Should we replace 'me' with your name?" Jordan asks.

I repeat the updated phrase in my head. "That messes up the meter. I think maybe 'her' works better."

Maggie speaks first. "Save her from this awful plight. Cleanse these deaths from her sight." Jordan joins in next, and then I add my voice to theirs. We're quiet at first, tentative, but then our voices blend into one and crescendo until my throat grows raw.

The temperature in the basement goes up and up and up. Sweat mixes with the oil and herbs on my skin as pressure builds inside my head. There's this sudden flare of heat and light that makes everything red from behind my closed lids.

Jordan screams.

Maggie curses and drops the pendulum against my forehead.

When I open my eyes, the basement is shrouded in darkness. It smells like smoke, and it takes me a moment to realize all the candles have gone out.

"Did it work? Is that it?" Maggie's voice trembles.

"I don't know." I sit up and block the glare of Jordan's phone light as it sweeps across the room. "I think I feel normal?"

"Here." With her gloved hands, Maggie helps me to my feet. "You're not dizzy or anything?"

"Nope," I say, and assess for signs of change. My skin is itchy, but I think that's the herbs. I feel fine, I guess, but there's only one way to find out for sure. "We should test it."

"Here." Maggie pulls off her gloves, but I step back, shaking my head.

"Jordan should do it," I say as gently as I can. "If it didn't work . . . His death hurts less."

"Hey! I'm right here."

"I don't mean it like that," I tell him. "Some deaths leave a lingering pain, like an echo. Yours doesn't, but Mag—"

Maggie holds up one hand. "Okay, now I *really* don't want to know." She steps back, but there's a shine to her brown eyes. "I'll grab a washcloth," she says, stepping over the salt line before I can warn her not to. The ritual is over, though, so it's probably fine.

She flicks on the light for us and is gone before I can thank her.

"So . . . How do we do this?" Jordan approaches slowly and holds out a hand. His fingers are long and slender, and I remember how well they used to fit between mine.

I hold out an herb-crusted arm and squeeze my eyes tight, bracing for impact. "A quick touch should do it."

"Here goes nothing." Jordan presses his fingers to my skin. Warmth spreads from his touch, but a moment later, he pulls away.

And I didn't see anything.

Cautiously, I open my eyes, convinced he didn't actually touch me. "Do it again." I watch carefully as Jordan presses his fingers to my arm. A flutter of hope crashes through me. "Hold tighter," I beg, the words broken on my tongue.

His fingers circle my wrist, dark brown skin against my green-coated paleness.

"It worked." My eyes sting with tears. "Holy shit, it actually worked!" Part of me wants to kiss Jordan until we're breathless, but this doesn't change the fact that our relationship is doomed.

"Really?" Maggie's excited voice cuts between us. "That's so great, Ellie!" She runs over with the washcloth and raises her arms to crush me in a hug. At the last second, she pulls up short and grimaces at the messy state of me. "Here, let's clean this up."

She wipes away the oil and herbs from my arm, and I can't stop smiling. It worked. It really worked.

I'm free.

Maggie runs the cloth over my skin again, and follows with her fingers, like she's checking that she got all of the oil. I think she did, the itching has already—

Pain rushes through me, and I close my eyes tight. Inside my head, I see an older version of Maggie walking around the edge of a pool. She raises a hand to greet someone, turning to continue a conversation. Maggie slips in a puddle of water, feet flying out from beneath her. The ground rises up. Her head smashes against concrete.

An echo of that pain explodes against the back of my skull as blood spreads out beneath her. The spark in her eyes disappears.

A scream tears from my throat. I rip away from her touch and collapse to the floor. I'm shaking all over, only vaguely aware of my friends beside me. Of Jordan asking what happened. Of Maggie guessing that the oil must have protected my skin. She puts on gloves to finish washing away the herbs while Jordan whispers empty reassurances.

Just one more day, the old refrain, the thing that kept me putting one foot in front of the other, rings hollow in my head. It was all a lie. A fantasy I concocted for myself.

This curse isn't going anywhere.

10

Claire

Night has fallen over Elmsbrook, and unlike the missing moon, I rise. Strength courses through every atom. My eyesight sharpens beyond mortal standards, and I drink in the carefree expressions of university students who dance without a care about tomorrow's classes. The air is thick with the scents of sweat and booze and *life*.

Hunger gnaws at my ribs and burns at my throat. My skin feels too tight, too thin, and I'm dizzy with need. It won't last long, though, not with Wyn's party in full swing. And it *is* Wyn's party. They handpicked students from the library, whispered ideas into their ears, and compelled them to throw a Tuesday-night blowout. Wyn has a special talent for identifying social linchpins every-where they go—all it took was a few key selections to pack the off-campus house with fresh blood.

I prowl the party, maneuvering through a sea of dancing bod-ies. My senses heighten to their predatory peak, and I scour the room for the perfect prey. This level of hunger would leave a lesser vampire desperate and sloppy, but control is everything to me. I maintain my composure even as I'm battered by the percussive beat of the music. Feeding is about more than blood refreshing my ageless body. It's about the hunt. The selection.

The chance, for one brief moment, to be seen.

Despite the dim lights, I catalogue every face in crystal-clear detail. A Latinx girl with a sharp jawline and beautiful brown curls. A genderqueer student with a face full of piercings and tattoos covering tan arms. Everywhere I look, soft cheeks, full lips, bright eyes. I search the crowd for a girl who will smile when she sees me, whose heart will flutter when I don't look away. Though I could compel anyone to host for me, that would only feed the physical need. What I truly crave, what I won't tell even Wyn that I desire, is something so much deeper than that.

Finally, when I'm so hungry I can't keep my canines from lengthening, I spot a girl sitting on the arm of an old denim chair. She smiles when she catches my eye, running a hand over the side of her head that's shaved tight to her skull. I drink in her smile as I make my move across the dance floor. Her skin is light brown, her eyes several shades darker. She's painted her lips a vivid plum, thick black eyeliner completing the look.

"Hey," she says when I approach, and her heart skips when I smile.

"Care to dance?" I offer my hand.

The girl accepts my touch, and I feel every line of her palm against mine. She steps past me, whispering, "Try to keep up," as she pulls me toward the center of the room. The song changes, the beat urgent and reckless, and the girl presses her body against mine. She moves like she's made of rhythm, and her hands find their way to the curve of my hips.

Vicious instincts urge me to sink my teeth into her flesh, to drink and drink until there's nothing left, but I want a few more minutes of *this*. Of her fingers finding a strip of bare skin beneath the edge of my shirt. Of her soft curls grazing my collarbone. One song turns into two, and when someone takes control of the play-list and provides a slower number, I make my move.

I shift back to meet her gaze, and when her eyes lock onto mine, I press my will against hers. The tether of compulsion locks in place, and I offer an apologetic smile. "Don't be afraid," I soothe. "Don't scream." She nods, her expression hazy and dreamlike in-stead of the sharpness that was there before.

She reaches for me to continue our dance, and I lower my lips to her neck. Her scent reminds me of warm summer nights, but then the hunger overtakes my rational mind, and I sink my teeth into her flesh.

The first pull of warm blood rushes through me, slaking the fire at the back of my throat. The second dulls the ache in my muscles, and the third rushes a flood of feeling *everywhere*. Every sense is heightened. Strength and power blooming where there used to be numbness and pain. The young woman presses tighter to me as we dance, and with a firm hand, I put space between us. She can't know what she wants while she hosts—can't consent to my touch—and I won't take advantage of anything beyond what I must to live.

I allow myself a final drink, and her blood warms my skin, fills my dead heart enough to make it beat once. Twice. I let go before I can take more.

My body protests—it's not enough, not *nearly* enough—but I won't hurt this girl. Not in a way I can't undo. I wipe the last beads of blood from the puncture marks before they seal shut, a by-product of vampire saliva that hides the truth of us mere sec-onds after we let go.

"Forget you ever met me," I say as I slip away. Her gaze is still unfocused, and I test the tether, make sure she won't remember my face, and then I let go. When I'm across the room, I turn to check on her. She rubs her neck absentmindedly, but the sharpness is back in her eyes as she scans the room. Her smile blooms when she spots her friends, and then she's gone.

I find a second girl.

A third.

Hunger finally satisfied, I go searching for Wyn. They're not in the living room or the kitchen. I reluctantly check the bedrooms and find them holding court over an audience of six college students. While I can only compel two or three people at a time, I've seen Wyn compel as many as eight people at once. A benefit of their additional years trapped in this existence. Their current half-dozen hosts sit fully clothed at the edge of the bed.

". . . the ambassador was *not* pleased to find that I'd introduced his wife to his mistress. Or that they were having far more fun without him."

"Seriously, Wyn?" I roll my eyes. "You lead with Paris every time."

"What? It's a great story. I'm a brilliant matchmaker," they say without looking at me. Wyn leans closer to the bed and mock whispers, "I didn't even get to the part where *I* seduced the ambassador's second mistress. It was a glorious weekend."

"It was two hundred years ago," I remind them. "You need new material."

"Why? They've never heard it before." Wyn steps closer to the bed and holds out a hand. The student on the end, whose blue hair reminds me of Elise's eyes, offers their wrist. "Much obliged," Wyn says and sinks their teeth into the soft, pale skin.

The scent of fresh blood stirs my hunger again, shifting it from manageable to aching in an instant. After several swallows, Wyn releases their host. "Amuse yourselves for a bit, friends. I'll be back." Wyn joins me in the open doorway, and somehow, their white shirt is still pristine. "Feeling better?"

"Yeah."

Wyn raises an eyebrow. "You're a terrible liar."

I cross my arms. "No. I'm not."

"Yes. You are," they say, mocking my tone, which makes me feel young and foolish. But then Wyn rests an arm over my shoulders and leads me into the narrow hallway. Out here, the thud of heavy bass reverberates through my bones.

"Claire, darling, do yourself a favor. Feeding is about more than staying alive. It can be *fun*. I don't want to see you again until your veins are bursting with excess blood."

"But—"

"If you say you have school tomorrow, I will kick your scrawny ass."

I glare at them. "But I *do* have school tomorrow, where I have to fix this mess with Elise." I lean against the wall and glance over my shoulder to make sure no one is close. "You said yourself that vampires have noticed Hazel's absence. The longer we go without a functioning Death Oracle, the greater the risk of mutiny."

Instead of agreeing with me, Wyn shoves me farther down the hall. "Which is precisely why you need to feed until you can't see straight. It'll buy you more time before you need blood again."

Before I can protest, Wyn disappears to hold court over the humans. I consider leaving the party and running home, but I didn't miss the command in their voice. Wyn can't compel me, but they still outrank me in the Veil. It's in my best interest to do as they say.

Plus, they do have a point. I guess.

So, I rejoin the party. I hunt and I dance and I feed. As the clock ticks toward midnight, I'm dangerously close to losing myself, drunk on warm blood and warmer dance partners. The string of girls is a blur, and I've lost track of how many there have been. My most recent dance partner, a pretty brunette with green eyes, laughs as I spin her, but when I blink, the girl in my head is blonde.

Her eyes as blue as the sea.

Despite the crowded room, despite the blissful absence of hunger, I feel suddenly alone. The kind of alone that crumples my soul like discarded paper.

In my haze, I wonder if I have a soul anymore. If I ever did.

And as I dance and spin and accept a kiss from a girl I didn't compel—didn't even drink from—all I see is Elise. Her sunlight hair. Her ocean eyes filled with shock and relief the first time our hands touched.

I was supposed to help her.

I failed.

But I won't fail again.

The next three days are a testament to the restraint I've spent decades cultivating.

In some ways, giving Elise space is easy. In our shared math class, she stares at the board and never glances my way. She bolts out of her seat the second the bells ring, and then continues to give me the cold shoulder each time we pass in the halls. Despite her avoidance, I can't help but notice subtle signs of distress. In gym, with her limbs exposed, she's jumpier than she was that first day, arms crossed protectively against her middle. Dark circles spread like bruises beneath bloodshot eyes, like she hasn't slept.

Guilt picks at me. She shouldn't have to suffer the effects of her untrained power alone. If she'd just agree to let me help, I could make things so much easier for her. Instead, I force myself to give her space. To respect the distance she keeps firmly between us. Then, at home each night, I speed through my homework and practice a thousand permutations of my second recruitment attempt. Later, I lose myself in the pages of a book while the stars burn overhead. Yet every day at school, the cold of her dismissal burrows into me like a splinter of wood.

On Friday, I can't stand the silence a second longer.

I can't even blame Wyn this time. They've checked in via text, but our conversations quickly turn from my lack of updates to the witch Wyn is seeing to an upcoming recruitment trip in Philly. I don't need Wyn to rush me, though. My own impatience is doing that.

At lunch, I sit with a group of juniors from my math class. The teens talk endlessly, trying and failing to draw me into their conversation, but my attention is locked on Elise.

She's actually in the cafeteria today, sitting with Maggie and Jordan. I don't know what Elise did to steal Maggie back from Kaitlyn, and I ignore the flush of hot jealousy that runs through my depleting veins. It won't be long before I need to feed again. Elise sits close to her friend, the nearest I've seen her sit to anyone— anyone who isn't *me*—but I note, with a satisfaction I shouldn't entertain, that she's still careful not to touch either of them.

Jordan smirks at something on his phone then holds it out for Elise to see. She watches the screen, her brows creased, then bursts into laughter. She gestures for Jordan to play it again, and curiosity gets the better of me. My ears tune effortlessly into their conversation.

". . . so much buildup, but then they don't go anywhere," Elise says through laughter. "Look at him!"

"I knew you'd love that one," Jordan says, turning the phone back to face himself. On the screen, a large cat prepares to jump onto a counter. When it launches, it barely leaves the ground.

What is it with humans and cat videos?

"I saved another one yesterday that you *have* to see," Jordan says, flipping through his phone.

Across the table, sitting next to Elise, Maggie swats at Jordan's arm. "We're supposed to be helping Elise, not distracting her."

"Distracting *is* helping. She hasn't laughed in days!" Jordan argues, but he sounds defensive even from here. And though his skin is too dark to show a blush, there's a tinge of adrenaline on the air. Serotonin, too. He still likes Elise, more than he wants her to know. He's a better actor than I would have guessed.

"I'm sitting right here." Elise taps her phone screen, and it lights up on the table. "Crap, I'm going to be late. Ms. Conrad wanted to see me this period."

"Why?" Maggie asks.

Elise shrugs and slips her bag over her shoulder. "I'm sure it's nothing important. I'll catch you both later."

There's a falseness to her tone, a worry that she's trying to hide from her friends, and I'm on my feet in an instant. This could be my chance to get her alone. I don't want to lose an entire weekend of potential shepherding.

"Claire?" One of the teens calls my name, but I glare at her until she presses her lips back together.

I slip out of the cafeteria and turn right toward the history wing. I move faster than I should through the halls, but they're mostly empty with everyone either in class or having lunch. If anyone does see me, I shouldn't be more than a blur of blue and green and white.

Footsteps sound behind me, soft soles against polished marble. Before I even see her, I can picture her blonde braid swinging with every step. I position myself, and when Elise finally turns the corner, I'm perfectly placed for collision.

She gasps when she crashes into me, and the softest of inhales catches in her throat when I reach out to steady her. I feel the moment she recognizes me, the stiffness in her body melting when she realizes there's no danger of seeing my death.

"You." She says the word accusingly, and I recalibrate.

I step away. "I'm sorry. I didn't mean . . ." I let the words trail off like I'd practiced, but being this close to her again, I feel giddy and strange and off-balance. The rest of my rehearsed words don't come. "I'm sorry," I say again.

"Are you following me?" Her blue eyes narrow with suspicion.

"Yes." The admission slips out, and I'm left scrambling to salvage the moment. Elise tries to circle around me, but I block her path. "Please, just wait."

She crosses her arms. "I don't have anything to say to you."

"I know. I fucked up the other day. I shouldn't have tried to stop you from leaving." I realize I'm doing the same thing I'm apologizing for, so I move out of her way. "I'm sorry, Elise. I really am here to help you. I didn't expect you to react like that, but that's no excuse for being a creep."

Though I expect her to stalk past me, she doesn't move. Elise's eyes sparkle with unshed tears. "I tried to get rid of it," she says, her words more whisper than substance.

I swallow the sudden panic and anger and relief. "Tried?"

"It didn't work." The anguish in her voice is gutting, and she wipes away the stray tear spilling down her cheek. "I'll never be normal again, will I? I'll never be able to touch anyone."

"But you will," I promise, holding out a hand. "You left before I could explain. There's so much more to your power than you know. I can teach you."

Elise glances from my outstretched hand to my face and back again. Slowly, she untangles her arms and rests her hand in mine. "I can train you to master your power," I whisper, stepping close so that my words are for her alone. "You could touch your family again. Your friends."

"But how?" she asks, voice breaking. "How is this possible? Why can't I see your death?"

Warnings clang inside my head, but I can feel the challenge of her words. I can sense the desperate need for truth—a need I once shared and fought for years to fulfill. "I'm not . . ." I struggle to find the right words. "I'm not . . . fully alive."

She tenses, but she doesn't drop my hand. "You're a ghost?"

"No, I'm—" The words die in my throat, and I'm the first one to pull away. I can't look at her. The last time I admitted this to a mortal, everything went to hell. "I promise I'll explain everything, but not here. We can meet tonight and—"

"Now," she says, cutting me off. "Now, Claire, or not at all. I've suffered enough. I've *waited* long enough. I want answers. Real ones."

Her glare penetrates my every defense, and I feel naked and exposed in a way I haven't in ages. Dueling desires—to run from her attention and to drink it in like life itself—battle within me. A flush of nerves prickles along my skin, desire pulsing deep in my gut. Fucking hell. If I'm not careful, this girl will destroy me.

"Promise you won't panic?" I ask, and she nods. I want to

trust her, but it's not like I have a choice. She's the Death Oracle. Once she's fully trained, Elise will have the power to completely unravel paranormal creatures like me. To deliver a slow and agonizing death to anyone who crosses the Veil. If this is what it takes to get her on that path, I'll tell her. Here. Now.

In the middle of a high school.

I take a deep breath, savor her scent—free, for now, from the acrid tang of fear—and take the plunge.

"I'm a vampire."

11

Elise

"Elise?" My history teacher, Ms. Conrad, peeks into the hall from her classroom. She's only two doors away, but I can't focus on her. Not when my world has been turned upside down. Again.

I turn back to Claire, positive I misheard her. "You're a—"

"A vampire," she says again, quietly enough that only I can hear. "It's not as scary as it sounds," she rushes to add. "And I promise I can explain everything if you—"

"Elise," Ms. Conrad says again, more insistent this time.

Despite my earlier promise, panic crawls up my throat. "I'm sorry, I have to . . ." I turn away from Claire and escape into my history classroom. I repeat the apology for my teacher. "I'm sorry, Ms. Conrad. Claire—" My mind races with all the things I can't say. Things I won't let myself believe. She's not a *vampire*. She can't be. "She's still learning her way around the academy."

Ms. Conrad, a white woman in her late twenties, maybe early thirties, settles behind her desk. She's the youngest teacher at the academy by at least a decade, but she dresses more formally than the others, like she wants to seem older. Today, she wears a cream silk blouse, black jacket, and matching slacks. "I'm glad you could help. Have a seat." She gestures to the chair she's already pulled up in front of her desk and tucks a loose strand of auburn hair behind her ear. "Do you know why I asked to speak with you?"

Even though I could list a dozen reasons, I shake my head and take a seat. Ever since the ritual failed . . . It's been hard to get up in the morning. Harder still to care about school. I'm starting to backslide without a plan forward. Which is precisely what Claire is offering me—hope that this will get better. But how can I trust her when I'm not even sure she's *alive*?

Except . . . she's also the only one with answers, strange as they may be. I thought I could figure this out on my own. I thought I could solve it, but I can't.

I hate that I need her. Hate that she must know that.

"Elise?" Ms. Conrad tilts her head to one side, and I get the feeling this isn't the first time she's said my name.

"Sorry," I say, staring at my hands. I push thoughts of vampires and curses out of my head. "There's been a lot on my mind lately."

"That's actually what I wanted to talk to you about." Ms. Conrad riffles through a stack of pages on her desk and pulls one from the middle. It's marked through with slashes of red.

Worry curls in my gut when I see my name on top alongside a sharply written *D*.

"Yesterday's quiz wasn't your best." Ms. Conrad slides it across the desk toward me. "I spoke with your teachers from last year. They assure me that you were an incredible student before . . ."

She trails off, and I can't stop the anger that rises up. "Before my brother died?"

Instead of getting upset, Ms. Conrad sighs and sinks deeper into her chair. "I'm not doing this right, am I?" She takes a deep breath and tries again. "You've been through a hurt no one in this school can fully understand." Her words surprise me. Most teachers pretend they miss Nick as much as I do. "I wouldn't be concerned about a single failed quiz—we all have bad days—but you're so disconnected during class. I worry this will become a trend."

"And if it does?" My question is equal parts curiosity and challenge.

"Dean Albro hosted a faculty meeting at the end of the summer. He wants us to keep a close eye on your progress," she admits. "Coach Cochrane tried to argue for more leniency, but the academy has certain standards to uphold."

Though embarrassment warms my face, I'm not surprised. It's a miracle the dean didn't kick me out last year, proof of my mom's amazing negotiation skills. "What are you saying?" Despite my cardigan, fear makes me shiver with cold. Maggie and Jordan say they've forgiven me for icing them out, but things are still . . . a little off. I can't afford to get kicked out, not when we're just finding our footing again. They're the only good thing I have left.

Unless there's any truth to Claire's promises.

Ms. Conrad watches me carefully for several seconds before leaning forward. "This isn't an ultimatum, Elise. I'm asking how I can help. I assume from your return that you *want* to be here. If that's true, you need to keep your grades up. I can help you find tutors or—"

"That's not the issue," I say, but now that the words are past my lips, I'm at a loss for how to continue. This wasn't the conversation I expected. At all. I glance out the door, where I'm certain Claire is lingering, waiting to ambush me the moment Ms. Conrad lets me leave.

Can Claire hear everything we're saying?

How can she be a vampire if I've seen her walking in the sun?

"Well, think about it." Ms. Conrad stands and rounds her desk, coming to a stop in front of me. "If you haven't seen a grief counselor, that might also be a good idea. I could help you research support groups in the area if you want." She smiles softly at me, and I'm surprised by the lack of pity there. It's like she actually wants to understand. Like she cares, despite how little she knows me. "If you like it here, I'll do what I can to help you stay."

"Thanks, Ms. Conrad."

"Anytime, Elise." She leans forward and pats my hand before I can stop her.

Fear turns my body to stone, making it impossible to pull away from the unwanted touch. Inside my head, I see Ms. Conrad. She's dressed in jeans and a blue silk blouse, her auburn hair loose around her shoulders. Ms. Conrad doesn't look any older, her hair the same length and color it is now. She stands frozen on a sidewalk, illuminated by a flickering streetlight.

Is someone there? Her voice carries through the dark, but no one responds.

Then, suddenly, there's movement at her back, arms wrapping tight around her trembling body. A hand presses against her mouth, smothering a scream. My throat aches from the strength of her stifled shout, and then there's pain *everywhere*. There's pressure at her back and searing heat as something slams into her again and again and again.

I see her fall—see the red blooming across her back—and then the living Ms. Conrad finally takes her hand away. My chair screeches as I scramble to my feet. My heart slams against my ribs as my body is flooded with pain and desperation and fear.

"Elise? Is everything okay?"

No. Nothing is okay. I just saw, just *felt*, my teacher get murdered, and—

Nausea twists in my gut. Bile burns at the back of my throat. Someone is going to *murder* Ms. Conrad, they're going to stab her, and I . . . I—

"I have to go." I stumble toward the door, and the second I pass into the hall, Claire is there.

"What's wrong?" The fierceness of her concern overpowers my fear, and she catches me when my knees give out. "Elise, talk to me. What happened?" She shifts, wrapping her arms around my waist, and I cling to her, to her solid body, to the cool touch of her hands, to the emptiness of my mind. I never want to let go. "What did you see?"

Tears slip down my face, and I'm shaking too much to speak with any coherence. I've seen so many deaths since I turned sixteen, but there's never been anything so violent. So intentional. So—

"Ms. Conrad . . . She's . . . She's . . ."

"Shh," Claire soothes, lifting me so only my toes graze the floor as she leads us farther from the classroom. "It's going to be okay."

"But it's not." I force myself to breathe until the tightness releases its stranglehold on my throat. When we finally stop moving, we haven't gone far, just enough to get around the bend in the hall. I've experienced so many deaths I can't change—illnesses and accidents—but I can't let Ms. Conrad get *murdered*.

She doesn't even get to grow old.

And the weather was still so warm . . .

I stare up at Claire, who's watching me with such worry and tenderness, I get an idea. "If I let you train me," I say slowly, noting the way her face lights up at the suggestion, "will you do something for me?"

"Anything," she promises, her hands still resting on my waist.

I grip tighter to her arms, force myself to hold her strange, hazel gaze. "Then you have to help me stop a murder."

12

Claire

"A murder?" The brief swell of victory crumbles inside me. Changing a death is complicated. It takes Death Oracles *years* to master that part of their power. But she's still holding tight to my arms, and each point of contact makes it hard to focus.

I shove down my emotions and step away from her touch. "Was it Ms. Conrad? Is that who you saw?"

Elise nods and scrubs her cheeks with her sleeves. "It was terrible. I mean, all the deaths I see are terrible, but this . . ." She shudders and hugs her arms around her middle. "I can't let that happen to her. We have to do something."

"We will," I promise, careful not to specify what that *something* will entail. There are too many variables. Elise needs time to sharpen her skills, and until we begin, there's no way to know how adept she'll be. "Do you have any idea when it might happen?"

"I don't know. She looked the same as she does now." Elise closes her eyes and winces. "It felt more like weeks or months instead of years."

"Then there's no time to waste." My words are punctured by the bells, and the hall fills with students. "Come on." I take her hand and lead her into the nearest classroom.

"We'll get in trouble for skipping," she whispers, drawing the attention of the teacher.

"Can I help you girls?" The teacher, a tall white man with a neatly trimmed salt-and-pepper beard and a steady pulse, stands from his desk.

"Do you have class this period?" I weave my voice with honey and light, and when he shakes his head, I smile. "Perfect." In a burst of speed, I cross the room and grip tight to his arm. It makes things easier, not having to hide myself—my *real* self—from Elise.

"Leave this classroom and stand guard in the hall," I say as the tether of compulsion finds a deeper hold. "Don't let anyone inside until both of us leave. Once we're gone, forget you saw us. Understand?"

"Perfectly." He walks past me, and as I turn to watch him leave, I notice Elise staring.

Her heart speeds in her chest, and the second the door shuts behind the teacher, she halves the distance between us. "What the hell was that? You can't just . . . just—"

"He'll be fine." I make a mental note to avoid mentioning that I compelled Kaitlyn the first day of classes. Somehow, I don't think that would go over well.

"But he's acting like a zombie! You can't just make people do whatever you want." She freezes out of reach, brows arching up her forehead. "Have you done that to me?"

"No, Elise. I would never—"

"But how can I know for sure?"

"Because it's impossible," I admit, voice rising. I take a deep breath and try again. "It's called *compulsion*. Vampires can compel humans to do just about anything. Some do it for their own amusement. Most do it to survive and to keep our existence hidden."

"And what about you? When do *you* use it?"

I think of the girls at the party earlier this week, compelling away their fear so I could feed without attracting attention. I think of all the girls over the years, over *decades*, who danced with me and kissed me yet will never remember my face.

"I do what I must for my job," I say at last. "Like this. We needed a private place to speak. I gave us one."

"Your job?"

This part is always tricky. Most paranormals—whether mortals like Elise, freshly turned vampires, or fae banished to the mortal realm—don't like being treated like an obligation.

I try to soften the blow.

"It's not as cold as it sounds. The Veil helps new paranormals understand our world. As your shepherd, I can help you control your power so it doesn't control you."

"But you're not a Death Oracle." Elise makes a face, like the title is bitter on her tongue. "How are *you* supposed to help me?"

Her words sting, but it's a logical question. "Most of the time, we're matched with our own kind, but there's only ever one Death Oracle."

"Which means the last one is dead, right?" Elise asks, and when I nod, she settles into one of the desks. "That doesn't explain the compulsion thing, though. Why can't I be compelled?"

"No paranormals can. Being the Death Oracle makes you one of us."

Technically, it's more complicated than that. Vampires can be compelled by our makers for the first year of our existence. Wyn says it's an evolutionary precaution to prevent the newly risen from draining entire towns before they learn restraint. Not that Rose ever used compulsion to help *me*.

"None of this makes sense." Elise groans and massages her temples. "Every question you answer makes me think of a dozen more. Like, how can you seriously be a *vampire*? You didn't bite me when I cut my arm, and I saw your reflection in the mirror. I've even seen you in the sun. You don't sparkle or burst into flames."

"You can't believe everything you see in movies." I sit in the desk to her left, weighing which details will answer her questions without scaring her away. "We do need blood to survive, but most of us can control ourselves around a cut. The reflection thing is just a handy myth. Direct sunlight is agonizing, but it doesn't kill us."

They're tiny admissions, little slivers of truth, but I still hold my breath when I'm done. An eternity of silence stretches between us, and I lose myself in the beat of her heart. It's fast at first, but eventually it slows and settles into a more natural rhythm. I let myself hope that this will actually go okay. That she won't see me for the monster I am.

That she'll see *me*, and she won't look away.

"About the blood," Elise says at last. "Is this a *Twilight* situation? Like, are you a vegetarian vampire who eats animals instead of people?"

I exhale a laugh that's more air than substance. "That's . . . not a thing."

"Why not?"

"It would be like . . ." I falter, looking for the right metaphor. This is only the second time I've had to explain vampire affairs to a human. Most of my shepherding cases were newly turned vampires whose creators abandoned them or were killed. Outside of witches—who train their own and generally try to stay out of Veil affairs—humans with paranormal gifts are rare.

"Claire," she prompts.

I sigh and try the first explanation that comes to mind. "Imagine you're on a deserted island. You're dying of dehydration and desperate for water. That's kind of what our hunger feels like. Our muscles ache. Our throats are on fire. It's hard to think clearly." I risk a glance at Elise and find her watching me. She nods, so I continue. "The island is surrounded by water, but since it's the sea, you can't drink any of it. The salt content will dry you out even faster. You'll die."

"Animal blood will kill you?" Elise's brow furrows with concern.

"Not immediately, but it won't stop us from desiccating, either."

Elise nods and fusses with the end of her braid. "So, you use blood bags, then? I mean, not all vampires, obviously. I'm sure there are some creeps who still kill people. But the good ones? They must use blood bags."

"Vampires do occasionally kill the humans who host for them. Sometimes accidentally. Sometimes on purpose," I concede, but from there, I don't know what to say. I stare at my desk rather than watch the inevitable shift from curiosity to understanding to horror play out across her face.

In the silence, I can't help but think of Fiona. She was the first human I told, and the shock made literal smoke curl from her fingers, a precursor to the paranormal power she possessed. Anger hardened her words when she told me to leave. It was a long time before she trusted me again. She did, eventually, but there isn't that kind of time with Elise. Not if she wants to grow her power fast enough to save her teacher.

"You didn't answer the question," she says at last, and I can't read her tone. I'm afraid to try. "You don't use blood bags, do you?"

"We can't. The way they separate the blood . . . It'd be like trying to survive off nothing but vitamins." The words scrape over my tongue, and I finally meet her gaze. "I take less than they would give at one of those donations, though, and I promise it doesn't hurt. There are chemicals in our saliva that—"

"I really don't need the details," Elise says, cutting me off. Instead of pulling away or running from the room, though, she takes my hand and squeezes tight.

A flutter of hope prods at my still heart.

"Just promise you'll never bite me." She shudders. "I don't want to be like you."

Despite the warmth of her skin, her words are ice. The conviction. The disdain for what I am. I would never wish this existence on anyone, but it still hurts. I pull my hand from hers.

"Sorry," she says. "I don't mean to keep touching you. It's just . . . It's been so long since I could touch another person."

"But I'm not really a *person*, am I?"

I stand and stalk toward the door. Her words shouldn't hurt, but all I can hear are the things she needs from me. Promises and assurances and a body without a death. I have no right to be upset, the Veil will require so much more from her, but I'm tired of feeling like a soulless cog in their machine. All the Veil's expectations—make her trust you, don't repeat your mistakes, never *feel* anything—batter against me on an endless loop.

"Claire?"

"Getting bitten won't change you," I say, the words as sharp as my teeth. When I turn back, Elise is sitting where I left her, cheeks flushed and her heart beating faster than it was moments before. "It's not a disease that spreads through our bite. Even if you *wanted* to become a vampire, you couldn't. The Veil needs you as you are, as the Death Oracle."

"Oh."

"If you want to save your teacher, we need to start training today." I pace the room, and with each step, I shove my emotions deeper inside me. I become the creature the Veil wants me to be. Calculating. Cold. Efficient. "I can compel your teachers to get you out of afternoon classes. We can use my apartment to—"

I stop dead when I turn and nearly crash into Elise. She's so close, the heat of her presses against me. Her heartbeat is loud in my ears.

"I'm sorry," she says, looking up with those ocean eyes.

The words squeeze the breath from my lungs. "You're what?"

Elise holds out a hand. "I said something that hurt you."

"You didn't."

"I did."

"Who said vampires have emotions?" I ask, even as I relent and slip my hand in hers. I lace our fingers and squeeze gently. "How do you know we aren't just blood-sucking machines?"

She raises one eyebrow and quirks up the corner of her lips. "Have you met you?"

Her question makes me laugh, which does terribly wonderful things to my insides.

"If we're going to do this," Elise says, still holding tight to my hand, "we need to work together. Okay? No delays. No secrets. No getting upset with each other for things we don't understand."

It's the most remarkable thing, the way she looks at me without flinching. Her determination to save her teacher, even with all the hurt she's carrying over her brother.

"Okay." I squeeze her hand once before I let go and head for the classroom door. "Lesson one—*no one* can know about this. Not that you're the Death Oracle. Not that vampires exist. None of it. Not even your parents."

"About that," she says, stalling me at the door. I turn back to find Elise fussing with her braid. "Maggie and Jordan . . . They sort of know. Already."

I sigh and lean against the closed door. "Of course they do."

———

I've never been more horrified by a trio of humans. While I pace the ripped carpet in my living room, Elise, Maggie, and Jordan detail the disastrous ritual they performed on the new moon.

"When the candles went out," Maggie says from her place on the couch, "we thought that meant the ritual had worked. We even tested it on Jordan."

Jordan nods, but he never quite meets my eye. "When I touched Elise, she didn't see me die."

"The oil and herbs must have created a barrier, because when I wiped them off, her curse came back." Maggie rests a hand on Elise's knee, where there's no danger of touching her skin.

I pinch the bridge of my nose. "You're lucky you didn't burn down the house." There was never any real danger of Elise losing her gift. Curses require a full coven to lift them, but as far as I know, nothing can take away a Death Oracle's power.

Except her own death.

Still, one of her friends must have a distant witch relative for the chant to have blown out the candles. The humans are lucky they didn't magic away their physical sight, too.

When I finally stop pacing, I turn and glare at the teens. Maggie and I are in matching skirts, while Jordan and Elise wear their academy slacks, but even though I'm dressed like them, it's clear I don't belong. "Anything else I should know?"

They share a series of looks, and it's like whole paragraphs pass silently between them. The familiarity of it, the intimacy, is a painful reminder of the connection I haven't had since my own mortality.

Not since Betty.

Her name knocks between my ribs, tender like a bruise that never heals. For decades I tried to forget her, but now it all comes rushing in.

Betty and I grew up together and spent every free hour at her parents' estate. When she was sixteen and I was seventeen, she fell in love with a boy in town.

One afternoon, lying in the grass with the sun a warm ball of possibility above us, Betty complained that she couldn't properly woo this boy if she were a poor kisser. I jokingly suggested that she practice. Except she didn't take it as a joke.

Betty was never good about asking permission. For anything. She leaned forward and pressed her lips to mine. The kiss lasted one second, perhaps two, but I lived a lifetime in those moments. My hands seemed to move of their own accord, and suddenly I was reaching for her. My fingers brushed her soft curls, and when she pulled away, I could hardly breathe.

Betty hovered over me, head tilted to the side. *Did you know*, she asked softly, *that this close, your eyes look like flowers?*

Yeah? I was afraid to breathe. Terrified to look away and break this sudden spell between us.

They're beautiful. A shy smile pulled at her lips, her cheeks flushed a rosy pink, and a thousand tiny clues knit together. The way she always reached for my hand. The way she leaned into me when she was tired. Her lips brushing my ear whenever she whispered sleepy confessions.

I dared to hope that we shared the same terrifying secret.

Before I lost my nerve, I captured her lips with mine. They were soft and sweet and so very warm. An unexpected passion bloomed within me, and I deepened the kiss. I gave her more of myself. My heart thundered and tried to leap from my chest to live inside hers.

But then I felt her stillness, and every brave thing inside me turned to glass.

Betty pulled away, looked at me with such horror . . . Even now, it stings, and not just because my love was unrequited. I lost everything that day. My best friend. My family. My future.

"Claire?" Elise's voice pulls me from the memory. "You okay?"

"Yeah, sorry." I rub a hand over my face. Elise reminds me a little of Betty, strong and determined and always reaching for my hand. In love with a boy, too. "Was there anything else?"

"No, that's it," Elise says, tugging on the sleeves of her sweater. "After the ritual failed, we didn't know what to do next."

"Although . . ." Maggie adds, "now that we've spilled *our* secrets, I feel like we deserve some answers."

"You can't read minds, can you?" Jordan asks, and Maggie elbows him in the ribs. "What? How am I supposed to know what she can do? Edward could read minds, and Alice could see the future. Though, I guess Elise can do that now, so maybe that's not a vampire thing."

I was wrong about high school. *This* is my personal hell.

"What about this organization you work for? What do they want from Elise?" Maggie adjusts her glasses and leans forward, studying me. "You can't expect us to believe they're helping out of the goodness of their hearts."

Jordan chimes in again, his leg bouncing with nervous energy. "If you lose a limb, will it grow back? And what about garlic? Does garlic kill you? Or wooden stakes?"

Fuck, this is going to be a long day. "Do you really think I'm going to outline all the ways to kill me?"

"I didn't mean . . ."

"We just want to understand," Elise says, picking up where Jordan trailed off. She stands and crosses the small space to me. "We want to trust you, but there's too much we don't know."

Technically, Maggie and Jordan shouldn't know *anything*. Wyn would never allow it, but Elise threatened to back out of training when I suggested compelling them to forget. And Elise . . . Well, as the Death Oracle, she'll learn all about paranormals—including how to destroy us—soon enough.

I really don't want to lead with that, though.

"Please?" She reaches for my hand, and her touch sends a jolt of wanting through me. It doesn't mean anything to her, though. She wants answers. She doesn't want *me*.

"Fine." I let go of her hand and gesture for her to rejoin her friends on the couch. "Garlic, holy water, and crosses have no effect on us. And despite what you may have read, we're not technically immortal, though we are ageless and damn hard to kill by your standards." I glare at Jordan. "But we're not *starfish*. We don't regrow limbs."

I leave out that a wooden stake to the heart *is* one of the ways to kill us, along with decapitation and being consumed by fire. Among other things.

Nothing is truly immortal. Everything with a beginning has an end. That's how Wyn explained this existence to me, when they found me wandering the streets of London, looking for Rose. When they recruited me for the Veil and took me under their wing, another orphan without a bloodline to claim them.

"Elise told us about compulsion on the way over," Maggie says, and it's like a splinter of wood beneath my nails. It's also a reminder that compelling her friends would be useless. Elise would tell them again anyway. "What about mind reading?"

"No mind reading."

"Any other powers we should know about?" Maggie presses. "How many vampires are there? And what about the Veil? They obviously want something from Elise."

I choose my next words with care. Elise needs to fully trust me before she learns that her service to the Veil will require constant supervision and protection. That she won't have time for mortal affairs once training is complete.

"Our numbers aren't massive," I say at last. "Most vampires cluster in northern cities with their bloodline, and only about a tenth of us are involved with the Veil. We keep the other ninety percent from overfeeding and terrorizing humans."

Maggie glares at me, unconvinced. "And Elise is supposed to help with that?"

"She's the biggest deterrent, yeah. The Veil is massively out-numbered. We've always had the oldest, strongest vampires among our ranks, but rebellions still pop up. Fully trained, Elise will have immense power over paranormals." I pause and watch as this information settles over the humans. Jordan looks nauseous as he bounces his knee in time with his heartbeat. Maggie's brow is furrowed, like she's lost in thought.

And Elise? Her blue eyes shimmer with worry and uncertainty that twists my stomach into knots.

"It's not all like that," I promise. "There are really wonderful parts of your power, too. You can save lives."

Elise's gaze flicks up to mine. "How?"

"There are . . . Actually, hang on." I slip into my bedroom, grab a notebook and pen, and return to Elise. "Okay, there are four main stages of Death Oracle power."

I draw a short horizontal line on the bottom-left corner of the page, then add three more, working my way to the upper right like stairs.

"This is where you are now. Level one." I write the word *touch* on the line. "Where you want to be, where you can touch other humans again, is here." On the third line, I write *shield.*

"What's in between?" Maggie leans forward and points to the empty second spot. Elise leans away from her sudden closeness.

I write *proximity* and draw a diagonal line from level one to two, then another from two to three. "Before Elise can shield, she'll need to expand her power." I turn my focus to my Death Oracle. "You'll need to learn to see death at a distance. Without touching them."

"What?" All the color drains from Elise's face. "I don't want to see *more* deaths. Isn't there a way to skip that part?"

My heart aches for her, but this is how it has to be. "If there was another way, I'd give it to you, Elise, I promise. You have to walk before you can run." I offer a smile that I mean to be reassuring, but the air is already thick with her fear. She trembles and leans into Jordan's touch for comfort. A flush of envy tears through me.

Focus, I chastise myself. *This is your one chance to earn a favor from the Veil.*

"What about saving Ms. Conrad?" Elise brushes her sleeves against her cheeks as Jordan rubs her back. "When can I do that?"

"I'll keep an eye on her until you're ready, but that gift is here." I draw a final slope to the fourth horizontal line on my page. This is the height of Elise's powers. Making new deaths for mortals. Unmaking a paranormal's gifts until they're nothing but a husk, a fate reserved only for the worst of the Veil's enemies. A warning to others to follow the rules.

I scrawl the final word across the page and hand the diagram to Elise.

"At the unraveling."

13

Elise

"I'm still not sure I trust her."

Maggie and I are at Elmsbrook Elementary with her kid sister, Vivi. The sky is dark with clouds, so we're the only people at the playground. Even so, I feel weird talking about this in public.

"What other choice do I have? Nothing else has worked." I grab one of the white bars on the merry-go-round and give it a spin. In the center, Vivi giggles, red pigtails bouncing as she turns.

"Is it actually helping?" Maggie raises a skeptical eyebrow.

My skin burns with embarrassment, and I pull the sleeves of my hoodie past my palms. "Not yet." I spent all Friday afternoon trying to see Jordan's death without touching him, but I didn't even get close.

Claire kept telling me to reach my aura out to his, but I couldn't feel anything. Saturday was more of the same, and by the time Claire sent us home, I was half-convinced I'd made up my power and imagined the whole vampire thing.

Except . . . I can't shake this bone-deep feeling that the murder I saw is barreling down on us. Thankfully, Claire has been keeping an eye on Ms. Conrad every night, despite my lack of progress.

"Come on, Elise. You have to admit she's shady." Maggie pushes the merry-go-round when Vivi shouts at us to go faster. "Every time we ask a question about your future, she gives some vague, semi-mysterious answer. We still don't know exactly what she wants from you."

"Technically, you and Jordan aren't supposed to know anything."

A flash of hurt and anger crosses Maggie's face, but Vivi yells that she's dizzy and we slow the merry-go-round. The four-year-old hops off and runs toward the slides.

"Just five more minutes, Viv!" Maggie calls after her sister, and as soon as she's out of earshot, Maggie glares at me. "How can you trust a dead girl more than your best friend? A dead girl who wants you to kill other vampires in, like, the grossest way possible."

Claire tried to downplay what it meant to unravel a paranormal, but the little she shared was awful. The same power that will allow me to change someone's death can also strip away a vampire's speed and strength. It destroys their ability to feed. They starve, desiccating until they're nothing but dust.

The memory makes me shudder. "What else am I supposed to do? Without Claire, I won't be able to save Ms. Conrad. I won't be able to give *you* a better death, either."

"I'm not telling you to ice her out. Just be careful." The wind picks up, and Maggie rubs her bare arms. "If you did want to cut her off, though, you've had plenty of practice." She doesn't look at me when she says it, but the pain in her voice cuts through the bitterness of her tone.

She's still hurting, and it's my fault.

"Mags, I—"

"Vivi! Time to go!" she shouts, cutting off my apology. When her sister doesn't come running, Maggie forces out a loud sigh. "I'll be right back." She jogs toward the other side of the playground.

I perch on the edge of the merry-go-round, feeling like the absolute worst friend. I hate this tension between us, hate knowing I'm the one that caused it. There has to be a way to earn back her trust while still letting Claire train me.

My heart quickens at the thought of Claire. Despite what Maggie said, Claire isn't *technically* dead, and even if some parts of unraveling are terrifying, there's no other way to save people. Claire actually understands this power. She's the only person I can touch without seeing their death.

How could I possibly ignore that?

"Elise?" Maggie shouts my name from the other side of the playground, hidden behind the equipment. "Can you come here?"

There's a tremor of fear in her voice that pushes me to my feet. I grab Maggie's discarded backpack—with the first aid kit inside—and hurry after her. If Vivi fell and scraped her knee, Maggie is likely to pass out.

When I clear the plastic slide, I find Vivi busy on the swings and Maggie standing beside a white woman I don't recognize. The stranger looks mid-twenties, with dark hair that flows in shining waves to the middle of her back. Her pale skin is accented by incredible contouring and the boldest red lipstick I've ever seen.

The woman rests a hand on Maggie's shoulder and smiles at me, flashing two exceptionally long canines.

My body runs cold as my brain screams *vampire*.

"You have quite a lovely friend, Elise. Such a strong pulse," the woman says, her voice smooth and warm, like honey. She leans close and inhales near Maggie's neck. "So much potential in these veins, don't you think?"

Fear sharpens into anger. "Get the hell away from her."

"Relax, young Death Oracle." She trails her fingers along Maggie's neck before finally letting go. "I'm not going to eat your little friend."

Maggie staggers away from the vampire and pulls Vivi from the swing. Vivi protests at first, but she must pick up on Maggie's fear because she settles quickly and clings tightly to her sister.

Adrenaline races through my body, but I clear my throat to draw the vampire's attention back to me. "How do you know who I am? What do you want?" My hands tremble, and I tighten them into fists. I glance at Maggie, silently urging her to get out of here, to get Vivi somewhere safe, but she doesn't meet my gaze. She doesn't move.

The woman flashes another smile, and her canines shrink to more human levels. "I know a lot of things, Elise. It's been, what? Almost six months since you came into your power? The Veil must have sent a shepherd by now. They like to swoop in early and brainwash you into joining their cult."

"No one is trying to brainwash me."

"Aren't they?" She examines her fingernails. "I'm sure they call it *helping*, but do you really think the Veil would train you as their greatest weapon just to let you lead an ordinary human life? You'll be far too busy for the likes of them." She gestures at Maggie and Vivi.

An icy chill creeps down my spine. Claire never said anything about leaving my life behind. "I won't abandon my friends."

"You won't even realize it's happening. Not at first," the vampire continues, like I haven't said anything. "They're good at their jobs, I'll give them that. The shepherds reel you in, make you feel indebted to the Veil. They'll ask for a favor, something simple at first. Something that feels noble and pure. But their requests will never end, and one day, you'll wake up and realize you haven't seen your family in years."

"That won't happen to me." I shake my head, pushing down the nausea climbing up my esophagus. "I'm going to save my teacher and help Maggie, and then I'm done."

"Your confidence is adorable."

I have to bite back a frustrated scream. "What do you *want* from me? Who even are you?"

The vampire smiles, bright white teeth against blood-red lips. "I've gone by many names over the centuries, but you can call me Delilah." She reaches into her leather jacket and pulls out a thick journal, held together by twine. "You and I have symbiotic desires, young Death Oracle. I doubt you want to sacrifice your freedom to serve the whims of ancient vampires. Henri and Luca *are* still in charge, yes?"

"I . . . have no idea." The admission is bitter on my tongue, and I glance at Maggie. She's busy soothing a squirming Vivi so she doesn't meet my gaze.

"Are you willing to give up your future to serve the Veil?"

"Definitely not." I don't know what my future holds—my dream of being a surgeon seems impossible now—but I want to be the one who decides, not Claire. Not her bosses. Not anyone.

"Wonderful. Because I would very much like to kill those controlling bastards, and I believe you are the key to doing just that." Delilah holds out the leather journal.

Cautiously, I step forward and accept the offering. The brown leather is smooth beneath my fingers, but the twine scratches my skin. "What's this?"

"Let's call it an advance payment for services to be rendered." Delilah crosses her arms and glances up at the dark, cloudy sky.

"I've been . . . preoccupied the last hundred years or so, which means my information is outdated. I need you to mine your shepherd for intel and funnel it back to me."

"And in exchange, I get an old diary that's falling apart?" I may not have gotten all the answers I want from Claire, but I won't spy on her, either. I try to return the journal. "I'm good, thanks."

"That *diary*," Delilah says, pushing it back against my chest, "was written by the previous Death Oracle, Hazel Elfring. Take it. Read it. I think you'll find Hazel's experiences with the Veil . . . illuminating. If you don't, forget we ever met." She circles me like prey, her steps silent on the ground. "But if you want more information like this, you'll tell me everything you learn about the Veil. Who's in charge. Where they're stationed these days. Everything."

"How will this keep the Veil from taking over my life?" I ask, even as I hug the journal tight to my chest. "Couldn't someone else tell you where they live? Why do you need me?"

"All in good time, Elise." Delilah moves with a sudden burst of speed, and in a blink, my phone is in her hands. She flashes it in my face to unlock the screen and types a number into my contacts. "I can't divulge my entire plan until I know you're willing to deliver. Read the journal." She presses send, and her phone chimes in her pocket. "I'll be in touch."

"Wait!"

But before I can say anything else, Delilah is a blur of color as she disappears into the trees.

14

Claire

*I*t's been a week since Elise agreed to embrace her gifts, but I haven't succeeded in teaching her anything. At least, nothing of consequence.

Elise was full of questions on Sunday. I answered as best I could, telling her about Veil leadership and the witches we used to find her. She wanted to know more about our world, so I told her about the fae, about the werewolf packs in the Midwest, and the different departments at the Veil. Each answer only spawned more questions, and eventually, we had to focus on her training.

Yet despite working all weekend and practicing every day after school, Elise still can't see death without touching someone. I know this training takes time—it's often years before a Death Oracle masters unraveling—but Wyn is breathing down my neck, and Elise hasn't made any progress on proximity.

I'm beginning to wonder if Jordan's death is the wrong motivator.

On Friday, I show up early to our first-period math class so I can sit next to Elise. She arrives right as the bells chime, and her brows arch up her forehead when she notices me next to her spot.

"I've been thinking," I say, keeping my voice low as she approaches.

"Yeah?" She doesn't look at me when she says it. Instead, she takes her seat and flips through her notebook. She straightens her pen at the top of the desk, like she wishes she were anywhere but beside me.

Don't be so dramatic. It's early, and we're in class. Her distance doesn't mean anything. I lean toward her desk. "I don't think you want to see Jordan die."

Elise glares at me. "Of course I don't."

This time, I can't ignore the bite in her tone. It's more than just being tired. But before I can say anything else, the teacher comes in and starts roll call. I pull out my phone and send her a text.

Maybe we need a different test subject.

All period, I ignore our math teacher and keep one eye on Elise. But she doesn't check her phone. Not once. She doesn't respond during the next class, either, and I start to worry that my message was unclear. So, I try again.

We could borrow someone else. Someone you don't know.

If it's a death that doesn't hurt as much, maybe it will be easier to learn.

By lunch, her silence feels deliberate, so I avoid the cafeteria. Elise has never invited me to join her table, and lately, it's gotten more crowded. Most of the time, it's still just her, Maggie, and Jordan, but on Tuesday, a couple girls from the swim team joined them. From across the room, I watched the girls sit far away from Elise, like Maggie had warned them not to get too close. I overheard them talking about a new horror movie and the latest team gossip before I tuned them out.

I should be glad for Elise, that she's getting a chance to mend broken connections before she leaves this place behind, but it makes my chest tighten and my stomach knot and I'm too damn hungry for that today. I'm too hungry to sit with random mortals and listen to their taunting heartbeats. Between training Elise and trailing her history teacher, it's been nearly impossible to feed.

Instead, I go to the library and search the shelves for old favorites, greeting each book like a long-lost friend. Reading *everything* is the one perk of this existence, and it's only gotten better over time. There are so many more books about girls with hearts like mine than there ever were before. While I search the shelves, I imagine what would happen if I told Elise I wanted to join her for lunch.

She would probably say yes, but only to be polite, and her friends definitely don't want me there. It's easier to stay away than sit through Maggie questioning my every motive and training tactic. Easier to avoid them than watch Elise laugh at Jordan's jokes and listen to his heart skip every time she looks at him.

Easier than watching her text someone who isn't me all period.

On the other side of the library, someone sucks in a sharp breath. A moment later, the tang of blood fills the air. My muscles ache, and my canines try to lengthen. I press the hunger down, cursing myself for caring about mortals and denying my own needs. I've waited too long if I'm reacting this much over a paper cut. I hate this. I shouldn't *care* that a bunch of mortals don't want me to sit with them. I shouldn't care that some girl won't text me back.

This too-young brain is such a fucking nightmare.

The bells toll, and I slide a copy of *Some Girls Do* back into its place, making a mental note to check it out later. Right now, I need to focus on the bigger picture. The Veil needs its Death Oracle.

Elise is a means to an end, nothing more. And once I've gotten my revenge, I . . .

I don't know what I'll do.

As I weave into the flow of junior girls heading toward the gym, I try to imagine what my future might hold. Once Rose is finally dead, do I stay with the Veil? I could go back to being a tracker and capture violent paranormals for the Death Oracle to unravel. But that path is hard and lonely and brutal, and eventually, Elise would die.

I don't want to train her replacement.

But what other option do I have? It's rare that anyone leaves the Veil to chart their own path. I'd lose my only claim to power and influence within the paranormal world. I'd lose access to financial resources and places to live. And with no connection to a blood-line, the Veil is the closest thing I'll ever get to family.

In the locker room, I change quickly. Kaitlyn glares at me, but she's inconsequential. She probably blames me for her teammates' reconciliation with Elise, but I had nothing to do with that. Elise and Maggie avoid my gaze, too, which is more troublesome. I fol-low them into the gym, but before the teacher can assign either of us to a team, I reach for Elise's elbow and lead her away from the group.

She pulls from my grip almost instantly. "What? Can't this wait until after school?"

The ice in her tone punctures deep into my chest. I try to recali-brate, but I can't shake the sudden hurt. "I'm only trying to help."

"Offering to *kidnap* people so I can see their deaths isn't help-ing," she whispers fiercely, glancing over her shoulder to make sure no one is near enough to hear. "I told you, I don't like all that zombie stuff."

"Compulsion isn't—"

"Can we talk about this later?" she asks when the teacher motions for us to come closer. Elise folds her bare arms protectively around her middle and steps away from me.

"Sure." I push the word up my throat, but everything hurts. My aching jaw and my blood-starved muscles and my foolish, long-dead heart. "You're still coming over to train after school, right?" I confirm as we join the rest of the class.

"Not until Jordan is done with practice. Maggie has a movie thing with the swim girls tonight, so it'll just be the two of us."

"You could come over before that, if you want. There are things we could—"

"I have homework to catch up on." Elise hurries past me and gets a team assignment from the gym teacher, effectively ending the conversation.

We don't speak again the entire class, though Elise and Maggie share pointed looks. I shouldn't care, but I can't help wondering what they say about me when I'm not around. Finally, after a brutally slow game of soccer, I change back into my school uniform. Out of habit, I check my phone, even though I know Elise hasn't texted. Even though I know she thinks I'm a monster.

For the first time all day, there is a text waiting for me. It's not from Elise—obviously—but it's not from Wyn, either. The message is from Abigail Winters, the head of the Veil's tracking unit. She begrudgingly took me under her wing when I switched departments ten years ago, and her training style was like a bucket of ice water after the ease and familiarity of working with Wyn. Abigail is short with praise and even shorter with patience. She also hates technology, so if she's texting, it must be important.

I open the message.

We found Hazel's body.

Oh. The news settles against my skin like a thousand tiny needles. It was only a matter of time before someone found the previous Death Oracle's body. Elise wouldn't have her gift if Hazel were still alive. But why is Abigail texting *me* about it?

Before I can ask, another message comes through.

She was murdered.

———

Peace among paranormals is a precarious thing.

The implications of Hazel's murder send fear prickling along my spine as the mortals around me change into their school uniforms. Given the freedom and space, paranormals keep to our own. Werewolves with their packs, witches in their covens, vampires with our bloodlines. The fae would flit between realms, causing mischief and mayhem but mostly staying out of our way—even if they did occasionally steal away humans with paranormal gifts.

But when the world began to shrink, when human populations and innovation threatened our continued existence, alliances had to be made. Rules put into place to keep our world hidden and prosperous and safe. The changes were easier for some than others.

I tuck my blouse into my skirt and scan the room, looking for Elise. She's already gone, so instead of going to class, I slip past the pool and escape through the rear exit. Outside, storm clouds block the worst of the sun's rays, but that doesn't stop my runaway thoughts.

When humanity forced our world to evolve, the wolves moved to remote areas where they could hunt freely on the full moons.

The fae spent less and less time in our realm, preferring to rule their own world rather than abide by our restrictions. Witches . . . they had good times and bad. Mortals themselves, they wove in and out of broader society depending on the tides of public perception.

But vampires need something none of the others do. While other paranormals can avoid humans and live as they see fit, we need humans to survive. Without a regular supply of fresh human blood, we wither.

Which meant we needed the most governing.

I cut through the woods toward home, my mind spinning with stories Wyn told me about the Veil's founding. Tagliaferro and Guillebeaux would never allow other paranormals to control vampires. Instead, they created the Veil to keep us in line. Later, they invited ambassadors from the wolf packs and the fae courts. They hired covens to work in research and development.

Over the course of centuries, the Veil amassed power and influence within the paranormal world, but they *really* took control when Henri discovered a young woman named Petronelle, the very first Death Oracle.

Henri gifted the girl to Luca, who shaped her into a weapon feared by all, unraveling anyone who threatened his power. It's a slow, painful, inevitable death. A fate so gruesome no one has mounted a serious rebellion in decades.

But to murder the Death Oracle is to declare war against the Veil . . .

Who would be courageous enough—*foolish* enough—to even try?

By the time I get to my apartment, I haven't come up with any answers and Abigail hasn't sent more details, either. I swallow my nerves and call her.

She answers on the first ring. "Took you long enough."

I wince at her tone but don't issue an apology. Abigail, a Black woman born and turned in England, doesn't suffer fools or weak-willed apologists. I rearrange myself into the tracker she created. "What do we know?"

"Check your email. Isaac sent you photos."

"On it." I put Abigail on speaker and open my laptop. My fingers fly across the keys, but then I have to wait while the screen loads. "Any idea which group was behind it?" I doubt the witches are involved. Their biggest complaint is that the Death Oracle isn't theirs to guide as they see fit.

Are the wolf packs rising up?

"Look at the files, Montgomery," she says as the email finally loads.

When I click the link, graphic, vivid photos fill my screen. I look through each one, unwilling to speak until I'm sure I've found what Abigail wants me to see.

Hazel is—*was*—a white woman in her late fifties, with dark hair shot through with gray. I saw her occasionally, when I'd drop off tracking assignments to headquarters. Even so, I hardly recognize her after six months of insect and animal activity have left her in a grotesque state of decomposition. Her hollowed-out body is sprawled on the ground, arms and legs bent in ways that suggest the bones are broken in several places. I click over to the next photo. This one is zoomed in enough to see that her neck is broken and—

"Are those puncture wounds?"

Abigail sighs. "Would I have called if they were fake?"

I know better than to answer, so I zoom in for a closer look. While most of Hazel's skin has decayed and slipped from the bone, the area around the bite looks untouched by insects. The tissue is still firm enough to broadcast deep, twin wounds.

Only vampires feed from humans, but the presence of teeth marks is rare. If we release a human before they're dead, the wound closes within seconds. Normally, bite marks point to another paranormal trying to pin the death on us, but insects and animals avoid flesh imbued with vampiric saliva.

Is someone sending a message? "I assume you already ruled out the Veil bloodlines?"

"Luca and Henri's lines are loyal."

"As is the Ayars line, I'm sure," I say, referring to Abigail's creator. According to rumor, Calum Ayars was very particular about who he turned. Abigail is only one of a dozen or so direct heirs to the line. Which, to be fair, might also be due to Calum's early demise. Those around at the time say he took up with a Salem witch in the seventeenth century and met an unfortunate, fiery end.

"Obviously."

I pinch the bridge of my nose. We're getting low on bloodlines, and I'm tired of the Veil using vampiric orphans—like Wyn and me—as their go-to suspects whenever something goes awry. Except . . .

"The von Bettenhaus line is too disorganized to pull off an assassination," I say, talking more to myself than Abigail. "Unless it was an accident or a prank gone wrong."

Fenna von Bettenhaus, the originator of the line, has been missing since the thirteenth century. Some say she died in a dispute with the fae realm, while others believe she preferred their way of life. It's technically possible the fae found her sordid humor and zeal for mischief entertaining enough to let her feed from the handful of humans they keep in their realm.

But because Fenna has been gone for so long, she has no immediate descendants left. All of her remaining line are at least twice removed from her, and even those are hard to definitively prove.

Abigail clears her throat, cutting through my silent considerations. "What about those photos says *prank* to you? We found Francesca's head strung up nearby, too."

I flinch at the mention of Hazel's bodyguard, even though it makes sense. Francesca would never let something happen to Hazel, not if she could stop it. But then I tick through the bloodlines we've listed and come up short. "You think it was someone unaffiliated, don't you? The Prathor line has been dead for centuries."

Wyn only mentioned the name "Jessamine Prathor" once, back when they taught me about the five major bloodlines. They wouldn't get into the details, but Jessamine and the vampires she created pissed off the Veil enough to earn the eradication of her entire line.

"It's more than a single stray," Abigail says, and the flippant term makes my blood boil. "Isaac found evidence that several orphans have joined together under the name 'Petal and Thorn.' We need you to infiltrate the group and find out what they're planning."

"Petal and Thorn? That sounds more like a poetry group than a rebellion."

Abigail ignores me. "We need an orphan to earn their trust. You're our best shot."

My phone buzzes before I can answer, and for the first time, I'm glad for an excuse to tell her no. There's no way a group like this would trust me. "I can't, Abigail. I already have a case."

"But—"

"Wyn's calling. I have to go," I say, and then I do something I've never done before. I hang up on Abigail Winters.

I don't answer Wyn's call, though. My mind is too busy. Even though I turned down Abigail's request, my brain won't stop spitting out theories as I click through the photos, looking for clues. I've never heard of Petal and Thorn, but if they're really behind Hazel's death, we're about to have the first major mutiny on our hands since the discovery of the Death Oracle.

Wyn calls again, and I send them to voicemail. No matter what comes next, Tagliaferro and Guillebeaux will be too busy to help me find Rose. And if there is a war? It could be decades before they care about anything else, and I am *not* waiting that long.

A few minutes later, Wyn calls again.

"Abigail already sent the photos," I say in place of a greeting.

"Of course she did." Wyn sighs, and then a door clicks shut, blocking out the sound of phones ringing in the distance. They must be at headquarters. "Please tell me you're not ditching. We need the new Death Oracle safe and fully trained."

Fully trained. As if I can snap my fingers and shove years of expertise into Elise's head. It's been a week, and she hasn't even progressed to the second stage.

"I'm not going anywhere. I promised to do this, and I will. But if you have a faster way to get her through training . . ."

Someone knocks on Wyn's door, and they cover the phone to shout a muffled reply. "I'll see what I can dig up, but for now, keep doing what you're doing."

It doesn't seem like enough, but I nod.

"Don't forget to submit your progress report tomorrow. I have to go. Henri called a meeting."

Wyn hangs up, but I only last a minute before I'm clicking through the photos again. Even if I stay in Elmsbrook, I can text Abigail if I think of anything concrete. I flip back to the beginning of the images, the one with Hazel's broken limbs sprawling in awkward directions, and fear digs into my chest.

Plenty of paranormals would like to control the Death Oracle's power, but if Petal and Thorn murdered Hazel . . .

Will they target Elise, too?

15

Elise

I saved a life today.

After so many years of training, I finally did it! It couldn't have been for a better kid, either. He's lucky his father managed to secure an audience with the Veil. Knowing the right people can make all the difference.

Now, thanks to me, that little boy will get to grow up. Fate resisted every effort to extend his life, his threads were so knotted and frail, but I did it. I was only able to get him to sixty-one, but that's so much better than six.

I wish I could tell my parents about this—about any of this—but at least Henri was proud. Francesca and Quinn are throwing a little celebration tonight, and there's even talk about an extended trip to Europe to see the sights while I remake deaths in Venice and Barcelona and Edinburgh.

Plus, the commission from today's assignment is more money than I've seen in my entire life. I think it's more than Dad ever made in a year. I am going to have the <u>best</u> wardrobe by the time we get back to the States.

"Elise?"

Someone knocks on the table, and I nearly jump out of my skin. I look up from Hazel's journal to find Jordan standing across from me, his messenger bag slung over one shoulder.

"Sorry," he says, keeping his voice low since we're in the academy library. He points to the journal. "Hazel partying with vampires again? Or was she at a fairy revel this time?"

"They're called fae revels, and no." I close the journal and slide it into my bag. Most of the early entries were just like Jordan said—Hazel getting to know the various members of the paranormal world. The girl *loves* to party, and she seems like she's having fun. She lives with Francesca—her vampire friend-slash-bodyguard—in Manhattan, and Hazel's shields are so strong that being around all those people doesn't bother her.

All week, I couldn't figure out what Delilah hoped I'd get out of the journal, but this entry . . . it feels different.

It's the first time Hazel has mentioned her family.

I shoulder my backpack and lead Jordan out of the library. We pass Ms. Conrad in the hall, and she waves at us. I offer a smile, hope blooming in my chest when I remember Hazel's words. Once Jordan and I are alone again, I continue. "Hazel actually saved someone's life. She changed their fate."

"That's awesome!" Jordan says, but then he glances back at me, and his brows furrow. "Is it not awesome? You don't look excited."

We push open the front doors and head down the steps. Above, the sky is heavy with storm clouds, and I'm grateful for my sweater. "I don't know. Something about it felt weird."

"Is anything about your life *not* weird these days?" There's this teasing note to Jordan's voice that feels dangerously close to flirting. It would be so easy to give in, to let myself fall back in love with him, but it's better for both of us if I ignore these feelings until they go away.

I kick a pebble down the sidewalk. "They charge people for it. Like, a *lot* of money."

Jordan shrugs. "So do doctors."

"That doesn't make it right. Life expectancy shouldn't depend on how much money you have." I glance at him, an unexpected smile pulling at my lips. "Remember when Maggie made us listen to that podcast about healthcare reform?"

He laughs. "At least that made sense! The stuff you listen to is weird."

"Medical history isn't *weird*," I argue. "We have blood thinners because cows ate moldy hay. It's wild!"

"Except half your podcasts are about people shoving poop into wounds to cure the plague. It's gross." Jordan shudders, and I can't help but laugh.

"That episode came on during your baking phase, didn't it?" I ask as the memory surfaces. A few summers ago, Jordan developed a baking obsession. Maggie, Jordan, and I were in the middle of kneading dough when that episode started. "Didn't they bathe in urine, too?"

"Gah, don't remind me!" He squirms and races up ahead to escape my laughter. I'm pretty sure that's when he banned me from playing podcasts at his house.

When I catch up to him, we walk in silence for a few blocks. It's a comfortable silence, though, and I wish it could always be like this. I wish we could flip a switch and go back to being friends without any lingering romantic feelings messing things up.

A few minutes from Claire's place, Jordan glances over at me. "So, what did you decide, with the whole Delilah thing?"

At the mention of her name, Delilah's warnings echo through my head.

Are you willing to give up your future to serve the Veil?

One day, you'll wake up and realize you haven't seen your family in years.

"I haven't decided anything yet, but I did text her last night." Delilah left me alone for a few days after we met, but then the texts started coming in, asking if I'd finished the journal. Telling me she needed information about the Veil if I wanted more.

"And?"

"I told her those vampires she mentioned are still in charge." I figured it wasn't much—it seemed like information she could get from anyone—but it still felt strange to share something Claire told me privately.

And then, not twelve hours later, Claire was waiting for me in trig and trying to get me over to her place early. At first, I was convinced that Delilah was a Veil spy. That Claire had arranged our meeting to test my ability to keep secrets. I expected Claire to be furious with me.

Now, I'm pretty sure I was a jerk for no reason.

"Everything okay?" Jordan asks when we turn the final corner onto Claire's street. "You look like you want to bolt."

"I'm fine," I insist, but when he gives me another worried look, I sigh. "Most people don't *want* to spend Friday night watching their friend die, but this is my life now." I make sure to emphasize *friend*, for his sake and mine.

A few houses down, Claire's front door swings open. She's still in her school uniform, but she's twisted her hair into a messy bun, and there's tension around her eyes that isn't normally there. "Oh, good, you're here. I was getting worried."

"We're fine," I say, hoping she didn't notice how strange I acted today. We follow her upstairs, and Jordan settles in his usual place on the couch.

"Ready?" I ask, even though Jordan doesn't have to do anything but sit there and try not to fall asleep. Still, I wait for him to nod before I attempt to see his death from a distance. Like Claire instructed last Friday, and every day since, I breathe deep and still my mind. Every time my thoughts wander to the boy Hazel saved and the price his father paid for those years, I nudge the memory away.

"Feel for his aura," Claire says, her voice gentle. "You can do this."

I remind myself of Hazel's earlier entries. Of her life in the city, with strong shields giving her the freedom to move through crowds without pain. This is how I get there, and Jordan has a good death. The kind of death most people would wish for. I reach for Jordan's energy, and there's this soft touch at my back.

"That's it." Claire's voice is soft against my ear. "Push the boundaries of your energy until it brushes against his."

"I believe in you, Ellie," Jordan says from the couch. "You can do this."

"And remember," Claire adds, her nearness stirring something in me that I can't name. "Once you master this, we can move onto the shield. You'll be able to touch the living again without seeing them die."

Tears sting my eyes, and I push harder, lured by the promise of freedom.

Suddenly, there's this pressure in my head, like two opposing forces coming into contact. Light brightens my mind's eye, and then I'm there. Jordan lies in bed, wrinkled and old. Eighty, at least. He's managed to keep most of his hair, but it's buzzed short and almost entirely gray. There's a wedding band on his finger, and beside him lies another man, smiling in his sleep.

Then there's a tightness in my chest—in Jordan's chest. His heart gives out, and he's gone.

I wrench away, pushing the images out of my mind. My knees give out beneath me, and I let myself sink to the floor as I gasp for air. It's the second time I've seen Jordan die, and though it's a comfort to know he'll live a long, long life . . .

It still won't be with me.

"Elise? Are you okay?" Claire kneels beside me and brushes my braided hair back behind my shoulder. "Did you see it?"

"Yeah." I pull my knees to my chest and stare at Jordan, absorbing his youth, his concern, the spark of life in his eyes. I lean into Claire's cool touch, to the steadiness of her presence beside me.

After I master this, I can learn the shield. After I master this, I can touch my parents again.

"Can we have a moment?" Jordan asks as he unfurls from the couch. He sits across from me on the floor, a good eighteen inches between us.

Claire looks like she wants to argue, but she sighs instead. "I'll go check the mail."

I doubt vampires *get* mail, but I appreciate the quiet that settles over the apartment when she leaves.

"You okay?" Jordan pulls his knees to his chest, mirroring me.

"Would you be?" The ache in my chest deepens. "If our places were reversed?"

"Definitely not, but you've always been the strong one in our relationship."

"Jordan—"

"Sorry. You know what I mean, though." He picks at a frayed bit of carpet. "How does it happen?"

"Do you really want to know?" I ask, and he nods. Though part of me wants to protect him from this, it's his death. He deserves to know it more than I do. "You're really old when it happens. You die in your sleep. I don't think you feel any pain."

He nods but doesn't say anything. He doesn't smile or crack a joke. I wish he would.

"If there's such a thing as a good death, that has to be it," I offer when he still doesn't say anything.

"Am I alone?"

I bite the inside of my lip. "No."

"That's why, isn't it? That's why you broke up with me."

"Jordan . . ."

He tugs harder on the frayed carpet, and a piece comes off in his hands. "Who is it?"

"I don't know." I weigh my next words carefully. Jordan came out to Maggie and me nearly a year before he and I started dating. The last time we talked about it, he was still searching for the label that fit best, but he was positive he liked guys and girls. Plus, there was this genderqueer YouTuber he thought was really cute.

Would it be wrong to tell him who he grows old with?

"Ellie, please." He looks at me with those deep brown eyes, searching my gaze like it holds the key to his future. "I just want to understand."

"I didn't recognize him." A series of emotions flits across his features as Jordan registers the pronoun I'm using. "You were both asleep, but you seemed happy."

His curiosity warps into concern. "Promise me that we didn't break up because you think I'm gay. I told you, I'm bisexual. Or maybe pansexual."

"I know, Jordan. I promise, gender had nothing to do with it. I'm just not your forever person." Downstairs, the front door slams shut, and footsteps draw near. "Claire's coming back. She'll probably want to try again." I pull myself to my feet.

"We don't need forever to be together right now." Jordan stands, too, and he towers over me. Even with a few inches between us, I can feel the heat of him, the pull I've always felt when he's near. "Elise, please. Just think about it. I still—"

"Break's over." Claire says, interrupting Jordan before he says something he can't take back. "Let's try again."

16

Claire

If I wasn't already on the verge of starving, stalking Elmsbrook Academy's history teacher would be enough to make me desiccate from boredom.

Amelia Conrad—twenty-nine, eldest of three sisters—lives a painfully predictable life. Every Monday, Wednesday, and Friday, she teaches an introductory history course at Elmsbrook University in the evening. On Tuesday and Thursday, Amelia takes an adult ballet class in town and is home before sunset, where she spends the entire night grading papers while she watches reality dating shows.

The only saving grace of this assignment is that the woman is murdered at night, when I'm strongest and there's no sunlight to batter against my blood-starved body.

Tonight, the day-old full moon is bright overhead while I loiter on campus, sitting on a bench outside the humanities building where Amelia teaches. That's the other benefit of Elise's vision. We know the teacher bites it outside, so there's no need to sneak into her class and risk getting caught.

If Elise hadn't gotten so upset when I suggested compelling the teacher to stay home, I wouldn't have to play stalker. I thought it was a perfectly reasonable solution, at least until we came up with something permanent. Elise disagreed. Loudly. Besides her usual misgivings about compulsion, she worried the change would trigger fate to kill Amelia faster. Elise even grabbed my wrist as she explained, holding my gaze until I promised not to compel the teacher.

Her skin is always so warm against mine . . .

"Reading something good?" A young woman wearing a mint-green hijab stands before me, a shy smile pulling at her lips.

I glance down at the novel in my lap. I've been staring at the same page for several minutes, but I show off the illustrated cover. "Always."

"Yeah?" She steps closer, like she might try to sit beside me. For a split second, a thrill of anticipation sparks like lightning, until I realize what's happening. Despite the flirty way she smiles, she's not interested in me. Not really. She's no different than all the teens at the academy, mortals drawn to danger like flies to a bug zapper. "Any favorites?"

As she nears, her pulse beats loud in my ears, and my jaw aches. Between school, training Elise, and tracking the teacher, I haven't had time to address my hunger. I shouldn't go so long between feedings, and I'm suffering for it now. Before Wyn and I parted, I'd only gone about a week without blood. Now, it's been more than two.

Just take a little . . .

My mouth waters at the suggestion, and the primal part of my brain urges me to feed. My teeth lengthen. Urgency tenses my muscles. It would be so easy. Just meet her gaze, flash a smile, compel her to offer her wrist so I don't mess up her carefully wrapped hijab . . .

I raise one hand to halt her approach. "I'm waiting for someone. You should go."

"Oh." The young woman stumbles back. She clears her throat

and glances around the mostly empty quad. "Right. Sorry." She scurries away, clutching a thick textbook to her chest.

A growl rumbles at the back of my throat as I watch her leave. I really am hungry. I should have taken a quick bite, just enough to take the edge off.

But I don't. I force myself to stay seated until the evening classes let out, and students flood the quad. At least one person has a small cut, the scent of blood on the air tantalizing and torturing me. A dull ache settles through my limbs. I won't be able to face the sun again until I feed.

As the thought crosses my mind, Amelia finally exits the building, talking with a student. I watch them until they've passed my bench and parted ways, and then I'm up and moving, keeping to the shadows so the history teacher doesn't spot me.

Amelia carries a bulging leather satchel at her hip, probably stuffed full with more papers to grade. I track her across campus, past old buildings and patches of trees with dying leaves, all the way to the parking lot.

Overhead, clouds shift to cover the moon, and the weak illumination of dying streetlights cast the world in patterns of gray. A sudden surge of hunger tears through me, and I stumble, collapsing against an SUV.

"Is someone there?" Amelia's voice carries through the parking lot, and I'm glad for the cover of the tall vehicle. I crouch low, trying to push down the hunger.

Except the hunger pushes back, begging me to throw it all away. I want to kill the teacher myself, drain every drop of blood from her veins. I could compel her to drive me home and feed just enough to think clearly again. No one would have to know. At least she'd be safe for another night.

Before I can step toward the teacher, Elise's words echo in my head. *Don't you dare compel her. You're supposed to protect Ms. Conrad, not turn her into a zombie.*

The disdain in Elise's voice is a slap in the face, even now.

Amelia climbs into her car and starts the engine. Behind me, footsteps approach.

"Excuse me," says a soft, sure voice behind me. "That's my car."

I turn and find a young white woman staring at me. Her hair is a deep auburn that curls where it reaches her shoulders, and she wears minimal makeup. Sorority letters dangle from the zipper of her designer purse, which she adjusts into the crook of her arm.

"Are you okay?" She looks me up and down, her brows arching. "Are you hiding from someone?"

Hunger roils inside me as I force myself to stand. "No, but I need a ride." I step closer, and the girl retreats to preserve the small distance between us.

"I'm sorry, but I—"

"You were about to offer help," I say, reaching out and ensnaring her mind. "Weren't you?"

"Yes," she says, her voice monotone and robotic now. "Of course."

She reaches into her bag and pulls out her keys. The moment the doors unlock, I climb into the pristine interior and direct my compelled chauffeur to Amelia's small home. When we get there, I have the sorority sister park along the street. There are a few lights on inside, and I spot Amelia through her kitchen windows, warming up a plate of leftovers.

She's home safe, which means I'm off duty for the night. Finally.

"Give me your hand," I say absently, still watching the teacher's house.

"Why?"

Pain claws at my insides. "Because I'm hungry." Though I prefer to feed from the neck, I only do that with girls who choose to hold me close. There's no way to know if my driver might have any interest, at least not when I'm this hungry. "Please."

Finally, she holds out her arm, and I grasp it, drawing her wrist to my lips.

"What are you—"

My teeth sink into soft flesh, and hot blood crosses my tongue as she sighs. I know the effect feeding has on hosts, but I never feel as guilty as when I snatch unwilling humans like this. The guilt doesn't stop me from swallowing again and again, though, filling my aching body with strength and life.

Survival outweighs guilt every time.

Drink it all. Bleed her dry.

Fear grips me, and I release the girl so fast that the seat creaks under the sudden pressure. My body feels like I've grabbed hold of a live wire, tense and electric. I'm desperate for more blood, but if I continue, I could go too far. I could kill her. *This* is why I can't risk waiting so long to eat. It's why parties and blood bars are so important. It's easier to let go, to move on, when there's another host just a few steps away.

"Take me back to campus. To your sorority house."

The girl stares at her wrist, at the puncture marks already closing up. "What—"

"No questions. Just drive." I wait for her to comply and pull out my phone. It rings four times before she answers. "I can't keep doing this."

"Can't keep doing what? Claire?" Elise's voice is quiet on the other end, slow and drowsy.

"I can't follow your teacher every night. I need a better idea of when she dies." I press my face against the window and watch the houses zip past. "There must be something else you remember."

Elise sighs. "I already told you everything. It wasn't winter, and she didn't look older, so it's probably soon. She was outside somewhere with flickering streetlights."

"It's probably campus. It's the only place she goes after dark." I lick my lips and find a drop of blood I'd missed. The hunger rises again, and I pinch the bridge of my nose, trying to force it down. "I can watch her on campus, but I need nights off. I have things I need to do."

"More important than saving a woman's life?" Elise's words are filled with challenge.

"Yes." A growl builds in my chest, and I squeeze my eyes shut. Fuck, I need to feed again. Now. I mute the call. "Drive faster."

"But the speed limit—"

"Drive. Faster."

"Claire?" Elise's voice draws me back, and I unmute the phone and backpedal as best I can.

"I know this is important to you, but I can't starve myself." I didn't mean to be so blunt, but it's hard to think with the kill-or-be-killed part of me so close to taking control. I should have known better. I should have gone to a blood bar *days* ago, but the closest one is over an hour away, and I wanted to focus on our training.

Another wave of hunger presses through me, and this time, I can't stop my canines from lengthening. It's so much harder to wait once I've had a taste. Once I've had a tiny bit of relief.

I hate this part of me.

I hate that I never had a choice in my monstrosity.

I hate that *Rose* made me like this.

"Are you okay? Are you safe?"

I'm not the one in danger. I think the words, but I can't say them. Even this desperate for blood, I know I can't give Elise reason to fear me. Well, more reasons.

"Claire—"

"I'll be fine. I just can't go this long without feeding."

My cautious driver turns on the blinker to pull into the parking lot, but I cover the phone. "Not here. Drop me in front of the house. And *no* arguments," I add when it looks like she wants to protest despite the compulsion she's under.

"Who are you with?"

"No one who matters." I grip the door handle as fraternity and sorority row comes into view. All I can think is how Rose did this to me. How I can't let her get away with it any longer. "Listen, I'm taking tomorrow off. No training. No trailing your teacher. I won't be at school, either. I'll see you Friday."

"Claire—"

The car comes to a stop in front of a massive house with Greek letters nailed to the front. "Goodnight, Elise."

I hang up and turn to my driver. "Come on. It's about to be a party."

17

Elise

*D*espite the advance warning, Claire's absence from trig puts me on edge. I shouldn't worry—between what Claire has shared and what I've read in Hazel's journal, not much can hurt a vampire—but last night's call plays over and over in my head. She sounded on edge in a way I've never heard from her, and I swear there was a thread of pain in her voice.

While Ms. Parsons explains the difference between sine, cosine, and tangent equations—something about SOHCAHTOA?—I pull my sleeves past my wrists and draw my aura as close to my body as possible.

Sitting through class isn't easy, but first period ends without incident. When the bells chime, dread creeps into my bones. Moving through the halls is harder. I'm constantly aware of my aura now, like a second layer of skin or phantom limb I feel but can't see. When other auras brush against mine, death unspools the same as if my classmates had grabbed my bare hand.

Most often, I'm battered by the fatigue of a drawn-out illness, but there's flickers of pain, too. Heart attacks. Car accidents. A bad fall.

Hazel is the only reason I see as little as I do. She spent most of her time in Europe incredibly drunk, and the alcohol messed with her ability to shield. A few entries from that trip mentioned relearning to compress her aura against her body.

Even so, by lunch my head aches and there's a lingering nausea that won't go away.

Jordan and Maggie are already at our usual table by the time I arrive. Though it probably looks weird to everyone else in the cafeteria, I sit as far away from them as I can.

"Bad day?" Maggie asks when I brace my head in my hands.

It's all I can do to nod. I'm afraid to lose focus on my aura. I don't want to see Maggie die or feel the impact of cement against the back of my skull.

"Do you think Delilah could teach you the shield?" Maggie blows on a spoonful of the cafeteria's chicken and dumpling soup. "You should text her."

Jordan makes a face, and he pauses mid pasta twirl. "I don't think asking vampires for help is a good idea."

"He's right. I don't want to owe any more favors." I massage my temples, trying to push all the lingering deaths away. "Besides, if it's this bad, I should be ready for the shield soon. Maybe Claire can teach me this weekend."

Someone walks by our table, and a fresh jolt of nausea pulses through me. I focus on shutting out everyone's deaths and lose track of my friends' conversation. When the pain finally relents, I find my thoughts drifting to Claire.

Worry tugs at my heart. Does she need time to recover after feeding? Does it hurt to wait so long for blood? My stomach cramps, and I can't stop picturing her eyes flashing red and her teeth lengthening and—

"Elise." Jordan waves a hand in my general direction, cutting off my thoughts.

"I'm sorry." I tighten my arms around my stomach. "What were you saying?"

A crease deepens in Jordan's brow, but he covers the expression with a smile. "Since you're not training tonight, could you come to our swim meet?"

Part of me wants to go, wants to stand on the sidelines and cheer until I'm hoarse, but I can't be that close to water without panic closing in. I don't think I could handle being on the outside, looking in at my old life.

I shake my head. "Crowds aren't a good idea right now." It's true, but it's not all of it. "I should probably get caught up on homework before the dean kicks me out, too."

"Yeah," Jordan says, but his expression dims.

Maggie rests a hand on his forearm. "That makes sense."

"You two are going to crush it, though. I know it." I offer a smile, but the bells ring before I can say anything else.

The rest of the day is a blur of pain and fatigue. Ms. Conrad's class is the worst. She's wearing a blue shirt under a bright white blazer today, but I don't have any idea what she's trying to teach. It takes all my concentration to keep my aura close. Despite my effort, echoes of fear spike my adrenaline. Phantom pain punctures my back. Hazel has written about saving dozens of people, but she never writes *how* she does it.

There has to be a way to speed up my training.

After school, I text Maggie and Jordan good luck and head home. My parents are still out, and Richard comes tearing down the stairs to greet me. She meows and weaves through my legs, nudging her head against my shins. The show of affection is just a ploy for treats, but I bend down to pet her anyway.

"Were you a good girl today?" I ask, adding a second hand

for the ultimate chin-scratch. "You didn't throw up in my clothes, did you?"

Richie turns and bites my fingers, which doesn't bode well.

"Just for that, no snacks until dinner." I go upstairs, Richard close on my heels. Her tail flicks against Nick's door in time with my fingers.

In my room, instead of homework, I pull Hazel's journal out of my bag and settle on the bed. The cat hops up, too, and kneads a section of the comforter. From this angle, the spot of orange on her back looks like a heart.

I spread the journal across my lap and flip to where I left off last.

August 8, 1990

Luca wants me to kill someone. He says it's important, that it'll save countless other lives, but I don't know.

It's definitely <u>possible</u>. I've woven enough new deaths to know I could change fate to almost anything. But I don't know if I could cross that line.

Not that he knows that. I told him I'd think about it, but who am I supposed to ask for advice? Quinn is a no-go—Luca said the witches alerted him to fate's current path. So many people will die if the target lives his full life, but why does it have to be me? Can't Francesca or one of the other vampires do it? Couldn't someone from the fae court take him over to their realm?

Henri always says that how I use my gift is up to me, but how am I supposed to know what to do? If everyone says it'll save more lives than the one I take . . .

Cold chills prickle along my skin, and this time, the nausea doesn't belong to someone's death. Is this what the Veil really wants from me? To give life and take it at their request? I don't want to be an angel of death.

Next to me, Richie decides the bed is kneaded to her standards and curls into a little ball.

I turn the page.

September 20, 1990

It was simpler than I thought.

The man's fate unraveled easily, and there was so much extra to snip away when I was done. Luca and Henri said it had to look natural, something that wouldn't draw suspicion from his allies. I didn't want it to hurt too much, either, but no one mentioned that concern.

Instead of another forty years, the man will have a heart attack before winter ends.

And the witches were right. As I cut away the extra years, changes rippled out like vibrations on a wire. Dozens of other fates shifted and lengthened, adding that extra time to their lives.

Luca promised that this kind of case is rare, but I have to wonder.

Is this the fastest way to save the most people?

I snap the journal closed in the middle of the entry. I am not doing that. I am not *killing* people so the Veil can change the world to suit their whims. I don't want to know what kind of expensive trinket or trip Hazel got in exchange for her services.

"Elise?" Mom knocks on my door and peeks her head in. "Can you help with dinner? I found the last bit of local corn. I need you to shuck it while I fire up the grill."

"You're grilling?" I slip out of bed and put the journal back in my bag. "Where's Dad?"

"He got called into an emergency surgery." Mom pushes the door open wide. "But we're strong, independent women. We're perfectly capable of grilling on our own."

I tug my sleeves past my wrists. "I mean, I know *I* am."

Mom glares at me, but there's a smile pulling at the corner of her lips. "Very funny. Now, get changed and come downstairs. The corn won't clean itself."

After Mom leaves, Richie close on her heels, I change into jeans and a long-sleeved T-shirt. In the kitchen, I get to work shucking the corn, but I can't stop thinking about the journal. How am I supposed to learn enough to save Maggie and Ms. Conrad without getting sucked into the Veil's world?

The thoughts trail me like a ghost while we cook—we only burn *one* of the sausage links beyond recognition—and during dinner, too. Mom is chatty enough for the both of us. Without Dad here to stop her, Mom shares all her favorite stories of Nick.

There was the time Nick came home from practice with his arm in a sling. Mom threatened to take him to the hospital for X-rays until Nick burst out laughing. He claimed it was an April Fools' joke, even though it was already May.

I thought Mom hated his pranks, but I guess she secretly enjoyed them.

"Do you remember the signs he made for your swim meets?" Mom asks, already laughing at the memory. "The crowd loved them."

"They were *embarrassing*." Nick knew enough Photoshop to stick my face on the most ridiculous fish he could find. "He put me on a sailfish once and stretched my nose longer than my body!"

"That was one of my favorites." Mom laughs so hard she snorts, but when she notices my scowl, she relents. "Nick said sailfish are the fastest in the ocean. It was sweet."

"If you say so," I grumble, but I'm glad she brought it up. We never get to talk about Nick like this when Dad is here. It's nice to remember the good times. The annoying ones, too.

But as dinner continues, a thread of fear keeps my body on edge and makes it hard to eat. I try to ignore the feeling, but when I clear the table, a jolt of pain slices through my back. I stumble, and my plate shatters across the kitchen floor.

"Ellie? You okay?" Mom calls from the dining room, where she's still finishing a glass of wine.

With our home's open concept, Mom has a clear view of me, so I can't blame it on Richard. I glance over my shoulder. "Yeah, my back just hurt all of a sudden."

"Cramps?" Mom points to the cupboard at the edge of the counter. "There are pills in there."

"No, I'm okay." I pick up the largest pieces of broken plate and toss them in the trash. As I reach for the broom and dustpan, fresh pain explodes across my back, higher this time, near my shoulder blade. The broom clatters against the floor.

"Elise?" Mom is on her feet now, crossing the room carefully to avoid the shattered plate. "Are you sick?" She reaches out to touch my forehead, and I jolt out of the way.

"I'm fine," I say, even as Mom's proximity brushes her aura too close to mine. Pain and fatigue settle over my limbs, and I stumble around her out of the kitchen. "I just need to lie down for a bit."

"If you're sure." Mom picks up the broom I dropped. "I'll clean this up and come check on you."

"Really, Mom, I'm good. I have homework to do anyway." I

escape up the stairs and make it to my room before the third rush of pain bursts in my back. It feels like an echo of death, but I'm not *near* anyone. This shouldn't be happening.

I shut the door and climb into bed. Adrenaline floods my system, and everything hurts. It's like all the deaths I've ever seen are rolling through me on an endless loop. Twice, I reach for my phone, but I stall in my messages. Do I text Claire even though she asked for the day off? Do I reach out to Delilah?

Before I can decide, my vision goes black, and I'm flung out of my body. I tumble into someone else's life, someone else's future. Ms. Conrad is there, dressed in jeans and a familiar blue blouse.

She walks down the sidewalk, and when we collide, my perspective shifts until I'm trapped inside my teacher's body. The cool air brushes against her skin, and we shiver.

Crack.

We turn our head. Search the dark for a figure.

"Is someone there?" No one responds. Fear and adrenaline flood our system. We need to run. We need to—

Suddenly, there's movement at our back. Our knees go weak, and we're trembling as arms wrap tight around us. A scream climbs up our throat, but a hand presses against our mouth, cutting off the sound. A deep voice rumbles in our ear, but we're too afraid to make out the words. Then there's pain *everywhere*.

Pressure and heat slam again and again and again into our back. We fall, crashing against hard cement. Something hot and wet pools around us. Blood fills our lungs. We can't breathe. We can't—

I'm thrown out of the vision, my insides roiling as I come back to myself. I suck in deep breaths, my lungs watery and weak with echoes of a death that's not my own. That's not—

My stomach clenches. I untangle my limbs and race for the bathroom. I barely make it to my knees before the vomit comes up, splashing into the toilet. I choke on bile and tears as the pain leaks from my body.

We're too late.

I can't explain how, but I know it deep in my bones. That wasn't the future. That was *real*. That was *now*. Why else would I see it on my own like this?

My stomach clenches again, expelling the last of my dinner. Tears stream down my face as I realize why I feel so certain. Ms. Conrad was wearing that blouse in class today, under her white blazer. It's too late. She's already gone.

"Elise? Are you okay?" There's a knock on the bedroom door.

"I'm fine, Mom!" I lie, knowing I'll never be fine again. Knowing I failed Ms. Conrad, just like I failed Nick.

Eventually, I pull myself to my feet. I wash my face, rinse my mouth, and stagger back to bed. But when I grab my phone, I don't know which vampire to call.

I don't know who to trust.

18

Claire

My bedroom wall has transformed into a collage of death. It turned out more gruesome than expected, but I was tired of staring at my computer screen, flipping from image to image. I caved, printed the photos Isaac sent, and stuck them to the wall. Red pen in hand, I've circled every injury I can spot—broken fingers, arms, legs, and finally, the neck wounds.

The final moments of Hazel's life were filled with pain.

Behind me, my phone buzzes on the desk, but I let it ring. Wyn can wait a day for updates. Their uncanny sense of timing grates on my nerves. They always call when I have nothing to share.

Or when I'm doing things I shouldn't.

When the ringing stops, I refocus on my work. I won't let Hazel's death derail the favor I'm owed, even if I have to solve the murder myself.

I tap the side of the pen against my chin as I study the images. The non-fatal injuries look systematic, like whoever did this wanted to inflict the maximum amount of pain.

Was it someone settling a grudge?

The nature of Hazel's work leaves a trail of possible enemies—families of people whose deaths she hastened or loved ones who couldn't afford the price to extend a life—but no one outside the

Veil is supposed to know who she is. How did they find her?

My phone rings again, vibrating against the desk. I lean my forehead against the wall and groan. What is so damn important that Wyn couldn't wait for me to call back? I snatch the phone on the fourth ring, a growl in my voice when I answer.

"This better be good, Wyn."

Instead of their typical retort or exasperated sigh, there are tears on the other end.

"Wyn?"

"We're too late." The soft, broken voice is not the one I expected.

"Elise?" Worry wipes away my annoyance, and I kick myself for ignoring her first call. "Too late for what?"

"Ms. Conrad," she says, and for a second, her voice is lost to sobs. "She's . . . She's—"

"She's what, Elise?" I ask, softening my tone, smoothing out all the harsh edges. "What happened?"

"She's dead."

"How? She doesn't go out on Thursdays." I abandon my wall of horrors and head for the apartment door. "Are you sure?"

"I saw it, Claire. I felt it." She sucks in a shuddering breath, and I can picture the tears spilling down her cheeks. Just imagining it, hearing it, is a sliver of wood beneath my skin. "Please. Come over. I can't. I can't do this alone. I—"

"Where are you?" I'm down the stairs in less than a second.

"At home."

The night is dark when I emerge from the old Victorian. "Don't move. I'm on my way."

I run to Elise's house, moving so fast onlookers will only see a blur of color and a burst of wind tossing fallen leaves. I make it there in less than a minute but falter on the front lawn.

It's been more than ten years since a human willingly invited me into their home.

Fiona's house was small, a quaint cottage in a town more rural than this. She made me explain while I stood on her porch, letting her assess and judge every word out of my mouth. I made promises I never intended to break—to keep her safe, to never cause her harm—promises the Veil would force me to shatter within a year. Yet standing here in front of Elise's home, Fiona's blood on my hands makes me pause.

Fiona wasn't supposed to get hurt, but falling in love with humans—especially the ones we're shepherding—never ends well. Our romance started slow, many months after she found out what I was, but I got so wrapped up in *her* promises—her kisses and her whispered declarations—that I failed to see *what* I was to her. A vehicle to immortality. A means to an end. And when I denied her, I became a problem to obliterate.

Before Fiona, I'd forgotten that humans can be just as devious, just as transactional, as vampires.

Please. Come over. I can't. I can't do this alone.

Elise's words tug at my insides. She might need things from me, but unlike Fiona, Elise won't pretend to want me. She won't fake romance so I'll turn her. She's made it clear that she detests vampires, and lately, it's like she barely tolerates my presence.

I text that I'm here, and her answer is swift. I'll be right down.

A light flicks on upstairs, and I force myself down the driveway and up the wide porch. Her footsteps, soft and sure, hurry down the stairs, and then the locks slide free and the door swings open. Elise stands inside, arms wrapped tight around her middle. She's wearing black leggings and an oversized gray sweater, the sleeves pulled all the way to her fingers. Her eyes are bloodshot, fresh tear tracks dampening her cheeks.

"I'm so sorry, Elise." Without thinking, I reach out to comfort her, but my hand slams against the invisible barrier at the center of the doorway. Pain ripples up my arm.

Elise studies me, her expression unreadable. "I guess Hollywood got that one right, at least. You can't enter without being invited, can you?"

"Nope," I say and shake out my hand.

"Why not? What stops you?"

"I never asked. I assume it's a *cosmic balance* thing. It gives humans a way to protect themselves."

She scowls. "Because otherwise we're easy prey?"

"Elise—"

"Not out here." She turns and heads for the stairs.

"Uh . . . Elise?" I call, still stuck outside. I press a hand against the barrier when she turns around. "If you want me to follow, you actually have to invite me in." I pull my hand away and step back from the door, feeling suddenly vulnerable. She watches me, those blue eyes darkened by the shadows of her dimly lit house. I imagine a thousand verbal blades she could wield. Telling me this was a mistake. Sending me home. Deciding she'd rather talk outside than let me enter.

She wipes the last of the tears from her cheeks as she approaches. "Is there a special way I have to do it?"

"No." I stare at my feet to hide my relief. "Any form of 'come in' is usually sufficient."

"Well then, please. Come in, Claire."

The air shifts between us, a sense of pressure dropping, and I step forward through the threshold. We exhale together as I come to rest before Elise, the toes of my shoes nearly touching her sock feet. "Thank you."

She glares at me and closes the door. "Don't thank me yet."

Before I can ask what she means, she's climbing the stairs. I follow, and we turn right at the top. Elise presses her fingers against the first door we pass, but she doesn't go inside. Instead, she continues down the hall and opens the second door on our left.

I step into her room, and I barely have a moment to catalogue it all—her hastily made bed, textbooks spilling from every surface, a desk covered with notebooks—before she closes the door and whirls on me.

"Why didn't you warn me that I'd see Ms. Conrad die when it happened?" Her hands are curled into fists, the edges of her sweater caught inside. Her voice is quiet, though, like she doesn't want anyone to overhear.

"What?"

"You promised Ms. Conrad would be safe, that she's never on campus on Thursdays. You said that you would protect her. You said—"

"She wasn't supposed to be there." I keep my voice calm, crushing the urge to match her anger. "I promise, if I thought she was going to be on campus tonight, I would have been there."

It doesn't make sense. Amelia doesn't teach on Tuesdays or Thursdays. For two weeks, she's gone to her ballet class and then directly home to grade. I haven't followed her long, but there was no indication the pattern might change.

"Are you sure she's dead?" I ask as delicately as I can.

"Of course I'm—" Her voice rises, and she cuts herself off.

"How can you even ask that?" Her words are a whisper now, fierce and full of hurt. "I *felt* it. All night I felt it coming, like a warning. I should have known. I should have recognized the pain in my back. I should have done something."

Elise is pacing now, her words picking up speed even as she keeps her volume low. Her parents must be home.

"There's no way you could have known. You can't blame yourself."

"And then it was like I was there, like I was *her*," Elise continues as if she didn't hear me. "Someone grabbed me, grabbed *her*. They stabbed us over and over. Everything hurt. And I was trapped there until she . . . Until she—"

"Hey," I soothe, reaching for her hand. "It's going to be okay."

"Stop *lying* to me. None of this is okay!" She rips away from my touch. "Is this what my entire life is going to be like? Is this what the Veil wants from me? To save people and kill people but no matter what, I have to feel their deaths? How am I supposed to live like this?"

"Elise . . ."

"Don't try to deny it. I'm smart enough to piece everything together. You said I'll be able to change deaths and save people. That means I can make them die faster, too. That's what the Veil wants. That's what *you* want."

"I don't want you to be a killer," I say, but left unspoken is a silent *like me*. The truth of it scrapes against my heart, tender and raw. I hope she has more say in that title than I did.

She studies me for several heartbeats. "You don't, but the Veil does?"

"The Veil can't make you do anything. It's always your choice,"

I say, which is . . . *technically* true. Elise can't be compelled, so no one can force her to use her power against her will, but Tagliaferro can be persuasive. Most of us can be.

What if that's what happened to Hazel?

The realization strikes like lightning. What if it wasn't someone upset about what Hazel had already done? What if the killer was trying to force Hazel to use her power for their own cause?

Elise settles on the edge of her bed, arms crossed protectively around her middle. "I can't believe Ms. Conrad is dead."

"We don't know that for sure." I sit beside Elise, even as part of me warns that she'll send me away. That she'll kick me out of her room, out of her life, leaving her unprotected until Wyn assigns a new shepherd. "I'll go to campus and find out what happened."

Elise leans into me, and the shock of her warm body against mine steals all rational thought.

It doesn't mean anything. She's just grieving.

"It isn't fair." Elise rests her head against my shoulder. "What did she do to deserve this?"

"That's the thing about death." I wrap my arm around Elise and lay my head on hers. She shudders, but she presses closer, her tears dampening my shirt. *It doesn't mean anything.* "We rarely get the deaths we deserve. The universe doesn't care about fairness."

She pulls away from my touch, slipping from the bed so she can glare at me fully. "Don't you think I know that? I've seen countless deaths. You don't need to . . . to *death-splain.* I get how unfair it is."

"That's not what I meant," I say, but whatever tenderness she may have felt is gone, leaving me alone with my guilt. I'm the one who demanded a day off. I'm the reason the teacher is dead, and yet here I am, upsetting Elise further instead of fixing things.

"I should go." I stand and head for the bedroom door. "I'll find out what happened."

"I'll come, too."

"No." The word comes out more harshly than I intended, and I try to soften the impact. "It's late. I'll text you if I find anything."

"But—"

"Goodnight, Elise."

I slip down the stairs before Elise can argue further. I consider going back and explaining what happened to Hazel, but the moment I step outside, the cool air brings me to my senses. There's no reason to scare her when Hazel's death might have nothing to do with Elise. Besides, I owe her answers about Amelia before I drop more worries on her plate.

Instead, I race to campus, but I'm not fast enough to get there first.

Students stand in clusters at the edge of a police line, illuminated by emergency lights. The scent of blood is heavy on the air. *Lots* of it. Even having fed last night, my insides twist with hunger as I maneuver through the crowd. I pass a girl from the sorority house, but she looks at me with no recollection of the moments we shared. It's a forgetting of my own making, yet it still makes me feel diminished and small.

I could walk ten thousand years on this earth, and no one will ever remember me.

What the hell is the point?

Rose, a voice says. *She deserves to pay for this existence.*

When I get to the front of the crowd, I find Amelia Conrad lying in a pool of blood, just like Elise feared. I take pictures to add to my wall of horrors. Amelia's death looks nothing like Hazel's—and no self-respecting vampire would leave so much blood behind—but it's yet another problem for me to solve.

Elise will want answers, and since I failed to save her teacher, I owe her that much.

When I finish with my photos, I pull up my text messages and send two to Elise.

You were right.

I'm sorry.

19

Elise

*E*lmsbrook Academy replaces first period with an assembly.
Students pack the auditorium, and the closeness of so
many future deaths presses against my defenses. My body carries
echoes of drawn-out illnesses and exhaustion as classmates file
into seats around me.

"Are you okay?" A sudden burst of pain at the back of my skull
follows Maggie's question. It fades into a dull headache, another
reminder of how I'll lose my best friend. I have to keep training
until I can fix it, until I'm strong enough to give her a better death.

Even if it means giving my own future, or part of it, to the Veil.

I tug the sleeves of my sweater past my wrists and cross my
arms against my chest. It's a useless gesture. No matter how hard I
recoil, I can't protect myself from her death when she's this close.
"Everything's been on hyperdrive since I touched Jordan's aura,"
I admit as we take our seats. Maggie is on my right, a boy I don't
know on my left. Being near him makes half of me tingle and go
numb.

"If it's that sensitive, maybe you can shield soon. Claire said
that was level three." Maggie crosses her legs and adjusts her skirt.
She purses her lips, a sure sign there's something she needs to say.

After a moment, she leans closer and whispers, "It's not your fault, you know."

The pain in my head deepens, and I fight the urge to wince. "What's not?"

"This," she says, pointing to the stage where several adults stand beside a podium. "You did everything you could."

Despite her assurances, guilt claws into my heart. Part of me was there when Ms. Conrad died. I can still feel her fear. The pain of someone stabbing her in the back. My throat tightens, and I wish Maggie was wearing gloves so I could reach for her hand. "She was so scared, Mags."

Before Maggie can respond, Dean Albro—a white man in his fifties with a stylish swoop of gray hair—crosses the stage and takes his place behind the podium. The sound system screeches as he adjusts the mic. "Good morning, students."

Around me, a handful of students say, "Good morning, Dean Albro," while everyone else continues their murmured conversations.

I say nothing. I know what's coming, and I still hate him for threatening to kick me out last year.

The dean clears his throat and glances at the line of adults behind him. A Latinx woman with light brown skin nods for him to continue. He makes a show of adjusting his glasses, despite not holding anything to read. "I regret to bear such news, but Elmsbrook PD found Ms. Conrad at the university last night. An investigation is ongoing, but I'm sorry to report that Ms. Conrad passed away."

His words hang heavy in the air. Aside from bits of whispered, panicked conversation, the audience goes unnervingly quiet. I carry the weight of their shock. The weight of their grief. I want to confess, explain that I knew this was coming and failed to protect our teacher. I wish Claire was beside me instead of the boy making my arm go numb. At least then I'd have someone besides myself to blame.

Claire promised to protect Ms. Conrad.

She failed.

Dean Albro turns the mic over to the Latinx woman, who introduces herself as Ms. Santino. She went to Elmsbrook Academy an *undisclosed* number of years ago and works locally as a social worker. While she talks about the additional support we'll have for the next week, the gruesome details of Ms. Conrad's death play on repeat in my head. I'm drowning under the weight of the things I know but can never say.

"We understand that this will be a challenging time for many of you," Ms. Santino says. "For others, you may not feel the impact for several days. We all process on our own timelines." She scans the crowd, and I swear her gaze settles right on me. "Dean?"

"Yes, yes. Thank you." Dean Albro takes Ms. Santino's place at the podium and gestures to the line of adults. "We're grateful to have Ms. Santino's team with us through the end of next week. If you want help processing this terrible news, please come to the main office for an appointment. Additionally, all after-school activities have been canceled. Instead, we will have a small memorial in the gymnasium following last period."

The dean dismisses us, and the masses bottleneck at the door. I fall back, trying to escape the crowd, but the guilt and shame weaken my defenses. Their deaths slip in—fragmented flashes of surgical suites, oncoming headlights, the loud shot of a gun. I carry it all, unable to identify the owner of each death, until finally, we're through the door. The halls are wide enough, despite students going in every direction, that I finally get the space I need to breathe.

Ms. Conrad will never breathe again.

I move through the rest of the day like a zombie, staring blankly at the whiteboard as teachers work. Their voices float above me, more rhythm and melody than actual words. Several ask if I'd like to speak with one of the counselors, but I never go. What's the point? I can't tell them the truth about what's bothering me. In biology, Mrs. Severson, the ancient science teacher with gray curls piled on her head, directs us to the lab tables, where dead frogs sit in trays beside laminated instructions.

"Pair up and identify the internal organs. Let me know if you have questions." Mrs. Severson sits behind her desk and picks up a paperback. She announced on the first day of classes that she was retiring in June, and she's been checked out ever since.

At least Maggie and I have bio together, so I'm saved from having to find a partner. We take the far-left table and settle by the windows. My former teammate, Grace, sits a table over, but thankfully, Kaitlyn is nowhere to be found. The sun warms my back as I put on the required gloves.

"I can't watch." Maggie covers her eyes.

"It's not that bad." I pat her arm, grateful that I can do something so small. I wish it wouldn't be weird to wear gloves all the time. "I can tackle the hands-on stuff if you take notes."

"Okay," she says, but she sounds uncertain even as she pulls out a pen.

"Really, it's not that gross." I scan the instructions, pin the poor creature to the cutting surface, and make the first incision. "See?"

Maggie glances at the opening. "Nope. Not looking again. No way." She shudders violently. "You must have inherited an iron stomach from your dad. That is *disgusting*."

I laugh, but then her words sink deeper. Before Nick moved away for college, Dad used to tell us all about his surgeries over dinner. Nick would beg him to stop, claiming it made his stomach hurt, but even as a little kid, I wanted more detail. I've always loved science, always wanted to understand how everything works. That's part of what makes training with Claire so frustrating. It's all feeling and intuition, and her being a vampire defies science altogether.

Dad hasn't shared any surgery stories since Nick died. He's barely even *looked* at me. Doesn't he miss it? Doesn't he miss *me*?

Thinking about it won't do me any good, so I focus on the frog. We identify the lungs, gallbladder, and stomach.

"Why do you think they need three livers?" Maggie asks when I finally find them. "I'm pretty sure they don't get wasted on Friday nights."

"They might. Weirder things have happened."

Maggie laughs, but her smile falls when Kaitlyn finally strolls in. She drops a late slip on Mrs. Severson's desk, and our teacher barely glances up from her book.

"This is ridiculous." Kaitlyn drops her bag and sits beside Grace. Her voice is quiet, but she's only one table away, so each word is crystal clear. "I spent all last period arguing with the counselor, but they won't un-cancel practice."

"Maybe we can have a make-up over the weekend." Grace passes the tweezers to Kaitlyn. "Could you do this? It's making me queasy."

"I can't this weekend. Mom is forcing me to have a *family bond-*

ing day with her new boyfriend." Kaitlyn scoffs and accepts the tweezers. Her entire face scrunches up when she looks at the frog, but she glances at the instructions and gets to work. "Look, I feel as bad about Ms. Conrad as the next person, but Dean Albro can't punish us for her mistake. The state invitational is in less than a month."

The blade slips from my hand and clangs against the metal pan.

"Elise . . ." Maggie says, her tone full of warning.

But it's too late. I'm already tearing off my gloves and turning to face my former teammates. "Mistake? Are you serious?"

Kaitlyn flips her hair out of her face and glares at me. "I'm not trying to be insensitive, or whatever, but swim actually means something to me. The dean shouldn't force us to attend the memorial."

"Insensitive? Ms. Conrad was *murdered*." I stand, and the tall stool screeches against the tile floor.

"Settle down back there," Mrs. Severson says in a bored monotone without looking up from her novel.

"Says who?" Kaitlyn asks. "The dean didn't say anything about murder."

"I . . ." Shit. There's no way to explain without looking super guilty.

Kaitlyn rolls her eyes and turns back to her table. "Everyone dies, Beaumont. The school shouldn't force us to mourn. They didn't even do this when your brother crashed his stupid car."

Grace shoots a shocked look at Kaitlyn, but I hardly register her surprise. Kaitlyn's words feel like a blade sliding into my back, and I can't hear anything else over the sound of blood racing through my system. The *whoosh whoosh whoosh* of my furious heart fills me with a punchy kind of energy, electric and bitter.

"Oh, so it's no big deal," I say, rolling up my sleeves. "Everyone dies eventually, so who cares? Want to know *exactly* how your life will end, Kate?"

Maggie grabs my shoulder. "Elise, no."

I shake her off and advance on Kaitlyn. "Maybe you'll even die soon. Swim practice wouldn't matter much then, would it?" I don't want to extend my aura and risk seeing Grace's death, so I reach out to touch Kaitlyn.

Before I can make contact, bare hands grip my forearm. Death explodes in my mind. Maggie walking around a pool. Slipping. Head smashing against concrete and bleeding out before anyone can help.

When Maggie finally lets go, Kaitlyn is standing several tables away. "What the hell is your problem?" Kaitlyn's voice trembles despite her scowl.

"Girls, that's enough." Mrs. Severson's crackly voice fills the room. She looks up from her book and scans the space between us. Satisfied that neither of us is holding a sharp object, she returns to her story.

Maggie pushes me back to our table, careful not to touch my skin this time, but the heightened tension leaves a lingering ache from the press of her aura. I watch Kaitlyn out of the corner of my eye. She and Grace switch to a table farther away.

My power is strong enough now that I could stretch my aura to hers, even from across the room, but I'd risk seeing every death between us in the process, and she's not worth that. Scaring her into being a decent human—if that's even possible—wouldn't be worth so many deaths, either.

So, I let it go. For now.

———

When I step into the gymnasium after the final bells, it's been fully transformed. The fluorescent overhead lights are off, the room lit instead by dozens of floor lamps that cast a soft, ethereal glow. On the far side of the room, there's a small in-memoriam area for Ms. Conrad. Her yearbook picture from last spring is blown up on a canvas, a table of candles flickering beneath.

I scan the crowd and maneuver carefully through the space. The press of death hangs heavy in the air, and it mingles with my guilt until it's this toxic, cloying thing. I spot Maggie and Jordan with the swim teams, Coach Cochrane among them. Kaitlyn is there, too, standing beside Grace, a deep scowl scrunching her face.

Kaitlyn's obsession with practice makes zero sense to me, especially after our teacher was *literally murdered*. Her callousness makes my blood boil. She was the same when Nick died. The entire team came to his funeral, but the first thing Kaitlyn asked me was how long before I'd be back at practice. As if that mattered more than the hurt and the guilt and the grief. As if I could ever swim again after my brother drowned.

Despite *years* of intense training, I still wasn't strong enough to save my brother. Not when it mattered most. After that, how could winning a mixed relay be anything but meaningless?

Familiar grief rises up, hot and choking, and I weave through the crowd to where candles are set up. I can do that much at least. I can light a candle for Ms. Conrad and get back to work. Claire wasn't in school again today, and I hope that means she's out investigating. If she's not, then I'll figure it out myself. I won't let a killer run free through our town.

Something cold slithers down my back. *There's a killer in Elmsbrook.*

My fingers tremble as I raise the long match. *There's a murderer in town.* I don't know why it took so long for that to sink in. Was Ms. Conrad in the wrong place at the wrong time, or did the killer target her specifically? I turn away from the candles and study the gym, filled to bursting with students, teachers, and administrators. Was this a one-time thing, or are all of us in danger?

As I turn to find a quiet corner to watch the ceremony, there's a flash of blond hair and blue eyes and a crooked smile.

Nick.

It's not possible, I *know* it's not possible, but I'd recognize my brother anywhere. His blond hair—the same color as mine—gleams in the soft lamp light, and he smiles when he sees me. My lungs constrict. It's hard to breathe. My heart races, and every muscle tenses with the need to run to him.

But the crowd shifts, blocking my view, and then he's gone.

Tears flood my eyes, the room a sudden blur of color. *Of course he's gone. He was never really here.* All the energy bleeds out of me. This happened to Mom for weeks after the funeral. She kept seeing Nick in every blond white guy who looked remotely like him. But Nick's gone. I saw him drown. I saw him—

I shut out the memory and stumble away from the candles. Yet, despite my effort, the past tries to overlay the present. Most of these people were at Nick's funeral. The same somber expressions and mascara-streaked cheeks blending then with now, the same guilt beating inside my chest.

I should have been able to save them. Both of them.

The diagram Claire drew our first day of training is burned into my memory. *Touch. Proximity. Shield. Unraveling.* Dozens of whispered deaths press against my aura, a constant reminder that I'm well into the proximity phase. Claire must have a faster way to do this. I need to master unraveling before anyone else I know dies. I wish I could trust the kindness in her eyes instead of worrying that it's an act to get me to trust the Veil as much as Hazel did.

As I pass the second set of doors, a strong grip tightens around my arm. I'm dragged into the hallway and shoved into another room. I suck in a panicked breath, ready to scream, but I'm choked by the tang of chlorine.

The pool sits empty before me. The hold on my arm relents, and I stumble back until I'm pressed against the wall. Flashes of memory threaten to drown me. Frigid water assaulting my skin. Heavy clothes slowing my strokes. Nick's panicked eyes as he slams his fists against the glass.

Go. Please, Ellie.

I can't be here. I can't—

"Relax, Death Oracle. You're not in any danger."

That voice . . . I force my gaze off the water and find Delilah. The vampire looks like something out of a fairy tale—pale skin, dark hair, blood-red lips—yet there's no sweetness to her.

"What are you doing here?" I mean for my words to sound harsh, but I can't keep the tremble out of my voice. "I've told you all I know. Luca and Henri are still in charge, but I don't know where they are. I can't ask more without Claire getting suspicious."

A smile tugs at the corner of Delilah's lips, and even that expression screams *predator.* "So, you *have* been reading Hazel's journal. Your shepherd isn't the savior you thought she was. Not quite so trustworthy anymore, is she?"

Her smugness grates against my nerves, and I cross my arms. "I don't trust you, either. You all want something from me."

"Smart girl. We do." Delilah reaches into her purse and pulls out another journal. "At least I'm up-front about what I want. Poor Hazel didn't realize how much she sacrificed for those ancient assholes. She was loyal to a fault, but she never knew how little they cared for her or how much they profited from her power."

I wish I could deny the vampire's claims, but I read the entries myself. I don't understand how Hazel could stomach only saving those with enough money to make it worth the Veil's while. And those entries were so old . . .

What else did she do over the decades? How many people did she kill? How many did she save? What am *I* supposed to do with this power? I can't possibly save everyone—the world is way too big for that—but how am I supposed to choose? How do I decide?

How can *anyone* decide?

My stomach twists, and my chest tightens. No matter what I do, people will die. But I can't ignore my power and pretend I'm like everyone else. Maggie deserves so many more years than she's slated to get. I don't want Mom to go through so much pain before she passes.

A deep ache creeps into my skull, and I tug on the end of my braid. "What do you need from me?"

"I told you before, Henri and Luca have long exceeded their expiration date. I plan to fix that." Delilah hands me the second journal.

It's thicker than the first, and I wonder how many lavish parties are within its pages. I wonder how many ways Hazel found to justify what she did. What trinkets she bought to soothe her guilt.

"If you want them dead, just kill them. You don't need me." I lean back against the wall, keeping my gaze away from the pool. "I won't unravel them for you."

"See, that's the thing." Delilah tucks her purse into the crook of her arm, and her eyes flash red. "I don't want you to kill them. I want you to *cure* them."

"I'm sorry, what?" I can't possibly have heard her correctly.

Delilah turns and paces, the *click-clack* of her heels echoing through the empty room. "I've spent a long time deciding how to end those fools. A wooden stake through the heart is too mundane. Decapitation is fun, but messy. I considered fire, but I could get hurt, too." She pauses and runs a finger along her cheekbones and down the length of her jawline. "This face is too pretty to risk."

I stare at her as she resumes pacing. The way she talks about murder like it's nothing . . . Are all vampires like this? Is that why the Veil had no trouble sending Hazel on mission after mission? Do none of them value life?

Is Claire like this, too?

How many times has *she* killed?

"Anyway," Delilah continues, oblivious to the way my stomach twists and my knees threaten to buckle beneath me, "none of those ideas felt right. I need something more poetic, something more *prolonged*, than just tearing out their hearts. That's where you come in."

"I'm not *murdering* for you." I hold out the journal. "If that's what you want, you can have this back."

The vampire lets out a frustrated sigh. "You're not listening, Death Oracle. You're not going to kill the Veil leaders."

"Then what *am* I supposed to do?"

She grins. "You're going to make them mortal."

20

Claire

"Don't rush."

I'm perched on the edge of the loveseat, eyes locked on Maggie and Elise. It's Saturday—a little over a week since Amelia died—and instead of her school uniform, Maggie wears yoga pants and a neon-orange T-shirt. Elise is in jeans and another bulky sweater, her golden hair in a tight braid.

The girls stand facing each other while Jordan watches from the couch. He offered to continue as the test subject, but Maggie's death is more physically painful. It's a better incentive for Elise to secure her shields. I wish there was another way. I wish I didn't have to trade progress for pain, but this is the only path I know.

Maggie holds up her hand and smiles encouragingly. "You've got this, Ellie. Just a little closer."

Elise nods, but her eyes are closed and her forehead is creased with concentration. Dark circles mark her pale skin like bruises, and I worry she's not sleeping well. I worry I'm pushing too hard, but whenever I bring it up, Elise insists she's fine.

"Just like we've practiced. Picture a shield of golden light guarding your aura."

She glances at me, eyes flashing with pain, then returns her focus to Maggie. Elise raises her hand until it's level with her friend's and pauses. One deep breath. Two. On the third exhale, she closes the gap, pressing their palms together. Neither of them moves for several seconds. Maggie holds her breath, heart hammering fast in her chest.

A slow smile blossoms on Elise's lips. "It worked," she says, the words breathy and full of wonder. "It worked!"

Maggie squeals and crushes Elise in a hug. Every atom in my undying body screams to join them, but I stay seated as Jordan takes the place I imagined for myself. Their joy doesn't involve me. My presence isn't wanted.

I don't know why I keep expecting that to change.

Beneath the sounds of celebration, Elise sucks in a sharp breath. She tenses and rips away from the group hug, pressing a hand to the back of her skull. Jordan reaches for her, but she shakes her head and steps farther back.

"It's my fault," she says, cutting off her friends mid-apology. "I lost focus. We can try again."

"No. You've done enough." I stand, cataloguing all the places her body screams exhaustion. The dark circles. The trembling fingers. The air tinged with sweat and fading adrenaline. I offer a smile, for what little good it will do. "You've earned a break."

"But—"

"Go home, Elise. Eat a good meal. Get some sleep." I usher the three mortals through my kitchen and open the apartment door. "We'll pick up again tomorrow."

Jordan never needs to be told twice. "Do you two want to come over for dinner? Mom was baking rolls when I left."

I abandon the mortals to their evening plans. I won't eavesdrop on lives that will never involve me, and Elise deserves to have fun with her friends while she can. Once she's joined the Veil, she'll be too busy for mortal life.

She'll be too busy for me, too.

Though the Death Oracle doesn't spend every waking moment remaking deaths or unraveling paranormals, leadership will keep her occupied. She'll be part symbol, part weapon, and between the social events, travel, and actual life-or-death assignments, she won't have time for mortal affairs. Once she's an active asset, the Veil will assign a full-time bodyguard, someone from one of the major bloodlines. Elise will have no use for me. It's another reason not to get attached. Another reason not to care.

At least, not about her.

I step into my room and focus on the gruesome collage. Most of the wall is dedicated to Hazel, though I did add a few photos of Amelia's murder scene. As far as I can tell, there's nothing paranormal about the teacher's death, which makes it beyond the Veil's interest.

"Claire?"

Elise's voice startles me out of my thoughts, and I find her in the doorway, fussing with the ends of her sweater. After a breath, she pushes her sleeves to her elbows.

We must be alone.

"Did you forget something?" I ask as a sudden, unexplained hope burns in my chest.

She shakes her head and steps into the room. Though we've been training for weeks, it's the first time she's been in here. "I was wondering . . ." She falls silent when she notices the printouts. "What's all that?"

I hurry to block her view. "It's nothing you need to see."

But Elise reaches for my arm and peers over my shoulder. I can tell the moment she spots Ms. Conrad, her fingers pressing against my skin, breath catching in her throat.

"The police are looking into Amelia's death, but I wanted to make sure it wasn't one of us." I shift to block the teacher's photos from view. Elise meets my gaze, and her blue eyes shimmer with tears. "I don't know if it makes it better or worse, but nothing about her death reads paranormal to me."

She nods, but her gaze flicks away, back to the wall. "What about that one? Who were they?" Instead of recoiling from the images, Elise steps around me to look at them more closely.

"Her name was Hazel."

Elise's heart skips a beat then races to catch up. "Hazel?" she asks, a thread of something I can't name woven through her tone. "What happened to her?"

"I never mentioned it because I didn't want you to worry."

She glances over her shoulder to scowl at me. "Claire, who is she?"

Guilt batters against my still heart, and I back away from the wall. "Hazel was the Death Oracle, the one before you." I hold my breath as my words land, watch as Elise turns to face me, and brace for her fear.

I get anger instead.

"Someone murdered the last Death Oracle, and you didn't think I should know?" Elise points to one of the images I've marked up in red. "What the hell happened?"

"That's what I'm trying to find out." *Not that I've been very successful.* I turn away and sit on the edge of my bed. "It's hard to investigate with only a few photos for clues."

"How long was she left alone to *rot* in the woods? I thought

Hazel was really important to the Veil. Why isn't someone else looking into this?" Elise pulls her sleeves past her wrists, treating the soft fabric like armor.

"They are. The entire tracking department is on it, actually."

"Then why are you investigating, too?" Elise turns back to the photos. "Her fingers look broken."

"I wanted to make sure you weren't in danger, too."

"Why am I sensing an 'and' in there?"

It's unnerving how easily she reads me, and I can't stop the truth from spilling out. "Attacking the Death Oracle is basically a declaration of war. I won't let Tagliaferro and Guillebeaux get distracted in a decades-long feud."

"Why not?" Her head tilts to the side, making her braid swing across her back.

"Do I need a reason to prevent war?" I sidestep the truth. I don't know if I can open those wounds. I don't know if I can let myself be that real, not with her. Not with—

"You don't need a reason . . ." Elise agrees, coming to stand beside my bed. "But I think you have one."

I stare at the floor, at the same ugly brown carpet that covers most of the apartment. "It's a long story."

"I'm not in a hurry to be anywhere."

Fuck. I let out a breath and stare at the ceiling. I could change the subject, I could ask why she isn't hurrying to Jordan's house for dinner, but instead, I let out a bit of truth. "I've spent a long time trying to find someone, but I need the Veil's help. If we get sucked into a war . . . no one will have time for me."

"Can I ask who?" She leans her hip against my mattress. "You don't have to say, but—"

"Her name is Rose." It's been so long since I've told anyone about her, about what happened to me, and the past claws its way up my throat. "She's the one who turned me."

"Oh." Elise worries at her lower lip, but there's no spike of fear or adrenaline in the air. "This . . . is maybe an awkward question, but you've never really talked about how you became a vampire."

"Most of us don't. It's incredibly personal."

Heat flushes Elise's cheeks until her pale skin turns crimson. "I'm sorry. I shouldn't have asked. You just seemed . . . I don't know, like you hate her."

"I do." The truth spills out, blunt and raw and aching.

But Elise doesn't flinch. Instead, she reaches for my hand, weaving our fingers together. "I'm sorry. You don't have to share anything, but if you want to talk, I'm here."

Pressure builds in my chest. No human has ever asked for my story before, not even Fiona. The rest of my secrets—the rest of my past—comes spilling out. "When I was seventeen, I was in love with my best friend. But as soon as she found out about my feelings, she rejected me. She tossed me out of her life without giving me a chance to explain."

Elise's eyes widen. I don't know what to make of her surprise, whether she didn't realize I was gay or if she's so much a product of her time that she's shocked to hear of such rejection. As if teens today aren't still cast out by the people they love, even in places like Elmsbrook.

"When Rose approached me," I continue, picking at my fingernails, "she acted like I *mattered* to her. She promised a world where we could be together forever. She . . ." The memory surges, and embarrassment forces my gaze to the floor. "Rose was the first girl who kissed me back. She helped me believe that my heart wasn't broken. But she never explained what she was, not until it was too late. Not until she'd turned me into . . . this."

"How does it work?" Elise's words are whisper soft, and she lets go of my hand. The rejection stabs at my heart, but before I'm crushed completely, Elise sits beside me on the bed.

I let myself relax. A little. "Not everyone survives the transition. We're only supposed to turn humans who understand the risks, who know what they're agreeing to." I shift further back on the bed and hug my knees to my chest. "The vampire drains the human of blood, and if the human survives long enough, they feed from the vampire. After the transition starts, we need fresh human blood within hours or else we perish forever."

"And that's what Rose did to you?" Elise looks horrified. "Without telling you what would happen?"

I nod, and unexpected tears spill down my cheeks. I wipe them away, burying the hurt beneath the rage I've carried for decades. "I don't even remember her biting me. She convinced me to run away, and we spent the night dancing to live music and kissing in the shadows. I'd never felt so free. So alive. But the next morning, when I woke up—the pain of bloodlust is unlike anything I'd ever experienced. Everything hurt so much, and when I stumbled out of bed, I . . ."

I can't speak the rest out loud. How I tripped and fell over a dead body. A girl, no older than I was, drained of every drop of blood. When the violent memory surfaced, I screamed and woke Rose. But she grew bored of my panic and disappeared, leaving me to figure out this new existence on my own.

"There are strict rules about how vampires treat the newly risen. Our creators can compel us for one year. Rose should have taught me to hunt without killing or raising alarm. She was supposed to help me embrace this unending existence." I rest my chin on my knees and look away from Elise. "Instead, she abandoned me in an unfamiliar city with a curse I didn't want or understand."

The mattress dips as Elise shifts closer. "That sounds terrifying."

I shrug as emotions I thought were long buried tighten my throat. "That's Rose. I've been looking for her ever since, but no one seems to know who she is."

"What will you do when you find her?"

"Nothing you'd approve of."

Instead of flinching away, Elise tugs at my arm until I give her my hand. She cradles it in both of hers, the heat of her skin warming through me. "I'm so sorry, Claire. You didn't deserve that. No one does."

Under her unyielding attention, my defenses crumble. "I hate it," I admit, tears spilling over my cheeks again.

"Hate what?"

"All of it. I hate the constant hunger. I hate living forever, watching everyone else grow old and die. I miss lying in the sun." A bitter laugh carves through my chest. "I hate being stuck at seventeen. Vampires . . . We're not like humans. We're not supposed to *feel* like you do."

"You won't convince me that vampires don't have emotions."

"We do, but it's different. Vampires . . . we can hold a grudge until the end of time, but our relationships are different than yours. We're loyal to our bloodlines, but if you don't have one, it's hard to find family. None of the others want to fall in love the way humans do. The prospect of forever isn't as exciting when it literally means *forever*."

"None of the others . . . But you do?"

The embarrassment is almost unbearable, but I nod. "We're not supposed to be turned this young. My brain is stuck at seventeen, and everything I feel is . . . heightened. It makes me too close to humanity. The others . . . They think it's foolish, the ability to love like this, to hurt like this, but I can't shut it off."

Her touch leaves my hand, and the loss of warmth hurts worse than the brightest sun. But then her fingers brush my face, wiping away tears I forgot were there. "I don't think it's foolish to want someone to love you."

The words hang between us, and time seems to slow. I find myself cataloguing every place we touch. Her knee against my hip. Her fingers lingering along my jaw. Elise drops her gaze to my lips before pinning me in place with the intensity of her blue eyes.

I hear it, the second her heart stops. Skips. Her breath catches in her throat.

BUZZZZ.

My phone vibrates violently on the desk, and we both flinch. I'm off the bed in an instant, my speed disturbing the air. Abigail's number glows on the screen.

"Yeah?" I answer, turning my back on Elise. *Don't feel. Shut it down. It doesn't mean anything.*

But my body is flushed, and I'm so very fucked.

Abigail cuts right to the point. "I have a lead on Petal and Thorn. You're the closest." She gives me an address for an unsanctioned blood bar over an hour away. "Ingrid tracked a handful of strays there. We think that's where they're recruiting."

I flinch at the derogatory term, but I don't say anything. If one of the witches picked up on the bar, it's worth checking out. Except . . . "I can't. I'm already on assignment."

"Consider it proactive protection for your charge." Abigail pauses, testing to see whether I'll deny her logic. I don't. "I want updates by dawn," she says, and hangs up.

I drop the phone and massage my temples as hunger flares. Visiting a blood bar wouldn't be the worst thing. My windows are covered by blackout curtains, but there's no rim of light around the edges. The sun should be mostly set.

No time like the present. "I have to go."

"I'm coming with you."

"No. You're not." I slip out of the bedroom, Elise close on my heels. "I thought you had dinner plans with your friends."

"We can reschedule." Elise steps around me and blocks the apartment door. "Look, I know you're practically indestructible, but you're upset. Someone should look out for you."

Warmth blooms in my chest, but I shake my head. "You don't even know where I'm going."

Elise crosses her arms and raises her chin. "You want me to join the Veil, right?"

"Yes . . ."

"Well, then, I should get to know your world. *Our* world," she corrects, and I can feel my defenses crumbling.

It's a terrible idea, and I tell myself I'm not doing this to spend more time with Elise. I tell myself it's to preserve the trust we've built, but I already know that's a lie.

"Fine. But you have to do *exactly* as I say."

"Can I ask you something?"

We've been traveling north for almost an hour, and it's the first time Elise has spoken since we hit the road.

"Sure." I tap the steering wheel, fingers moving in nervous patterns. I shouldn't have said so much. Whenever I crack the lid of my emotions, everything comes spilling out and makes a mess. Under the night sky, which normally brings comfort and power, I feel exposed. Vulnerable.

Weak.

"Why are you still a vampire if you hate it so much?" Elise fusses with her phone, flipping it round and round. She spent most of the ride texting, and this is the longest stretch the phone's been silent.

"It's not like I can snap my fingers and be human again." My knuckles pop as my grip tightens on the steering wheel. "The only way to stop being a vampire is to stop existing."

Elise's forehead crinkles. "But the Veil has witches and fae and all sorts of things. Someone must know how to make you mortal." She sounds so sure, and every inch of me wishes she were right.

"If there was a way to be human, I'd do whatever it takes." The rawness of our earlier conversation flares. "It's just not possible."

She nods, but her lips are pressed together like she's holding back another argument. The GPS chimes in before I can decide whether to press for more detail.

In two miles, take the exit.

Up ahead, city lights crest the horizon, and with the brightness comes sudden clarity. What the fuck am I doing? I can't bring Elise into a blood bar. *Especially* not an unsanctioned one. And if Ingrid is right, if Petal and Thorn is recruiting here, Hazel's killer could be among them.

You're upset. Someone should look out for you.

I can't believe that's all it took for my ridiculous brain to throw caution into a wood chipper. That's all it took for my dead heart to override basic fucking protocols.

In one mile, take the exit.

"We can't do this. I'm turning around."

"What, why?" Elise shifts in her seat until she's facing me. "We're basically there."

"You're the Death Oracle, Elise. I'm supposed to keep you safe, not dangle you in front of rogue vampires who want you dead."

She crosses her arms. "Fine. I'll wait in the car."

In point-five miles, take the exit.

"I'm not leaving you alone in the car."

"Then I guess I'm going with you."

Take the exit.

I curse under my breath and pull off the highway. Elise is quiet while I follow the directions to the downtown bar and find a place to park. Once I've paralleled into a spot, I cut the engine.

"Are you sure about this?" I unbuckle and turn to Elise. "Blood bars thrive on compulsion, and there might be vampires feeding in plain sight. If you act grossed out, by any of it, you'll blow our cover."

Elise opens her door. "You said the Veil needs to know who killed Hazel, and *you* need the Veil to find your maker, so let's do this. In and out, no fuss."

"It's not that simple." I'm out of the car and standing beside Elise before she closes her door. "You'll have to pretend that I've compelled you, which means you can't look at anyone else directly."

Her brow crinkles. "Why?"

"It's a side effect. When compulsion is active, humans can only hold eye contact with the vampire who compelled them."

"Active?" Elise shivers in the early October evening and pulls her sleeves to her fingers.

There isn't time for a detailed lesson, so I stick to basics. "Remember the teacher who guarded the classroom for us? He was compelled for an immediate task, so it was active the whole time. We can also set parameters for future actions. The compulsion will go dormant and undetectable until the conditions are met."

Elise glances down the street. "So, literally anyone could be compelled without me knowing?"

"We can only hold a few minds at once, so it's not as widespread as you're thinking." I lock the car and lead Elise toward the bar. "The older the vampire, the more nuanced and powerful their compulsion gets, though. The more minds they can hold at once."

"Are you considered old?"

"By vampire standards? Not even a little." I pause us a few buildings away from our target. "When we go inside, follow my lead. Okay?"

"Okay." Elise raises her gaze to mine, and her pulse jumps in her throat. The flicker of movement draws my gaze and makes my jaw ache. I really should have left her home. I can't feed while she's here.

I take a steadying breath, but it only fills my lungs with her scent—fresh laundry and spearmint. It stirs a hunger that's about more than blood. A hunger I can't risk acknowledging. I clear my throat and lead us the rest of the way to the bar.

At the front door, a bouncer asks for IDs, but his heart isn't beating, so I flash my canines. He waves us inside without another word.

Music batters against me when we step through the door, but it's nothing compared to the heavy scent of blood on the air. There are at least a dozen humans hosting somewhere out of sight.

"Are you sure this is the right place? It looks like a normal club." Elise leans in close, wincing. Probably from the press of so many humans and so many deaths.

"There are usually private rooms in the back to feed." There is at least one vampire feeding among the dancers, though. My knees threaten to buckle, but I shove down my hunger and lead Elise toward the quiet bar.

The only bartender, a Black vampire wearing jeans and a tight-fitting tank top, slides a menu in front of Elise. "For the human, we have wine, cocktails, and beer. There's also a full dinner menu on the back."

"Oh, thanks." Elise accepts the menu and flips it over.

"And for you," he says, sliding a very different kind of menu in front of me, "we have a great selection of premium hosts tonight. Or, if you prefer the hunt, you can work the dance floor. Pricing runs by the quarter-hour."

I feel the weight of Elise's gaze as the bartender leaves us to review our options.

"What are all those initials?" She leans close and studies the host menu. "And what is 'ethically sourced' supposed to mean? These are *people*."

My face burns, but this place isn't nearly as unsavory as it could have been. "It means the humans were interviewed before they were compelled, and they're being adequately compensated for their time. The initials indicate which activities they've consented to."

"Activities?"

"Some hosts find the process exciting. The code indicates whether they're interested in . . ." I have to pause and clear my throat. "In releasing said excitement."

Elise stares at me, one eyebrow arching up her forehead. "Wait, like sex?"

I push the menu away. "We need to focus on the reason we're here." I wave the bartender over rather than risk Elise's judgment.

"Found something you like?" he asks.

"We're actually after something else tonight." I lean against the bar, examining the other vampire. The intricate braids sitting tight against his skull. The quick smile. The flash of silver around his neck, a pendant with thorn-covered vines and a flower with curling petals.

Petal and Thorn is recruiting strays.

I flash the bartender a fresh smile. "I've heard this place is kind to orphans."

He looks from me to Elise. "We don't offer discounts, if that's what you're after."

"No, nothing like that." I lower my voice and glance over my shoulder, like I want to make sure no one's near. "I heard about what happened to the Death Oracle. Rumor has it I owe someone at this bar a thank you."

A flash of recognition lights up his eyes, but the bartender shakes his head. "I don't know what you're talking about."

"Come on, we all know what she did to orphans like us," I say, hedging my bets that the bartender wouldn't work here if he belonged to a bloodline. "When's the last time the Veil unraveled one of their descendants?"

The man's eyes flash crimson. "Not since Petronelle destroyed the Prathor line." He says it with such certainty, but he can't be right. There's no way the Veil has only unraveled orphans for hundreds and hundreds of years.

I would have noticed.

Right?

"Wait here. There's someone you should meet." The bartender squeezes his necklace and ducks under the bar.

Elise watches him disappear into the crowd, and the second he's out of sight, she grips my arm. "How screwed are we if he realizes who I am?"

"He won't find out," I say, but even I don't believe my words. All he'd need to do is try to compel Elise. The moment he couldn't touch her mind, he'd realize she's not fully human. I scan the dance floor and find the bartender talking to someone behind the DJ booth. The bartender points in our direction, and the DJ's eyes flash red. A feral scowl twists shadowed features.

Fuck.

"Do whatever you can to stay calm." I reach for Elise's hand and lead her farther down the bar. "They can smell fear."

"What?" Her voice pitches high with worry, and her adrenaline is already spiking.

So much for staying calm. I glance behind us, and the vampires leap over the DJ booth.

"Run!"

I drag Elise after me, weaving through the dancing crowd. Each time we near a mortal, Elise flinches and loses her footing, but we don't have time to be careful. The bartender shouts at us to wait as I crash through the kitchen doors.

Everything is chaos, compelled humans busy tossing pizzas and throwing fresh meat on the grill. They're oblivious to our intrusion, which makes it hard to weave through the cramped workstations.

"Stop them!"

An unfamiliar voice fills the room. The cooks freeze. Their compulsions shift. Elise crashes into the nearest one and falls to her knees, pressing her hands tight to her temples. I draw her into my arms and shoulder through the line of cooks. There are flashes of silver. Long knives. The bite of metal against my skin.

And then we're through, crashing out the back door into a shadowy alley. We need to get out of here. We need to disappear before the other vampires find us. We—

"Wait." Elise grabs my arm and pulls me back. "Kiss me."

"What?" My question is breathless as she presses her back to the brick wall and draws me close.

"Kiss me." She puts my hand at her waist and rises onto her toes. "Hurry."

Elise's fingers brush my cheek, and then I'm falling. I press my lips to hers as the kitchen door slams open. A rush of wind tugs at our clothes, footsteps race away, but none of that matters. Elise is kissing me, and it's everything I wouldn't allow myself to imagine.

It's tender and gentle and so very warm. I haven't felt this alive in years, haven't felt this seen in decades. Her fingers thread through my hair, and I tighten my hold on her waist. Her kiss is sweet and soft and sure and—

She pulls away suddenly and presses her forehead to my shoulder. "Are they gone?" she asks, sounding breathless and dazed.

I can still taste her kiss on my lips, and my brain won't think of anything else. "What?"

"The vampires," she whispers, pulling away. A flush of pink warms the bridge of her nose and cheeks. "I figured they'd be looking for someone running away, and even if they saw us and still smelled adrenaline, they might think it was . . . not the kind they were looking for?" Elise steps back, putting further distance between us as understanding settles over me like sudden frost. "They are gone, right? We're safe?"

"Yeah, they're gone." I head for the car as everything inside goes brittle and tender and raw. Of course it was a ruse. Of course it meant nothing to her. "We should go before they come back."

Elise nods, but neither of us speaks until we're safe inside my car. Until we're alone on the highway. Until I'm half-convinced I imagined the whole thing.

"I'm sorry. About the kiss, I mean." She stares at her hands, her profile lit by the last of the highway streetlights. "I hope it wasn't too weird. I—"

"It's fine. It was a clever idea." Listening to her explain away the kiss, knowing it was tactical and nothing else, shouldn't be a surprise. I should have known that was her intention the moment she suggested it, but I was caught off guard and part of me—

No. Shut it down, Claire. You're not allowed to like her. You're not allowed to care.

She's quiet the rest of the way to Elmsbrook, and I try to erase the memory of her touch. Erase the taste of her kiss. I should focus on the mission Abigail set for me. The bartender's necklace might be the symbol for Petal and Thorn. The DJ might have been the one who killed Hazel. Abigail will be furious I didn't find out more.

Yet no matter what I try, my thoughts slip back to Elise. I still can't believe she kissed me, even to avoid a fight. I've never known her to be a good actress, so she must have felt *something*.

Right?

21

Elise

*E*very time I think my life can't get more complicated, it does.

It was already too much, trying to balance school and Death Oracle training and the guilt over Ms. Conrad's death. I didn't need anything else, but then I found out Hazel was *murdered*. Why does everyone connected to me keep turning up dead?

My brain is stuffed full of worries and fears. It takes all my concentration to strengthen and hold my shield. And in those rare moments all the noise in my head fades away? Well, that's an entirely different problem.

I shouldn't have kissed Claire at the blood bar.

She said it was fine, but she's been distant ever since. She was at school all week, and she continued my training, but she keeps space between us now. I didn't realize how much I relied on her touch until it was gone.

No matter what I try, the memory won't fade. I can't stop thinking about the cool press of her lips, the pressure of her hands on my back. The thrill of it shocked me, the way my entire body lit up inside, but I pulled away before I could tell if any of it was real.

But it doesn't mean anything. It *can't*. It's just been so long since I could touch anyone. Kissing Jordan felt like that, so I know I'm not gay. I just wish I could stop *thinking* about it long enough to—

"Elise!" Maggie snaps her fingers in my general direction, and I escape my runaway thoughts. Even though I can shield semi-reliably now, I sit across the room so I can relax.

"Sorry, Mags." I shake my head to clear away the memories. "Did you find something?"

It's Friday night, and Jordan invited us over to study and watch movies. Both his parents are lawyers—his mom works for the NYCLU and his dad is a law professor. They're out tonight, celebrating Mrs. Wallace's recent victory.

I texted my parents about our plans after school, but only Mom responded, sending a thumbs-up and a reminder to be home before midnight.

Despite our intention to study, my friends and I haven't cracked open a single textbook. Instead, we've been going through Hazel's journals, looking for anything that might explain how to make vampires human again.

And by *we*, I mean Maggie.

She's the fastest reader, so she's been tackling the journal while Jordan tries to convince his chonky chihuahua, Biscuit, to play fetch.

Maggie puts a sticky note on the page and tosses the book to me. "Didn't Claire call the final stage 'unraveling'? I think this is that."

The journal lands in front of me, and I pull it into my lap.

January 25, 1995

I used to think humans had the greatest capacity for evil.
Humans commit all sorts of atrocities, not to mention all the
centuries of war. Yet in all my years with the Veil, I've never
met an unkind paranormal. Sure, the vampires have to feed
from humans, but deaths are rare, and often accidental. They do
what they must to survive, and like 99% of the time, the hosts
never remember anything happened.

But then Luca introduced me to Bartholomew Colardi.

Bartholomew didn't belong to a major bloodline, and he
resented the Veil's rules. He hated our power, claiming we were,
and I quote, "self-important bureaucrats with no legitimate
authority." That alone wasn't a problem—people, even vampires,
are entitled to their opinions—but Bartholomew was gathering
support for an assault against the Veil.

Luca warned him to back down. Henri even tried to explain
how the rules protect all of us, but Bartholomew wouldn't listen.
He kept pushing boundaries until, finally, he went too far.

He left a trail of dead bodies up and down the east coast,
massacring humans without attempting to hide them. He had
to be stopped, and Luca asked me to unravel the vampire to
send a message.

I'd never done anything so intricate. His threads were thick
and knotted, and it seemed an impossible task. When I finally
pulled them apart, the vampire was a shadow of himself. He
didn't die, not right away, but I'd stripped everything that
made him paranormal. He couldn't feed. He barely had the
strength to stand.

Luca said he'd desiccate and crumble to dust within the year.

My stomach twists into horrible knots, and not just because what Hazel described is awful. It's strange to read her words knowing how she dies, knowing someone murdered her and left her to rot in the woods.

Was her murder revenge for something like this?

Biscuit shoves her nose into my palm, and the cold startles me out of my morbid thoughts. I scratch behind her ears, letting the presence of the little dog soothe my nerves.

"That can't be the key to mortality." I kiss the top of Biscuit's head, which seems tiny compared to Richard's. "I don't know what Delilah expects us to find. Claire said it's impossible to make vampires human."

Jordan tosses Biscuit's teddy bear to me. "When did you talk to Claire?"

"You didn't tell her about Delilah, did you?" Maggie asks.

"Of course not." I pick up the teddy and dance it in front of the dog. I remember the hurt in Claire's voice when she explained her turning, the conviction when she said there was no way to be human again. It feels wrong to expose that part of her to my friends, so I keep it locked inside. "And I . . . I asked about it after training last week. I kept it all theoretical, but she said it wasn't possible. If Hazel knew how to do it, you'd think Claire would know."

Maggie picks at the carpet, but she has this look on her face, the same one she gets before a breakthrough for the school paper. "What proof do we have that Claire actually works for the Veil?"

"Why would she lie?"

Jordan shrugs. "She said your power was valuable."

"And Hazel never mentions a vampire named Claire, right?" Maggie adds.

"That doesn't mean anything," I argue, and my mind slips back to last week, to Claire's hurt, to her lips against mine and—
"Forget Claire for a second. What am I supposed to do with the mortality thing if we find it? I trust Delilah less than I trust Claire."

Maggie scowls. "Why?"

"Seriously? She *smelled* you the first time we met." I shudder at the memory. "Who knows what she could have done to Vivi."

"Vivi's fine," Maggie says, but she sounds less certain now. "Look, here's how I see it. If you make the Veil dudes mortal like Delilah asked, they won't be a problem anymore. Then you can repeat the process until all the vampires know to leave you alone. Boom. Normal life."

"It can't be that easy." I tug on my braid, and my brain flits back to my shepherd. Claire said she'd do anything to be human again. I can't keep hiding this from her. "What if I tell Claire? If we warn Tagliaferro and Guillebeaux about Delilah's plan, maybe they'll let me have a normal life."

"I vote for whatever plan doesn't steal you away from us," Jordan says, raising his hand.

But Maggie shakes her head. "What's to stop them from adding this to their list of threats? Based on that," she says, pointing at the journal, "I bet they'd love to hold the threat of humanity over other vampires."

"Ugh!" I tip my head against the wall and stare up at the ceiling. "Why does everything have to be so complicated?"

"Ellie—" Maggie starts, but Jordan cuts her off.

"I think we need a snack break." Jordan stands and reaches out to help Maggie to her feet. He shoots her a meaningful look I don't think he meant for me to see.

"I'll get it." She pushes her glasses up her nose and finally meets my eye, a bright smile warming her face. "You two stay here." She's out the door before either of us can say anything.

When we're alone, Jordan stretches his long limbs and sits on the edge of his bed. He watches me, rich brown eyes full of concern.

"Whatever it is, Jordan, you might as well say it." I perch on the edge of his desk, across the room from the boy who suddenly feels more like an ex and less like the friend I desperately need him to be.

He folds his arms, muscles flexing beneath his brown skin. A smile filled with regret pulls at his lips. "I wish I could make this better for you. I hate that I can't hug you without it hurting. You don't deserve any of this."

I shrug, trying to keep things casual. "At least Kaitlyn isn't the Death Oracle. Can you *imagine* what a nightmare she'd be?"

Jordan laughs, and it fills the room with warmth. "God, I miss you, Ellie. I miss *us*."

Memories of our relationship, memories I've tried so hard to avoid, come rushing in. Jordan sticking a glob of frosting on my nose while baking in his kitchen, his parents spying on us from the living room. Huddling up together after we finished our races, his towel wrapped around me as I soaked up his body's warmth. Late-night video calls where Jordan listened to my latest medical history obsession.

He used to complain that his future wasn't as clear as mine. I've always wanted to be a surgeon like my dad. Jordan's parents have hinted at him being a lawyer, but he's not sure. Since I've known him, he's entertained being an engineer, a baker, a famous

YouTuber—a dream his parents promptly squashed—and he even toyed with the idea of going to trade school and becoming an electrician.

His future is suddenly far clearer than mine.

A stab of nostalgia presses into me, but this time, the familiar longing doesn't rise up. I miss the way we were, I miss knowing what he was thinking and hanging out and talking about our futures, but the desire to take his hand? The desire to kiss him? For some reason, that isn't there anymore. I just miss my friend.

Even so, I offer him a smile. "We were pretty great, huh?"

"We could be great again," Jordan says, but uncertainty raises his voice, turning it into a question. Hope radiates off him stronger than chlorine after two hours in the pool. I'm sure he misses the girlfriend I used to be, but I'm not that person anymore.

I couldn't be her again, even if I wanted to.

Jordan sighs into the silence between us. "I'm sorry. I shouldn't have said anything. I just keep thinking that once the shield is easier—"

"It's not about the shield," I say as gently as I can. There has to be a way to keep the friendship we had. There has to be a way to get rid of this hope he clings to without hurting him. "A lot has changed since we broke up, at least for me. I can't go back to how things were."

"Because we're not forever?"

"Not only that," I say, but maybe this is what he needs from me. A reason that isn't about falling slowly out of love, so slowly I don't even know exactly when it happened. "I guess it's a little bit that, though. I know there's someone better out there for you. Someone you get to grow old with."

Jordan nods and scrubs at his cheeks. His eyes shimmer with hurt, and I wish I could fix it. "What about you? Will you have a forever?"

I shrug, but my mind flashes to Claire. To her lips on mine. To every time she's ever reached for me. Something warm and strange flutters in my chest, but I shove it down. It doesn't mean anything. It can't. Even though my feelings for Jordan have changed, they were still *real*. I loved him, even if I don't anymore.

"If we figure out the Veil problem," I say, forcing a smile, "I can be your cool spinster friend with, like, ten cats."

He laughs. "There's nothing wrong with being a cat lady." He stands and crosses the room to me, pausing just out of reach. "Besides, if you wanted to wait, oh, I don't know, until you're thirty to date, that would be cool, too."

I roll my eyes at him. "You mean wait until you've found your happily ever after?"

"That's not what I meant, but if you wanted to . . ." He grins.

"You're ridiculous." I laugh and playfully push him away, careful to raise a shield and avoid his skin, just in case. "Don't worry, I have way more important things to figure out than who to take to prom."

Downstairs, the smoke detector goes off, screeching through the house.

"Sorry!" Maggie yells up the stairs. "Everything's fine! Don't panic!"

"Well, that sounds promising." Jordan points to the door. "Should we save Mags from herself?"

"Do we think popcorn or . . ."

"Oh, definitely popcorn."

Jordan goes downstairs first, waving smoke out of his face. I follow, laughing while Biscuit barks at Maggie, who is holding a very burnt bag of popcorn with a pair of metal tongs. The pup loves popcorn, a habit Mr. Wallace encouraged.

As we pass the front door, someone knocks.

"I'll get it." Jordan spins back toward the door. He swings it wide while I head for the kitchen to rescue Maggie. "Um, Elise?" Jordan calls after me. "Your dad's here."

"Dad?" My heart skips in my chest, and it's suddenly hard to breathe. What is he doing here? I didn't think he read the group chat, but there he is, standing on Jordan's front porch, still wearing his scrubs. "Dad, what's wrong?"

He glances up, and for the first time in months, he actually looks at me. "It's about your friend. Kaitlyn."

Kaitlyn is *not* my friend, but I don't correct him. "What about her?"

"She's dead."

22

Claire

I need to stop looking at photos of dead people.

I need to stop thinking about the kiss at the blood bar. The *fake* kiss. The meant-nothing-to-her kiss.

But I'm failing on both accounts.

"Montgomery." Abigail's voice fills my room, distorted from the speaker phone. It sounds like she may have said my name more than once, and I wince, swallowing an apology.

"Can you repeat that? The line cut out." It's dangerous to lie to the lead tracker, but it's better than admitting I wasn't listening. Especially since *I* called *her* this time.

"Research already reviewed decades of old cases. We tracked down everyone noteworthy, but none of them were involved."

"Has Petal and Thorn officially taken credit for the murder?" The bartender knew *something*—or, at least, suspected I was snooping and wanted me gone—but I haven't been back since Elise and I escaped.

Abigail lets out a sigh that's equal parts disappointment and irritation. "How many times did your phone cut out?"

"The reception in this town sucks." I approach the wall of photos, scanning the injuries again. Broken fingers. Broken limbs.

Preserved bite mark. "Someone definitely wanted us to find the body. They wanted us to know a vampire was involved."

"We might understand why," Abigail says, an edge to her voice, "if *someone* hadn't tipped our hand and sent half the strays Ingrid was tracking underground."

"Ingrid lost them?" Only the most skilled witches get invitations to join the Veil, so for a group of vampires to evade their tracking . . . "Do you think they have a witch on their side?"

"We're already looking into that possibility." The line goes dead for several seconds, and I worry Abigail hung up on me. A moment later, she's back. "Listen, Montgomery, you're a decent tracker, but your performance at the blood bar hurt our cause more than it helped. Unless you're willing to rejoin the team and give this mission your full attention, I think it's best if you stand down. My trackers will handle this."

"But—"

This time, when the line cuts out, I know it's permanent. I bite back a scream and throw the phone as hard as I can. It shatters against the wall, raining broken bits of glass and metal and plaster onto the carpet.

Abigail is just doing her job. It isn't personal. The reminder rings hollow, even though it's technically true. I'm so tired of nothing being personal, of nothing about me mattering except the results I can produce for the Veil.

Hurt and anger harden around my heart like armor. I need to focus on the real reason for this miserable existence. I need to blame the cause, not the symptoms.

Rose.

I spare a glance for the ruined phone before opening my laptop.

Just because Petal and Thorn hasn't officially declared war against the Veil doesn't mean they won't. I pull up the video chat and send an invite to Wyn.

They answer almost immediately.

"How's my favorite forever-seventeen vampire?" Wyn teases, using the screen to straighten their tie.

"I need you to set a meeting with Luca and Henri."

Even over video, I see them tense. "Why? Something wrong with Elise?"

"No, Elise is . . ." I falter, her voice suddenly in my mind. *Kiss me. Hurry.* I shake my head. "She's fine. This is about Rose. I need a commitment that the Veil will help me find her."

"Claire, we talked about this." All the teasing is gone from Wyn's voice now, but so is the worry. Instead, they sound almost pitying, and it grates against my nerves. "Someone like us getting a favor from the big bosses is rare. Waiting until Elise is fully trained is your best shot."

"You said they would owe me for this."

"And they *will*, but your job's not done. They won't agree until the Veil has a fully functioning Death Oracle."

"She's not just a tool." A growl rumbles deep in my chest. "She's a *person*."

Wyn stares at me, fingers steepled beneath their chin. "Please tell me you're not getting too attached again. We can't afford another Fiona."

"It's not that," I say, but it is. A little. The shame of it is enough to bury me alive. "Look, Elise may be the Death Oracle, but she's only sixteen. It could be years before she masters unraveling, and I can't wait that long. I can't keep doing this until I know Rose's death is guaranteed. She has to pay for what she did to me."

etween us falls silent, and Wyn doesn't move a muscle.
eathe or blink or sigh.

you freeze up?"

runs a hand down their face. "Is your life really that aw-
softness warms their tone. "I know I haven't been around
this past decade, but we have a good time. Surely something
t the last seventy years has been worth experiencing."

Wyn . . ." There's this sinking feeling inside me, and I can't
blame it on hunger. "You know this isn't about you. It's not
en about the Veil." But I don't know how to explain without
rting Wyn's feelings.

There are a lot of great things about immortality. Though vampires have never held the same obsessions with gender binaries or
heteronormative nonsense as western human societies, it's been
nice to witness the mortal world's evolution. This decade has been
so much better for humans who love like Wyn and I do, who experience gender the way Wyn does. There's language for us, now.
Pockets of community that feel so much like home, even if those
moments are fleeting for vampires.

I'm lucky that I didn't have to grow into adulthood in the 1930s
and '40s and '50s. I'm glad my parents were denied the chance to
marry me off to a man I could never love. If Rose had offered me a
choice, if she had explained everything and given me time to make
a decision . . . I might have chosen this when I was old enough to
be a normal vampire.

But she didn't. I woke up a murderer with a hunger for blood I
could never satisfy.

"Please, Wyn," I say, emotion thick in my throat. "Set the meeting. I have to try."

For a moment, I think they might disagree, but Wyn nods. "I'll

ask Henri first. He's generally the more agreeable ⟨
They run a hand through their dark hair, and it flops o⟨
side. "You do realize this is your one chance, right? You a⟨
want to do this now?"

"Yes."

"Fine." Wyn stands and leans over so their face is still in f⟨
"I'll let you know in a couple hours."

23

Elise

A numbing sensation settles over me, like my body is stuffed with cotton. At Jordan's, Dad explained that someone found Kaitlyn's body on campus this morning. He didn't provide details, just enough to know it wasn't natural. That police think it might be connected to Ms. Conrad.

And then he made me leave, abandoning my friends as they were falling apart.

We didn't speak in the car, and when we got home, I tried to escape to my room. Dad wouldn't let me, though. He told me to wait for him in the den. Asked if I needed tea or soup or cocoa, like I'm a little kid home sick from school. I shook my head, my throat tight and my chest aching in a way I didn't expect.

Kaitlyn is dead.

Now, Dad is back, perched on the edge of his recliner. He changed out of his scrubs, swapping them for light-wash jeans and a dark polo. I sit on the couch, curled into the cushions, trying to wrap my head around this new reality where Kaitlyn is dead.

How can she be gone? It doesn't seem real. I didn't see it. I didn't know it was coming. It's been less than seven months since I lost my brother, and it's like I've forgotten that people can die without warning.

Somehow, it feels worse. The not knowing.

"Are you sure it was her?"

Dad nods and drags a hand down his face, like he's trying to wipe away the memory. His knees bounce with nervous energy, and then he launches himself out of the chair.

"I thought it was *you*," he says, pacing in front of the couch. His voice catches, and he rubs the back of his neck. "I overheard a nurse say the police brought in a girl from the academy, and my first thought was that it was you."

"Dad—"

"And all I could think was that I'd failed you. I think . . . I think part of me believed that if I didn't love you so damn much, it wouldn't hurt if something happened to you. If you left us like your brother. But for that minute I thought you were gone, it was so much worse." Dad falls still, his dark eyes shimmering with tears. "I'm sorry, Ellie Bean. I was supposed to be the adult. I should have been there for you."

His words hang between us, but I can hardly breathe. My chest feels too tight. My throat too raw. I knew things were bad between us. I knew he wasn't looking at me, that he hadn't touched me.

I guess some part of me hoped I was overreacting. That I was making it worse in my head than it actually was. But to hear Dad say it, to know it was all *real*.

"Fuck you." The words come out small, but they light a fire inside me.

Dad's eyebrows creep up his forehead. "Excuse me?"

Tears slip past my lashes, and now I'm the one who can't sit still. I leave the soft embrace of the couch and stand before my father. "Do you have any idea what you did? For *months*, I've been blaming myself for Nick's death, and you've barely looked at me! Do you know that you haven't hugged me? Not at the funeral. Not at the burial. Not once!"

"Ellie . . ." He steps forward, arms outstretched.

"Don't *touch* me." I back away, but that fire burns brighter. Hotter. "I don't even know what to say to you right now. I tried so many times to fix things. You can't just apologize and make everything better. You can't spend months blaming me for Nick's death and wave it all away because you got scared."

This time, Dad stays where he is. He keeps his arms pressed to his sides. "Ellie, I never thought you were responsible for your brother's death."

"His name was Nick, Dad. You can say it."

"It wasn't your fault."

"But it *was!*" I shut my eyes, and I'm there again.

Rain batters against the windshield. My hands shake on the wheel. I've only had my driving permit for a few hours, only practiced with Nick a couple miles, but I know the way. Lightning flashes and thunder rumbles so loud it shakes the car.

And then it's there. The bridge.

At first, everything looks okay. I pull over, just to be sure, and climb into the rain. That's when I see it. The bent rail. The tire tracks in the mud that go all the way to the water. I don't remember making the decision. I don't remember removing my shoes and running for the shore. But then I'm in the water. I'm taking a deep breath and diving down into the dark.

The light is on inside the car.

Nick's face is full of panic. He pounds against the window. He can't get out. I can't get him out. I can't—

"I was there," I say at last, and I can't stop the shudder that works through me. I can't stop the tears. "I knew it was too dangerous for Nick to drive to school in the storm. I tried to get him to stay, but he wouldn't listen. I had to follow him."

"Jesus, Ellie."

"I tried to get him out, but I couldn't break the glass. The water was so cold. My clothes were too heavy. I wasn't fast enough. I couldn't hold my breath long enough to get him out. He told me to go. I didn't want to, but my lungs hurt so much and I—"

"Baby girl . . ." Dad steps forward, but I shake my head.

"No, Dad. You don't get it. Everyone around me keeps dying. First Nick, then Ms. Conrad, and now Kaitlyn." My stomach clenches, and I wrap my arms around myself. "I should have been able to save them, but all I do is fail and fail and—"

"Elise, stop." This time, Dad closes the gap between us and holds tight to my upper arms. "Look at me. I'm the one who fucked up. Okay? You don't have to forgive me, but you cannot blame yourself. I was wrong. I should have done better. But *you* are not responsible. For any of it."

"You're not listening," I say, but some of the anger bleeds out of my voice. There's no way to explain how he's wrong. Dad will never understand my world. There's no proof that would make him believe in vampires and witches and Death Oracles.

And there's a part of me—a tiny, too-small part—that desperately wants to believe him. That wants to believe being the Death Oracle doesn't make me responsible for all the deaths around me. It would be so much easier if that were true. It would wipe away the guilt that claws at my ribs.

Except . . . he's wrong. Every choice I make has the potential to kill. If I had touched Kaitlyn that day in bio, I would have known she was going to die. I could have protected her. If I worked harder at my training, maybe I'd already know how to unravel fate. But for every person I save, hundreds—millions—are beyond my reach.

How am I supposed to do this?

I wipe the tears from my cheeks and back away from him. "I can't be here right now." I check that my phone is in my pocket and turn toward the front door.

Dad is close on my heels. "You're not leaving this house with a murderer loose in Elmsbrook."

"Why not?" I whirl around to face him. "Why should I sit home with a father who spent six months pretending I didn't exist? I need to help my friends. At least *they* never abandoned me." I choke back the reminder that I ghosted Maggie and Jordan over the summer, but that's not the point. And besides, Dad wasn't paying enough attention to know that.

He probably doesn't even know Jordan and I broke up.

"You have every right to be upset with me, but that doesn't mean you can wander the streets by yourself!"

Behind me, the electric lock unlatches, and Mom steps through the door. "You're home early, Phil. Did one of your surgeries get canceled?"

"Hey, Mom," I say and focus on shielding my aura. I give her a quick, death-free hug. "I'm actually on my way out. Can you feed Richie tonight? I might be back late."

"Oh. Okay, sweetie. Have fun." She presses a kiss to my cheek, and I freeze. But the shields hold. I don't see her die. My heart doesn't stop beating.

"Love you!"

"Elise, wait—" Dad starts, but I slam the door closed before he can finish. It's his turn to be ignored.

Maggie was still at Jordan's place when Dad dragged me home, but I can't go there. It's the first place my parents will look.

When I hit the sidewalk, I turn left and pull out my phone.

I stare at the number for an entire block before I finally dial.

24

Claire

The doorbell screeches as I'm reaching for the last photo. If Abigail doesn't want my help, fine. I don't need images of Hazel's decaying body on my wall.

I drop the picture in the garbage and head for the kitchen. I'm not expecting anyone, and I wasn't paying attention to the sounds of traffic, so I have no idea who it might be.

Before I can open the apartment door, the impatient visitor rings again. Irritation rumbles in my chest, but I swallow it down. I don't need to scare a lost delivery driver or someone looking for my landlady. When I reach the front door, I realize the guest doesn't have a heartbeat.

"Come on, Claire. I can hear you." Wyn knocks on the door. "Let me in."

I slide the lock free and swing the door wide. "I thought you were at headquarters."

Wyn slips past me and saunters up the stairs. "I was at a regional office. Thought I'd pop in for a bit."

"Did you talk with Henri?" I follow close on their heels. "You said you'd have answers soon."

"I do." Wyn's voice is carefully neutral, which doesn't bode well.

In the kitchen, they pull open cupboard after cupboard, looking for who knows what.

"And?"

"Don't you keep any booze in the house?" Wyn opens the cupboards under the sink, which are as bare as the rest. "What self-respecting vampire doesn't stock their kitchen with alcohol?"

A sinking feeling pulls at my insides, and I collapse into one of the chairs at the table. "Guillebeaux said no, didn't he?"

"I tried calling you." Wyn comes to sit beside me at the table. "Three times, actually."

I think it's best if you stand down.

My trackers will handle this.

Shame prickles across my skin. "I may have . . . broken . . . my phone."

"Anyway, I'm here now. We can hit up the bars near campus, drown your disappointments, then find you a host or twelve." Wyn pats my cheek. "You'll be right as rain by morning."

I swat their hand away. "I don't want to feed. I want a commitment. We have to ask again. There has to—"

"He's not going to change his mind, Claire."

"You don't know that." I push away from the table and the chair clatters to the floor. All my hopes—all my plans for revenge—are on the verge of collapse. "Was it because Elise isn't ready? It doesn't have to be now. I can wait. I just need his promise that the Veil will help me."

Wyn shakes their head. "Henri was adamant."

"Then we ask Luca! I *need* this, Wyn. Please."

"Listen to yourself." Wyn stands and grabs my shoulders, holding me in place. "Think about what you're asking the Veil to do.

They won't help you kill your maker, Claire. Henri won't set that kind of precedent."

I pull away from their touch and pace the kitchen, frustration itching under my skin. Absently, I scratch my bare arms, trying to relieve discomfort only feeding can fix. "Then what the hell is the point? Why should I even train Elise?"

When I turn again, Wyn is blocking my path. Their brown eyes search mine, and they grab my hand, pulling my nails away from skin that's started to bleed. "*This* is why I came," they say, voice softer now. "You always jump to such extremes. Take a breath and think this through."

"I don't—"

"Think it through, Claire," they interrupt. "You are shepherding the Veil's most important asset. You *will* be rewarded for your efforts, but you have to pick a different prize."

I hold their gaze, fighting the pressure building in my chest. "What if I don't want anything else?" The words come out small, and I feel young and naive and useless. "I didn't ask for this existence, Wyn. I didn't choose it. The only thing I've ever wanted is to end Rose's life the way she ended mine."

"It's not all bad, is it?" Wyn reaches out and brushes my cheeks, wiping away tears I didn't realize were there. "We've had all sorts of fun together. And the hunger wouldn't bother you so much if you fed more often."

"Except every time I feed, I end up hating myself."

"This is who we are. It's how we stay alive. There's nothing to hate."

I wrap my arms around my middle and step away from them. "But I didn't choose this. I never wanted—"

"None of us choose this. Not really." Wyn sits down at the table. "We're told what will happen. We agree to attempt the change. But none of us *really* know what it'll be like."

"Do you enjoy it? Being like this?"

Wyn shrugs. "We all have bad days, but yeah. I do."

Before I can respond, before I can ask how they handle the bad days—or if the bad days ever turn into bad decades—the doorbell rings again.

"Expecting someone?" Wyn asks.

"No. I wasn't even expecting *you*." A moment later, I recognize the quiet pulse of a familiar heartbeat. My own heart clenches in response, like it wants to match the rhythm. "I'll be right back."

I leave Wyn in the kitchen, and when I pull open my front door, Elise is on the porch, backlit by streetlights. Stress pulls at her features, and there's a tang of salt on the air.

"Is everything okay?"

Elise tugs on the end of her braid and glances over her shoulder. "I'm sorry. I didn't know where else to go. I tried to call but . . ."

"No, that's my fault. My phone's broken."

She nods, and tears spill over her lashes. "Is this what my life will be like? Everyone dying around me and being completely useless to stop it?"

"Of course not." I step out onto the porch, but I don't let myself reach for her hand. We haven't touched since the fake kiss, and my dead heart can't handle the possibility of Elise flinching away. "I know it feels slow right now, but I promise, you will be able to change deaths. You will save so many people."

"But it's already too late! I lost Nick and failed Ms. Conrad and now even Kaitlyn's dead."

"Kaitlyn?"

Elise nods and wipes the backs of her wrists across her cheeks. "My dad told me. Someone found her on campus this morning." Elise sucks in a deep breath and reaches for my wrist. The touch might be steadying for her, but it knocks me off balance. When she looks up to continue, though, shock widens her eyes. "Who's that?"

I turn, not sure who she's referring to until I spot Wyn coming down the stairs. Wyn drops their gaze to where Elise holds my wrist, and I pull away as naturally as I can. "This is Wyn. We work together."

"At the Veil?" Elise asks, uncertain.

"Yeah. They're kind of my boss." I hope she understands the gravity of what that means.

A second later, Wyn joins us on the porch. "You must be Elise." Wyn holds out a hand, and after a hesitant pause, Elise shakes it. "Claire has nothing but wonderful things to say about your progress. The Veil is very excited about your future."

Elise drops Wyn's hand and nods, tucking bits of loose hair behind her ears.

"I'd love to stay and chat, but I'm needed at the office." Wyn clasps me on the shoulder and squeezes tight. "Walk me to my car?"

There's no point denying their request, but I pass my keys to Elise. "I'll meet you upstairs." Once she's inside, I follow Wyn to the car. Their silence makes me squirm, and a jumble of panicked words come tumbling out. "It's not what it looked like. I promise. She's scared."

"You're only lying to yourself, Montgomery," Wyn says, and I cringe. They only default to my surname when I've fucked up in a truly spectacular fashion. Plus, Wyn reads human emotions better than most vampires I know. "If things go south like they did with Fiona, the Veil won't eliminate the Death Oracle. They'll eliminate *you*."

The words are a punch to the gut, and I bury the memory of Fiona's blood on my hands. "I swear, Wyn, there's nothing going on. Elise is straight." At least, she's never said otherwise. The kiss didn't mean anything. It was a clever distraction, nothing more. Besides, even if she *were* queer, she could never love a creature like me. Fiona never did, despite how many times she lied and said otherwise.

Wyn unlocks the car and fixes me with a stern look. "For your sake, I hope you're right." A smile quirks up one side of their lips, and they punch me hard on the shoulder. "You're a pain in the ass, but you're twice as fun as the other shepherds."

"So glad I continue to amuse you." I roll my eyes as Wyn slides into the driver's seat, but that's truer affection than most vampires can muster, and it makes me warm and buzzy inside. Although, that might also be the lingering heat of Elise's touch or the fact that I'm edging toward a serious need to feed.

At the thought of Elise—alone and worried in my apartment— I turn and race back up the stairs. I find her in the living room, but it's like something has changed in the brief moments I spent with Wyn. The tears are gone, replaced with an almost frantic determination.

"I'm ready," she says the moment she sees me. "I want to learn the next part of my power. I'm tired of letting people die."

"One thing at a time." I hold up my hands when she starts to protest. "How is your shield?"

"Better," she says, though her tone isn't as confident now. "It still takes a lot of focus, but I . . ." Elise trails off, a soft smile pulling at her lips. "I hugged my mom without seeing her die."

Her relief unravels something in my chest. "That's a wonder-ful step, but we can't move on until the shield is as automatic as breathing."

"But we can't wait that long!" Elise lets out a frustrated noise and paces the living room. She's silent for several passes, and I wish I could peer inside her head. If I could see her thoughts, maybe I could help. "How many more people have to die before the police figure out who's doing this? There has to be more we can do."

"Human murders aren't our jurisdiction." I step into Elise's path the next time she comes my way and reach out to steady her. My hands rest on her upper arms, the sweater warm from her skin. "I know it's hard, but we have to stay focused."

Elise sighs and rests her hand over mine. I shouldn't keep do-ing this to myself—reaching for her, letting her touch throw me off balance—but it's like I'm drawn to her before I even know I'm doing it.

"What if we investigated?"

I don't like the sound of that. "We can't."

"Says who? You were looking into Hazel's murder. You know how to investigate." Elise steps away from me, pacing again. Her movements are faster this time, more frantic. "We should go to campus and look for clues."

"Elise . . ." Abigail's earlier dismissal, her declaration that I'm not good enough, weighs heavy on my chest. "We can't afford to get distracted."

"I'm already distracted." Elise takes my hand and tugs me toward the door. "Catching the killer will help me focus on training."

"But the Veil—"

"We don't have to tell them anything. If we figure it out, you can compel a police officer to think they solved it."

Her suggestion makes me freeze, and I pull away from her touch. "You'd be okay with me compelling someone?"

"We need to get there soon, before the police collect all the evidence." Elise grabs my keys from the counter.

"There is no *we*." I block her path to the door. "You're going home, where it's safe. Two people have already died on campus, and the last time I brought you with me . . ." I can't finish the thought. I can't even look at her.

"It'll be fine." Elise tries to step past me, but I move and block the door. "Come on, Claire. This was *my* idea. I'm not letting you go alone."

"And I'm not letting you wander around campus with a serial killer on the loose."

Elise props her hands on her hips and glares at me. "I'm the Death Oracle. You can't compel me to stay home."

Her defiance should annoy me. I should take Elise home and barricade her inside the house. Instead, there's this strange fluttering in my chest that makes it hard to breathe. I don't need oxygen to exist, but I need air to speak, and there's not enough in my lungs to push a single objection past my lips.

"Good." Elise takes my silence for agreement and jingles the keys. "Can I drive?"

25

Elise

Claire does not let me drive.

It ends up being a good thing, since the closer we get to campus, the more nervous I become. I keep worrying that I'll feel Kaitlyn's death in the atmosphere, the way I felt the moment Ms. Conrad died.

The not knowing makes it hard to relax.

Once we reach the college, we park in one of the large lots, and Claire leads me through campus. Before I can ask how she knows where to go, we reach an area marked off by bright yellow police tape.

There's also an officer standing guard.

"What do we do now?"

Claire glares at me. "*We* don't do anything. You wait here," she says, but there's a flicker of amusement in her eyes before she speeds away. I blink, and she's suddenly in front of the officer, holding his arm and leaning close. A moment later, she slips beneath the police tape.

I inch closer, but the officer holds out a hand to stop me. Even from here, I can see the blackish pool of blood. Claire kneels beside it and presses three fingers into the grass. The wind picks up, tossing her hair over one shoulder.

She looks different in the dark of night, with the moon a tiny sliver in the sky. During the day, there's something about Claire that separates her from the rest of us, something that screams *more*. But now, under the cover of darkness and the glow of the moon, she's radiant. Powerful.

Dangerous.

Her eyes flutter shut, and creases appear on her forehead. Claire leans closer to the ground, and even from here, I notice the way her nostrils flare. Is she . . . Can she smell the attacker? Can she tell if they were human or vampire or something else?

I want to ask, but even though the officer is compelled, it feels wrong to mention the paranormal world in front of him. Whether it's fear of exposure or feeling foolish, I'm not sure, but the result is the same. Questions bubble up from my chest and die on my tongue.

After what feels like forever, Claire stands and turns her back on the crime scene. As she approaches, I can't help but imagine what it looked like before the police arrived. Was Kaitlyn stabbed in the back, like Ms. Conrad? What was she doing here on a school night?

Claire ducks under the yellow police tape, but she stumbles when she tries to stand, like her knees are buckling beneath her.

"Are you okay?" I catch her by the elbow, and Claire leans into my touch for several breaths before stepping away.

"I'm fine." The words seem to scrape up her throat. They're harsh and breathy, and she seems more pale than usual.

"You're not fine. You're—"

"Hungry," she says, cutting me off. "I'll survive." She grabs the officer's wrist, and when he turns to meet her gaze, the way she looks at him makes me shudder. Her pupils expand, and though

I can't *feel* anything, I know she's taken over his mind. "We were never here. You won't recognize us if we meet again. You won't report anyone coming to visit the scene."

The young officer nods, and Claire releases him, stalking away.

I chase after her. "What did you find? Did a vampire do it?"

Claire shakes her head. "A vampire wouldn't leave so much blood behind."

"So . . . it was a human?"

"Probably." Claire stumbles again, and I grab her arm.

"You're definitely not okay." I lead her to the nearest bench and make her sit. Claire breathes deep and massages her temples. Her discomfort seems so . . . human, so vulnerable. I settle beside her. "Is it always like this? When you're hungry?"

"Not like this, no." She leans forward, pressing her forearms against her thighs. "Being around the stale blood made it worse than I expected."

"It looks like it hurts."

"It does."

Claire raises her gaze to mine, her hazel eyes full of pain and sorrow and regret. The same pain I heard when she told me about the vampire who turned her. When she told me how much she hates her existence.

I should tell her about the cure.

The thought shoves its way into my brain, all pointed elbows and knobby knees. It tries to argue that it makes sense, that it would take away all of Claire's pain, but I recognize the danger. The lies. I can't say anything until I know it works. I won't dangle something like that in front of her. I won't be the cause of unfounded hope.

But maybe . . . Maybe I can still help.

I reach for my sleeve, rolling it up to my elbow. "You shouldn't have to hurt this much." I rub a thumb against my bare wrist, then hold it out to her. My body trembles with fear and anticipation. "You can feed from me."

In a blink, Claire disappears from my side. A burst of wind pulls at my clothes, and I look up to find her standing several feet away, panting. "Absolutely not." Her voice is tight. Strained. "Never."

Heat creeps into my cheeks, and my eyes burn with embarrassment. I tug the sleeve down and stand, but I don't know where I'm supposed to go. Claire drove me here, and it's too late to walk home alone. I fold my arms across my chest, and every part of me wants to fall into the earth and disappear. "Sorry. I didn't realize I grossed you out."

"Elise—"

"Forget I offered. It was stupid."

"It *was* foolish, but not because there's anything wrong with you." Claire returns to my side, closing the space between us. "Protecting you is the most important part of my job. Accidents are rare, but they happen. You could get hurt, even die. The Veil would never let you host. Not even for Guillebeaux or Tagliaferro."

Well, that's . . . still weird, but some of the heat fades from my face. "But you're hurting."

Claire winces, like my reminder makes the pain worse. "I can hunt after I bring you home."

I shake my head. "You can go now. I'll be okay."

"I'm not leaving you alone where two women were murdered."

"And I'm not going anywhere until you take care of yourself."

Claire sighs and pinches the bridge of her nose. After a moment, she drops her hand and tilts her head to one side, like she's listening.

"I can hear a party, maybe two, happening across campus," she says at last. "I can feed there, but you can't watch."

"I'm not afraid of who you are."

"*What* I am, you mean."

"I meant what I said."

Claire shakes her head, but I catch the flash of a smile before she hurries past me. It doesn't take long for the sounds of the party to reach my ears. A few blocks later, the large house comes into view. It's lit up inside with twinkle lights, and there are several dozen people crammed into the first floor.

Fear pulses through me at the thought of so many people, but I have to trust that I can do this. It's gotten easier to keep death out of my aura since I started developing my shield.

Claire gets us past the guy trying to charge a cover, and we crash through a wall of sound. We're separated by the crush of dancing students holding red cups over their heads, and I'm tossed like a pebble in an undertow, dragged further into the house. I pull my sleeves past my wrists and tuck my aura in close. *I can do this. Just stay focused.*

Behind me, someone squeezes past, and their fingers brush the back of my neck. The sudden touch jolts me, and I'm overcome with dizziness, the taste of sick in my mouth. I suck in a breath and put all my focus into my shield. I shove away their final moments, and then they're moving deeper into the crowd.

"There you are." Claire appears before me, one hand resting protectively on my arm. "Are you okay? Is it too much?" She still looks too pale, and her fingers tremble.

"I'm fine," I yell over the music. "Now, go! Find someone and feed so we can get out of here!"

"Are you sure—"

"Claire, go!"

She nods and turns, scanning the party before slipping back into the fray. The music changes, and people partner up, bodies grinding and writhing to the beat. My face burns, and all I can think is how much my teachers would panic if they saw this.

I search the sea of faces until I find Claire. She's dancing with a girl with pale skin and buoyant red curls, the pair of them laughing as the girl hooks her fingers into the belt loops of Claire's jeans. A flare of something hot and sharp digs into my chest, but then there's this shift.

Claire holds the girl's gaze just a moment too long before brushing curls off her neck and leaning in close. To anyone else, it might look like a kiss, but I know what's happening.

Piercing teeth.

Flowing blood.

A stunned smile spreads across the girl's lips, and that sharp feeling digs deeper into my chest. It only gets worse when Claire moves on, feeding from girl after girl after girl. Never boys, I realize, remembering what she said about falling for her best friend. Always girls who agree to dance with her, who touch her, who kiss her, well before they're compelled.

I know it makes no sense, but my brain keeps screaming that this isn't fair. That she's dancing with them. That her hands are around their waists. That she kisses them deeply before drawing her teeth to their necks. I remember the taste of her kiss. The press of her hands against my waist. The music beats around me, and all I want is to dance. To let my body move with a freedom I don't get with anyone but her.

Claire releases her fourth host, and I find myself weaving through the crowd, desperate to get to her. She goes still, like she can sense my approach, and turns to look at me. There's a flush of color in her cheeks, the tiniest bit of red still clinging to her lips. *Blood*, I realize. *There's blood on her lips.*

But I don't stop until we're toe-to-toe. She peers at me, pupils wide and gaze unfocused, almost hazy. "What are you doing?"

"I want to dance."

The pulse of music works through my bones, and I give into its call. I dance, pretending not to care if she'll join in. After seconds that feel like an eternity, Claire reaches for my hips and draws me close. I rest my arms around her shoulders, my fingers grazing the nape of her neck. I shiver when her hands find the bit of exposed skin along my lower back. We move together, the music binding us into one, and my gaze drops from her eyes. It lingers on her lips.

When I wasn't looking, she must have licked away that final drop of blood. I wonder if I'd still taste it, if I kissed her now.

"Elise . . ." Claire's hands tense at my hips. She tips her forehead to mine. "What are we doing?"

"Isn't it obvious?" I flick my gaze back to hers. I mean to finish the thought, to tell her that we're just dancing. That of course we're just dancing, because the way I'm staring at her lips doesn't mean anything.

Instead, my whole body freezes up.

Over her shoulder, I see a ghost. Except he's solid and real and staring right at me. I blink hard, trying to make the hallucination go away. It can't be real. He can't be here. It's another illusion, another blond-haired boy with a passing resemblance to my brother.

Yet when I open my eyes, he's still there. Walking closer. Features coming into stark clarity.

Blue eyes, shining even from a distance.

Blond hair like mine and Mom's before she dyed it.

A smile quirking his lips.

"Nick?" My voice catches. It can't be real. He can't be *here*.

The smile blooms brighter, and he stops, still six feet away. "Hey, Elise."

His voice breaks me. It shatters every doubt. I tear away from Claire's touch and reach for my brother. My brother, who's here. Who's alive. Who's looking at me like he missed me every second that he's been gone.

But then the music stops. The room goes still.

And strong arms circle my waist.

26

Claire

Danger screams across my skin. I drag Elise away from the quiet rumble of a predator's growl.

A predator who used to be her brother.

"Let go of me!" Elise thrashes against my hold, and already, the air is thick with her tears. "It's Nick. He's alive. He's okay." Her voice catches, and she yanks uselessly against my hands.

I don't know how to tell her she's wrong.

It's going to break her heart.

"Claire, *please*," she begs, but I only tuck her closer against my chest.

"It's not him." My voice comes out louder than I expect. "He's not the Nick you remember."

"But—"

"His heart isn't beating." The moment my words land, her body goes slack in my arms. "I'm so sorry, Elise."

Around us, the room is a terrible kind of quiet. My eyes adjust to the dark, and every college student has gone utterly still. Their hearts flutter with life, but they stand frozen with solo cups held tight. There's no way Nick compelled them all. Not on his own.

Nick grunts, cutting into my thoughts. "That wasn't your secret to share."

At the sound of his voice, Elise strains against my grip. "Nicky, tell her she's wrong. Tell her you're fine." She digs her nails into my hands, but I can't let her go. The heavy scent of stale blood has me on edge.

Nick steps closer. "I missed you so much, Ellie."

"I missed you, too." Her voice catches in her throat. "How did you survive? How did you get out? Where have you been?"

"I—"

"He didn't survive, Elise. That's what I'm trying to tell you." If my heart wasn't already dead, it would break for her now. "He's not human anymore. He's a vampire."

A growl erupts from Nick's throat. "Who the hell even are you? I'm trying to talk to my *sister*. I'm trying to explain." Nick approaches, and with him comes that familiar stench of stale blood. "It's a long story, Ellie Bean," he says, voice softer now. Almost sweet. "I wasn't sure you'd understand."

"I will. I promise." Elise tries to step forward. "I know about vampires. I understand what's happening. We can fix it."

A smile tugs at Nick's lips, but it's missing the warmth his sister has. "That's my Ellie. Always the problem solver."

Elise laughs, but it's a watery, broken thing. "That's me." She wipes tears from her cheeks and takes a steadying breath. "Claire, let me go. Nick isn't going to hurt me."

I hesitate.

"Claire," she says, sharper this time.

Even though every instinct still shouts *danger*, I loosen my hold on Elise. I don't understand how Nick compelled so many people. He's too young for that. It should take dozens of vampires.

Or someone truly ancient.

The second my grip loosens, Elise tears away from me and crashes into her brother, wrapping him in a hug. Nick returns the embrace, but he stares at me over her shoulder, a feral smile pulling at his lips. His eyes flash red and his canines extend. The scent of stale blood hits me again, and I finally realize why it's so familiar. I realize where I've smelled it before.

"Elise . . ." I try to keep the alarm out of my voice, but I must not succeed. She releases her brother and glances over her shoulder.

"What now?" she asks, raising a brow.

"He—" My throat closes. How can I say it? How can I tell Elise that there's blood all over her brother? Weeks ago, we promised not to keep secrets, but I never thought I'd hold a truth that could break her. But now she's glaring at me with such hatred in her eyes, her hand clasped tight in Nick's, and I don't know what else to do. "I think he . . . I think he killed Kaitlyn."

Her expression dissolves into shock then disbelief, and Elise shakes her head. "Nick would never do that." She looks to her older brother. "Tell Claire she's wrong."

Nick only offers a half-hearted shrug. "The transition changes us."

"What?" Elise stumbles away from her brother and bumps into one of the compelled college students. She squeezes her eyes tight, and I've seen that expression enough to know she's been sucked into their death.

"Don't blame him too harshly." A new voice pierces the quiet, and the familiarity of it steals the strength from my limbs. It leaves me off-balance and cold. So very cold. "Nicholas was only doing as I asked."

The crowd parts, and my maker steps into view. Though she's updated her wardrobe since 1937, I remember the high-waisted floral day dress she wore then. The press of her kiss in the shadows.

The burn of bloodlust tearing through me for the very first time.

"Rose." I force her name past my lips, and it's all I can do to keep standing.

"Do I know you?" She tilts her head to one side.

Her confusion, her lack of recognition, pierces me like a wooden stake. All the years I've spent trying to find her, desperate to get my revenge, and she doesn't even *remember* me?

Before I can say anything, Elise extracts herself from her vision. "Delilah? What are you doing here?"

Delilah? Something hot and acidic pulses through me, and somehow, this betrayal hurts worse than Rose's indifference. "You *know* her?"

Tears slip down Elise's cheeks, but she doesn't look at me. "This whole time . . . You've had Nick this whole time, haven't you?"

Rose smiles, and it's cruel, how beautiful she is. "I've been planning my revenge since before your parents were born. I wasn't about to leave loose ends."

I'm trembling as my worlds collide. The past I spent so long burying overtakes the present. Rose smiling at the human version of me, kissing me, promising a future of adventure and companionship. Rose abandoning me the second things didn't go her way. And now Elise. Elise, who I thought I could trust. Who makes me feel things I know I shouldn't.

And all this time, she's been talking to the creature who ruined my life.

"How do you know her?" I cover the hurt and pain with anger, letting a growl rumble through my chest. Elise flinches away, and I let her. I don't care if she fears me. "How do you know Rose?"

Elise shakes her head, her expression twisting from anger to confusion. "I don't—"

"Your Death Oracle hasn't been terribly helpful yet, but I'm confident she'll join my cause in the end." Rose flashes a wide, satisfied smile.

"What *cause*?" I turn back to Elise. "How could you do this? How could you help the vampire who did this to me?" My voice breaks, and I hate that my weakness is leaking through. It's not supposed to be like this. I'm supposed to find Rose on my terms. I'm supposed to rip out her throat, but I can't move. I feel like I'm falling apart.

"I didn't know. She said her name was Delilah." Elise looks from me to Rose, and fresh fury rolls off her in waves. "Wait, if you had Nick this whole time . . . Did you orchestrate the crash, too? Are you the reason my brother almost died?" She advances on Rose, oblivious to the danger. "How did you even know I'd be the Death Oracle?"

Rose rests an arm over Nick's shoulders. "The Veil isn't the only one with access to adept diviners. I have my fair share of loyal witches. They suggested I might need some insurance to get your cooperation."

"Insurance for *what*?" I ask, and it feels like I'm falling. Like I'm grasping for solid rock while sand slips through my fingers.

Attack her.

Kill her.

End this.

I think the words, over and over, but I can't move. I can't even draw the breath I need to demand answers.

"Delilah thinks the Death Oracle—She thinks that *I* can make vampires mortal again."

Elise's words land like a slap across the face, and I stumble back. "That's not possible."

"Oh, it most certainly is." Rose compels Nick to stay put and approaches Elise. "The Death Oracle can do a great many things, but Hazel was too loyal to the Veil. She wouldn't even try to help me, and I worked so hard to convince her." Rose pats Elise's cheek. "I decided to start with a fresh one."

Horror accompanies my sudden understanding. "You murdered Hazel."

"Murder is such a harsh term, don't you think?" Rose waves away the thought. "I simply *shepherded* her gift to the next person in line." Rose circles Elise like she's prey. "And just to make triple sure, I devised a truly enticing reason for her to uncover the key to mortality."

"My brother," Elise says, glancing back at Nick.

"Exactly." Rose claps her hands, like this whole thing delights her. "I'm so glad you're finally catching on."

A white-hot hope burns inside me. If it's true, if Rose is right about a key . . . I could finally leave seventeen behind. I could create a life for myself, build connections with people who actually care about me, who see me as more than a means to an end.

But the vampire I knew all those years ago never wanted those things. Why is she even looking? "What could you possibly want with mortality? It's not possible. If it were, the Veil would know about it."

Rose's eyes flash red. "Who says they don't? Why would Luca and Henri tell a lowly shepherd about their greatest fear?"

"They—" My words die on my tongue, and I feel the surge of hope turning brittle like spun glass, hardening around my heart, threatening to burst. Elise knew about this, and she said *nothing*. Even after I told her how much I hate this existence.

Did she tell Rose what I said? Did they laugh about it?

"I'm not making *anyone* human for you." Elise tightens her hands into fists. "Not unless I can save Nick first."

In a blur of speed so fast even I have trouble tracking it, Rose wraps her hand around my throat. She lifts me into the air like I weigh nothing, and the extent of her strength is terrifying. The bones in my neck shift and crack. If she squeezes much harder, she could remove my head.

She could end me.

"You don't have the power here, Death Oracle. I do." Rose tightens her hold, and I scratch at her hands, desperate to escape her iron grip. "You will do exactly as I ask, or I'll send your brother rampaging through town. He'll kill everyone you've ever cared about."

Rose snaps her fingers at Nick, and he's a blur of movement. He pauses beside Elise and grips tight to a young man's jaw.

"Nick, don't . . ."

"Do it," Rose commands, and Nick hesitates for only a second before snapping the man's neck.

Elise's scream fills the room, and she collapses to her knees. Despite everything she's done to me, despite every lie, I want to comfort her. But I can't. Rose has a death grip on my neck, and my toes barely reach the floor.

Rose pierces the tips of her nails into my skin. "How many people do you think Nick can murder before the brother you knew is gone forever? Two? Twenty? A hundred?" Rose flings me across the room like a rag doll, and I crash into a group of compelled college students. "Tick-tock, Elise. We'll be in touch."

I untangle myself from the humans, my neck healing rapidly with all the fresh blood in my veins. But in the second it takes to rise, the music has resumed, the students are dancing . . .

And my maker has disappeared.

27

Elise

*L*oud music batters against me as I struggle to breathe. Nick was *here*, but he just . . . He—

What has Delilah done to him?

Grief closes my throat, and I can barely see through the blur of tears. College students dance and drink around me, but then someone notices the dead body. Their scream carries above the noise, and people are turning. Looking. The music stops, and someone is calling 911, and I have to go. I have to get out of here.

I stagger to my feet and search for Claire. If anyone can help me rescue Nick, it has to be her. We can figure out how to save him. Together. And then after, I can make her mortal again, too.

"Claire?" I call her name over the screams and sobs around me. Finally, I find her beside a group of drunk girls, looking unsteady on her feet. She presses a hand to her neck, and fresh worry pulses through me.

But then Claire notices my approach, and her expression twists from shock to rage and back again.

"Claire!" I push my way through the crowd, but I'm battered by panicked auras. Death is heavy in the air, suffocating and raw. Claire's eyes flash red, and she bares her vampiric teeth before disappearing in a blur of motion. "Claire, wait!"

I chase after her, scrambling to shield my aura as I dodge through the crowded room. Sweat spills down my back, and guilt joins the grief that twists my stomach. I shove the feelings down as I spill out into the cold night. The air kisses across my face, but I don't see Claire.

Focus. Nick was here. He's still alive.

I thought he was gone forever, but he's not. He's still alive. He's—

The horrible memory surfaces, blotting out my relief. The blur of speed. The hesitation. Delilah's demand, and the *crack* filling the quiet room as Nick snapped the boy's neck and stole his life.

I didn't want to believe Claire. The Nick I grew up with never would have killed Kaitlyn, but to see him following orders without any sign of remorse . . .

He probably killed Ms. Conrad, too.

The thought makes me stumble, but I have to keep moving. I have to fix it. This isn't his fault. The death, my power, his transformation into a vampire . . . None of that blame belongs to Nick. Delilah is the reason I'm like this. She's the reason Nick has killed again and again.

She has to be stopped.

Sirens wail in the distance, and I retrace my steps, heading back to the parking lot. Claire might be upset, but she's not going to abandon me here. Minutes later, an earsplitting *crack* punctures the quiet, and I finally spot Claire. She's off the main path, her fist buried in a tree trunk. She curses loudly and eases her hand from the jagged bark.

I race toward her as she picks pieces of wood out of her skin. "Claire."

She whirls around, tears streaking down her cheeks. "How long did you know?"

The anger in her voice stops me short, and shame burns my face. "Know what?"

"That you could fix me!" Her anger gives way to anguish. "How long did you know you could make me mortal again?"

It feels like forever and yet no time at all. "I didn't know for sure that I could. I still don't."

"Elise."

"Not that long," I promise. "She told me at Ms. Conrad's memorial. Before that, I only knew she wanted my help."

Claire's eyes widen like my words are a strike to the face. "How long have you known her?"

I do the math as fast as I can. ". . . about a month?"

"A month! You've been keeping secrets the *entire time* you've known me. You've . . ." Claire falters, and she stares at the stars rather than look at me. "You knew all of this when I told you about Rose, didn't you? You knew when I told you how much I hate this existence, and you said *nothing*."

"That's not true. I asked you in the car. You said it wasn't possible."

But Claire is shaking her head, like I haven't said a thing. She brushes tears from her cheeks and lets out a bitter laugh. "Did you call her, after, to gloat about it? Was it funny for you, knowing you had the power to make me human but never would?"

"It's not like that. At all. I was—"

"You were *what*?"

The sharpness in her tone grates at me, and I squeeze my hands into fists. "I have no proof this is possible! I wanted to make sure it *worked* before I gave you false hope." The second the words leave my lips, Claire scoffs and rolls her eyes. It picks at my already bruised heart. "Don't pretend I'm the only one who kept secrets. You act like mastering my power will solve all my problems, but the Veil won't let me have a normal life. They'll decide who I save. Who I *kill*. I'll be a well-paid prisoner!"

"And what," Claire asks, voice filled with bitter hurt, "you think you're better off helping *Rose*? Why does she even want to be mortal?"

This time, I'm the one averting my gaze. "She doesn't."

"Then what did she want?"

I don't want to admit the truth. I don't want Claire to know I've considered doing what Delilah wants, but I need her help to save Nick. Secrets will only make things worse.

"Delilah—Rose. She wants revenge. She wants them human before she kills them."

A low growl rumbles through the air. "Who?"

"Luca and Henri?"

The names hover between us, a dangerous declaration.

"All this time . . ." Claire approaches slowly, her words quiet yet filled with betrayal and hurt. "All the weeks I've helped you, you've been plotting to kill the Veil leaders?"

"No," I say, but even I hear the uncertainty. The lie.

"Well, then." Claire shakes her head and backs away from me. "Maybe Rose had the right idea."

I follow her, confused but not wanting to be left behind. "What do you mean?"

"Maybe it would be better to kill you and start fresh with a new

Death Oracle." Claire turns her back on me and continues toward the parking lot. "Maybe the next one won't stake me in the heart."

Panic blots out the anger and indignation, and I race after her. "You don't mean that."

"Why not? You haven't even mastered the shield yet. It would be easy enough to start over."

"Claire." I reach for her arm, but she yanks away from my touch like it burns her. "I'm sorry I didn't say something sooner, but you can't just leave. We have to rescue Nick."

"I don't *have to* do anything. I quit." She turns to face me, and her pale skin is flushed. Her beautiful features pull into a sneering, vicious expression. "I'm not your shepherd anymore. Find someone else to fuck over."

Her dismissal makes me feel small. I don't know why it hurts so much, but it does. Everything she's done for me—every touch, every encouragement—shifts in my memory, twisting until it becomes something else. This feels different from the threats. It feels real. True.

"Was I only ever a job to you?"

Claire doesn't even bother to meet my gaze. "What do you think?"

When she turns to go, I stumble after her. "How am I supposed to get home? How do I save Nick?"

"Ask someone who gives a damn."

———

Though I want to say I handled Claire's dismissal by making a logical plan forward . . .

I did not.

Claire disappeared, and like a fool, I chased after her. My lungs burned. My legs ached. The physical pain was a nice distraction from emotions I did *not* want to feel, but when I got to the parking lot, she was gone.

Her car was gone, too.

The tears came fast then, and I let myself cry about being stuck on campus rather than feel everything else.

And there's just so much *else*. Betrayal and fear and worry. This terrible ache in my heart that feels like emotional whiplash. I wish I could rewind to the moment I thought Nick was here and alive and himself, before he murdered a guy at Delilah's command.

Eventually, I manage to call Maggie and beg her to pick me up. She doesn't ask questions, just grabs her dad's keys and promises to be here soon. Thankfully, it's not a Mom Week. There's no way Ms. Sullivan would let Maggie drive after dark, not even for me.

I sit on the stone curb to wait, and the cold seeps through my jeans by the time she pulls up next to me and rolls down the passenger window.

"What are you doing out here?" Maggie's voice sounds raw, like she's been fighting tears ever since she found out about Kaitlyn.

Has it really only been a few hours? It feels like a lifetime.

Maggie unlocks the doors. "Come on, Elise. I don't want to be here. Not after . . ."

"I know. I'm sorry." I wipe the tears from my face and climb into the car. "Thank you for coming to get me."

She nods and pulls away from the curb, signaling even though there isn't anyone around. Even though we're in a *parking lot*. When we finally leave campus and pull onto a main road, she speaks. "What is wrong with you? Why were you *alone* on campus after what happened to Kaitlyn and Ms. Conrad?"

Fresh tears spill down my cheeks, and I don't know why I bothered wiping them away. "I know who killed them, Mags. I know what happened. It was Nick."

The moment I mention his name, my throat closes and Maggie has to pull over. I tell her everything. That my brother is a vampire. That he *killed* someone in front of me. That he murdered Ms. Conrad and Kaitlyn. And then Maggie is crying, too, and I don't know how to comfort her when I'm too shaky to raise a shield.

Why does everything have to be so awful all the time?

Maggie pulls herself together first, and she dabs at her cheeks as she gets us back on the road. "How did this happen? Why is Nick doing this?"

Anger chases away my tears. "Delilah."

I explain the rest, how Delilah is the one who turned my brother and forced him to kill. How she'll make him kill again if I don't figure out the key to mortality. I tell Maggie that Claire is pissed at me for not telling her Delilah's plans. For some reason, that makes my chest ache so much it's hard to breathe. I don't understand why, and it's too raw to look at more closely.

By the time Maggie parks in front of my house, I've told her everything. "What am I supposed to do, Mags? I can't do this without Claire." I don't specify what *this* means. There's too much. Saving Nick. Figuring out the key. Escaping a life controlled by the Veil.

Maggie presses her wrist to her eyes and shifts to reporter mode. "The plan doesn't have to change. Helping Delilah means you get Nick back. And if she destroys the Veil, you don't have to work for them."

"I don't know . . ." I stare at my house, where the worst thing in my life used to be Nick's terrible singing. "Can I really help her murder someone?"

"You don't have to decide tonight." Maggie pats my knee, and when she glances up at me, she smiles. "Either way, you still have Jordan and me. We may not be paranormal experts, but we love you. You won't be alone."

My chest squeezes tight. "Love you, too, Mags." I want to embrace her, but I'm too worn out to risk it. "I'll call you tomorrow."

"You'd better," she says as I climb out of the car and shut the door.

The house is quiet when I enter. I flip off the exterior light and relock the door behind me. My stomach twists with hunger, but I'm too exhausted to eat. What I need more than anything is sleep. Tomorrow, I can come up with a new plan. I can deal with the fallout from my fight with Dad. I can figure out how to fix everything.

Hopefully.

At the top of the stairs, I let my fingers graze Nick's door. My insides twist again. *My brother is a vampire*. No matter what he's done and who he's hurt, at least he still exists. There's a chance he can be human again. A chance my family could be whole.

I push open my bedroom door and step inside, peeling out of my sweater. When my head emerges from the soft fabric, a loud hiss erupts by my feet.

"Don't be such a dick, Richard. It's only me." I flip the light switch, but when I turn around, Richard isn't where I expect her. "Ridiculous cat," I mutter, throwing my sweater in the general direction of the closet.

"That's no way to talk to my fluffy baby."

I freeze at the sound of the familiar voice, and tears slip past my lashes. I force myself to look at him, to believe he's really here.

"Nick." My voice shakes, and when I spot him across the room, he has Richard tucked in his arms.

My brother moves with a burst of supernatural speed, closing the door and covering my lips with his cool hand. "Waterworks aren't necessary. We don't want to wake your parents."

I nod, but I can't shove down this kind of emotion on command, no matter what Delilah has forced him to do. "I can't believe you're here." I reach for him, but Nick steps out of reach, a snarl rumbling in his chest. That stops me more than his retreat, the feral, in-human noise. His words *don't wake* your *parents* suddenly make me cold. "What did you do to them?"

He smiles, but it's not the kind, lopsided grin I know. Even as he cradles Richie and scratches her head, Nick's expression is a mocking, cruel thing. "Nearly gave the old man a heart attack when he saw me on the front porch, but once they invited me in-side, I compelled them to sleep until their alarms and forget they saw me."

"They're okay? You didn't hurt them?" I hate that I have to ask, but though he looks like my brother, this version of Nick is a stranger. *Your parents. The old man.* He never talked about our family like that.

The brother I grew up with would show off his new powers, doing impossible soccer stunts or one-handed push-ups. He'd promise that everything would be okay and goof around until I cracked a smile. Did the transition make him like this—cruel and cold instead of laughter and warmth? Or is this Delilah's doing?

Fear twists in my gut when I realize he still hasn't answered. "Nick, please."

"I didn't feed from them, if that's what you're worried about," Nick says as Richie butts her head against his knuckles. He sounds bored by our conversation. By *me*. The only thing that holds his attention is the cat.

"Then why are you here?" Despite everything, hope grows in my heart. "You want my help, don't you? You don't like what Delilah makes you do."

"I—"

"It won't always be like this," I say, cutting him off. "She can only compel you for the first year. That'll wear off in a few months. I have connections at the Veil. I could—"

"*This* is why I came," he snaps, and this time, even Richie startles. She hisses and leaps out of his arms. "This isn't a problem you can fix, Elise. If you screw over Delilah, people will get hurt. You need to do exactly as she says."

"So, you're here to keep me safe?" I can't keep the hope out of my tone. "You still care what happens to me."

"No, I don't." He steps closer, and I have to crane my neck to meet his gaze. "I'm here because if you mess with Delilah, she'll make me kill everyone you love." His voice is soft, and it sends a terrible chill down my spine.

But I won't let this hope die. I won't stop searching for his humanity. "You don't want to hurt them."

"No, I don't want to hurt *me*. When she makes me kill, Delilah doesn't let me feed." Nick's canines lengthen, pushing past his lips. "Do you have any idea how much it hurts to spill blood without getting a taste?"

My entire body trembles, and I shake my head.

Nick's blue gaze goes hard. "Delilah is the only reason I'm still alive. You will not fuck her over."

It's like diving into the river all over again. My lungs constrict, and I feel impossibly heavy. "I—"

"Don't make me kill our parents," he says, turning away. "Do as you're told."

And then he throws open the window and disappears.

28

Claire

I wish I hadn't destroyed my phone.

The engine roars as I accelerate down the highway. The trackers were wrong. The orphans in Petal and Thorn had nothing to do with this. It was all Rose. *Of course* it was her. Guillebeaux may have denied my first request for revenge, but he'll have to reconsider now that she's the one who killed Hazel. Now that I'm warning him of the plan to destroy him and Tagliaferro.

My dead heart tries to constrict in my chest. This is about more than revenge now. There's a way out of this unending existence. I could be human again.

Why would Luca and Henri tell a lowly shepherd about their greatest fear?

Rose's words echo in my head, and a snarl rips from my throat. If the Veil has known all this time that we could be human again, I . . .

I don't know what I'll do.

A flush of betrayal twists inside me, and it destroys the lock I'd chained around my emotions. The hurt and hope breaks free and bubbles to the surface. All I can see is Elise's face. All I feel is the touch of her hands on my neck.

The rest of the world fell away when her gaze fell to my lips. For a moment—one brief, tantalizing moment—I didn't feel alone. I felt seen and desired and wanted.

I slam my palm against the steering wheel. I am such a goddamn fucking fool. Elise has been working with Rose this entire time. She knew she had the power to make me human, and she said *nothing*.

As the clock slides past midnight, trading Friday for Saturday, I finally make it to Manhattan. To mortals, our headquarters looks identical to the office buildings around it, and that's if they notice it at all with the refraction spell averting their attention.

Hurt and hope duel inside my chest as I riffle through old receipts and find my badge for the underground garage. I flash the card, the gate raises, and I shove down every part of me that isn't cold and calculating. Emotions mean nothing to Veil leadership, only evidence.

I park and take the elevator to the lobby, swiping my badge again. The doors open, and I'm greeted by marble floors, clean lines, and open space. My footsteps echo faintly, swallowed by the soft conversation of my colleagues. I don't look at any of them, and no one stops me. I've worked here long enough that they know I belong.

At least, as much as a too-young, orphaned vampire can belong anywhere.

I take the stairs to the third floor. Wyn already failed to deliver my revenge, so I head for Abigail's office. I have something the lead tracker desperately wants, which is all the leverage I need.

Abigail's door is open when I arrive, but she isn't here. I lean through the doorway and inhale deeply. Her scent is strong, and when I step back into the hall, I follow a faint path into the building.

After the second turn, I recognize where I'm headed. There's a conference room this way where Abigail hands out assignments. Despite the complete disaster of my night, confidence blooms in my chest. Delivering information Abigail's entire team couldn't collect is exactly the boost I need.

Doors at every Veil location are spelled to prevent eavesdropping, so I don't bother listening in when I arrive. Instead, I burst into the room like I own the place . . .

And instantly regret my decision.

A handful of people sit around the long table, and though one of them is Abigail, the others make my entire body freeze over.

Henri Guillebeaux sits at the far end of the table. He looks up when I enter, and his impossibly light brown eyes narrow. Henri dresses in tailored three-piece suits that make Wyn's fashion look amateurish, and his gentle dark curls graze the nape of his neck. "Are you lost?" Remnants of a French accent color Henri's words.

Wyn, sitting a few seats from Abigail, comes to my rescue. "This is Claire Montgomery. She's the shepherd assigned to the Death Oracle."

Guillebeaux flashes a warm smile, but it doesn't meet his eyes. "Wonderful! Luca, she must be here for you." He gestures toward the other end of the table, and fresh dread settles in my chest.

I've met Luca Tagliaferro many times, but I doubt he'd remember my name if Wyn hadn't mentioned it. The Italian vampire shifts in his seat but doesn't look away from his notes. "Is the Death Oracle's training complete?"

"No, I—"

"Then what are you doing here?" Luca leans back in his chair and scowls at Wyn. "I told you to assign your best shepherd."

"Claire is perfectly capable—"

"I know who killed Hazel." My words silence the room and

draw the weight of their attention. Speaking so bluntly to Luca and Henri should be terrifying, but my heart is too broken to care.

There's a better future out there, and all I have to do is grab it.

"Did you find Petal and Thorn?" Abigail prompts.

"It wasn't them." I step farther into the room and shut the door behind me. "Rose killed Hazel when the Death Oracle wouldn't comply with her demands."

"And what demands were those?" Luca asks, smoothing a hand over his neatly trimmed beard.

Wyn catches my eye from across the table and shakes their head, but I know I'm not making this up. This is *real*. "Rose wanted the Death Oracle to attack the Veil. She wanted to make you human." I turn from Luca to Henri. "You, too."

"I'm sorry about this," Wyn says, appearing by my side in the space of a breath. "Claire is a brilliant shepherd and tracker, but her brain is a bit underdeveloped." They knock on my skull. "Poor thing is stuck at seventeen."

Wyn tries to drag me out of the room, but I hold my ground. Concerned looks pass between Luca and Henri, and I see the fear they're desperate to hide. "It's true, isn't it?" A surge of wild hope rises within me. "It's possible to be human again."

Luca stands, his chair clattering to the floor. "Out. Now." He points to the door, but when I fall back, he shakes his head. "Not you."

"There's no need for alarm, friends." Henri stands and motions for Abigail to pass in front of him. "We understand the challenges of our youngest colleagues. Luca and I only need a moment to explain. You may leave, too, Mx. Sulyard."

I shoot Wyn a panicked look. I've never been alone with Luca and Henri, but maybe this is my chance to get what I want. What

I *really* want. Wyn squeezes my upper arm before slipping away, closing the door behind them.

Once we're alone, Henri pats my shoulder. "Why don't you have a seat. It's Claire, right?"

"Yes, sir." I allow Henri to lead me to the nearest chair, and he takes the spot beside me.

"This Rose . . . Is she the same vampire Wyn mentioned? Your creator?" There's a thread of pity in his voice, and I bristle even as I nod. "I understand Rose denied you the year of guidance all newly risen deserve, but we've trained you better than to believe such outlandish theories."

"I'm not making this up," I say, failing to keep the emotion out of my voice. "Rose wants to make you mortal. She killed Hazel when she wouldn't do it."

Luca leans against the table on my other side and stares down at me. "What about the new Death Oracle? Do we need to start over?"

Start over. As if killing Elise is a simple reset. But then guilt digs into my ribs. I said something similar. I didn't mean it, though. I could never mean it.

"She's not our enemy. Elise will be an exceptional Death Oracle." I say the words with conviction, but Luca merely nods. "Let me help you capture Rose. I've been a tracker for a decade. I just need some backup and—"

"I appreciate the initiative," Henri cuts in, patting my hand. "We will handle this on our own."

"But I'm already in Elmsbrook."

Henri raises an eyebrow. "I know Ms. Winters didn't train you to question orders."

"No, sir."

"Good." He stands and returns to the head of the long table. "As for this mortality nonsense, there's no need to worry. We would never allow a Death Oracle such latitude."

The last of my hope crumbles to dust inside me, but when I stand, a small voice whispers all the things Henri *isn't* saying.

He didn't say it was impossible.

He didn't say it couldn't be done.

He said he wouldn't *allow* it. Which means it *must* be possible. It must be real.

Luca reaches for the door. "Return to your charge. I want a fully functioning Death Oracle before year's end."

"You will be well rewarded when you've finished," Henri adds. "Promotion. Vacation. Whatever you'd like."

I nod, afraid that if I speak, all my real thoughts will come spilling out. That I don't want a promotion or riches or anything else they'll offer. I want to be *human*, and I won't let anyone—not even Henri or Luca—stop me.

When I step through the door, I find Wyn waiting in the hall. "Your heart is still in your chest." They fall in step beside me. "That's promising."

A growl rumbles up my throat as I turn the first corner. Elise's betrayal is a paper cut compared to this new pain. Everything I've worked for, decades of sacrifice and training and service to the Veil, comes shattering down around me.

I'm not allowed to get revenge against Rose, even though she murdered the previous Death Oracle. Even though she turned me too young. Even though all the other vampires think I'm a joke. Someone else gets to bring her in. Not me.

What is the fucking point of any of this? Why should I dedicate my entire existence to the Veil if they'll deny me the only thing I've ever asked for? I don't care what they say. I'm going to find Rose. I'm going to figure out the key to mortality.

And then I'll leave all this bullshit behind.

"Claire." Wyn grabs my arm at the top of the staircase. "What's gotten into you? What happened in there?"

"Nothing." I pull away from their touch. "I just finally realized how inconsequential I am."

"Claire—"

"Don't bother, Wyn. I'm done." I start down the stairs, but Wyn stays right on my heels. "I quit."

"You what?"

I jump over the rail and hurry to the lobby, but Wyn is faster. They grab my arm and haul me around to face them.

"Let go of me."

"Not until you listen." Wyn keeps their voice low, but they glance around. We're far from alone, though none of the other paranormals seem interested in our conversation. "Stop acting like a child and *think* about what you're doing. The Veil gave you everything. You can't turn your back on us."

I meet their glare, and anger lengthens my canines. "Watch me."

"Damn it, Claire." Wyn tightens their hold. "Getting revenge against your creator isn't worth throwing away the only good thing you have."

"It's not just her," I say, though that's part of it. I lower my voice, so only Wyn could possibly hear. "There's a way to be human again. Henri all but confirmed it."

"That's not possible."

"It is." I jolt away, finally breaking their hold. "I won't let *anyone* keep this from me. Not Rose. Not the Veil. Not even you."

Wyn stares at me a long time before running a hand through their hair, making it stand taller. "Look, don't make any decisions right now. You're not thinking clearly." They glance back at the stairs. "I can buy you a few days to calm down, but you need to pull it together and finish your job."

"How many times do I have to say it, Wyn? I quit. Assign someone else."

"Claire . . ." they say, warning laced through the drawn-out syllable.

But they don't stop me when I turn. They don't say anything when I raise both middle fingers and flip them off as I leave the Veil behind forever.

———

I spend the next forty-eight hours feeding until my vision blurs. Manhattan blood bars have an endless supply of hosts, and I feed in luxurious back rooms until my veins are ready to burst. When I can't hold another drop, I escape to the dance floor, desperate for a connection I know I'll never find.

The faces of my dance partners blur until all I see is blonde hair and blue eyes and a hesitant smile. I can't remember the last time I fed so many days in a row, but I'm too damn miserable to enjoy it.

When the sun rises Monday morning, I compel myself a hotel room and collapse into dreamless sleep. I wake around noon, and for a blissful moment, all I know is that I'm warm and comfortable and my bloodlust is still sated. But then memories of the weekend surface, and I make a mental list of everyone who has fucked me over.

Wyn.

Abigail.

The Veil.

But above them all, orchestrating my misery, is Rose. Without her, I wouldn't be a vampire. I wouldn't know it was possible to be mortal. I wouldn't know that Henri and Luca decided none of us could have the key. That they never even gave us a choice. That Elise is disposable to them.

Elise . . . Her name makes my chest ache, which is infuriating. Even before all this, she was always going to age and die and leave me. I never should have cared, but her betrayal is tied to Rose, too.

At least one thing hasn't changed: I will get revenge on my creator.

The *how* will just have to be a little different.

I mold that certainty into purpose and passion on the way back to Elmsbrook. Rose is stronger than I am, and without the Veil's support, I'll have to be smart about this. I'll need to track her, learn everything she knows about the Death Oracle's power. Before this is over, Rose will be dead, and I'll have the key to mortality.

And then I'll *finally* be free.

I arrive in Elmsbrook long before I finalize my plans, passing through the wealthy neighborhoods before turning onto my street. As soon as the house comes into view, I spot a figure sitting on the front porch, golden hair bright despite the overcast sky.

My hands tighten on the steering wheel, and for a second, I consider driving past the house and hiding until Elise disappears. Instead, I pull into the driveway. If I want to find Rose, I can't continue to delay. I need to act.

When I cut the engine and climb out of the car, Elise stands. She's still dressed in her school uniform, sleeves pulled past her wrists. I don't remove my sunglasses, even though the agonizing orb is hidden behind thick clouds. They become a shield, the wide frames blocking a third of my face from view.

"If you came to apologize, it's too late." I head for the porch. "You might as well leave."

Elise presses her lips into a thin line and stares down at me. "We have a common enemy. We can help each other."

"Who says I need your help?" I climb the stairs, and once we're both on the porch, I'm the one looking down at her. "I can kill Rose without you."

She flinches, but she doesn't run away. If anything, she seems to hold herself taller. "Nick came to see me that night."

The emotion in her voice is contagious. I feel her grief, and my heart responds in kind. My fingers twitch by my side, the reflex to reach out and comfort her echoing through my limbs. It only lasts a second, though, until I remember the truth. Elise isn't here because she's sorry or because she cares about me. She's here because she wants me to rescue her brother.

She needs me, but she doesn't *want* me. She never did.

"Let me guess, your undead brother wants to be human again." I pull out my apartment keys. "He can get in line."

"Just stop for a second and listen to me." Elise grabs my wrist, but I growl and yank my arm away. Elise gives me space, but she doesn't avert her gaze. "I get that you're mad, but none of this is how it looks. I *want* to help you. I have since the moment you told me about your past."

I feel myself soften, but I don't let myself speak. I can't afford to trust her, not after she lied for so long. Not after what Luca said.

Elise tugs on her braid as the silence stretches between us. "I still don't know for sure if it's even possible."

"It is."

Surprise widens her eyes. "Are you sure?"

Though I can still barely believe it myself, I nod. "Henri confirmed it."

"That's great!" A smile blooms across her face.

"No, it's not." I turn and fit my key into the lock. "The ability is banned. The Veil won't let you do it. Not for me. Not for Nick. Not for anyone."

"Screw what they want!" Elise reaches for me again, and this time, it's like her touch turns me to stone. Her fingers fall over mine, stilling the key. "We can figure it out together. We'll save Nick and you can get your revenge and then—"

"No." I shove open the door and step through the threshold, putting space between us. "I won't help you save your murderous brother just so you can turn around and fuck me over again."

"You don't have a choice. I'm the only one who can help you."

"Don't." I whirl around to face her. "You can't hide this for *weeks*, then try to use it to get your way."

"I wouldn't have to if you weren't so stubborn." Her voice rises until she's nearly shouting. "If you could just trust me—"

"The last time I trusted a mortal, she tried to kill me." I step in close until Elise has to crane her neck to look at me. Until we're close enough that in another life, we could kiss. I raise my sunglasses so she can see the flash of red in my eyes. "Do you know what happened after that?"

Elise shakes her head.

An impenetrable cold digs into my chest. "I ripped out her heart."

I stay just long enough to see my words land. To see the way they contort her face into shock and confusion and pain. Then I disappear into the house, slamming the door between us. Despite the barrier, I still hear her voice catch. I hear the tears start as I fit the key into the apartment door upstairs. Guilt snakes through my ribs, slithering through every corner of my mind.

Stop acting like a child and think about what you're doing.

Nick came to see me.

I'm confident she'll join my cause in the end.

The only thing I know for sure, the only thing that *matters*, is that there's a way out of this existence. I can't afford to care about anything else. Not Elise. Not the decades I've spent working with Wyn. Not even the Veil's betrayal. I'll learn everything Rose knows about the key, and then I'll destroy her. If Tagliaferro and Guillebeaux won't let me be human after that, then I'll dismantle the Veil, too. And when the wreckage of this existence has burned to ash around me, I'll convince a Death Oracle to make me mortal.

If that's not Elise, so be it.

I'm good at waiting.

29

Elise

I stand frozen at the bottom of Claire's front steps, feeling lost and hurt and alone.

The Claire I know wouldn't rip out someone's heart. I've seen her feed. I've *kissed* her. She's always so careful. She wouldn't do something like that. She couldn't. I shiver as a stiff breeze cuts down the street, sending falling leaves skittering across the sidewalk. Her voice was colder than the autumn air, though. Her jaw set. It felt like she meant it, every word.

Which means she isn't going to help me.

I pull my sweater past my fingertips and cross my arms tight against my chest. If Claire doesn't want to listen to me, fine. I'm tired of being a pawn for ageless creatures, anyway.

It's time I used *them* for a change.

With a final glance at Claire's front door, I pull my phone from my pocket. Even without her, I'm not alone. I have my friends. I have Hazel's journals, even if they've been unhelpful so far.

Maggie and Jordan don't answer their phones when I call, and guilt flushes my cheeks when I realize why. They're probably still at the memorial for Kaitlyn.

Dean Albro held an assembly this morning, like he did for Ms. Conrad, except this time most everyone already knew. Still, the official announcement shattered the room, emotions raw and sharp and *loud*.

With everything so heightened, I barely kept myself shielded from their auras. And knowing Nick was responsible for their pain? That *I* was responsible? It only made things worse.

If Delilah didn't need me for the key, none of this would have happened.

A block later, my phone rings.

"Everything okay?" Maggie asks, voice pitched with concern.

"Claire isn't going to help us." The rejection sits heavy on my chest, but I don't deserve to hurt this much when Maggie is still grieving her friend. "How was the service?"

"It was weird." Her voice catches, and Maggie clears her throat. "The team is going to swim laps in Kaitlyn's memory. She'd want to be in the pool if it were one of us."

"Can we meet after?" I continue toward the school.

There's mumbled, far-away conversation on Maggie's side, and then she sighs. "Does it have to be today?"

"I'm sorry, Maggie. I know this sucks, but I wouldn't ask if it wasn't urgent." Sharp pain digs into my chest, a toxic mixture of worry and fear and panic. "We need to save Nick. Now. Delilah will make him hurt everyone I love, and I can't risk him going after you or Jordan."

Another sigh. "Fine. Meet me at school. I owe Kaitlyn at least a few laps."

My heart squeezes. "Of course. Whatever you need, Mags."

She hangs up, and a chill works through me that has nothing to do with the wind. The Nick I grew up with—goofy and kind and *human*—would never hurt someone. If I hadn't seen him kill that guy at the party, I wouldn't believe it. Nausea twists my insides.

How many lives has he destroyed for Delilah? How many more will he take before I figure out how to save him?

And when I finally do, which version of my brother will I get back?

By the time I arrive at the academy, the parking lot is almost empty. I still circle the building and enter near the gym. The air is heavy with chlorine, the familiar scent filling me with longing and dread. Part of me misses the weightless feel of the pool, muscles aching and warm from exertion, but I can't think about being submerged without remembering that night in the river.

I pause at the door to the pool, memories coming in swift, trying to drown me. The frigid, fast-moving water. The burn of my lungs. Nick's car sinking, sinking, sinking while I failed to break open the glass.

Go. Please, Ellie.

I saw him die that night. Or, at least, I thought I had.

Somehow, Delilah knew where to be. Maybe she even caused the accident, lying in wait on the bridge. She may have saved his life, but she damned him to an existence that has brought Claire only misery.

A flush of anger burns in my veins, and I curl my hands into fists. I'm going to fix this. I have to.

With a fortifying breath, I push through the door.

The gentle splash of a solitary swimmer sends a very different cascade of memories rippling through my brain. The starting whistle during swim meets. Coach's voice raised louder than everyone around us. Cheering for Maggie and Jordan, Karen and Jenn, and everyone else on the team during races.

"Maggie?"

A quick scan of the room shows no other signs of life except for the swimmer heading toward me in a nearby lane. "Mags, is that you?"

The swimmer touches the side of the pool and pops up their head. Maggie raises her goggles to her swim cap. "Sorry. I needed a few extra laps." She wipes her face and climbs out of the pool. Water sloshes onto the cement between us.

I try to stop it, but my brain supplies images of Maggie's death, the same kind of cement opening her skull and stealing her life. I shake the memory away. "No, I'm sorry. I wouldn't ask if it wasn't urgent."

Maggie crosses to a bench where her towel is waiting. "Are you sure double-crossing Delilah is the way to do this? She'll let you fix Nick after the Veil is gone. Those other vampires won't let you use that power." The emotion bleeds out of Maggie's voice as she shifts gears.

The pool's surface has gone glassy and still now that she's no longer in it. "I'm tired of being a pawn. I want to save my brother and live my life on my terms. I'm done helping them."

"That's too bad."

"Why?" I ask, and then the rest of Maggie's words register. "Wait, how do you know Luca and Henri won't—"

Maggie crashes into me and shoves *hard*. I stumble and lose my footing, falling into the pool. Panic clutches my chest. All my air comes out in a rush. Lungs burning, I manage to find my bearings. I break the surface, gasping for breath.

"What the hell, Maggie? I—"

A hand fists in my hair and shoves me under. I thrash against the hold, but my mind is filled with visions of Maggie bleeding out. She dies over and over while I fight to break the surface. My lungs scream. Every atom begs for air. I try to shield myself from

her death, but I can't focus and I can't breathe and I can't I can't
I can't—

Maggie's touch disappears, and my mind goes blank. Before
I can break the surface, someone hauls me out of the water. I'm
dropped onto the cement, gasping for breath, choking on water
streaming down my face, coughing until my entire body aches.
When I roll onto my side, away from the pool that nearly claimed
me, I find Maggie's bare feet standing a few yards away. Behind
her, there's a pair of heels and familiar gray oxfords.

I force my gaze up. Maggie stares straight ahead, her eyes glazed
over. Behind her, Nick stands with his arms crossed, his attention
fixed on the floor. Even with his face turned away, the memory of
his last human moments, so full of fear, superimpose over reality.

"Nick." His name comes out broken as I struggle to my feet.

Delilah steps forward, blocking my view. She glares at me like
she wants to slit my throat and drink every last drop of my blood.
"This isn't a family reunion."

"What did you do?" I'm weighed down by soaking wet clothes
as I approach Maggie, but she doesn't look at me. "What did you
do to her?"

"You really ought to know the signs of compulsion by now."
Delilah slinks forward and trails a hand across Maggie's shoulder
blades. The nails slice Maggie's bare skin, and Delilah licks the
blood off her fingers. "This one has been keeping an eye on you.
She was *supposed* to steer you to the right decisions, but you're even
more stubborn than your predecessor."

"You can't do this." Even as my world crumbles around me, I
remember Claire's warning. Actively compelled humans can't look
anyone else in the eye, but some compulsions can go dormant.
They can lurk under the surface, waiting for the right situation

to activate. Anger overrides my fear. "You can't turn my entire life upside down and expect me to help you."

"Except that I absolutely can." Delilah tilts Maggie's head back, exposing her neck. "If you don't help me, I'll kill the people you love until you change your mind." She snaps her fingers, and Nick appears by her side, teeth lengthening. He shoots me an apologetic look before lowering his head toward Maggie's throat and—

"Wait!"

"That's what I thought." Delilah releases Maggie and crosses her arms. "This shouldn't be complicated, Elise. Your brother would have died without me. The Veil would have manipulated you into lifelong servitude without those journals."

I shake my head, knowing she's wrong but lacking the words to prove it.

"All you need to do is learn one power for me. Just one." Delilah softens her voice and approaches slowly. "You make Luca and Henri human, and I'll handle the rest. You'll be free to save your brother and anyone else you choose."

"Not *anyone*," I say, looking past her at my brother. "You made Nick a killer. I can't bring those people back."

Delilah shrugs. "Well, then, I guess you'd better get to work if you want that list to stay small."

"Why are you doing this?" My voice fills the cavernous space, fury overpowering self-preservation. "What could possibly be worth all this suffering? You're as bad as the vampires you want dead."

Pressure circles my throat before my eyes register Delilah's sudden closeness. "I am *nothing* like those monsters," she whispers as her grip tightens, cutting off my air. "They took everything from me. They don't deserve to rule the paranormal world."

"Let her go, Delilah," Nick says, and the sound of his voice picks at my heart. "She can't help you if she's dead."

"Fine." Delilah releases me, her face twisted with disgust. "You have one week before Nick kills someone else."

Panic pounds against my ribs. "A week? That's not possible. Hazel never wrote about a key."

Delilah slips a hand into her back pocket. "So, just contact her directly." She holds out a folded piece of paper.

"How?" I ask, even as I accept the paper and pinch it carefully between my wet fingers.

"Death Oracles can contact those who held the gift before them." Delilah examines her nails. "Witches do it with their ancestors, too, but there's a cost."

"Of course there is." Everything about this world seems to cost something, but maybe I can charge my own price. "Fine, but only if you leave Nick with me."

Laughter echoes through the room, and Delilah turns away. "You are so delightfully outmatched, little one. Now, be a dear and talk to your predecessor." She snaps her fingers, and Nick hurries to her side without hesitation.

"You won't get away with this."

"One week, Death Oracle. One week," Delilah says, waving goodbye without turning around.

And then they're gone.

The doors slam shut, and the sound ricochets throughout the room. Maggie blinks and shakes her head, and her eyes finally focus on me. "Oh my god, Elise! What happened? Why are you soaking wet?"

My heart aches, and I have to hold back tears when I realize her compulsion is still there, just dormant. "I fell in."

Her brow arches with concern. "How'd you manage that?"

"Just clumsy, I guess."

Maggie doesn't look like she believes me, but I don't know how much of that is her normal inquisitiveness or some lingering part of Delilah's compulsion. What activates it? Delilah's name? Any talk about the Veil or saving Nick?

Is this version of Maggie nothing more than a carefully crafted trick?

"Come on," she says, waving me toward the exit. "I have an extra towel in my locker."

I follow my best friend away from the pool, feeling like I'm sinking. The number of people I need to save keeps going up. First Nick, and now Maggie. Is Jordan one of Delilah's pawns, too?

Do I have any allies left?

30

Claire

"Come on, Greg. You owe me." I pace my bedroom—earbuds in, newly purchased phone safe in my pocket. "You don't even need to help directly. Just connect me to your supplier."

"You know I appreciate everything you did for me back then," Greg says.

"But . . ."

"If I put in a request for this many solar grenades and an arsenal of wooden stakes, people will ask questions, Claire."

"And who answered all *your* questions in 1973?"

Greg sighs. "You did."

I turn to my wall—now covered with large maps of Elmsbrook. "Damn right I did. When your creator got himself staked by a newbie vampire hunter, *I* showed you the ropes. I taught you how to blend into society and feed without raising suspicion. The least you could do is connect me to a supplier."

"Why can't you get this stuff from the Veil? Wouldn't that be easier?"

The question stalls me, and I pause. This part trips me every time I make my pitch to old contacts who owe me a favor. My options are limited, with everyone currently working for the Veil out of reach. But I was a shepherd for a long time, and most paranormals tend to think fondly of the ones who guided them.

Unfortunately, they tend to be more afraid of upsetting the Veil.

"Claire?"

I scramble for a way to explain that won't scare off the vampire. "This is a personal project. The Veil only lets us use their resources for assignments."

"Did they approve it?"

"For fuck's sake, Greg, can you connect me with the dealer or not?"

"I don't know. I can't really afford to burn bridges right now, and there's only the one guy—"

A vicious snarl fills the room.

"Sorry, Claire," he says, and then the useless asshole hangs up on me.

"No, no, no!" I rip out the earbuds and let a frustrated scream tear from my throat. Greg was the last of my contacts, and despite two days focused on this, I haven't made an inch of progress.

I don't know where Rose is staying. I have no idea how Death Oracles are supposed to make vampires human again. My only plan for killing Rose isn't so much a plan as a desire to tear out her throat. Except, with her centuries of additional strength and speed, that's very likely to fail. Which is why I wanted to arm myself with solar bombs and stakes and anything else I could get my hands on.

Without any of that? I'm screwed.

My phone buzzes against my leg. Another text from Wyn, no doubt. They pretended to be my friend for decades. Convinced me to join the Veil. Mentored me. Assigned me to this cursed case. Wyn can fuck the hell off.

A sudden knock on my apartment door startles me. I freeze, straining to listen for a sign of who might be here. The heartbeat says they're mortal, and I move through the apartment in a blur. At the door, I notice the unmistakable old-lady scent of patchouli, pain cream, and freshly baked cookies.

There's another knock, then my landlady's creaky voice. "Claire? I know you're in there."

I open the door, intending to compel the old woman to go downstairs and leave me the hell alone, but I falter when I see the plate of chocolate chip cookies. "Mrs. Tihy, can I help you with something?"

My landlady pushes into my apartment, blush bright on her wrinkled cheeks, and sets the plate on my table. She takes a seat. "Those stairs are not made for old ladies, I'll tell you that."

"You didn't have to come all the way up. I could have come down."

"Nonsense." She waves me off. "My hearing isn't what it used to be, but it sounded like you were having a bad day."

"I'm sorry, Mrs. Tihy. I didn't mean to disturb you." It never occurred to me that she could hear me downstairs. "I'll be more quiet."

Mrs. Tihy adjusts the plate so it sits in the center of the table. "Your friends haven't been over for a few days, not since you yelled at the blonde one. Are you having a fight?"

I cringe at the memory. "You heard that?"

"Dear, the front door is right outside my bedroom. When it slams, I know about it."

"Sorry."

The landlady clucks her tongue. "I'm not looking for an apology." She picks up a cookie and breaks it in half, handing one section to me. "Will you indulge an old woman's unsolicited advice?"

Basic math says I've been around longer than my landlady, but I nod. "Sure."

Mrs. Tihy glares at me until I take a bite of the cookie. I don't even have to fake enjoyment. It's the best kind—gooey, scratch-made, with just a touch too much chocolate. She smiles. "When you get as old as me, you'll learn there's nothing quite as special as friendship."

"It's a little late for that." I shove the rest of the cookie in my mouth. "I'm not sure we were ever really friends."

"Know how you find out? You apologize. Call the blonde and say you're sorry."

"But—"

"No one is blameless, dear. I've been around long enough to know that. Getting upset and yelling loud enough that even *I* hear you isn't going to solve anything."

The fear in Elise's eyes when I threw my violent past in her face haunts me. "I know I'm not blameless. It's just . . . I'm not sure I deserve to be forgiven. I'm not sure I know *how* to forgive."

No matter how much I wish it were different, the facts remain. Elise kept so many secrets. She made me believe it was okay to share my most vulnerable truths, and the whole time, she was plotting to destroy the Veil.

Not that they deserved my loyalty, either.

Mrs. Tihy grabs my arm and pulls herself out of the chair. "You can't know for sure until you try. Call your friend. You'll feel better, I promise."

There's no point arguing with her, so I offer my elbow. "Let me walk you back down."

She scoffs. "I got myself up here, didn't I? You be good, dear." Mrs. Tihy waves and steps out of the apartment.

I wait until Mrs. Tihy is safely back in her part of the house before I close my door. My phone buzzes in my pocket, and I pull it out, half expecting to see Elise's name. Instead, I find another text from Wyn. I unlock the phone and check messages that date back to Monday.

Status report.

Come on, Claire. It's been three days.

Be smart about this.

I can't keep stalling for you. The Veil needs an update on Elise's progress.

If you don't check in soon, I'll have to drive up there myself.

I scroll through half a dozen similar messages. Not a single one mentions the meeting I interrupted. None of them contain an apology. I don't understand why Wyn can't see how fucked this is. How can they be so unquestioningly loyal to the Veil? How can they know how badly I want to be human and still side with Henri's decision to hide the possibility?

While I'm holding the phone, another series of texts comes through, and I realize my read receipts are on, which means Wyn knows I've seen their messages.

We're out of time.

If I send another shepherd, that'll be it for you, Claire.

The Veil will cast you out.

Don't make me do this.

Please.

Fear pools in my stomach, and even though I fed over the weekend, I'm suddenly itching for fresh blood. I erase the entire thread and return to my bedroom. If I'm running out of time, I'll make every moment count.

I have to find Rose.

Now.

31

Elise

I've been collecting supplies ever since Delilah gave me the instructions, but I'm not sure this is a good idea.

The last time I tried a ritual, it didn't do anything, and I'm not eager for a repeat of my failure. It's already Friday, though, so I have to do *something*. Delilah may have picked Nick's next target already, and I won't have more blood on my hands.

A knock on my door makes me jolt, and I shove the box of herbs under a pile of dirty clothes. "Just a sec!"

No one jiggles the door handle, so it's probably not Mom. My stomach twists. I really don't want to deal with Dad right now. He's been hovering ever since his attempted apology.

When I open the door, he offers a tight-lipped smile. "Hey, Ellie Bean."

The nickname tugs at my emotions, but he can't erase months of distance with a few kind words. I cross my arms. "What's wrong? Does Mom need help with dinner?"

"No, nothing like that." Dad shifts awkwardly, and Richie sneaks up behind him, whining for food. "Has she always been so vocal?"

"You don't know the half of it." I bend and scoop up the cat, cradling her in my arms. I step out of the way so Dad can come in. "She spends half the night screaming if I don't give her enough treats after dinner."

Dad chuckles, and the sound is so unexpected that my throat tightens. "That must be why your mother keeps the cat locked out at night."

Richie twists and tries to gnaw on my finger, so I put her down.

"So . . . What's up?" I can't remember the last time Dad came looking for me.

"Nothing really." He perches on the edge of my bed, like he's unsure of his every move. "I just wanted to apologize again. I should have been there for you long before you lost your friend." Dad tilts his head to one side, considering me. "How are you holding up?"

I shrug. At the beginning of the school year, I would have done anything to get Dad's attention. Now, I worry it puts him in more danger. No matter how upset I am, I don't want him to get hurt. There's so much I wish I could tell my parents—about vampires and Death Oracles and my plan to save Nick—but they wouldn't believe a word of it.

"And school is going okay?" Dad presses when I don't say anything.

Barely. I'm staying on top of coursework, but it's not the quality the school expects. No one has said anything yet, and I'm half-convinced Claire compelled the dean to ignore my academic failures. The school might be going easy on us since we lost both Ms. Conrad and Kaitlyn, but Dean Albro never went easy on *me* after Nick died.

Or, when we all thought he died, anyway.

"I'm trying my best," I say, which is true enough. It's just hard with all my time devoted to solving paranormal problems I didn't want.

"That's all your mom or I ever ask." Dad reaches for me, and I manage to put up a shield before he squeezes my hand. His dark eyes shimmer. "I'm so sorry I wasn't there for you, Elise. I—"

The doorbell saves me from more of Dad's apologies. I won't hold this against him forever, but I'm not in a rush to forgive him, either. With everything else going on, I've barely had time to think about my fight with Dad.

"Elise!" Mom calls my name from the bottom of the stairs. "Jordan's here!"

A tremor of fear works through me. I've been avoiding Jordan ever since Maggie tried to drown me at school on Monday. Whenever I see my friends, they act normal, but Maggie's been under Delilah's compulsion for weeks, and I'm afraid to find out if the vampire ensnared Jordan, too.

"Elise?" Mom calls again when I haven't answered.

Dad groans as he stands. "I'll send him up for you." At the doorway, he pauses and turns back. "Unless you're not up for visitors?"

"No, it's okay." I force out a slow breath. I'll have to face Jordan sooner or later, and if he isn't compelled, having help for the ritual isn't a bad idea. "You can send him up."

"You got it, kiddo. Door stays open, though."

"We're not dating anymore."

"Door still stays open," he says as he steps into the hall. I roll my eyes, but the normality of it is grounding after everything we've been through.

Faint sounds of Dad greeting Jordan trickle into my room, and I pull the box of supplies from my closet. Jordan and I may not be dating anymore, but he doesn't need to see the piles of dirty laundry in there. I shut the closet and turn in time to see Jordan arrive.

"Hey, Elise." He stands in the hallway, hands shoved into his pockets. "Your dad said I could come up."

"What are you doing here?" The question comes out harsher than I intend, and Jordan's gaze flicks to mine.

"You've been weird all week. I wanted to make sure you were okay." He steps into the room and holds my stare. His face softens with concern. "I know everything with Nick is super messed up, and that you and Claire are fighting, but Maggie and I are here for you. We can't help if you won't let us, though."

"Did Maggie send you?"

Jordan scowls. "I know how to be a good friend, Elise. I don't need Maggie to remind me."

He's still holding my gaze, but Maggie can, too, so long as I'm not talking about Delilah. I have to know if this is the real Jordan, or some puppet version. "Would you really help me betray Delilah?"

His brows arch up his forehead. "Is it considered betrayal if you were blackmailed into helping in the first place?" Jordan asks, and he never breaks eye contact. Not once.

"Oh, thank god." A tension in my chest releases. "You're still you." I fortify the shield I raised with Dad and crush Jordan in a hug. Even through his shirt, his body is a furnace.

"Of course I am. Why—"

"Maggie's compelled," I say, and then I lose myself to tears. It's the first time I've seen Jordan one-on-one since the pool incident, and it takes several minutes to explain everything that happened. How Maggie tricked me into going to the pool. How she held me under until Delilah got there. The intricate compulsion that turns on and off depending on the topic. The impossible timeline Delilah gave me.

"I was afraid you were compelled, too," I say, trying to pull away from the wet spot I've created on Jordan's shirt. "I'm really glad you're not."

"Me, too." Jordan hugs me tighter before finally releasing me. "At least this explains why Maggie was all *Team Delilah*. I just assumed she knew something I didn't."

The fact that Jordan realized something was off before I did fills me with shame. "Am I a terrible friend?"

"What? No. You've got a lot going on." Jordan rests a hand on my shoulder. "When a vampire is training you to be a paranormal warrior, you're allowed to be distracted from normal teen stuff."

"I miss normal teen stuff."

"Don't worry. Your life will be boring again before you know it." Jordan grins. "So, what's the plan?"

"Delilah gave me this." I grab the ritual instructions from my desk and pass them to Jordan.

"What is it?" Jordan unfolds the page and runs a hand over his head while he reads. As he gets near the end, his eyes widen. "You're not seriously considering this, are you?"

"I don't have much choice," I say, even though his concern is a mirror of my own. "Hazel didn't write about making vampires human. The only way to find out is to go back to the source."

"But she's dead!" Jordan whispers the words, but his intensity isn't lost. "You said the vampire killed Hazel. What if this is a plot to kill you, too?"

"Most of these ingredients were already in my kitchen." I had to go back to Heart & Stone for a few of the supplies, but both the internet and the owner confirmed everything was safe to consume in small amounts. "Besides, you know CPR from lifeguarding. If something happens, you can help."

Jordan shakes his head. "This is a terrible idea."

"If you know how to cure vampirism, I'm all ears." I take the instructions back from Jordan and check through the list again. Freshly squeezed apple juice, basil, and mint. Cinnamon, amaranth, and acacia seeds. Wolf's paw, which is just another name for club moss. "It's simpler than the first ritual we tried."

"Yeah, but you didn't drink it last time."

"Please?" I tuck the paper in my back pocket and reach for his hands. The shield holds, which is a small miracle in itself. "I have to do this, Jordan. I'm willing to do it alone, but it'll be safer with you there."

It only takes a moment before Jordan sighs and squeezes my hand. "Fine. I'm in."

"Are we sure this is a good idea?"

Jordan hovers over me while I simmer the mixture of apple juice and herbs. His parents are out for their usual Friday date night, so we've taken over the Wallace kitchen.

"Good idea or not, we're doing it." I stir the mixture and glance up at the timer. Two minutes left.

"It smells like you dumped salad into moldy apple cider." Jordan waves the steam away from his face. "With a hint of toothpaste."

I suppress a laugh. "At least *you* don't have to drink it."

"Fair."

We fall silent as the mixture bubbles, watching the clock. When the timer beeps, I cut the heat and move the small pot to another burner to cool.

Jordan opens a cabinet near the sink and grabs a giant coffee mug. "Assuming this works, what next? Delilah probably won't let you near Nick until you do what she asks."

"I know."

"And it sounds like Claire is *super* pissed at you, so I don't see her helping. Plus, even if you do what Delilah wants, you know those dudes will fight back. Claire is already scary, so I bet those guys are terrifying."

I roll my eyes and watch steam dance above the gross, clumpy mixture. "Claire isn't scary."

"Uh, yes. She is." Jordan hops onto the counter next to me, his long legs dangling off the edge. "All she does is glare at me and talk about how I'm going to die."

"Only because she had to train me to see it," I say, a tightness forming in my chest. "I know she's weird about death sometimes, but I don't think she realizes since she's basically immortal. She's kinder than she seems."

Jordan looks at me like I've lost touch with reality. "She threatened to kill you so she could train someone new."

"She was hurt," I argue, that pressure in my chest building. "She—"

I cut myself off. There's no way to explain the things I know about Claire without divulging her secrets. The story of the night Rose—*Delilah*—turned Claire was heartbreaking. No matter what else she's done, I can't deny the pain in her voice. I still feel it echoing in my heart.

"Elise?"

I shake the memory away. "We should do this before the potion gets cold." I take the cup from Jordan and pour in the mixture. It's gritty and thick and altogether unappealing.

"Do you need a puke bucket?" Jordan hops off the counter and bends to grab a large bowl from under the sink. "Mom used this one when I was sick as a kid."

"Gross." I shudder, but then I notice which bowl he's holding. "Wait, haven't we used that for popcorn?" I ask, and the way Jordan goes silent is answer enough. "All the bowls in this house and you use the puke bucket for popcorn? What is wrong with you?"

"It's the only bowl that holds two bags at once!"

"I don't know, Jordan, that might be grosser than this." I raise the mug of chunky potion and try not to think too hard about what's inside or the cost Delilah warned I'd have to pay. "Here goes nothing."

"Ellie, wait. Shouldn't you lie—"

Before Jordan can finish, I toss the liquid back and fight my gag reflex. The potion is thick in my throat, but I get it down in three big gulps. It's sweet and tangy and earthy in all the worst ways. I reach out to put the mug on the counter, but a heaviness settles over me. The cup slips from my fingers. It shatters across the floor. My legs give out and I'm falling and—

I jolt awake.

Except . . . I'm not at Jordan's house anymore. At least, not all of me. I'm surrounded by white, unrelenting light and swirling mist that curves along my skin. I blink, and suddenly I'm standing. Gray mist clings to my calves as I take a tentative step forward.

"Hello?"

My voice disappears into the open, empty space. It's like it travels on forever, never reaching a boundary, never bouncing back. The vastness of this place prickles at my skin, leaving me unsettled and uncertain. *Focus, Elise. You need the key.*

I take another tentative step forward. The ground beneath me is soft yet firm, like stepping across moss. "Hazel?" I really hope

Jordan was wrong. I hope this isn't a weird hallucination before Delilah's concoction kills me.

"Hazel Elding?"

"It's *Elfring*," an irritated voice says behind me. "Not off to a good start, newbie."

Embarrassment floods my body until I realize what this means. I whirl around to face the previous Death Oracle, braced to see the same decomposed skin and exposed bone. Thankfully, none of the trauma of her death is reflected in the Hazel standing before me. She looks a little older than my mom, her dark hair pulled into a bun. Strands of gray streak through her hair like highlights.

"Well?" Hazel's voice is harsher than I expected. She's clearly not the same carefree young woman who wrote the journals I read, and I'm afraid to know what made her this way. "What is so important that you're bothering me in the first year of my retirement?"

"Retirement?"

Hazel rolls her eyes. "What do you want, newbie? Spit it out."

My face burns, but I force myself to meet her icy stare. "I need a cure."

"There's no cure for this, cupcake. Once you're the Death Oracle, you hold that power until you die." Hazel waves her arm to the side. The gray mist around her feet bends and grows until it forms an armchair. Hazel sits and glares up at me. "You'll have to get used to it."

I shake my head, even as a desperate kind of panic claws at my throat. "That's not what I meant. I need to make vampires mortal again."

Hazel's glare sharpens. "Excuse me?" But there's no question in her tone, only challenge.

"I need—"

"You *need* to do as you're told. Forget about this cure nonsense." Hazel stands, and the vapor chair vanishes into mist. "Go back, kid. If you're quick, you may only lose a couple weeks."

I have no idea what she's talking about, but when she turns to leave, I lunge after her. "Wait! You don't understand."

When I reach Hazel, she whirls around and grabs a fistful of my sweater. Her strength rattles me, and she pulls me close. "Enlighten me, then, newbie. A vampire tortured and killed me for this so-called key. What reason is good enough for my death to be in vain?"

"My brother," I say without hesitation, even as she glares at me. "Delilah turned him. This is the only way to get him back."

The former Death Oracle shoves me away. I stumble and collapse into the mist, but I can feel her disappointment like a weight against my chest.

"Please, Hazel. I can't abandon him."

"Even if I wanted to help you, I couldn't. I don't know anything about making those creatures mortal again."

"But Delilah—"

"The vampire was wrong. I don't know how to do this."

"But—"

"Goodbye, newbie." Hazel kneels beside me and holds a hand over my forehead. "Get your loyalties straight before you return. I can make this place *very* uncomfortable for you."

Hazel presses her fingers against my temples. Pressure builds inside my brain, like my head might actually explode, and then—

I jolt upright, gasping for breath. The real world comes into focus around me, and Jordan lets loose a string of profanities.

"Oh, thank god." Jordan slides to the floor beside me. "I warned you to lie down first. You okay?"

My head is screaming, and my elbow feels like it took the brunt of the fall, but all the physical pain in the world couldn't compare to this jagged gash in my heart.

"She doesn't know how to do it." I wipe my sleeves across my face, and my breath catches in my throat as the swell of grief overtakes me.

"Ellie . . ."

"I can't save him. I can't fix it." I bury my head in my hands. "Nick will keep killing, and there's nothing I can do to stop him."

32

Claire

My apartment is in shambles. I've been researching non-stop, and my space shows every sign of neglect. The fridge is full of half-eaten containers of takeout—fried rice and pizza, mostly. Though the food doesn't temper my hunger for blood, it's a decent distraction.

In my bedroom, I've pinned photos of vacant homes to the maps of Elmsbrook. I don't have a plan for how to kill Rose without ending up dead myself, but I can at least figure out where she's staying.

As soon as the sun dips below the horizon, I head out on foot. I can't cover all of Elmsbrook in one night, so I focus on the neighborhoods closest to campus, since that's where Nick made his kills. I'm even dressed the part, wearing dark jeans and a black-and-gray flannel over a black cami—*break-in chic*, Abigail used to call it. Disparagingly.

My phone buzzes in my back pocket, and I wonder if it's Abigail, summoned by my thoughts. Maybe she needs more details about Rose so her team can find her. Maybe she convinced Guillebeaux and Tagliaferro to let me help.

The phone buzzes again, and I slip it out to check. Streetlights glint off the glass as I read the messages. They're both from Wyn.

You're out of time, Claire.

As soon as I finish here, I'm driving to Elmsbrook.

The breeze kicks up around me, but the sudden cold isn't what makes me shudder. Wyn's right. I am running out of time, but I won't let them stop me. I will find Rose. I will learn everything she knows about the key, and then I'll end her.

The road turns and climbs a hill toward campus. I've spent so many years pushing down painful memories, but now they all come spilling out. So many of them have a mortal's face.

Fiona's face.

My last charge was unique. Though her gift wasn't as special or rare as a Death Oracle's, the Veil still wanted her power controlled and concealed. They wanted her loyal in case they ever needed her skills. When Fiona was eighteen, a senior in high school with plans to attend the University of Georgia, she came into a dangerous power.

She could create fire.

For two years, I shepherded Fiona and helped her control her gift. She panicked when I told her what I was, but she eventually came to trust me again. I went with her to college, and the summer between her first and second years at UGA, we fell in love. Or, at least, I did.

What would happen if you bit me? Fiona asked one day while we were picnicking under the full moon, the sky full of stars above us. Her voice was hushed and reverent, her body snuggled against mine.

Nothing, I said, pulling away from her. *Because I never would.*

Why? Would it make me a vampire? She sat up, and there was this gleam in her eye that turned my stomach.

Becoming a vampire is more complicated than that. In an instant, I was standing. *Vampirism isn't transferred like a disease.*

Hey, she said, voice soft and sweet. *I'm sorry. Of course it's not.* Her hands rested against my back, and when I didn't pull away, she slipped her arms around my waist. *But what if you* had *to bite me? Like if you were injured and needed blood to heal? What would happen? What would it feel like?*

Why are you even asking? I pulled from her touch again. I could feel my temper rising, and I didn't want to take it out on her. *Do you want to know if I'd lose myself and kill you? Are you curious how tempting your blood is?*

I—

We don't drink from other paranormals, even if they're mortal.

She smiled a seductive smile, the one she knew I had a terrible time denying. *But what if I wanted you to?*

Her question sent a strange thrill through my body. No one had ever asked this of me, not in all the decades I'd been a monster. I could feel my defenses cracking, but I couldn't give in. *What are you asking me?*

Fiona shrugged. *I'm just curious about your life.*

Life. Such a loaded word.

I don't have a life. I have an existence, Fiona, one filled with terrible, aching hunger that I struggle every day to control. I wouldn't wish this on anyone.

Undeterred, she stepped forward. Trailed her finger along my exposed collarbone while the moonlight danced in her hair. *It can't be all bad. It brought you to me,* she said, and I shivered under her attention. *Hunger seems like a small price for an eternity together.*

Her words left me cold, and I stepped away. *You don't know what you're saying.*

But I do. Fiona pulled a knife from her pocket and flicked it open. *I want this. I want to be like you.*

No, you don't. I couldn't keep the growl out of my voice, low and harsh. I couldn't stop my teeth from lengthening at the suggestion of feeding, and she flushed, the heat of her blood pooling close to the surface. My throat tightened, and I stole the blade from her hand, throwing it as far as I could.

Fiona fell back a step, the flush draining from her cheeks. She crossed her arms and scowled, her entire demeanor changing in an instant. *What's the point of us if you won't turn me?*

Her words tangled up in my brain like knotted chains. *What?*

If I can't even convince you to bite me, you'll never turn me, will you? Her voice rose until she was yelling, furious tears streaming down her face. Smoke curled off her fingertips. *Don't claim to love me, then hoard immortality for yourself.*

Her words twisted my insides, and the sparks crackling between her fingers sent a rush of fear through my limbs. *Fiona, you're only twenty. You have your whole life ahead of you. I won't destroy that.*

Then what is the point of you? She spit the words as full flames erupted from her palms.

My own anger rose to meet hers. *Is that all this was? An elaborate ploy to get me to turn you?*

The flames in her hands flickered in the light breeze. *Not all of it.*

And there it was.

Another crack in what was left of my heart.

Just used and used and used. Until one day, I was all used up. I tried to leave the field, tried to abandon her there alone, but she attacked. I escaped with nothing worse than singed hair, but Fiona didn't stop. She broke every one of the Veil's rules of secrecy, using her powers openly and recklessly.

She attacked the tracker sent to stop her. Burnt him to ash.

She set fire to her residence hall, killing two of her classmates. I never found out if she meant to hurt them or if their deaths were an accident.

The Veil sent me back to Fiona with an ultimatum. Only one of us was allowed to leave the meeting alive. I called her. I lied.

Fiona met me in that same field where we'd had our picnic. She wore a white sundress with yellow flowers, her hair braided into a crown along her head. I kissed her. I promised to turn her, said the Veil made a mistake.

And then I ripped out her heart.

I blink away tears. Wyn burned the body for me, and I swore I'd never shepherd again. I buried my feelings and let the Veil shape me into a weapon. For a decade, I built armor around my emotions. I learned to question everything, to trust no one. I turned into a shell of a monster, drinking just enough to survive, but never enough to feel whole.

But as soon as I met Elise, all of that came crumbling down around me. And for what? So she could betray me, too?

A bitter cloud hangs over me as I approach the first house on my list. It stands dark and quiet, the lawn unkept. I'm done caring about the Veil. Once I find Rose, I'll plan my revenge. One step at a time.

Though the house seems abandoned, I hurry across the front yard and around the corner until I'm out of view. I walk the perimeter, looking for signs of occupation, and find nothing but a family of grazing bunnies.

In the back, I open one of the kitchen windows, breaking the lock in the process. I try to press my hand through the opening, but I'm blocked by an invisible barrier. Despite being for sale, someone still has enough claim on this property that I can't get inside.

Which means no vampire can enter without invitation.

Rose has to be somewhere else.

I pull out my phone and check off the address. One down. Eleven to go.

It's going to be a long night.

———

Okay, maybe *long night* was a bit of a stretch. After two hours, I've checked all the houses on my list and come up empty. My young brain wants to rage with frustration, but I tap into my tracker training. I stay focused. I move forward.

I've crossed an entire neighborhood off my list, which means I'm that much closer to finding Rose. And I will find her. It's only a matter of time.

With the final vacant house behind me, I turn west to avoid the heart of Elmsbrook. It's almost nine on a Friday night, and the downtown bars are sure to be packed. I'll need to feed soon, but I don't have time tonight. Not with Wyn on their way. I need to make sure my hunt for Rose isn't disturbed.

As I make my way through town, I realize I'm closer to Elise than I've been since I slammed a door in her face. A bitter sting of regret pulses through me. I try to shove it down, but I remember my landlady's advice.

No one is blameless, dear.

Call the blonde and say you're sorry.

I'm not sure I want to apologize. Even if she forgives me, I'm not sure I can forgive her. Besides, without the Veil, there's no reason to see Elise. She was only ever a job. I'm not her shepherd anymore.

But I keep walking toward her place instead of mine, the streetlights a metronome of bad decisions. Up ahead, someone turns and comes toward me. The figure is tall, all lanky arms and legs. When he looks up and notices me, he stops short.

"Claire?"

Jordan sounds surprised, and the air between us grows heavy with adrenaline. He's right to fear me, despite the weeks we've spent together. Yet somehow, it stings. I consider compelling him to forget he saw me this close to Elise's house, but she'd never forgive me if I did. Despite everything, that alone makes me pause.

"I'm not going to bite you," I say, when he's still frozen several feet away.

"What are you doing here?"

"I could ask you the same thing." I glance behind him at the road he turned from. "Let me guess, you were visiting Elise."

The boy clenches his shaking hands into fists, as if that'll hide his fear. "Don't stand there and act like you care."

"I'm not—"

"Do you have any idea what she's been through this week? That other vampire compelled Maggie." Jordan's voice catches, and he clears his throat. "Maggie tried to drown Elise."

"What—"

"I'm not done," he snaps. "Delilah gave Elise one week to figure out the key to mortality. Just one week until Nick starts killing people again. She risked poisoning herself to contact the old Death Oracle, but even that didn't help. And despite you completely ghosting her this week, for some reason, she still gives a shit about you."

His words land with a jolt of pain, and I try to focus on what he's saying. "Wait, she talked to Hazel?"

"Delilah gave her a recipe to contact ancestors," Jordan says with a shrug. "I don't understand how this mystical crap works. Elise said Hazel doesn't know anything about making vampires human, though, so now we're *screwed*."

Jordan's outburst makes my head spin, and I try to see past his unexpected backbone to figure out my next step. If Hazel doesn't know how to make vampires human, why was Henri so sure it was possible? How is Elise supposed to figure it out on her own?

And if she does . . . would she help me after all the things I said? After I abandoned her to deal with this on her own?

"Well?" Jordan says, rubbing his bare arms. There's still a hint of fear on the night air, but it's mostly dissipated now. "Do you really have nothing to say? You were supposed to help Elise, not make things worse."

A growl rumbles in my throat. "*She* wasn't supposed to conspire to kill my bosses, either." *Former bosses*, I correct silently.

Instead of backing down, Jordan rolls his eyes. "You don't know her at all, do you? Elise wouldn't force someone to be human. She was never going to betray the Veil. Not that she owes them anything, since they want to steal her away from her normal life."

"That's not . . ." I start, but I trail off. Jordan isn't exactly *wrong*, and a thread of shame weaves between all the layers of hurt. I know better than to let this kind of emotion color my judgment, but I can't wash it away. "She hates me, doesn't she?"

"She should." Jordan says it with no hesitation, but after a moment, he sighs. "I don't think she does, though."

The reluctance in his voice makes his words feel undeniably true, but it doesn't matter. It's too late. Even if Elise won't help

Rose attack Guillebeaux and Tagliaferro, the Veil will never teach Elise the key. She won't stop looking, though, not until she saves her brother.

"Where is she now?"

"I walked her home. Her parents were out, but she wanted to be alone." Jordan rubs his arms. "I think the ritual was hard on her."

"That's too bad," says a voice behind me. I whirl around and find Nick Beaumont grinning in the glow of the streetlights. "Still pining after my sister, Wallace?"

I shift in front of Jordan, blocking Nick's line of sight. "What are you doing here, errand boy?"

Nick stalks toward us, his movements slow and unhurried, but his gaze never meets mine. Elise's brother is physically here, but Rose is in complete control. "My sister ran out of time. Now someone has to die." He flashes vampiric teeth and lets a growl fill the night.

"You're not touching him," I say, stepping into Nick's path again. "You might as well leave now."

"Who said I was after Jordan?"

There's a blur of motion. Nick's arm moving fast, something long and dark grasped in his hand.

Then there's pain. Everywhere. I'm burning and freezing and my legs crumble beneath me. My fingers curl around the wooden stake as I fall.

I don't have the strength to grasp it. To pull it free.

My back slams against the ground.

And the world goes dark.

33

Elise

The doorbell jolts me from the edge of unconsciousness, and I force my eyes open. I stay in bed, though, hoping my parents will deal with it.

A second later, it rings again. And again. And again. The urgency sends a wave of adrenaline through my body, and I check my phone. It's only been a few minutes since Jordan left, which means I'm still alone.

Worry settles in the pit of my stomach as my feet touch the floor, but the bell rings again. "Just a second!" I hurry downstairs, worry pulsing through every part of me. My fingers shake as I flip the deadbolt, open the door, and—

"Holy shit."

Jordan stands on my front porch. He's soaked with sweat, and there's blood spattered on his shirt. His entire body trembles, and cradled in his arms is . . .

"Claire?"

"She's hurt," Jordan says, shoving past me into the foyer.

I shut the door and follow him into the dining room. Jordan stumbles, but he catches himself in time and lays Claire gently on the floor. A wooden stake protrudes from her chest, blood soaking her dark clothes. "What the hell happened?"

"Nick." Jordan collapses to the ground, gasping for breath like he just finished the 200-meter backstroke. "He attacked us. Claire . . . she protected me, and Nick . . . He—"

My hands hover frozen and uncertain over Claire's still body. I don't need Jordan to finish to guess what happened next. Nick stabbed Claire. Jordan carried her here. But how do I fix this? How do I save her?

Is it already too late?

Jordan runs trembling hands over his head. "If anyone had seen me . . . Black kids get shot for so much less. If anyone saw and called the police, I could've— They would've—"

"I know," I say, crossing the short distance between us and reaching for his hands. I can't focus enough for a shield, but I squeeze tight anyway. For once, the familiar scene of his death is comforting. "But I promise, you have a very long life ahead of you."

For a moment, Jordan doesn't say anything. Just squeezes my hands, letting his death run on a loop in my head. Then he looks past me to Claire, where she lays unmoving and bloody and probably dying. "She tried to protect me, but I wasn't the one he wanted. Nick went right for her." Jordan shuts his deep brown eyes, and tears slip down his cheeks.

"Nick won't hurt you. I promise, I won't let him. Okay?" I wait for Jordan to nod before taking a deep breath. "I need to help her. Are you good?" When he nods a second time, I hurry over to Claire. I wish I knew *anything* about vampire biology, but step one has to be getting this out. "Can you get me a few things? I need a towel to grip this. There are some in the kitchen."

"On it." Jordan pulls himself up and stumbles toward the kitchen on shaky legs. He grabs all the towels from the drawer and drops them beside me.

I wrap one around the blood-soaked stake and grip it with both hands. It makes a terrible sound as it shifts inside Claire's chest. If she were human, I'd call 911 and wait for the paramedics. They'd probably leave the stake in her chest until they got to the hospital, to a surgical suite, but that's not an option. Not for us.

And maybe . . . Maybe if I get it out, her body can heal. That's a thing, right?

God, I hope so.

"One. Two . . ."

"What are you—"

"Three!" I pull the wooden stake with all my strength. For a second, it seems stuck, but then it comes tearing out of her chest, slick with blood. The momentum nearly topples me over, and I drop the stake to the floor.

"—doing?" Jordan steadies me as my knees threaten to buckle. "Were you supposed to do that? Won't she bleed out?"

"I don't know. It's hard to see." I grab a fresh towel and kneel beside Claire, pressing the clean cloth to the wound like they always do in movies. There's no pulse, though. No blood trying to pour through my fingers. Is that a good thing? Is it bad? Does her heart normally beat, even though she's not technically alive? I've never noticed. I've never thought to ask. I should have asked.

"Is she going to be okay?"

I pull away, but there's still too much blood to see anything. "Can you get wet paper towels?"

"One sec." Jordan rushes back to the kitchen.

"Come on, Claire," I whisper, brushing strands of dark hair out of her face. "You have to wake up. I don't know what I'm doing."

"Here." Jordan appears beside me with dripping paper towels. I wipe gently at Claire's chest, washing the blood away. There's a gaping, deep wound where the stake was moments before.

"She's not healing." My voice shakes, and I try to remember everything Dad has ever said about surgery. He works on humans, though, not ageless creatures. "Why isn't she healing?"

Jordan picks up the discarded stake and examines it. "There's a sliver missing. Maybe there's a piece still inside?"

Horror turns my stomach. I stare at the wound. Angry. Bloody. Deadly. "Shit." *It's just like bio class. It's only anatomy.* I hold my hand over the wound. "Let's hope vampires can't get infections."

"What are you—"

I plunge my fingers into the wound. It's unsettling how cold her insides are. How still she is. Jordan spews profanities behind me, but I shut my eyes and focus on what I'm feeling. Soft flesh. Smooth bones. Hard muscle.

Something sharp pokes into my forefinger, and I flinch.

"What is it? What happened?"

"I think I found it." Carefully, I feel for the press of wood and trap it between my fingers. I retract my hand slowly, afraid to hurt her, but she's still unconscious. Unmoving. I drop the sliver of wood on the floor, my skin covered in her blood. "Come on, Claire. Wake up." Nothing happens, and panic settles behind my ribs. "Was that the only piece missing?"

Jordan fits the splinter to the broken part of the stake. "Yeah, that should be it."

"Then why isn't she waking up? Why isn't she healing?" Claire isn't supposed to die. There's no death in her future. All those times she touched me and I saw nothing . . . She can't just *die*. Not now. Not like this. "There has to be something. There has to be—"

The answer comes in a rush, and it's so obvious, I don't know how I didn't see it before.

I drag myself back to my feet and race to the kitchen. The tap runs hot as I scrub her blood from my skin. When my fingers are clean, I grab a knife from the block on the counter.

"What are you doing?"

"She's a vampire," I say, running back to the dining room. "She needs blood."

"Elise—"

I draw the edge of the blade across my wrist. The cut is uneven, and it stings worse than I expect, but blood beads quickly along the edges, which is the point.

"No way. You can't let her bite you." Jordan stands in my way, blocking me from Claire. "What if she starts drinking and doesn't stop?"

"She protected you, Jordan. She doesn't deserve to die." I push past him and kneel beside Claire, leaning over her still form. She said once that the Veil would never let me host, but I can't lose her. Not like this. "I have to try."

"Wait—"

I press my bleeding wrist to Claire's lips, ignoring Jordan's plea, but nothing happens. A surge of fear builds inside me, woven through with shame. I'm too late. I was foolish to think I could save a vampire. If I had warned Claire about Delilah the moment she first showed up, maybe—

Sudden pressure against my wrist stops the swirl of panicked thoughts. Twin pricks of pain make me gasp, and then I'm warm and tingling all over. The whole world falls away except Claire's lips against my skin and the pull of blood from my veins.

My brain feels buzzy even as my whole body relaxes. I sigh as I lean into her, wishing this could last forever. I feel powerful. Wanted. Like I'm the sun she orbits. It's intoxicating. It's freeing. It's—

It's starting to hurt.

Claire bites down harder. She draws my blood faster and faster as her wound begins to close. The room spins out of control. The edges of my vision go black. Her hands curl around my arm, fingers digging in deep. Bruising. Crushing.

Distant and muffled, I hear Jordan yelling. There's a touch at my shoulder. Pressure on my arm. Death in my head. The sound of wood striking flesh.

And then I'm free-falling into unconsciousness.

34

Elise

Someone calls my name, pulling me from sleep. I shift. Softness cushions the ache in my body as my eyes flutter open. The light is harsh, but Jordan kneels beside me with a bottle of water.

I reach for it, and a blanket slips from my shoulders. My left wrist is wrapped in bandages. I stare at the white fabric, stained red, and memories come racing back.

"Where is she? Did it work? Is she okay?" I sit up too fast, and my head swims.

"She's fine." Jordan sits on the edge of the couch and uncaps the water. "At least, I think so. Her wound is mostly closed."

Jordan stares over my shoulder, and I turn to follow his gaze. Claire is propped up in Dad's recliner, a blanket over her lap. The skin on her chest has knit together, but it's still angry and red. I shudder, remembering her teeth in my flesh, her lips against my skin, but it's not a bad feeling. Not exactly.

Especially when I remember the first time I felt the press of her kiss.

"Come on. You need to hydrate." Jordan hands me the bottle and makes me take a sip. "Do you want something to eat?" He stands and heads for the kitchen.

I follow on unsteady legs. From the granite-top island, I can see most of the first floor, but it's like looking through a fun-house mirror. There's a vampire in the living room, unconscious in my father's recliner. The dining room floor is covered in blood, and the white kitchen towels are so saturated they look more black than red.

We'll have to clean before my parents get home. They can't see this.

A wave of nausea rolls through me, and I slide onto a stool. Jordan searches the cupboards, pulling out bread and a jar of crunchy peanut butter. He assembles a sandwich, but I'm not sure I could stomach one right now.

"What happened?" I ask, laying my forehead against the cool granite. A pounding ache pulses at the front of my skull. "The last thing I remember is Claire feeding from me. How did you get her to stop?"

Jordan freezes with the knife poised over the bread. "I . . . uh . . . I may have hit her with the stake. In the head."

"You what?"

"She wouldn't let go! I couldn't let her kill you!"

I should be upset that he brained the vampire I was trying to save. Instead, uncontrollable laughter bubbles up from deep inside, shaking me until my whole body hurts. Jordan glances over his shoulder at me. A sheepish smile pulls at his lips until my laughter grows contagious, and he doubles over, too.

"What the hell are our lives?" I ask as I finally raise my head off the counter.

Jordan slides the peanut butter sandwich in front of me. "Really, really weird." He says it so matter-of-factly that I burst into laughter again. Except this time, he doesn't join in.

I swallow fresh nerves as he studies me, his brown, nimble fingers drumming against the counter. "What is it?"

"Nothing." But he says it too quickly, dropping his gaze. He picks up half the sandwich and takes a huge bite, like he's buying time while he chews.

"Jordan."

"It's probably nothing," he says after he swallows, and I wait him out. Finally, he drops the sandwich on the plate and glances into the living room. "It's just . . . Is there something going on between you and Claire?"

"What?" The question catches me off guard, but my cheeks flush with heat. "Why would you ask that?"

"I don't know. I just get a vibe between you two."

"A vibe. Seriously?" Yet even as I deny his claims, something uneasy twists in my chest. I never told my friends about the kiss at the blood bar, but only because it wasn't a real kiss. It didn't mean anything. "Jordan, you know I'm straight."

He fidgets with the plate, turning it round and round. "No, I know. It's just that I thought *I* was straight . . . until I didn't. And the way you stood up for her at my place, and the way you look at her . . . I don't know. I just get a vibe."

"But shouldn't I know by now? You realized you liked multiple genders when you were twelve. And it's not like I think there's anything wrong with being queer. I would know if I liked more than just boys." I'm rambling, but Jordan can't possibly be right. There's no reason I would hide something like this from myself.

Except . . . There are all those times I reached for her hand, all those times I was desperate for her touch. I told myself I missed touching *anyone*, that I only reached for her because I couldn't see her death, but what if I was wrong? Even that night on campus, I felt drawn to her like gravity.

I keep telling myself that kiss at the blood bar meant nothing, but maybe it did. Maybe it shifted something, somewhere deep down. Or awakened it. Or . . . however this works.

Jordan rests a hand on my bandaged wrist. "Maybe I'm wrong, but it's okay to realize you're not exactly who you thought. There's no expiration date on coming out." He grins. "Besides, it's always nice to have another member on Team Bisexual."

All I can offer is a weak smile. I don't know what to say. Everything I thought I knew about myself is reorganizing inside me. Part of me thinks he can't possibly be right—that I should have *known* by now if I was into girls.

And yet.

"You're alive." Jordan's hand slips from my wrist.

"Not exactly," says a sleepy voice behind me.

I swivel around on the stool and find Claire. She still looks paler than normal, but the wound on her chest has fully disappeared. Her hair is a mess, and her eyes are blurry with sleep. Or perhaps a concussion. Can vampires get concussions? Maybe not.

"How are you feeling?" I slip off the stool and close the few remaining steps between us. "Are you okay?"

"Are *you?*" She reaches for my arm and traces her fingers along the edge of the bandage. My heart gallops in my chest, but that doesn't mean anything. "You shouldn't need this. Can I check?"

I nod, and she peels away the bandage. Underneath, my skin is smooth. There's no sign of the knife wound. No sign of teeth marks. There isn't even a scar.

Claire traces my healed wrist with her thumb. "I am so sorry, Elise. I never should have bitten you. I never meant to hurt you."

Her voice catches, and when I glance up, there are tears in her eyes.

"You didn't hurt me," I say, even though by the end, it did hurt a little. "I chose this. I knew the risks."

"But why? I've been an absolute ass this week."

"You weren't the only one who messed up." I brush the tears from her cheeks, but when I remember Jordan standing behind us, I drop my hand. "Besides, even if you were, I still wouldn't let you die."

Claire shakes her head. "I'm already dead, Elise."

"No, you're not. Not to me."

The front door slams, and all three of us flinch. I whirl around to find my parents standing in the foyer. Richie comes tearing down the stairs and sprints around the corner, heading for her food bowl. The cat slips in the pool of blood, meows indignantly, and runs off, leaving a path of bloody paw prints in her wake.

"What the hell is going on here?" Dad demands in a voice I haven't heard since Nick crashed the car into the garage.

I glance at Claire, who looks as horrified as I feel. What are we supposed to do? My parents can't know about this. I can't put them in Delilah's path.

Richie jumps onto the counter, and I scoop her up before she can get blood anywhere else. Guilt tightens my throat, but I know what I have to do, how to keep them safe. I reach for Claire's hand and squeeze tight.

"I need you to send them away."

35

Claire

"Are you sure?" I understand what Elise is asking, but I can't believe she'd want this.

Elise nods, tears filling her eyes as the cat squirms in her grip. "Please. They can't know."

"We're not going anywhere." Philip Beaumont kneels beside the pool of red and glares up at us. "Why is there blood all over the floor?"

"You didn't join a cult, did you?" her mother asks.

"She's not in a cult, Christina."

"How would you know? I've been the only one keeping an eye on her since Nick died!"

Philip stands and turns to his wife. "How many times do I have to apologize?"

The cat yowls, like she wants to join the argument, and my head throbs with pain. This is getting us nowhere. In the space of a heartbeat, I cross the room and stand before Elise's parents.

"Don't move. Don't speak." I tether my mind to theirs, but the aching in my skull deepens. It shouldn't hurt like this after feeding. It shouldn't hurt *at all*. I don't remember smacking my head when I fell . . .

The memory rushes in, and I turn around to glare at Jordan. "You hit me."

Jordan backs away until he's pressed against the fridge door. His elbow hits the ice maker, and several cubes come tumbling out. "Sorry. Please don't bite me."

"I won't hurt you for protecting Elise." I mean for the words to come out light, but the admission leaves me raw in a way I didn't expect. Especially when Elise is staring at her frozen parents with a mixture of curiosity and horror.

Her reaction pummels my bruised heart. I don't understand why she bothered to save me if she's embarrassed by my existence. If she—

No. I can't keep doing this. I can't keep spinning off into the worst possible conclusions. Not after Elise risked her life to help me.

It's a good thing her brother has terrible aim. A few inches lower, and I would have died right there on the sidewalk.

"Come on." I walk toward the sliding glass door off the kitchen. "Let's talk outside."

Elise hands the cat to Jordan and hurries after me. "We don't need to talk," she says when she catches up. "I know what I want."

Though it's not what she means, my mind goes to the brush of her fingers across my face. The concern in her eyes. The things Jordan said to her as I came back to myself.

There's no expiration date on coming out.

I push the words out of my head. That conversation wasn't for my benefit. Even if Elise is bisexual, that doesn't mean she has any interest in me.

"Elise, compelling your parents—"

"It's the only way," she says, cutting me off. The fenced-in back-yard feels secluded despite the houses on either side, but she still keeps her voice low. "I won't let Delilah hurt them. As long as they're here, they're not safe." Elise stares at the starry sky, but that doesn't hide the grief that creases her brow. It doesn't hide the tremble in her bottom lip. "Please, Claire."

The way she says my name picks at my heart, but every time Elise yelled at me for using compulsion rings through my head. Of all the inhuman parts of me, compulsion was the thing she hated most. Even more than the blood. This can't be what she wants.

"Are you sure?" I ask again, resting my hands on her shoulders. She meets my gaze and nods, but she looks cold and miserable and so very alone. Before I realize what I'm doing, I draw her close. "I'm so sorry this is happening to you."

Elise leans into my embrace, wrapping her arms tight around me. "I'm going to fix it." Her words are fierce, like she's trying to convince herself as much as me. "I'll figure out the key. I'll save you and Nick and make the Veil leave us alone. I'll give Maggie a better death. My mom, too." She pulls away and stares at me with those ocean eyes. "I just need you to send them away until it's safe."

My dead heart constricts, and I squeeze her hands in mine. I still worry she'll regret it, that she'll resent me for agreeing, but she's right. They'll be safer out of town until all this is over. "Okay."

Inside, Jordan is losing the battle to wash my blood off the cat's paws. He nods at me, and it's like our relationship has shifted, like we've bonded over our desire to protect Elise. Her parents are still frozen in the dining room, and I grab hold of their minds as I approach.

"When you came home tonight," I begin, compelling the

Beaumonts as one, "your daughter was in the living room doing homework with Jordan. Elise was happy to see you, and the house was exactly as you left it."

"They're such good kids," Christina says, her eyes glazed over. Her husband nods.

I lower my voice so Jordan won't hear where I'm sending them, for his safety as much as theirs. "You've planned a trip to visit the eastern shores of Maine. You're leaving tonight, while your daughter remains safe at home. You will stay away until Elise calls and asks you to come home. Understood?"

Christina smiles at Philip. "I'm so glad we're finally doing this."

"And Elise will be okay until we get back," he says, kissing his wife gently.

Guilt twists through me, but this is what Elise wanted. "Go pack your things. You want to be on the road in five minutes."

The parents hurry upstairs, and I let the tether between us drop, confident the compulsion is secure. When I turn around, Elise is in the kitchen with Jordan, helping him dry off the cat.

Elise seems so sure that she'll figure out the key, but I can't let myself believe it. Henri and Luca will never allow her to master that kind of power. It'll be safer if she doesn't try. She could still have her brother back, if she's willing to accept this new version of him.

I skirt around the pool of blood and sit at the kitchen island, a new plan taking shape. If I can kill Rose, she won't be able to force Nick to murder Elise's friends. He'll never be the boy he was before, but he should be closer without Rose's influence.

Maybe that will be enough.

The cat finally escapes Jordan, and it saunters across the counter to me, smashing its head against my knuckles. I pick it up and scratch the top of its head. "Who's this little fluff ball?"

"Her name is Richard," Elise says, and when I glance up, there's a flush of pink across the bridge of her nose. "She also goes by Richie."

I lean forward to kiss Richie's head, but the cat puts her paw on my face and pushes me back. She's still purring like a lawn mower, though.

"Well, that's just perfect." Jordan dabs a fresh paper towel to the scratches on his arms, courtesy of Richie's bath in the sink. "She tears me apart, then falls in love with a vampire. These cuts are going to suck in the pool."

"She probably just likes me because I smell like Elise." I say it without thinking, and embarrassment clogs my throat. "After . . . well, you know."

"That's not it." Elise reaches for Richie, but the cat buries its face in my neck. "See, she doesn't like me that much, either. She liked Nick, though, that night he came to warn me." At the mention of her brother, Elise draws back. "I still can't believe he tried to kill you."

"You know that's not him. Rose—" I start, but before I can finish, Elise's parents come back down the stairs.

Her mom unlocks the front door and swings it wide. "Bye, darling! No parties while we're gone!"

"Come here, Ellie Bean." Phillip waves his daughter over and hugs her tight. "Be good until we get back."

Elise manages a nod, but she's stiff now. Her adrenaline spikes. And when her parents close the front door, Elise turns and races up the stairs.

36

Elise

For the first time since he left for college, I pass Nick's door without touching it. My vision is blurry, everything a mess of whites and creams before I make it into my room and close myself inside.

I know my parents will be safer away from Elmsbrook, but the guilt claws at my chest anyway. What if I can't figure this out? What if Delilah kills me, and they never get a chance to say good-bye? Because I stole it. Because I—

There's a knock at my door, soft but sure. I expect it to be Jordan, but it's Claire's voice that calls my name. "Elise? You okay?"

It doesn't matter if I'm okay. I have to keep it together. Everyone is counting on me—Nick, my parents, even Maggie. Oh god. *Maggie.* There has to be a way to break the compulsion she's under. I won't lose her, too. I can't.

"I'm fine," I call, wiping my cheeks on the ends of my sleeves.

The door creaks open, and Claire leans in to check on me. She doesn't step past the threshold, though. She's paler than normal, and there are dark bruises under her eyes. Her hair slides past her shoulders like curtains of silk.

She still looks dangerous, but I see the vulnerability now. There's sadness behind her hazel eyes. Questioning in the rise of her brow. The curve of her neck. I rub my thumb along my wrist, remembering the press of her lips. The bite of her teeth.

Heat flushes my face, but it doesn't mean anything. Even straight girls can tell when other girls are beautiful. I'm overthinking everything because of what Jordan said. Besides, even if I *did* feel something, I don't have time for that. I have to figure out how to save my brother and put my family back together.

But Claire is still standing in my doorway, and there's this fluttering in my chest. I clear my throat. "It's okay if you come in."

She enters slowly and closes the door. Though it's only the second time she's been in this space, Claire doesn't let her gaze wander over my things. She's focused on me, and her attention makes my insides do strange things. "I made sure your parents will be happy. They'll enjoy the trip."

I nod. Emotion tries to rise up, but I shove it down. "Where did you send them?"

"It's probably safer for everyone if you don't know." Claire closes the space between us. My breath catches in my throat, but she doesn't reach for me. I wish she would. "They'll come back whenever you're ready. All you have to do is call, and they'll come home."

"So long as they're safe—"

"They are."

"Then we have to make Elmsbrook safe, too. We have to deal with Delilah and save Nick so I can bring our parents back." I turn on my heel, putting space between us as my conviction deflates. "I . . . I talked to Hazel. She doesn't know anything about a key."

I risk a glance at Claire, but she doesn't seem surprised.

"Jordan mentioned that," she says. "Before Nick stabbed me."

"Right." I flinch at the reminder of my brother's violence. "What do I do? If Hazel doesn't know, how am I supposed to uncover the key? I'm still too new at everything, and who knows when Delilah will force Nick to kill again or if he'll try to come after you."

When I turn to pace the other way, Claire steps into my path. She rests her hands on my shoulders, the cold from her touch penetrating all the way to my skin. Goosebumps raise along my arms. "You're not alone anymore. We'll figure this out together." Her words are whisper soft, and I want so desperately to believe her.

"But if Hazel doesn't know, and the Veil won't teach me—"

"Forget the Veil." Claire brushes a loose piece of hair behind my ear.

A strange warmth settles in my gut, but it can't erase the guilt nagging at the back of my mind. "I swear I didn't know that Delilah and Rose were the same person. I never meant to hurt you. I was just trying to figure out what to do with this . . ." I hold up my hands between us. "This curse. I'm sorry I never said anything."

Claire takes my hands in hers, and a thrill spreads through me. "I'm sorry about a lot of things, too. Anything you want to know, just ask. I'll tell you every detail."

As she speaks, my gaze drifts to her lips. I want to see her smile. I want— No. Claire and I, we're . . . friends. There's nothing romantic brewing between us.

"Is there anything you want to know?" Her hands leave mine, but her touch doesn't stray far. It skims along my forearms before coming to rest at my waist.

I suck in a breath, and my body seems to move on its own. The space between us shrinks to almost nothing. I look up to meet her gaze, and the tilt of my head brings her lips so close to mine. Her touch shifts to my back, and the tiny space between our bodies disappears. "Questions can wait."

We were this close while we danced, but this feels different. The silence around us is electric with possibility, with intention, the way the crowded dance floor never could have been.

What are we doing? she'd asked then, the same fire in her eyes that's there now.

Isn't it obvious? But it wasn't obvious, not even to me. I wanted so much more than I let myself believe.

If I was straight, would my heart still beat this hard?

Would my hands stray to her neck like this? Would my fingers twine through her hair?

I catch myself holding my breath, waiting for the moment when she leans forward and kisses me. When we kissed before, it didn't feel like this. That moment was born out of panic and worry. But this . . . I feel like my heart will shatter into a thousand pieces if she doesn't close this final space between us.

"Please."

"Please what?" she asks, and it's the most exquisite torture.

"Kiss me."

Claire studies me, her hazel eyes like flowers in the soft light, and a tentative smile pulls at her lips. She tips her forehead against mine. "Are you sure?"

I'm not sure of anything right now, but my heart is screaming at me, and my mind is a kaleidoscope of fast-moving memories. Every time Claire has touched me. Every time I've reached for her hand. Every argument and apology and the desperate panic I felt when I thought she was dying.

Instead of answering with words, I tilt my face to hers and wait, giving her a chance to pull away, a chance to make a different decision. Claire hesitates, but before rejection can fully infect my heart, she presses her lips to mine.

Our first real kiss is gentle. Tentative. It's like we've torn out our hearts and are waiting to see if the other person will crush it or keep it safe. But then there's this hitch in my chest, this fire in my veins, and I lean into the kiss. I pull her close. I want so much more.

My bedroom door bursts open, slamming against the wall. Claire and I spring apart, and I'm gasping for breath like I've been swimming for hours. Jordan stands in the threshold. I'm about to yell at him for barging in, but then I recognize the fear in his eyes.

"What is it?"

"There's . . . There's someone downstairs," he says, redirecting his attention to Claire. "I think they're a vampire."

37

Claire

Fear erases the very different feeling that was buzzing through me moments before. "Is it Rose?"

Jordan glances out the doorway. "I don't know. Does she wear a lot of suits?"

Fuck.

The front door is open, but Wyn is trapped on the other side of the threshold. They stand under the glow of the porch light, dressed in their usual tailored suit and tie. As I descend the stairs, I assess my strength. The wound in my chest is closed, but I'm still healing. Wyn is older than me, and they feed more regularly, too. I won't stand a chance if it comes to blows.

"What the hell are you doing here?" I ask, coming to a stop before the doorframe.

Wyn looks up from examining their short fingernails. "I told you I was on my way. Better me than someone else." They peer up the stairs, and without turning, I hear the flutter of two heartbeats drawing close. Elise's steady and strong. Jordan's, as ever, a bit panicked. "Elise, nice to see you again."

"Leave her out of this."

My former boss sighs and runs a hand through their floppy hair. "I can't very well leave out the Death Oracle. She's the whole point." Wyn returns their attention to me, and after a moment's examination, they groan. "How many times did I warn you not to fall in love with your charge?"

Behind me, Elise's heart skips a beat, and I shove down the surge of embarrassment. "I'm not letting you kidnap her so she can serve the Veil."

"No one said anything about kidnapping. The Death Oracle deserves to have full control of her power. If you won't shepherd her, I will." Wyn glances over their shoulder at the neighborhood around us. "Look, why don't we have this conversation inside. Elise?"

"Absolutely not," I say. "You can stay out there."

There's movement behind me, and then Elise is by my side. "If I let you in, do you promise not to harm anyone in this house?"

"You have my word." Wyn inclines their head.

"Elise, you can't trust—"

"Then please, come in."

The moment the words pass her lips, there's pain. Wyn grabs me by the throat and slams me against the nearest wall. "Why are you always so stubborn? I'm trying to help you!" Wyn snarls, and a bone-deep fear washes through me. But then they pause, nostrils flaring as they breathe deeply. "Why does this place reek of your blood?"

"Because my brother tried to kill her," Elise says, slamming her front door and whirling around. "Let her go. Now."

"What?" Wyn turns and notices the blood all over the dining room floor. They release me, and concern softens their expression. "Nicholas Beaumont is alive?"

"Rose turned him." I push away from the wall and press two fingers against the tender, freshly healed skin below my collarbone.

"She compelled him to jam a wooden stake into my chest. He's killed humans, too."

Elise flinches. "I can't leave my brother like this. I have to make him human again."

"Which Henri and Luca *confirmed* was possible," I say before Wyn can object. "But they won't allow it. Not for Nick. Not for me. Not for anyone."

Wyn glances from me to Elise, but then their gaze travels up the stairs and their brow creases. "Who the hell is that?"

"Oh, I'm—" Jordan's voice cracks and he clears his throat. "I'm Jordan."

"You're *human*." Wyn snaps their attention back to me. "Why is there an uncompelled human listening to our conversation?"

"That's my fault," Elise says, blocking the foot of the stairs. "I told my friends everything before Claire warned me not to. But they've been helping with the training and—"

"Friends? Plural?" Wyn sighs and pinches the bridge of their nose. "Are there any shepherd protocols you *haven't* broken? Maybe I shouldn't convince you to stay."

Even though I have no intention of helping the Veil, it stings to hear the disappointment in Wyn's voice. "How can you support Luca and Henri when they lied to everyone? How can you choose them over me?" I lower my voice so Elise won't hear this next bit. "Luca was willing to kill her to keep mortality a secret."

Shock registers in Wyn's eyes, but they shake their head. "I'm sure he has a good reason." But they don't sound sure, and I seize the opening.

"But what if he doesn't? What if neither of them do?" I think of all the paranormals I've tracked for Luca over the years, creatures who dared seek a future outside the bounds of what the Veil deemed appropriate. I think of Fiona, whose blood will forever stain my existence, all because I didn't think I had a choice.

All because Luca and Henri said it was her or me.

I can't live like this anymore. I won't let Elise's future get tied to theirs.

"Why should two vampires make the rules for the entire paranormal world? Why should they decide whether I can be human? What have they done to earn our loyalty?"

"Claire—"

"We do all the work, anyway! We're the ones who shepherd new vampires. We're the ones who risk life and limb to enforce the rules they create." I'm pacing now, a frantic energy pulsing through me. "And the *one* time I asked for anything in return, Henri said no. They don't deserve our devotion."

Wyn steps into my path and grips my shoulders. "Would you listen to yourself? You can't mount a one-vampire revolution and end up anything but dead. Or worse, completely unraveled."

"Elise would never do that." I knock Wyn's hands away. "And if you're willing to let Luca kill her so the next Death Oracle can dismantle me, then you might as well rip out my heart right now."

A growl rumbles in Wyn's throat. "You are such a pain in the ass!"

"They argue more than you and Nick ever did," Jordan whispers when he reaches Elise.

"No one asked you," I snap, but Wyn bursts out laughing. "What could possibly be funny right now?"

"It's completely absurd." Wyn braces their hands on their knees. "I've known this human for all of three minutes and already he can tell you're my reckless, impulsive kid sister."

"I am not."

"You definitely are, but it makes you fun." Finally, Wyn stops laughing. "Well, it did, anyway. I don't know how the hell I'll get you back in the Veil's good graces after this."

"Why don't we all just take a deep breath?" Elise cuts in before I can explode at Wyn for not listening. "There has to be a way to save my brother without declaring war against your bosses."

"My parents negotiate compromises all the time," Jordan adds. "We just need to figure out what each party *needs*, and what you're willing to give up."

Elise raises her hand. "They need to let me save my brother." Her ocean gaze settles on me, and blood rushes to her face. "Plus anyone else who wants to be human again."

Her attention makes me feel warm inside, but a quiet voice warns that she doesn't want me like this. That she could never truly care for a vampire. "Rose needs to pay for the damage she's done," I add.

"They might go for that, but Luca and Henri need a Death Oracle who's loyal to the Veil." Wyn crosses their arms. "They won't budge on that. Ever."

"Absolutely not." I shake my head. "I won't let them take over Elise's life."

Wyn raises an eyebrow. "Do you not get how negotiations work? It'll be hard enough getting them to agree to the brother thing, forget letting *you* become human again. They have to get something out of it, too."

"But—"

"Claire, it's okay." Elise abandons Jordan on the bottom step and reaches for my hand, lacing her fingers between mine. "I won't help Delilah kill your bosses, which means they're not going anywhere. If I have to work for them, I might as well get something out of it."

"Are you sure?" It feels like failing, letting her do this.

Elise squeezes my hand, and I wish we were alone. I wish I had time to talk her out of this. But then she nods and turns to Wyn. "There is one problem, though. I already tried contacting Hazel, and she doesn't know how to make vampires mortal. I can't agree to anything until I know how to save my brother."

A mischievous smile pulls at Wyn's lips. "Then we go back to the beginning."

38

Elise

A lot can happen when there are two highly motivated vampires in your house.

Claire and Wyn are a blur of motion as they clean blood from the dining room and push the table against the wall. Wyn dumps salt into a lopsided circle on the floor and sets pillar candles at the four cardinal directions.

"Does it matter that it's crooked?" I sit on the stairs with Jordan while the vampires work. I've changed out of my bloody clothes, replacing them with my most comfortable hoodie and leggings.

Wyn laughs. "You don't get bonus points for symmetry." They light the candles and shoo Claire toward the kitchen. "We just need a few minutes to brew your spiritual cocktail. You might want to work on your pitch. It's been awhile since Petronelle met a living Death Oracle."

"Right." According to Claire, Petronelle was the very first Death Oracle, and if anyone knows the key to mortality, it'll be her.

I abandon the stairs and stand outside the salt circle, letting the flicker of tiny flames ease the tension from my shoulders. So much depends on this ritual being successful. If I screw this up, I'll never convince the Veil leaders to let me save my brother.

Or Claire.

In the kitchen, Claire and Wyn tend to a small pot on the stove. They add an obscene amount of dried herbs to the mixture, arguing the entire time. At least, it looks like arguing. I can't hear them, but Claire keeps glaring at Wyn, who mostly looks annoyed. Then every so often, Claire's gaze meets mine, and my insides feel like they're on fire.

"So," Jordan whispers, joining me in the dining room, "are we going to talk about what happened in your bedroom?"

"There's nothing to talk about," I say, even as my face burns. "A certain *someone* burst into my room."

"Sorry about that," he says, except he doesn't actually sound sorry. He grins and waggles his eyebrows at me. "It looked like you were having fun, though."

"Jordan."

"What? She obviously likes you. Why else would she keep staring?"

From the kitchen, Claire clears her throat. "I'm *concerned* because I don't think this is safe." She turns her attention to Wyn. "Are you sure this is a good idea?"

"Of course I am." Wyn turns off the stove and pours a muddy green mixture into a mug. It looks—and smells—worse than the one I made. "If Elise wants to make your scrawny ass human, Petronelle is her best bet."

Claire rolls her eyes. "She isn't doing it for me. She's doing it for her brother."

Beneath the irritation, there's a sadness to Claire's words.

"Not just him." I wish we were alone. I wish I could help her see how much I care. That I want her to be happy, whatever that looks like, but I don't have the courage to say that out loud, especially with an audience.

"Are there any side effects?" Jordan asks. "She won't fry Elise's brain or anything, right?"

Wyn shrugs. "Probably not."

A low growl rumbles through the room, and Claire moves in a blur, blocking me from Wyn. "We didn't agree to *probably*. I'm not letting Petronelle melt Elise's mind."

"I'll be okay." I reach for Claire's arm and turn her to face me. "If this is what it takes to get the key, I want to do it."

"Are you sure?" Her voice is impossibly soft, and it makes my heart skip a beat. "We can find another way."

"This *is* the other way. Trust me. I can handle this. I already talked to Hazel, how much worse can Petronelle be?"

"See? It's fine." Wyn brings me the mug of foul-smelling potion. "Drink this."

I accept the drink and step into the circle. Wyn closes it behind me, adding more salt as I sniff the contents. It's so violently bitter and earthy that I barely suppress a gag. "On a scale of one to ten, how gross is this?"

"I've never tried it," Wyn says. "Only Death Oracles and witches can contact their magical line. But Ingrid said it tastes worse than it smells."

"Wonderful." I sit on the floor so I don't collapse like last time. "Anything I need to do besides drink this?"

"Nope. It'll be as easy as falling asleep." Wyn settles onto a chair and props their feet on the table. "You'll want to drink that before it gets cold. I hear it gets worse."

"Great." I brace myself and toss back the hot, sludgy, herb-infused mixture. It's bitter, gritty, and smoky all at once, and it's a miracle I don't choke on it. My entire body shudders when I manage to swallow.

Wyn laughs, and Claire smacks their shoulder. They start to argue, but the words feel far away. The room spins, and a weightlessness settles over my limbs. Then I'm falling, my back hitting the floor, and the world goes stark white behind my eyelids.

When I manage to open my eyes, pastel mists—blues and pinks and purples—swirl around me. The air tugs at my limbs until I'm standing, and it nudges me along. This place feels different, more vibrant, than the one where I visited Hazel. It feels bigger, somehow, too. The colorful mist urges me forward, like I'm late for a meeting.

"Petronelle?"

My voice gets sucked into the mist, swirling around me like a thousand tiny reverberations. Like ripples in a pond.

A cascade of whispering voices, dozens of them, ebb and flow around me, but I can't make out the words. I whirl around, searching for their source, but there's only fog.

"Please, I need your help." I spin again, looking for any change in the colorful mist. "I need the key."

The voices die, and the sudden silence hangs heavy in the air. My heart beats loud in the quiet, the rush of blood through my veins like the whoosh of a far-off river. In front of me, purple mist curls in on itself, contorting from one face to another. Some old. Some young. I recognize Hazel in the mist, her expression twisted into a scowl, before the purple fog transforms into someone else.

Then a flash of light burns away the color, leaving me alone.

"It's been a long time since one of us learned about the key," a clear voice says behind me.

I turn and find a white girl standing a few paces away. She doesn't look much older than me, but there's this sense of agelessness about her. She wears her brown hair in loose braids that circle her head like a crown, and her dress looks like something out of the 1600s, with puffy upper sleeves, tailored bodice, and a floor-length skirt that hides her shape.

"Petronelle?" I ask, and she nods as she continues her approach. "Do you know how the key works?"

"I do." She stops in front of me, her gaze flickering to my outfit. I glance down, feeling underdressed in my hoodie and leggings. "You may call me Petra, but we must hurry. The longer you remain here, the shorter your life becomes."

"What?" No one said anything about that.

"Hazel should have warned you when you met. Contacting us should be a last resort." Petra offers a sympathetic smile.

Go back, kid. If you're quick, you may only lose a couple weeks.

I shudder, realizing for the first time what Hazel meant by those words. "But you know how the key works. You can help me."

"I do, and I will, if you're willing to pay the price." Petra runs her fingers through a growing curl of purple mist. "I discovered the key, actually. I didn't realize it would cause such tension among the founders."

"Founders?"

Petra tilts her head, like she's confused by my ignorance. "Henri Guillebeaux, Luca Tagliaferro, and Jessamine Prathor."

That last name picks at a fuzzy memory, but I can't remember where I've heard it. "What happened to her?"

With a flick of her wrist, Petra shapes the purple mist into a large circle. The center glows bright before settling into a single image. Three vampires, wearing outfits from a similar era as Petra's dress, stand at the center.

"Henri and Luca despised the very concept of the key," Petra says, pointing to each vampire in turn. "Jessamine fought them on it. She wanted to make the option available to all."

I step closer, examining the image. Something about Jessamine is so familiar, with her long dark hair and confident smile. "What happened to her?"

"She disappeared. The remaining founders claimed Jessamine grew bored of her role and defected to parts unknown. They labeled her a traitor and said the Veil was stronger without her. As for the key, I was told to forget the possibility existed." Petra tugs at the edge of her dress sleeve. "I never found proof, but I believe Henri and Luca killed Jessamine to ensure the key remained secret. They even made me unravel what was left of her line."

"What?" Panic pounds in my chest. "Why?"

"The official reasons were numerous, but I believe now that it was merely a precaution. Luca feared they'd question Jessamine's absence and retaliate." Petra shakes her head, the grief in her eyes unmistakable. "I didn't think I had a choice, but I've regretted it ever since."

Horror and revulsion grow toxic inside me, but I can't upset Petra before she gives me the key. I step closer to the image, memorizing the faces of Luca and Henri, the vampires I'll have to serve if I want my brother safe. Vampires who were willing to destroy their own kind to keep the key hidden.

My gaze shifts to Jessamine, her pale skin and dark hair and sharp eyes. I imagine what she'd look like today, in modern clothes instead of the puffy dress, and my heart stops.

I've gone by many names over the centuries, but you can call me Delilah.

Henri and Luca are still in charge, yes? I would very much like to kill those controlling bastards.

My hands shake, and I step back from the image.

I am nothing like those monsters. They took everything from me.

"Elise?" Petra grasps my trembling hands. "Are you well? Should I send you back?"

"No." The word scrapes over my tongue, and I focus on the reason I'm here. Everything else can wait. "I'm not leaving without the key."

Petra nods, but there's suspicion in the arch of her brow. "I can give it to you, but there's a cost."

"Anything."

"Never agree until you know the price, especially in our world." Petra waves her hand, and the image of the founders disappears. "Taking this path will change your fate."

It doesn't matter. So long as I get Nick back, I don't care what happens to me.

Petronelle holds out a hand, and I place mine in hers. She closes her eyes and breathes deep. "If I give you the key, the threads of your fate will unravel. Death will come for you far sooner than it should."

I pull my hand from hers. "How soon?"

"It's hard to know. Our fates are not as tightly woven as the humans we help." Petra offers a sympathetic smile. "Our threads slip and change often, but accepting the key will break some of yours."

Part of me wants to ask what broken threads mean, but I know enough about our power to understand it's not good. If Claire were here, she wouldn't allow this. Jordan and Maggie wouldn't, either. Even the vampire version of my brother wouldn't let me do this.

But they aren't here to stop me.

For the first time since I inherited this power, the choice is fully my own.

39

Claire

I don't like this. At all.

Elise seems okay—she hasn't moved since her eyes fluttered shut—but with every minute that passes, my worry grows. I hate not knowing what Petronelle is saying to her. I hate not knowing if Elise connected with the original Death Oracle at all. It's equally possible Hazel is giving her hell.

Nervous energy vibrates through me. "How long should this last?"

"It takes as long as it takes," Wyn says, which isn't helpful.

"That's not a real answer." I pace toward the front of the house, and my attention turns to Jordan. He's sitting on the stairs, elbows braced against his thighs, head resting in his hands. I pause in front of him. "Is it?"

The boy glances up then looks over his shoulder at Wyn. "I . . . probably shouldn't get in the middle of this." Jordan rubs the back of his neck. "It has been a long time, though. Are you sure this is safe?"

I find myself softening toward Jordan, and not just because what he said to Elise might have led to the kiss in her bedroom. He's clearly uncomfortable around vampires, yet he stuck around for Elise. He didn't try to talk her out of liking me. He gets some credit for that.

"I'm sure she's fine." Wyn examines their nails. "Ingrid has used this ritual herself. Most of her coven has. Granted, there's always a cost for contacting the spirit realm, but—"

"A *cost?*" A growl rumbles in my throat. "What do you mean, a *cost?*"

"You know how witches are about balance. Of course there's a cost."

"Damn it, Wyn!" If they were anyone else, they'd get a fist to the nose. "You should have told me."

"Elise already talked to Hazel. I assumed you knew the risks."

"I didn't." I skirt around the edge of the circle, hands clenched into fists. "Wake her up. Get her back, *now.*"

Wyn sighs. "I really wish you hadn't fallen for her."

Their words stop me in my tracks, and a strange feeling curls through my chest. Heat flares in my face. "I didn't. I—"

A piercing scream cuts me off, the sound reverberating through my bones. Elise's face twists with pain as her back arches off the ground.

"Elise." I rush forward, desperate to get to her side, but a strong grip tightens around my wrist.

"You can't break the circle, Claire. Not until she wakes up."

"We can't just stand here." I force my gaze past Elise, to where Jordan waits at the base of the stairs. His brown eyes reflect my fear, and I know he's as worried as I am. "Do something, Jordan. Please."

"Kid, if you move a muscle, I will snap your neck." Wyn drags me farther from the circle, and though Jordan glances from Wyn to Elise, ultimately, he stays where he is.

The screams stop, but only long enough for Elise to draw a breath. They begin again, the sound raw and terrible, and I can't let it continue. I pull as hard as I can, trying to break Wyn's grip. "She's dying!"

"I don't think so." Wyn is calm, which makes no sense. "Just wait."

"Wait? I'm not going to—"

A sudden silence settles over us, and this time, it stays quiet. Elise lays impossibly still, and I strain to listen for her heartbeat. For sounds of breath. Sounds of life.

Thump-thump.

Thump-thump.

The relief that rushes through me is so strong, it would send a lesser being to their knees. This time, when I tug from Wyn's grip, they let me go. I stumble forward, brush away a portion of the salt border, and drop to my knees inside the circle. I hold my breath and keep my hands pressed to the floor, afraid to hurt her.

Finally, Elise opens her eyes.

"Welcome back." My throat is tight with worry, and I'm vaguely aware of Jordan coming to stand beside us. Elise smiles up at me, and I brush the hair from her forehead. Her skin is burning hot. "How are you feeling?"

"Terrible," she says, but she sounds like herself. She sounds okay.

"You scared the hell out of me," I say, offering a hand to help her sit up.

"Sorry. Petra warned it might hurt." Elise massages her temples. "I didn't realize it would be like this."

Wyn finally seems interested, and they help Elise to her feet. "Did Petronelle give you the key?"

Elise sways a little, but before I can stand to steady her, she reaches for Jordan, gripping his bare hand with hers. Jealousy flares inside, but I let it burn out. They're friends. Besides, she can seek comfort from whoever she wants.

After several seconds, Elise smiles. "She did more than that. Petra taught me everything she knows about our abilities."

Jordan grins. "So, that means the shield . . . ?"

"Is as natural as breathing," Elise confirms, and the relief in her voice is palpable. Jordan crushes her in a hug, and she laughs as he picks her up and spins her around.

When he finally puts her down, Elise reaches for both of my hands and squeezes tight. "I know how the key works. I can make you mortal again. Nick, too. But we have to find Delilah." She looks over my shoulder at Wyn. "Call the Veil. It's time to negotiate."

———

The Veil is sending negotiators in the wake of Wyn's call, and the wait is terrible. I pace the first floor of Elise's home, worried and flustered and filled with an anxious energy I can't release. If we don't want to spend the rest of our lives hiding from the Veil, we need to secure their blessing for so many things they've already refused. To use the key. To stop Rose. To release Maggie from compulsion. I worry what they'll require in return.

Once I'm sure Elise is safe, I convince Wyn to help me search for Rose. If we know where she's hiding, that'll be one less excuse for the Veil's negotiators.

We leave Jordan in charge—he's proven that he'll do anything to keep Elise safe—and scour the neighborhoods of Elmsbrook. Wyn and I check all the vacant buildings, but we can't find Rose anywhere. The failure leaves me irritable, but as the sun peeks over the horizon, I'm too worried about Elise to continue the search.

As we pass through a park, the first rays of sun scorch across my skin, and I hiss with pain.

"You need to feed," Wyn says.

"I'm fine."

"Do you *want* Rose to rip out your heart?" They shoot me a look, and I kick a pebble down the path. "Stop being so stubborn. You need to replenish your strength." Wyn tilts their face to the sky and sniffs the air. "There are at least six joggers in the park already, the masochists."

"Fine," I grumble and step off the path. It's not long before two runners come our way, and we snatch them both. The blood is warm against my tongue, but it lacks Elise's power. Still, it does what it needs to do. Some of the ache leaches out of my body.

"Forget this ever happened," I say, compelling the jogger and sending her back on her run. The blood is enough to face the sun, but Wyn convinces me to drink from three more before we leave the park.

As much as I hate it, the blood helps. With any luck, this will be the last time I ever need it.

I hold on to that dizzying hope all the way back to Elise. She gave me the code to the electric lock, and when we slip through the front door, she and Jordan are asleep in the living room. Jordan is curled up in the armchair, like he dozed off while keeping watch. Elise is on the couch, a blanket tucked to her chin, her hair loose around her shoulders.

I lean against the wall as I watch her sleep, and the steady rise and fall of her chest brings immeasurable comfort. Her heart is strong. Her breathing even.

"You've got it bad for her." Wyn's voice is quiet behind me.

Though I expected judgment, their tone is carefully neutral. "I know," I say, glancing at Wyn. "I've never met anyone like her. She's curious about everything and incredibly clever. She's kind, too, even to me. And if she can make me human . . ." I don't dare speak the rest out loud. That maybe, just maybe, she could love me if I were mortal like her.

"Can she do this?" Wyn brushes a drop of blood from the corner of their lips. "The whole plan rests on her ability to wield the key."

There's a not-small part of me that wants Elise to wait at home. It feels reckless to bring her to Rose. Foolish to risk her life, but she's the Death Oracle. No one else can take her place. "If Elise says she can do it, I believe her."

"I hope you're right." Wyn turns on their heel and rolls up the sleeves of their button-down. "I'll pick up the compelled friend. Maggie, right?" They wait for my nod. After Wyn called the Veil, we agreed it was safer to have Maggie here while we negotiated. Elise didn't want Rose to compel Maggie again or make her do something terrible. "While I'm gone, stay focused on the *mission*, Claire. Now isn't the time for confessions of love."

"Goodbye, Wyn." Once the door closes behind them, I roll my eyes. I'm perfectly capable of staying focused.

Probably.

While my mortals sleep, I worry what the day will bring. I don't know who the Veil will send to negotiate—Henri?—but I think through every possible rejection and argument the Veil could make. Thankfully, now that Petra has given Elise complete control over her power, Luca should be less willing to start over with someone new.

I hate that he ever considered it. I hate that our best-case scenario still leaves Elise working for him. Tagliaferro doesn't deserve her. None of them do. Not even me.

"Good morning." Elise's voice pulls me from my thoughts. She untangles herself from the blanket and sits up.

"Good afternoon."

She winces. "That late, huh?"

"Wyn should be back with Maggie soon." I gesture to Jordan. "He should probably go home, though. The Veil won't let Jordan keep his memories if they find out."

"I'll wake him up in a bit." Elise rubs the sleep from her eyes and studies me. "You look better." Her face flushes with sudden heat. "Not that you looked bad before. It's just— You don't look as pale now."

Her heart rate speeds up in time with her jumbled explanation, and despite Wyn's warning, I feel warm inside.

"I fed while I was out," I admit, and she doesn't flinch. She doesn't look away. Even so, worry tugs at my insides. "Are you sure you want to do this? We can find a way that doesn't tie you to the Veil."

Instead of offering reassurances, Elise wakes Jordan and sends him home. He tries to argue, but she shoos him out the door and makes him promise to stay away until this is all over. She only faces me once we're alone.

"Petra taught me a lot about how the Veil operates," she says, still standing by the front door. "I won't—" Elise cuts herself off, shaking her head. "For the first time since I turned sixteen, I feel like I'm in control of my future. At least, part of it."

"But—"

"Please, Claire. Let me do this." She steps onto the first stair and leans against the railing. "I'm going to take a shower. If Maggie gets here before I'm done, keep her company for me?"

"Of course," I say, even though everything inside still screams at me to protect her from the Veil. There's not much I can do, though, especially once I'm human again.

Elise disappears upstairs, and a moment later, her cat comes running out of the office. She slams her head against my shin and squeaks up at me, weaving between my legs.

"Sorry, kitten. I don't know where your momma keeps the food." As I bend to pick up the fuzzy creature, the keypad beeps and the deadbolt slides free. When the door opens, Wyn has Maggie thrown over their shoulder.

"Excuse me," they say, pushing into the house.

I shut the door. "This is not what Elise meant when she asked you to pick up her friend."

Maggie's hands are bound, and Wyn gagged her with their tie. Maggie glares at me, her red glasses slipping to the end of her nose. She slams her fists into Wyn's back.

"It's not my fault. The compulsion makes her very disagreeable." Wyn sets Maggie on one of the kitchen stools. "She went straight into attack mode."

"I'm pretty sure that's a normal human reaction to kidnapping," I say, and Maggie rolls her eyes. "I don't think the compulsion is active anyway. She's looking right at me."

"Is she?" Wyn steps back to examine Maggie, who mumbles something unintelligible. "Huh. Would you look at that." Wyn unknots their tie and removes the gag.

"What the hell is wrong with you?" Maggie raises her bound hands to wipe saliva from her lips. "Where's Elise?"

"She's fine," I promise. "She's just getting changed."

Wyn leans over and whispers, "Are you sure this is the right one? I thought you said Rose compelled her."

"Of course I'm sure," I whisper back, the words hissing through my teeth. I turn my attention back to Maggie. "I'm sorry about Wyn. They don't always remember how to interact with humans."

"Clearly." Maggie tries to pull her hands apart, but Wyn's tie holds strong. "Can you take this off? I shouldn't be a hostage in my best friend's house."

"Sure." I pause a few inches away, though, remembering what Jordan said about Maggie trying to drown Elise. "It's good you're here, actually. We need help finding Delilah."

"Yeah?" Maggie's gaze drops to the floor.

"We can't let her attack the Veil," I continue, watching as the compulsion takes hold. Her gaze becomes unfocused, and anger twists her features. "You're going to help us kill her."

Maggie lunges for me, but Wyn catches her shoulders and guides her back to the stool.

"Well, I guess you were right." Wyn bends to examine Maggie, but she won't meet their gaze. "That's a clever bit of compulsion."

"Don't give Rose that much credit." Above me, a door creaks as it swings open. Footsteps approach the stairs.

Elise appears a moment later, wet hair hanging loose around her shoulders. When she spots Maggie, she rushes down the final few steps. "Mags, you okay?"

"Delilah is going to be furious with you," Maggie says, struggling against Wyn's hold. "She'll make Nick kill everyone."

"Maggie . . ." Elise reaches out and holds tight to Maggie's hand. "We're going to fix this," she whispers. "I promise."

Before Maggie can respond, the doorbell rings. The loud chimes fill the house, and a moment later, the visitor knocks for good measure. Elise tucks her loose hair behind her ears and turns to the door.

"No, let me." I reach for her hand, her skin burning-hot from the shower. Her touch distracts me for the space of her heartbeat, but then the impatient visitor knocks again, and worry claws at my chest.

Did Henri come? Luca? And if not them, who would they send to negotiate on their behalf? I hurry to the door and peer through the peephole, my worry shifting to fear. "Abigail?" I open the door. "What are you doing here?"

"What do you think?" Abigail levels a disappointed glare at me. "Despite all the *years* I spent training you, you haven't learned how to properly follow orders."

"You're the negotiator?"

Abigail narrows her brown eyes. "Did I mumble?"

"No, ma'am."

"Good. Come on, Ingrid." Abigail motions to a petite white woman standing off to the side, who waves at Wyn through the doorway. "Invite us in."

40

Elise

"Let me get this right." The vampire Claire introduced as Abigail—a Black woman with a faintly British accent—sits across from me, consulting a scribbled list of my requests. "You want permission to make two vampires mortal *and* you want us to free this human from compulsion?"

I sit tall in my seat and try to channel Jordan's mom. She does this kind of thing all the time. Minus the vampires and witches. "Two specific vampires, yes. Claire and my brother, Nick. Plus, the Veil can never harm them or interfere with their lives. I also need you to call off your hunt for Delilah—Rose, I mean. We need her for the key."

"The key to mortality," Abigail says, sounding uncertain. "What exactly are you offering in exchange for these outrageous demands?"

Across the room, Claire keeps watch over Maggie. Ingrid gave her a sleeping potion to keep her calm while we handled negotiations, but I can't stop worrying. So much hinges on me getting this right.

"I spoke with Petronelle last night. She taught me everything she knows about our powers. I'm fully trained and ready to serve the Veil."

"That's—"

"I'm not finished," I say, which earns me a smirk from Wyn. "I will work for the Veil, but I will continue to live at home with my family. I will have a normal life between missions. And I get to decide which ones I accept."

Abigail stares at me for several seconds, like she's making sure I'm not going to interrupt again. "Well, you've imagined quite the ideal little future for yourself, haven't you?" She doesn't smile, and I don't reveal the high cost I already paid to get this far. "What leverage could you possibly have that's worth all this?"

Sweat prickles my palms. This part is a gamble, but it's all I have. I raise my chin and hold the negotiator's gaze. "I know what happened to Jessamine Prathor."

The name hangs in the air, and no one moves. I don't think any of the vampires are even breathing. Claire breaks the silence first.

"But the Prathor line was lost. Her descendants went rogue after she abandoned the Veil. They were destroyed. How could you—" Claire is cut off when Wyn smacks her arm. Neither of them is supposed to participate in the negotiation. This is all on me.

"Jessamine disappeared after Petra uncovered the key, but she didn't abandon anyone. Not intentionally." I don't have definitive proof that Delilah and Jessamine are the same person, but the picture looked so similar, and Delilah's hatred of Luca and Henri fits the story Petra told. "If the Veil agrees to my terms, I will only use the key on Claire and Nick. No one else will know about it unless I get explicit permission."

"In writing," Abigail adds, but she seems distracted now.

"Fine." I pretend the condition is an inconvenience, but I

doubt I'll ever get permission again anyway. "As for your bosses, if they agree to this, I won't tell anyone what actually happened to Jessamine. I won't share the real reason Petra unraveled her line."

Abigail doesn't seem impressed, but she scribbles something on her list and stands. "I need to make a call." She disappears into the backyard.

I let out a long sigh, all the tension that kept me upright melting from my muscles, and I rest my head against the table. There's movement next to me. Someone pulling out a chair and reaching for my hand. I recognize her touch immediately, and my heart gives a little leap in my chest. I don't know how I ignored these signs for so long.

Jordan will be insufferable when I tell him he's probably right about the whole bisexual thing.

"That went better than expected," Claire says, rubbing her thumb along my wrist. Her touch sends goosebumps all the way up my arm.

"We don't have an agreement yet." I pick my head up and squeeze her hand. "It could still fall apart. There's plenty that could go wrong with the key, too."

"One thing at a time." Claire brushes a loose strand of hair behind my ear. "It looks nice down like this. Longer than I expected, too."

My face warms, and I suddenly wish Ingrid and Wyn weren't here. At least they're not watching. They're in the living room, standing close, whispering to each other. Ingrid blushes, and I imagine I look much the same. Rosy cheeks and warmth in my eyes.

I wonder what it'll be like when Claire is human. Will her skin still be cool against mine? Will her touch still make my heart race?

The back door slides open, and Abigail comes in. She groans when she sees Claire holding my hand, but she slaps a blank sheet of paper on the table in front of me. "Ingrid?" Abigail waves the witch over, and Ingrid hurries to her side. "For reasons unclear to me, Guillebeaux and Tagliaferro have agreed to your terms, Miss Beaumont. Sebastian is drawing up the contract."

Ingrid reaches into her pocket and pulls out an intricate fountain pen, the black body covered in shiny silver swirls. "It'll take a moment to connect to Sebastian," she warns and poises the pen over the blank page. For several seconds, nothing happens, but then the color leaches from her eyes, leaving behind a shimmering silver pool that matches the metal of the pen. Unfamiliar words spill from her lips, and a moment later, ink drips to the paper.

The red ink expands to cover the entire page, shining like blood. Then Ingrid flicks her wrist, and the ink returns to the pen. Left in its place is a contract written in tiny font.

Two flourished signatures mark the bottom.

A thick line awaits my name.

Ingrid blinks, and the green in her irises returns. "Here you are, Elise. All we need is your signature."

"Read it first," Wyn warns from across the room. "Make sure everything you wanted is in there. Once signed, it's impossible to break."

With shaking fingers, I reach for the document and turn it around to face me. I read each line with care, but everything I asked for is here. Permission for Claire and Nick to become human again. An ironclad promise that they'll be safe. Assurances that I can have a normal life so long as I complete at least one mission every month.

The monthly minimum requirement wasn't part of my plan, but it's a small thing compared to all that I'm getting.

Besides, who knows how long I have left.

I rub my chest. The spot has been tender ever since Petra taught me the key. Ever since some of my threads were torn away, my future altered and shortened.

It'll be worth it, I remind myself when fear tries to harden my heart. *If I get Nick back, it'll be worth it.*

At least this decision was *mine*, instead of someone else making it for me.

"Any time now," Abigail prompts. "The offer won't last forever."

"Right. Sorry." I adjust the pen in my hand and press it to the page. "Here goes nothing . . ." I hold my breath as I sign my name. When I finish the final letter, there's this tightness in my chest. I gasp for air, but it feels like someone knocked the wind from my lungs.

The contract glows, far brighter than the lights above us, and in a blink, it's gone.

Disappeared.

"Okay, then." Ingrid claps her hands together and rubs them like she's cold. "First order of business, removing the compulsion from your friend."

I want to watch more of Ingrid's magic at work, but the vampires join me at the table, making plans for the attack on Rose. There's talk of stakes and solar grenades and questions about how many other vampires she'll have on her side. If it's more than Nick. If she has werewolves or fae or witches as backup.

"What about Petal and Thorn?" Abigail asks. "Could they be involved?"

"There's no sign of other paranormals in town." Claire leans back in her chair. "I don't think she sees us as a threat. Rose kicked my ass when it was just the two of us."

Wyn snorts a laugh, and Claire smacks their arm. I don't fully understand their relationship, but I hope I'm around long enough to figure it out. Wyn reminds me a little of Nick—the *real* Nick— though he never thought it was funny when I got hurt.

He did, however, find it hilarious whenever I got myself grounded.

"Your human is good to go," Ingrid says, joining us in the dining room. She looks tired now, dark circles forming under her eyes. "Shall I take her home?"

"I've got her," Wyn says, standing. "I need to pick up a few supplies anyway." They don't clarify further, but I have a feeling it has something to do with the solar bombs Abigail wanted.

Wyn picks up Maggie from the couch and tosses her over one shoulder.

"Could you not?" I say, pushing back my chair. "There has to be a more dignified way to carry her."

"Sorry." Wyn shifts Maggie so she's being cradled like a baby. "Better?"

"Not really."

"Don't worry. I'll be quick." Wyn sprints to the door and is out of sight before I can react.

I groan and slide back into my seat. I am *so* going to owe Maggie when this is over. But then I realize what else my bargain with Petra means. I can change Maggie's death. I can give her all the years she deserves. That alone is worth a few broken threads.

"As soon as Wyn comes back," Claire says, her leg bouncing with what looks like nervous energy, "we search for Rose."

Abigail's phone pings, and she pulls it from her pocket. "No need. Isaac has the address."

Claire rolls her eyes at the mention of Isaac, and I make a mental note to ask her about that later. But then she smiles.

"Good. Then as soon as Wyn comes back, we get the key."

———

"Of course this is where she's staying."

Claire tightens her ponytail and folds her arms across her chest, glaring at the vacant home across the street.

The place is massive, perfectly clean white siding accented by navy shutters and trim, and there's a full wraparound porch and ornately carved columns, too. Inside, the first floor is warm with light. For a moment, I wonder why Delilah would risk someone catching her squatting there, but then I remember she can compel any human who discovered her.

Any human, except me.

"So, what's the plan?" Wyn hands Claire a wooden stake. "Enter through the back door and split up until we find her?"

"If you want your head ripped from your shoulders, sure." Abigail wraps a tie around her braids, securing them out of her face.

"Well, we can't just waltz through the front door."

My phone vibrates against my thigh, and I pull it out while the vampires argue about the best way to break in. Another text comes through, and my body runs cold when I see who sent the messages.

Delilah.

No need to be dramatic about it.

The front door is unlocked.

Three dots bounce as she types something else, and I grab hold of Claire's arm.

"What's wrong?" she asks.

Nicky says hello 😵

A surge of anger drowns out my nerves. I shove the phone into my pocket and cross the road.

"Where do you think you're going?" Claire is at my side in an instant, but she keeps pace with me instead of blocking my path. "You can't just barge in."

"Delilah already knows we're here." I don't bother lowering my voice. Shouldn't *one* of these vampires have realized Delilah would overhear them? "She invited us in."

I climb the stairs, and the door swings open before I reach the porch.

Nick stands inside the threshold, his gaze unfocused. His face expressionless. "She's expecting you."

Wyn and Abigail hurry past me, leading the way into the house while Claire stays close to my side. The four of us follow Nick down a hall with an ornately patterned rug that spills into a large sitting room. Flames crackle in the fireplace. Delilah lounges on a formal couch, dressed in dark-wash denim and a silk camisole.

Delilah smiles at me, but when her gaze flicks to Claire, she scowls. "I thought I told Nick to kill you."

Claire snarls. "He tried."

"I should have been more specific." Delilah shrugs and swings her legs off the couch. "Come, Nicky." In a blink, Nick appears at Delilah's side. He turns toward us, but his gaze doesn't leave the floor. "Now, since you've chosen to visit, little Death Oracle, I assume you figured out the key?"

It takes all my self-control not to race across the room to my brother. "I did."

"Very good." Delilah gestures to the team around me. "Unfortunately, I have a feeling this little entourage isn't here to help me dismantle the Veil."

"No one is destroying the Veil." I step forward, holding out a hand to keep my team from following. "But I understand why you're upset. What Luca and Henri did to you was awful. You have every right to be angry."

Uncertainty flickers across Delilah's face. "What are you talking about?"

"I know who you were. Before you became Delilah. Before you were Rose." I pause, positioned between the two factions of vampires. "I met someone you used to know. Petronelle."

Delilah's eyes widen and flicker red as she stands.

"Petra knew you by another name, back when you helped create the Veil." My heart races as horror and recognition light across Delilah's face, and it's the final confirmation I needed. "I'm sorry for what they did to you, Jessamine, but I can't help you hurt them."

A snarl tears from Delilah's throat at the mention of her original name, and Claire flanks me in an instant.

"That's not possible," Abigail says as she approaches. "Jessamine Prathor defected. She hasn't been seen for centuries."

I want to explain my theories, how Jessamine escaped Henri and Luca's attempt to kill her and went into hiding. How she became Rose and then Delilah, biding her time and planning her revenge. How she used witches to find me. Killed Hazel to transfer the Death Oracle power. Her past must be too closely linked to the attempt Luca and Henri made on her life, though, because the magic from the contract prevents me from forming the words.

"That day at school," I say, shifting gears until the contract allows me to speak. "You told me Luca and Henri took everything from you. That making them human was the poetic justice they deserved."

Delilah shakes her head, but there are tears in her eyes that I didn't expect.

"Petra thought you were dead." I remember the pain in Petra's eyes, and I feel myself soften despite all Delilah has done. "She missed you."

"Missed me?" Delilah lets out a humorless laugh. "She unraveled my entire line! Petra destroyed every vampire I ever created, for no other reason than their connection to me."

This time, it's Abigail who scoffs. "You expect us to believe that? Death Oracles only unravel vampires who have committed a grave offense."

"I don't know, Winters," Wyn adds, casting me a curious look before returning their attention to Abigail. "What are the odds that *every* vampire Jessamine created deserved that fate?"

Delilah wipes away fresh tears. "I chose my line with such care. They were incredible artists, witty and clever and passionate, so full of potential." Her gaze lands on Claire, and a bitter sort of sadness settles over her features. "If they find out you're a Prathor, they'll unravel you, too."

"No, they won't," I promise. "I made sure Claire was safe. And I know you wanted to share the key. You wanted vampires to have a choice. Luca and Henri had no right to—" My throat tightens as I skirt too close to the things I can't say. How they buried the secret of the key, destroying anyone who might reveal the truth of what they'd done. I force myself to redirect. "Even if I wanted to, I couldn't make them human. Petra said their makers are long dead. Vampires must drink their creators' blood to initiate the key."

"You're lying." Delilah shakes her head. "Feeding from another vampire is deadly."

I step forward, but Claire grabs my wrist, keeping me a safe distance from Delilah. "I'm not. That's why you need me, so I can change the death. Without their makers, it's impossible for Luca and Henri to be human again."

"No!" Delilah screams, the terrible, broken sound filling the space. She grabs the couch and flings it across the room. A window shatters, and the wooden frame smashes against the wall. When the broken furniture and glass settles against the ground, Delilah smooths the front of her shirt and blows out a sharp breath. "Fine. If I can't make them human, I'll sever their heads."

"I don't care who you were," Abigail says, pulling a wooden stake from her belt. "You're not getting anywhere near Luca or Henri."

"Wait! Don't kill her," I say, grabbing the tracker's wrist. "We need her blood for the key."

At that, Delilah does something very strange.

She laughs.

The sound is a shock to my system, and dread erases all the sympathy and hope I had moments before. Abigail, Wyn, and Claire step closer to me, their nerves amplifying mine.

"Did you really think I'd just hand over my blood?" An eerie smile pulls at her lips, her long canines bright in the firelight. "Are you sure there's enough of me to go around? You might have a tough choice to make, Elise."

I shake my head. "Petra never said—"

"Nick?" Delilah snaps her fingers. "It's time to kill your sister."

41

Claire

Nicholas Beaumont tries to resist the compulsion. The veins in his neck bulge. His eyes burn red. But in the end, he's still too newly turned.

He lunges for Elise, and I surge forward, checking my shoulder into his ribs. The impact sends Nick flying, and then everything is chaos.

"Don't let Rose escape!" I risk a glance away from Nick. Abigail is already trading blows with Rose, Wyn circling into position to launch their own assault. I focus on Nick in time to see him barreling toward me, arms outstretched.

We collide, the crash loud as thunder. I shift low. Take advantage of Nick's momentum and fling him over my back. He lands hard on the stone floor, and I pin him there before he can rise. Press my forearm tight against his throat.

He squirms beneath me, a terrible growl rumbling deep in his chest. Nick looks so much like his sister, but there's a predatory coldness to his eyes that she could never match. He scratches at the arm that holds him. Rivulets of blood spill down my skin.

"Don't hurt him," Elise says, stepping dangerously close to the brother that wants her dead.

"You need to choose." I release Nick's throat and grab his

shoulder, flipping him onto his stomach and pinning his hands behind his back. "If Rose is right, if only one of us can have the key, you need to decide. Now."

The *crack* of splintering wood steals my attention, and I look up. Rose is sprawled on the floor in front of Wyn, a broken chair shattered beneath her. Abigail raises a stake, poised to plunge it through Rose's back.

"Stop!" Panic rips through me. "We need her alive!"

Abigail hesitates, for only a second, but it's enough for Rose to grab a broken chair leg and plunge it into Wyn's thigh.

Wyn cries out and loses their footing. They crash to the floor, and Rose uses the distraction to climb to her feet. She runs. She—

Nick shoves up from the ground, and I tumble off him. My elbow slams against the floor. Pain ricochets up my arm, but I grab his ankle and pull. Nick falls again, just inches from Elise. I will *not* let him hurt her. Ever. I drag Nick back, but he's a flurry of furious limbs. I catch a kick across the chin. A knee in my stomach. Nails tear across my face, but then I finally regain control.

I wrap my arm tight around his neck.

"Kill me," he says, the words scraping up his throat even as he fights for his freedom. "Kill me before I can hurt her. Please."

His words are too quiet for Elise, but I hear the boy he used to be. The *brother* he used to be. Something painful cracks deep inside my heart. "Elise, you have to choose!"

She shakes her head, tears spilling down her face. "I can't. There has to be a way to save you both. Petra didn't say anything about how much blood we—"

A solar grenade explodes behind me, painful light burning against my skin. When the light fades, I risk a glance in that direction. Wyn drags Rose back into the room but takes an elbow to the gut. They double over, but then Abigail is there, driving a stake into Rose's shoulder.

"Don't—"

"Kill her. I know, Montgomery!" Abigail glares at me as she puts Rose into a tight chokehold. "Get your ass over here and finish this. We can't hold her off indefinitely."

Wyn tugs on their trouser leg. "Preferably before she pokes more holes in my suit or breaks a rib!"

"Elise, please." I say her name gently, but I know the moment her gaze meets mine that I can't make her do this. I can't make her choose between the brother she's known all her life and a vampire she met two months ago. Because in the end, it's no choice at all.

It was always going to be Nick.

I pull Nick to his feet and twist his arms tight behind his back. "You're positive you can complete the key?"

Elise nods.

"Good. Get ready."

I summon all the resolve I have left, bury every hope about being human. Even if Nick has to drain Rose completely, even if him going first means there's nothing left for me, I can do this for Elise. I can let her believe she wanted to save us both, let her believe she had no hand in dooming me to be forever seventeen.

Nick lashes out as I drag him toward Rose. I weather every impact. His blows are nothing compared to the hurt in my heart.

"Hold her still!" I say as I approach. Abigail and Wyn have Rose pinned to the floor. My maker—the head of the lost Prathor line—screams and squirms in their combined grip.

"You can't do this." Rose twists her neck to glare at me. "Without me, you wouldn't even know about the key!"

"We wouldn't *need* the key if you hadn't turned us." I snarl and shove Nick down beside our maker. "You brought this on yourself."

"Wait." Rose tries to throw off her captors, but she can't over-power the Veil's head tracker and lead shepherd. "Destroying me won't save the Veil. There is so much more in motion than you could possibly know."

"I'm sure we'll figure it out."

Rose snarls. "You've suffered for decades. Why should he get the cure first? You won't give up your chance to be human."

Her words tug at a deep hurt, but I've already made my decision. "Watch me." I pull the stake from Rose's shoulder and press Nick's face to the wound.

Rose screams as he begins to feed.

42

Elise

I stumble forward when Claire releases my brother. Nick doesn't let go, though. He grabs hold of Delilah and bites harder, vicious snarls reverberating through the room as he feeds from his maker. Delilah tries to pull herself away, but it's three against one now, and she's not going anywhere.

Even after everything she's done, it's awful to witness.

But this is only the beginning.

Claire appears beside me, her cool hand on the small of my back. "How much blood does he need?" Her voice tickles my neck, but I hear the question she isn't asking—if there will be anything left for her—and I don't know.

"Why did you let him go first?" I didn't mean to ask the question out loud, and I wish I could take it back. The flash of pain in her eyes is unmistakable. A vicious growl draws my attention back to my brother, and the violence of his feeding twists my insides into painful knots. I bury my face in Claire's shoulder.

What if this part of him persists after he's human again?

What if this violence survives the change?

"Elise," Claire says, voice raw with a jumble of emotions I can't decipher. "Try to remember. Did Petronelle say *anything* about—"

A terrible scream splits the night, and I look over in time to see Nick release Delilah. His eyes shimmer red before returning to their natural blue, but he's clutching his throat. He collapses to the floor.

"Nick!" I rush forward and turn him onto his back. He scratches at his throat, unable to pull a full breath.

He's drowning.

Again.

THWACK.

I glance up in time to see Delilah drop a smoldering log beside Wyn before she takes off in a blur, Abigail close on her heels.

"Don't let her escape!" Claire calls after Abigail, but she kneels beside Wyn instead of giving chase. Wyn screams as they clutch their face. "We still need her!"

Nick reaches for me, drawing my attention back to him. The panic in his eyes is so familiar, and it's like I'm there. In the river. Nick's car sinks deeper and deeper as he tries to smash the window. I see his lips, forming the words I couldn't hear.

Go. Please, Ellie.

I can't do this. I can't lose him again.

Just like Petra taught me. I reach for my brother, press the palms of my hands flush to his cheeks. His death rolls over me in waves, that night in the river superimposed over the death trying to take him now. I sink into the pain and the fear and the agony. I search for the separate threads that weave it all together.

And then I start to pull.

The threads of his fate fall apart in my mind like tiny beams of light. I undo my brother's death, piece by piece, and when it's nothing more than a pool of light in my hands . . .

I freeze.

There isn't time to delay. I know that. Everything Petra showed me when she poured decades of power and memories into my mind made that clear. Time is crucial. Every second I waste brings me closer to losing the brother I love for good. But what kind of death do I give him? How do I choose the way he'll die?

The lights in my hands begin to dim, and fresh fear spurs me into action. I nudge the lights in new directions. I weave together a new fate, the best one I can imagine for someone I love. I push everything I have into this new death, and as the final strand of light slides into place, I hear the most glorious sound in the world.

Nick finally inhales.

My fingers slip to his neck, and I feel his pulse against my fingers. Steady. Strong.

"Ellie?"

I open my eyes, and Nick is there. He's smiling, his gaze unfocused as tears spill down his cheeks. Blood stains his lips, but he's alive. He's human.

A shocked laugh tumbles out of me, and I crush Nick in a hug.

He laughs, too, and reaches up to hug me back, but the embrace feels awkward. His arms barely touch my shoulders. They circle my neck. Squeeze tight. I can't breathe. I can't—

There's a loud *thump*, and then the pressure releases from my throat. Nick crumples in front of me, and I gasp for breath.

"What was that for?" I glare at Wyn—whose face is red but healing quickly. They drag Nick away from me. "Where are you taking him? I just got him back!"

"He'll be fine." Wyn lets Nick go when there's several feet of space between us. "Unfortunately, Rose's compulsion survived the key. We can't have him axing the Veil's newest Death Oracle, can we?"

Delilah's voice echoes in my head.

Nick? It's time to kill your sister.

"What do we do?" I press a hand to my throat and pull myself to my feet.

"Ingrid will fix him up, just like she did for your friend. Don't worry." Wyn glances over their shoulder, attention stolen by something I can't hear. Their expression falls. "No luck?"

Claire comes through one of the doorways, Abigail close on her heels.

Delilah isn't with them.

Abigail picks up a discarded stake from the floor and fits it back into her belt. "Rose escaped, but she won't get far. As soon as Tagliaferro gives the command, my team will track her down." There's a strange tremor in her voice when she says Luca's surname, and I wonder how much she pieced together about what her bosses have done. If it changes how she sees them or the organization she serves.

Claire's expression is carefully neutral, like she's been carved from stone. She leans against one of the columns in the grand room and closes her eyes.

My heart breaks for her, and I know she must be devastated, even if she won't show it. While Abigail and Wyn argue over who's going to carry Nick home, I approach Claire. I stop a few paces away, far enough that I can't touch her without stepping closer.

"Claire?" My voice cracks, but she doesn't open her eyes. "What you did for me, for *Nick* . . ."

"Don't mention it." Claire's voice is cold as she pushes away from the column. She meets my gaze, but the look lasts only a second. A heartbeat. "Wyn can take you home."

"Claire, wait!" I reach for her, but there's a blur of motion and a gust of air.

And then she's gone.

———

"Ready?"

Maggie shifts on the kitchen stool, but she nods. "Make it a good one, okay?"

I roll my eyes, but I'm not sure it covers my nerves. "Obviously." I press my fingers to Maggie's temples and let out a slow breath.

"Ooh, can she die the same day as me?" Jordan asks, making me flinch. He stands over my shoulder, watching my every move. "Then we wouldn't have to miss each other."

"Quiet, the both of you." I shoo him back a few steps. "No one say anything until this is done." I return my fingers to Maggie's temples and shut my eyes.

Inside my head, the threads of her life come into view. I unravel them with care and lengthen each thread as long as I can. They glow with brilliant light, and I weave together a new death for my best friend. A better one. A much later one.

When it's done, a rush of exhaustion floods my system. Jordan reaches out to catch me when I sway, and my shield stays firmly in place with barely a thought.

My bargain with Petra may have shortened my life, but at least I can actually live it now. I can hold my friends again. I have my brother back.

"Is that it? Is it done?" Maggie slips from the stool and holds out her arms, like she's expecting to see something. "I feel the same."

"It worked. I promise," I say, and then I'm surrounded, my friends squeezing me in a tight embrace. I hug them back, but my heart says something is missing.

Someone is missing.

Claire hasn't answered any of my calls. Not one in the three days since she gave up her chance at mortality for Nick. Delilah is still out there, somewhere, which means there's still hope, but she was so close to getting everything she wanted. I still can't believe she gave it all up for Nick.

Upstairs, my brother cries out in his sleep. The panicked, pained sound fills the house, and my friends release me.

"He's still not sleeping well?" Jordan asks, glancing up at the ceiling. Maggie smacks his arm. "What?"

"Of course he's not," Maggie says, and a shudder visibly shakes her. "Being compelled to do awful things . . . there's no way to describe how that feels. I can't even imagine how much worse it is for him. Delilah made him kill people."

Jordan shoves his hands in the pocket of his hoodie. "This whole thing just sucks. How are those families supposed to get closure when a vampire causes all this suffering and then just disappears?"

I bristle. "It's not Nick's fault."

"No, I know," Jordan says. "I meant Delilah."

Maggie grabs his arm. "Come on, Jordan. We promised to take Vivi to the playground." She drags him toward the door and swings it open.

"Tell Vivi I said hi," I say, following them to the door. "I'll text you after my parents get here."

"Good luck." Maggie hugs me again, and whispers in my ear. "Thank you. For everything."

I watch my friends until they reach the sidewalk before I close the door. Upstairs, the shower turns on, which means Nick is finally up for real. *About time.* Our parents are due home within the hour.

Thirty minutes later, the kitchen is in chaos. I timed lunch a little too perfectly, and now everything is beeping at me. The garlic bread in the oven is perfectly golden. I need to release the steam from the Instant Pot. The radio blasts behind me as I reach for an oven mitt. A piercing, off-key falsetto grates at my nerves.

"You could help, you know." I glare over my shoulder as Nick finally comes downstairs. I flip the release valve on the Instant Pot, and steam shoots into the air, filling the room with the bright tang of spicy marinara sauce. While that's depressurizing, I click off the oven timer and open the door. The rich scent of butter and garlic fills the room, mingling with the spicy spaghetti and meatballs Nick requested.

My brother finally stops his singing—aka wailing noises—and leans against the counter island. "Are you sure I can be trusted in the kitchen?" He flashes a grin that everyone besides me finds charming. At least, that's what Nick always said.

"Can you at least grab the parmesan from the fridge?" The pin drops, so I remove the Instant Pot's lid and give the whole thing a stir. Normally, our parents don't like pasta this way, but it's Nick's favorite. Besides, once they see him, I doubt they'll even taste lunch.

"Here you go!" Nick drops the cheese on the counter and reaches for a slice of garlic bread.

"Be careful. You'll burn—"

He yelps and pulls his fingers back.

"—yourself." I roll my eyes. "You're not invincible anymore, Nick. You need to be careful."

"But I'm so *hungry*," he whines, opening the snack cabinet.

"You'll spoil your lunch."

"Impossible." Nick grabs a granola bar and tears the wrapper. He eats half of it in one bite and talks while he chews. "Trust me, if you'd spent seven months surviving on blood, you'd be starving all the time, too. And everything tastes so *good* now."

I dump a bunch of the freshly grated parmesan into the pot. "But other than being hungry, you're sure you feel okay?"

Nick has woken up screaming every day since we brought him home. Ingrid removed all traces of Delilah's compulsion, but Nick wouldn't let anyone remove the memories of the things he'd done. He said he deserved to remember, even if it hurt.

Every time I ask about it directly, Nick brushes me off. He even leaves the room if I keep pushing. He says he's fine, but we agreed to wait two days before I called my parents and asked them to come home. I didn't say anything about Nick. I'm not sure they'll believe it until they see him with their own eyes.

And they're due home any minute now.

"Ellie, I promise. I'm fine."

"But you'd tell me if something was wrong?"

"You've already done the hard part." Nick ruffles my hair, which hangs loose around my shoulders. "I can handle the rest. I promise."

Outside, car doors slam. Nick flinches at the noise, eyes darting to the front door.

"Hey," I soothe. "It's going to be fine. I promise." I shoo him into the living room, where he'll be out of sight. I don't want Mom to faint on the front porch. "We all missed you. They're going to be thrilled when they see you."

"There's no way they believe our amnesia story, though." Nick perches on the arm of the sofa. "They'll figure it out."

I roll my eyes. "Even if they don't believe us, they're not going to guess you were a *vampire*." The lock beeps with a four-digit code, and then the deadbolt slides free. "Stay here." I rush through the kitchen and dining room as the front door swings open.

Dad smiles when he sees me, his skin tan from time spent outdoors. "Hey, kiddo." He seems happy. Lighter than he's been in months. A twinge of uncertainty twists through me. Maybe Nick's right. Maybe this whole thing will be a disaster.

I wish Claire were here. For so many reasons, reasons that are going to include some seriously stressful conversations with my parents. But at least she'd know what to do. She could help me explain. She could fix things if I messed it up. She could hold my hand and—

Mom follows Dad into the house, dragging her rolling suitcase and clutching several shopping bags. Mom always picks up weird knickknacks from locally owned shops when she travels.

I back up to give them room to enter, but I can't stop fidgeting. Mom stares at me, her gaze sharp. "Elise Beaumont, if you've been doing drugs while we've been gone . . ."

"*Mom*," I say. "I don't do drugs."

"There was that one time—"

"I just need to show you something." I take her hand, and I don't even have to think about the shield. It's just there, keeping her death out of my head. I pull Mom toward the kitchen, Dad trailing us.

"Since when do you cook?" Mom asks.

"YouTube does exist. But that's not what I want you to see." I turn at the sound of Nick's footsteps.

He comes out of the living room, his hands shoved deep in his pockets. Mom gasps when she sees him, dropping my hand to cover her mouth. "Nicky?"

Nick forces a smile, but there's tension in his jaw. "Hey, Mom. Hi, Dad."

Our dad stumbles and grabs my shoulder for support. "How is this possible?"

"It's kind of a long story . . ." But before I can say anything else, everyone is crying. Mom is hugging Nick, and Dad is hugging me like he's never been prouder. There will be time later for our made-up explanation of near-death-related amnesia. For now, I let myself cry with my family.

A good cry.

A cleansing one.

Because our family is whole again. Everything will be okay.

And if some of my tears belong to the vampire who stole my heart and won't answer my calls, no one can tell but me.

43

Claire

I've packed my meager belongings a hundred times before, but this feels different.

It feels final.

Wyn hovers by the desk as I fold my clothes and lay them in a suitcase. "Are you sure about this?"

"You can ask a thousand times, Wyn, but I'm not changing my mind." I say it with fondness, though, not irritation. Wyn doesn't want me to leave the Veil, but I don't see how I could possibly stay. If what Rose said is true, if she's really Jessamine Prathor, then I'll be safer on my own.

Petra destroyed every vampire I ever created.

If they find out you're a Prathor, they'll unravel you, too.

After decades of being treated like an outsider because I had no bloodline, I never imagined knowing my origins would make things worse. I shove my last shirt into the suitcase and zip it closed. Really, I shouldn't be surprised. Rose never brought me anything but misery. Why should this be any different?

At least she's still out there. There's still a chance for mortality.

I shove the thoughts away. I can't risk the swell of grief and regret and rage that rises every time I think about what happened that night. I was so close to being free of this unending existence.

I was one choice away from ridding myself of this bloodlust. One last bite from a heartbeat and warmth and an actual life.

It was right there, and I gave it away.

Wyn pushes my suitcase aside and flops onto the bed. "I promise, I'll never make you shepherd a teenager again. No more high school. Ever. You could even go back to Abigail! She secured a special assignment to track down Rose. I'm sure she'd let you help!"

"I'm leaving the Veil, Wyn, not you. I'll still visit." I reach for my suitcase, but something in my chest tightens. "Besides, you're family. You couldn't get rid of me if you tried."

"Damn straight." Wyn looks up at me from the bed, one brow raised higher than the other. "What exactly are you going to do with all your newfound free time?"

I shrug. "I don't know. Figure out how to enjoy my life, I guess."

A sly smile quirks up the corner of Wyn's lips. "Your *life*?"

"You know what I mean." I drag the suitcase out of my room, but Wyn is close on my heels.

"If you're not going to work with Abigail, promise you won't waste more than a decade looking for Rose."

"I'm not—"

Wyn speeds around me and blocks my path. "There's no sense denying it, Claire. I know it's eating you up inside, what you sacrificed for Elise."

"It wasn't for her."

"Oh, really?" Wyn crosses their arms, leaning back against the door. "You expect me to believe you gave up your first real shot at mortality on a whim? That kind of sacrifice doesn't come out of nowhere. You did that for her."

Pressure builds in my chest. My eyes burn. "Elise was always going to choose her brother over me. All I did was speed up the process."

"Maybe." Wyn shrugs. "Or maybe, she would have found a way to change you both. You didn't give her a chance to figure it out."

The pressure twists into pain, and I think of all the texts I've ignored. The calls I've sent to voicemail and deleted unplayed. "What are you saying?"

"Nothing. I just think it's a mistake to leave Elmsbrook without saying goodbye." Wyn rests a hand on my shoulder. They lower their voice to a barely there whisper. "I know I've teased you, but that girl cares about you. A lot."

I shake my head. "She has her brother back. She mastered her power when she met Petra. She doesn't need me." It's bad enough knowing I'm irrelevant. I don't need to see the proof of it in her eyes.

"That doesn't mean she won't *want* you, Claire." Wyn squeezes my shoulder a little harder than necessary. "If you keep up this *I'm worthless* act, I will kick your ass. At least have the decency to tell the girl goodbye."

"She—"

"It's not about her." Wyn finally releases me and swings open the apartment door. "You owe it to *yourself*."

———

I park a block away from the Beaumont house and cut the engine. Overhead, clouds block out the glow of the moon and stars, but the streetlights are bright, illuminating the well-kept homes. I can't help but remember the first time I walked down this street, trailing Elise while Wyn complained about my lack of check-ins.

It feels like a lifetime ago, but it's been less than two months.

A flood of memories washes through me. The first time Elise reached for my hand. The sting of her fist across my jaw after I told her what she is. The concern in her eyes when I told her secrets not even Wyn knows.

That first kiss.

Our first *real* kiss. The one she actually meant.

The one after she'd saved my life.

Wyn's words echo in my head. *You owe it to yourself.* I really hate when they're right. With a steadying breath, I force myself to leave the car. If closure is possible, maybe I do deserve to try.

When I reach the sidewalk in front of her house, I find myself frozen in place. The first-floor lights are on, and I can see through the gauzy curtains that cover the bay window.

Her family is gathered around the dining room table—moved back to its proper place, centered under the light fixture instead of pushed against the wall. These aren't the same people I studied in newspaper clippings and funeral photos. Each and every one of them wears a radiant smile. Philip laughs and claps his son on the shoulder. Christina squeezes her daughter's hand, face glowing with gratitude. Elise tucks a strand of hair behind one ear.

It's kind of nice, actually, to see them like this. I give myself the tiniest bit of credit for bringing them back together. I let myself imagine that part of the smile on Elise's lips is because of me.

An ache settles in my chest, but there's warmth to it, too. Nick's return may never fully erase their memories of grief, but Elise succeeded in putting her family back together. She repaired the hole in their lives when she gifted her brother with the mortality he'd lost.

A sharp pang throbs in my chest, and when I reach up to wipe my face, my fingers come away damp.

I won't regret letting Nick go first, but I want what they have. I want that kind of love and laughter, that kind of deep, unquestioning sense of belonging. I want someone who will carry the most secret parts of my heart, who will keep every broken piece safe and warm.

Maybe, someday, I can figure out how to do that for myself. How to *be* that for myself.

Elise will be okay. Even though she committed herself to the Veil, she gets to keep her family. She has her friends. Her whole life is stretching out before her.

And I won't get in the way of that.

Wyn was wrong. I don't need to say goodbye. This is enough.

I can carry this moment with me to whatever adventure I choose next.

44

Elise

Mom squeezes my hand. Dad is still laughing at a story Nick told about a pre-accident party at college, and honestly, everything feels . . . perfect.

Well, mostly perfect.

My phone still sits silent in my pocket. I haven't heard from Claire, not once, since she helped me save Nick. Just thinking her name makes my heart ache. What she did for Nick—for *me* . . . I can never repay her for that. And even though I have no right to want more, even though I'm sure she's grieving after Delilah's escape, her silence hurts.

I thought we were more than shepherd and Death Oracle. Or, at least, I hoped we were. I've gone through so many moments again in my head, looking for clues, dissecting every touch and word and glance. I even told Maggie about the kiss—Jordan, too. I know I felt something that day in my room. Something real. I thought Claire did, too.

Maybe she was just being polite.

Maybe all she ever wanted was the key.

Mom squeezes my hand again. "Everything okay, Ellie?"

"Yeah. I'm good," I say, squeezing back to prove it. And it's mostly true. I'm still the Death Oracle, but my bargain with Petra was worth it. However long I have left, I get to be in complete control. I have my life back. I have my *family* back.

The only thing missing is Claire.

I push her name out of my head. If she needs more time, she can have it. She deserves it. I have plenty to deal with on my own. Too much, even.

My parents were skeptical of our amnesia story, but they haven't pressured us for another explanation. We haven't told the rest of our extended family quite yet, and we're not sure what Nick's future will look like.

Dad thinks it would be easiest if he transferred to a school where no one knew him, but Mom wants him here, at least for now. She's been researching amnesia specialists and trauma therapists since she got home. I'm letting them handle the logistics. I have enough to worry about, waiting for the Veil to assign my first official mission.

A shiver of cold prickles along my skin, and I glance out the front windows. Though I can't see anything in the dark, there's this feeling in my chest that I can't quite explain. It's like a thread has wrapped around my heart, and it's tugging me to the door.

"Elise?" Mom asks when I stand up.

"I'll be right back," I promise, dropping my napkin beside my plate and hurrying for the door. I flick on the porch light and step into the cool evening air. A breeze kicks up, blowing loose hair away from my face, and I pull my sleeves past my wrists. This time, though, it's for no other reason than the cold.

That's when I spot her walking away in the dark.

"Claire!"

I hurry down the steps, afraid that she'll disappear. Claire has the speed to escape if she wants to, but she pauses at the end of the driveway. When she glances over her shoulder, her expression is twisted with pain and hope and something I can't name. It's only been a few days since I saw her last, but it feels like a lifetime. My gaze falls to her lips, and my mind flashes back to that moment in my bedroom.

My heart beats just a little faster.

I wonder if she hears the change.

I wonder if she knows what it means.

Finally, she faces me fully, her expression hidden in shadow. "Hey, Elise." She sounds almost . . . guilty.

Why would she be guilty? Why—

"You're leaving. Aren't you?" Anger shoves past the hurt in my heart when she nods. "And what? You weren't going to say good-bye? You were just going to disappear like I mean nothing to you?"

Claire winces. "I didn't want to complicate things. You have Nick back. You have your agreement with the Veil." She shrugs. "I thought it would be easier if I just disappeared."

"Easier? Why the hell would that be easier?"

"Elise . . ." There are so many emotions wrapped up in the way she says my name, and I know I'm not imagining it. I know she's hurting, that this is hard for her. My anger deflates as she steps closer, and when she tips her forehead to mine, it dissipates like smoke. "You already have everything you wanted. You don't need me."

"Who said anything about needing you?" I rest my hands on the back of her neck and raise onto my tiptoes until my face is level with hers. "I *like* you, Claire, and I'd really, really like you to stay."

"But I'm not human," she says, even as her hands find my waist. Even as she pulls me close.

"I know."

"And there's no guarantee we'll find Rose again. I might always be like this."

Claire is so close now, I can feel the coolness of her through my shirt. My heart skips in my chest, and I grab hold of every brave thing inside me. "Are you going to stand there and list everything I already know, or are you going to kiss me?"

Claire laughs, and it's the most beautiful sound I've ever heard. "I'm overcomplicating things, aren't I?"

"Just a bit."

She smiles, and then she *finally* leans forward and presses her lips to mine. It feels different this time, better somehow, knowing that we've chosen this, chosen *us*.

Our future is uncertain, and there's an unknown expiration date on my life, but isn't that true for everyone?

Isn't that the beauty of life, making choices and falling in love and embracing the good things—no matter how small—even when you have no idea what will happen next?

"Oooh," calls a voice behind me. "Ellie's got a girlfriend."

I pull away from the kiss just long enough to give my brother the finger. "Shut up, Nick!"

"Don't worry," Claire says, kissing me again. "He can't ruin this moment. Nothing can."

"Elise Beaumont! What are you doing?" Mom's voice is loud in the otherwise quiet neighborhood. I groan and bury my face against Claire's neck. "Get inside."

"You had to tempt fate, didn't you?"

"It'll be okay." Claire kisses the top of my head. "I promise."

"You say that now," I mumble, reaching for Claire's hand. "Ready for Meet the Parents, Take Two? Compulsion-free edition?"

Her smile lights up the night. "Absolutely."

Acknowledgments

I finished drafting *The Coldest Touch* during the beginning of the COVID-19 pandemic and completed my biggest edits during the height of US cases that winter. Falling into this story was such a welcome escape from reality, but it wouldn't be in your hands today without the help and support of some wonderfully badass people.

Thank you first to my agent, Kathleen Rushall, who believed in this story when it was a tiny seed of an idea and helped me find the right soil to make it grow. To my brilliant editor, Julie Rosenberg, who always knows the right questions to make me dig deeper than I thought the story could go. And to everyone at Razorbill who had a hand in bringing *The Coldest Touch* to life—Simone Roberts-Payne, Casey McIntyre, Katie Bircher, Abigail Powers, Shelby Mickler, Jayne Ziemba, Bri Lockhart, Felicity Vallence, Alex Garber, Jennifer Dee, and so many others—you have my eternal thanks.

I'm forever in awe of artists who work in visual mediums, so huge thanks go to Muna Abdirahman, whose illustration beautifully captures Claire and Elise, and to Samira Iravani, who designed the stunning cover.

Naming characters is one of the hardest parts of writing for me (seriously!), so I'm hugely grateful that several friends and colleagues graciously offered up old family names for this book. Thank you to Jaimee Morrissey, PJ Connell, Jena Curtis, Beau Harbin, Deborah Fadeley, Pam Gillow, and Nicole Miner for letting me borrow some fantastic surnames (and being game when I wanted to make some of them villains!). Additional thanks go to the teens in our Gender Sexuality Alliance who (aside from being amazingly awesome humans) helped me rename a character at the very last minute.

To my local writing group, who provided insightful and encouraging feedback throughout the entire first draft, I miss you! I hope by the time you see this, my schedule has slowed down enough that I'm attending meetings again!

To Karen Strong and Jennifer Dugan, I can't imagine navigating this industry without our little writing coven, even if your horror references go over my head. I can't wait until we're back in person again, writing our books, talking to readers, and lounging on the beach!

I'm incredibly lucky to have such a wonderfully supportive family who's always in my corner (whether about books, career, or general life stuff). I appreciate you more than you know. An extra special thanks goes to my wife, Megan, who has loved this story (and me) through every stage of the process.

And finally to you, dear reader: thank you for letting Claire and Elise into your heart.